A Crown of War

Whill of Agora Book 4 (Legends of Agora)

Michael James Ploof

Join the Legends of Agora <u>mailing list</u>. Get updates on
book releases, contests, giveaways and more!

Other Books by Michael James Ploof

<u>Legends of Agora</u>

<u>Talon</u>

<u>Whill of Agora</u>

<u>A Quest of Kings</u>

<u>A Song of Swords</u>

<u>A Crown of War</u>

<u>The Sock Gnome Chronicles</u>

<u>Billy Coatbutton and the Wheel of Destiny</u>

<u>Billy Coatbutton and the Ring of Sockchild</u>

DEDICATION

This book is dedicated to Paul Fiacco,
the first wizard I ever met.

CLARIFICATION:

As stated in *Whill of Agora: Book 1*, elves name their blades the opposite of themselves. Hence, Zerafin's blade is Nifarez. Other examples include: Aramonis–Sinomara, Avriel–Leirva, and Eadon–Nodae. In particular, some confusion has been expressed regarding the name of Adimorda's blade, Adromida. Though obviously similar, it is not a typo or mistake.

A CROWN OF WAR

Do the bards sing of a hero's fears?
A hero's scars?
A hero's tears?

CHAPTER ONE

I Have Seen Your Heart

Aurora walked with Zander out of the tent and into the bitter wind. Fat snowflakes whirled in the afternoon light, and the clouds above glowed in stark contrast to the dark storm around the rift.

"Your army waits," said Zander, indicating the rift beyond the tents of the armies of the Seven Tribes.

Aurora's reply was lost as she gazed upon Azzeal. A thin fog surrounded him as the snow was singed by his energy shield. "You will die before you join Eadon?" The accusation in his voice ripped through her.

"Decide now! Shall you die with your honor intact, or will you become yet another of Eadon's puppets?" Azzeal screamed as he began to glow.

"You offer me only death!" she cried.

Zander stepped past her to face Azzeal. He regarded his sun elf cousin with disdain. "When you strike my enemy, my strength shall guide thy hand."

Aurora knew the words that he spoke, for Eadon had said such a thing as they sealed their deal with flesh.

When you strike my enemy, my strength shall guide thy hand. The promise came to her again.

The fourteen elves that had disguised themselves as spirit animals stepped forth out of the swirling snow to stand next to Azzeal.

"You are clearly outnumbered, dark elf. Surrender, and we may find an excuse to let you yet breathe," Azzeal snarled.

Zander laughed in Azzeal's face. "To the rift!" he bellowed in Elvish.

There was a sudden rumbling that shook the ground. Far beyond the army of the Seven, the rift crackled and buzzed with lightning. The winds picked up, and, soon, a blizzard surrounded the encampment. Before any of the elves could retaliate, Zander had turned to shadow and swirled to the ear of Aurora.

"The Draggard horde pours forth, m'lady. What will it be? Do you mean to send your tribesmen to their deaths against us in the name of honor? Or, will you join our ranks and storm the beaches of Agora with a mighty army at your back?" Zander whispered.

Azzeal awaited her reply with a hard-set chin.

"Bring me to the front line so that I might calm my armies," said Aurora.

As she was whisked away by Zander's spell, the face of Azzeal–the face of the betrayed–stared after her with tear-filled eyes.

At the base of the storming rift, the barbarian armies prepared for the imminent attack. Aurora stood before her legions and raised her arms to the sky. With Zander's help, her voice rang out loud and clear.

"Hold!" she said with authority.

The thousands of barbarians stirred, and many complaints found her ears. Behind her, the hulking form of a dwargon came through the rift. Alarms and calls to arms rose up above the tumult as a host of Draggard and dark elves followed.

Aurora could not believe that the beasts were now her allies, but once again the power of Eadon coursed through her. Her decision had been made, and it had been rewarded.

"The dark elves and their hordes are our allies!" she told her people.

"Allies?!" a barbarian cried, and many angered voices rose up.

"These beasts have been a scourge upon our lands for decades!" yelled another.

Aurora yelled over them. "It is true, we have had our differences. But a deal has been stuck. They would have ravaged Volnoss, leaving none alive, had it not been for me. With the dark elves as allies, we shall know the glory of the past. We will retake our homelands of old, and once again we shall know honor!"

"There is no honor in this!" yelled Winterwind, Chief of Eagle Tribe. "These beasts are an abomination!"

"You would rather we die defending this frozen rock?" asked Aurora.

"I will fight before I join with the dark elves," Winterwind proclaimed.

"Do you challenge my authority as Chieftain of the Seven?" Aurora asked. Behind her hundreds of Draggard had filed out of the rift and fanned out wide. Many dark elves came to stand by her and Zander.

Winterwind answered her with a war cry and charged across the frozen ground. Aurora met the charge with a cry of her own and sped to meet him. Eadon's words played in her mind as Winterwind raised his massive war hammer and came on fast.

"When you strike my enemy, my strength shall guide thy hand."

The dark elf's power coursed through her, lending her speed and power. She thumbed a gem upon the Dragonlance of Ashai, and the blade extended to ten feet with a shriek. The tip shot forth in a blur of enchanted steel and impaled Winterwind through the neck. His body convulsed as Aurora heaved him high at the end of her lance and threw him through the air to land at the feet of the dark elves.

With three sharp clicks her lance retracted into the shaft. Aurora stalked toward the barbarian line and eyed each chief in turn. "I ask one more time: who here would challenge my authority?"

"I would!" A voice rang out, and the barbarians parted for the speaker. Aurora recognized the voice, and her heart broke as Azzeal and his elves, now in their true form, walked toward her.

Aurora shook her head and trained the lance on Azzeal's chest, her thumb hovering above a gem. The elf paid the threat no mind and was soon standing before her. He offered her a sympathetic smile. Zander came to stand beside her. She could sense the other dark elves at her back.

"You can still do the right thing," Azzeal begged her.

"Kill him," said Zander in her ear.

"Be gone from here, sun elf. There is not but death for you now," Aurora bade him with a whisper. "You offer me only death," she reminded him.

"I offer you honorable death: freedom of your soul!" Azzeal erupted. Behind him, the fourteen druids unsheathed their curved blades in unison; the drawn swords of the dark elves at Aurora's back rang out in answer.

A tear found Aurora's cheek as Azzeal's voice came to her. *I have seen into your heart Aurora Snowfell; you are a good person. You cannot do this.*

Zander stared at her from the right. The dark elf had taken a step back. "Defy thy master's will, and you shall share his enemies' fate. The barbarian warriors will be slaughtered, the women will be ravaged by Draggard, and your children will be their food."

Eadon's words echoed in her mind. *When you strike my enemy, my strength shall guide thy hand.*

Coward at your back, the voice whispered from her dreams.

"Choose," said Azzeal.

As the single tear fell from her face, Aurora made her choice. Power coursed through her body and into the Dragonlance of Ashai as it shot forth into the energy shield and sank in Azzeal's chest. Chaos erupted as Zander and his dark elves engaged the Elves of the Sun. Time slowed for Aurora as Azzeal's dying gaze locked her in a stare. Spells erupted around them, and the clamor of blades rang out; Azzeal's blade fell to the frozen earth as his power was leached from him by the Dragonlance. His face became taut and his eyes bulged as his strangled voice uttered words that would haunt her forever. "I have seen…your…heart."

"Be still!" A voice boomed, and the world became silent.

Everyone froze. Aurora turned to gaze upon the portal. There, floating at its center, was Eadon. In an instant, he was before her.

"You have chosen well my Lady of the North," said Eadon with a lingering grin. He turned to the Elves of the Sun and extended a hand. They cried out and withered to ash. Their essence was pulled forth into Eadon's clenched fist and absorbed. Aurora retracted her Dragonlance, horrified at what she had done. Azzeal fell dead to the ground. The barbarians watched silently as Eadon stalked the line taking a measure of the armies. Their shoulders, once proud and strong, now hung down as they cowered before the dark elf's power.

"Stand tall barbarians of Volnoss!" he cried. "Chieftain Snowfell has secured your place in the New Agora."

Behind him, the rift churned and lightning lashed out from all sides. The Draggard army had reached the thousands. Overhead, scores of draquon circled, swirling like a gathering whirlwind, and sending phantom shadows swimming across the frozen landscape. The ground shook with the heavy steps of lumbering dwargon as they approached with dark elf riders saddled on their hunched backs.

"Kneel before me now, and prove your allegiance!" Eadon bellowed. The barbarians began to comply, and soon only a handful of brave souls remained standing. Eadon studied the two dozen barbarian warriors, men and women alike, and his gaze fell to Aurora. She straightened under that stare, her heart hammering all the while.

Eadon reached toward the standing barbarians, and they were pulled to him by an unseen force.

"Chieftain Snowfell, what do you suggest we do with these…traitors?" he asked.

Aurora considered them as she walked the line. One of the women spat in her face, but quickly regretted it. She was lifted by Eadon's mental grip, and tossed high into the churning mass of draquon. Soon her blood and torn body were raining down upon the crowd.

"The tribes of Volnoss have no place for those that would not help us thrive. If you are not our allies, you are our enemies," said Aurora. "Zander!"

"Chieftain?" he smiled.

"Dispose of them."

"As you wish," he said and turned to the group. He arched his back and tensed as his many gems and crystals began to glow. He threw out his right hand and blue lightning snaked forth and engulfed them all. After half a minute of thrashing and screaming, the barbarians lay dead and smoldering.

Aurora watched her kin die and felt nothing. Whatever goodness Azzeal had seen in her had died with him. Her choice had been made; there was no turning back now. She would lead her barbarians and the hideous hordes of Draggard in an attack on Agora, and reclaim the ancient lands and the mountains of the north.

Eadon followed her gaze to the crumpled form of Azzeal. He walked to the elf and turned the body over with his boot. With an outstretched hand over the corpse, Eadon began to chant in a hissing language unknown to her. Azzeal's body lurched and convulsed and rose into the air. A lightning bolt crashed through the snowstorm and slammed into the body. A strangled cry issued forth from Azzeal, and Eadon grinned at Aurora.

"Rise, Azzeal of Drindellia. I yet have use for you," said Eadon as Azzeal descended to the ground and stood weakly. His eyes were milky white. Aurora recognized nothing of the elf she had known in them.

"The undead elf will lead you to the southern coast; there you will find the waters frozen to the Shierdon shores. Near Orenden, you shall join forces with the armies of Shierdon, and reclaim your lands."

"Yes, my lord," said Aurora with a bow.

Eadon turned with a jerk, alert to something. Aurora recognized surprise in his face. He leapt from the ground and flew like an arrow toward the rift, but before he could reach it, there was a deafening explosion and the rift winked out of existence.

CHAPTER TWO
A Prison for the Mind

The Other peered out over the ash-covered land and shuddered as the power of Adromida coursed through him. He sheathed the ancient blade and turned to his army. He had done what Whill would not; he had destroyed the entire Draggard force. The elves and dwarves stared at the destruction, dumbfounded. The horde that once stretched for miles was gone, as were the monolithic crystals, and, more importantly, the rifts.

The dwarves burst into cheers, and the elves quickly joined in the celebration. But, soon the cheering subsided and the reality of the situation set in, and they found themselves trapped somewhere in Drindellia. They knew that thousands of miles away and across the sea, the dark elf armies wreaked havoc.

"Ye did it, lad, you destroyed 'em all," said Roakore, as he came to stand next to Whill.

"It is good to see you again, Roakore."

Roakore eyed him oddly and noticed the cuts and scars, the bloody nose and eyes.

"Yer hurt a bit, lad," he said, looking uncharacteristically concerned.

The Other shrugged. "From the blast. It shall pass."

Avriel and Zerafin approached and gazed out over the destruction. Avriel noticed the Other but said nothing. If Zerafin recognized a change in Whill, he did well to hide it.

"The rifts have been destroyed; we are trapped here," said Zerafin.

Roakore beheld the smoldering battlefield as if for the first time. He had been so caught up in the victory he missed the ramifications of the rifts being destroyed.

"We be trapped?" he yelled, looking around frantically. "And thousands o' miles away?"

Roakore grabbed the Other by the armor and gave him a shake. "Open it back up. The rifts, they be leading to the Dwarf Mountains, I tell ye. We gots to be gettin' home!"

The Other swung his arms up, loosening himself from the distraught dwarf.

"Calm yourself! We will find a way," he said.

"Across the sea be the only way. Ye plan on buildin' us a magic boat?" Roakore huffed.

"Upon the castle grounds of Del'Oradon is a tomb. Within lies one of Arkron's lost gates, which leads here," said the Other.

Roakore squared on him once again. "And this be a chunk o' land how big? Nearly five times the size o' Agora!"

"Then we had better start looking," Whill said, ignoring Roakore's gaze. "This was likely Eadon's main force; he will not have ventured far. Where we find the portal, we find him."

"You mean to face him then?" Avriel asked from behind him.

The Other turned to her and grinned. "I mean to kill him."

Zerafin stepped forward. "Whill is right. Eadon will be close if he is here at all. We are trapped, but the rifts have been closed–we can only pray there are not more. I shall set the Ralliad to the task of seeking out Eadon's base."

He turned back to a waiting general. "Gather the Ralliad for a briefing. Set everyone else to procuring a defensible location."

The general bowed and went off to carry out his orders.

"Zorriaz and I shall begin scouting to the north," Avriel suggested.

"And we be searchin' to the south," said Roakore, referring to himself and Silverwind.

"Very well," said Zerafin. "Whill, you should–"

The Other shot into the air and flew out to the east so quickly he soon disappeared from sight.

Roakore mounted Silverwind and took a long pull from his water pouch. Holdagozz followed him and scowled up at his king with worry not befitting a dwarf.

"I ain't likin' this, me king, I ain't likin' this at all. Rifts and portals and jumpin' to another land with a footstep. Dark magic we be meddlin' with, and we be trapped. Our rations won't last a month. Naught but death be here. As we speak, our kin be fightin' a likely invasion."

"Aye, I be agreein' with ye. We be up shyte creek. But we ain't gonna complain ourselves out o' this. I made our feelings known, but now is time for action. We find the portal, we find a way home. You just keep these knuckleheads busy till then," Roakore ordered.

"Yes, me king!" Holdagozz had to yell over Silverwind's flapping wings.

"I be countin' on ye, General," Roakore yelled as he and Silverwind took to the sky.

Avriel and a host of elven druids took flight also, and began their assigned scouting missions. The elves took the form of eagles, hawks, falcons, and owls. Some branched out into groups; others flew alone.

Upon each of their heads, the elves wore a small gem; with them, the general of the Ralliad would scry their progress, seeing through their eyes. Roakore and Avriel too had been given such a gem, attached to a circlet and using the same magic as the Looking Glass of Araveal.

Heading north with the others, Avriel wondered about Whill. She knew his alter ego had taken control, but she had not determined if that was a bad thing. He destroyed the entire dark elf army with one massive spell, the likes of which few had ever seen. She knew Whill now had the full backing and confidence of not only the elven armies, but also her brother. He was Whill, or at least, a part of his mind. She believed the Other was Whill's tortured self, the one who remembered it all. She had no way of knowing Whill was a prisoner within the Other's world of nightmares.

The Other was fulfilling the ancient prophecy, and Avriel decided that no matter Whill's current plight, it did not outweigh the good that would be done by his alter ego. Only a flicker of doubt nagged at the back of her mind, warning her of danger, but again, the results quieted those thoughts for the time being.

Whill screamed, and his tortured voice echoed throughout the dark chambers of his mind, chambers that once held the Other. He fell so deep into the memory illusions of his prison, he began to forget what was real. Chained to the wall, he remained helpless to the ever-shifting memories of torture. The most brutal sessions replayed in living color, and, ever so slowly, Whill lost himself to the pain. The Other had not only gained control, but would soon destroy him.

Whill found himself laid out on a table. A cage of seething rats and a large assortment of knives lay on the opposite table. Above him, his hated dark elf torturer grinned down on him.

CHAPTER THREE
Spirit-Elf

Eldon Island remained as quiet and peaceful as Dirk remembered. The only people who called it home were the tribal Eldonians, and no trouble was to be found from them. They stayed to themselves and lived mostly on the northern and eastern shores of Eldon. Krentz had flown Dirk to the southern coast, and they had yet to be discovered by anyone.

Morning had come, and Dirk gazed upon Krentz in the light of the new sun. She was fading. The beams penetrated her body, illuminating it softly from within. The tattoos on her body swirled and danced lazily as she smiled up at him.

"I am tired, Dirk. I must return to the spirit world."

Dirk turned his head in sorrow and reached for his cloak. From an inside pocket, he retrieved the relic.

"What is it like there?" he asked.

"Like a dream," she purred. "Chief's spirit home is a dark winter forest teeming with streams and wild game. I was there for only minutes, but I spent hours."

Dirk gave a smile hearing the experience was at least pleasant for her. "I could come with you."

"Are you mad?" she said, aghast.

"You say I die because of you," he reminded her with an arched eyebrow. "Perhaps we can be rid of the cursed vision also. Suppose I can be taken by Chief as well. We might watch the ages pass, together."

"Who would summon us, who would keep us? If another obtained the trinket, would we have to obey them? Should the trinket become lost, would we be trapped in the spirit world forever?" she asked.

"You can't emerge from the relic at will?" Dirk inquired.

"No," she admitted. "Had you not summoned me, I would not have gotten out. I heard your words loud throughout the spirit world. Your beckoning drew me forth, and, before me, a doorway to this world opened. When I came through, I found you on the ground, disoriented, and you soon passed out."

Dirk remembered seeing her fighting the dark elf and dwargon as flames leapt all around them. Krentz had shifted in and out of spirit form, disorienting and getting under the guard of her enemies.

"Shifting to spirit form during combat…how did you learn that?" he asked, interested in the concept.

She chuckled. "Chief taught me. Did I mention he can talk in his spirit realm?"

"Yeah." Dirk shook his head unable to imagine the conversation. Krentz had become almost entirely translucent, and her whispered words became nearly inaudible. Dirk moved to push back the hair from her face, but found no form. His hand went through her and found only dancing sunlight.

"Goodnight, my love," she smiled.

"Back to the spirit world, Krentz," Dirk managed to utter. She turned into a wisp and spiraled into the timber wolf relic.

He let her stay in the spirit world all of the day, not knowing how much time she would need to recuperate. He noticed the more she or Chief held their physical form, the longer they had to remain within their own realm.

He spent the day inspecting and repairing his gear. The cloak's enchantments had been drained protecting him from the explosion of the dark elf war machine. His weapons and darts had been spared any serious damage, but he was running low.

Night came, and he could wonder no more about Krentz. He summoned Chief, and the spirit wolf solidified, bounding around Dirk like a puppy.

"Is she well?" Dirk asked hesitantly.

Chief trotted and barked and was distracted by the smells of the world. Dirk snapped his fingers to get Chief's attention.

"Hey, is she ready or not?"

Chief barked once and went about sniffing the perimeter. Dirk held the relic aloft and called to his beloved.

"Join me once more, fair Krentz."

The relic glowed bright as a glowing mist swirled out and around his body. Krentz solidified before him; she seemed to have rested well. He reached out and touched her face, amazed that, once again, they were free.

"Did it seem a long time?" he asked.

"T'was days," she said, kissing him. She noticed the nighttime. "How long has it been?"

"I sent you back just this morning," he told her.

"The waiting is unbearable," she pouted. "Do not leave me to wait so long again."

Dirk nodded. "I believe you will tire less easily in the physical plane if you remain more often in spirit form."

"Yes, I suppose," she admitted sullenly and shifted out of physical form. She became a wisp of light, which danced around Dirk and to his ear.

"But you will miss looking upon me," she teased with a faraway giggle.

Dirk smiled as her spirit brushed against him and a warmth seeped through.

"Show me how you can fight now," he said as her spirit wound around his body. Dirk felt a kick to the back and dove into a roll with the momentum. He spun as he came up and was ready with a sweeping kick, but she was gone. He circled and backed into the shadows of the forest, and, even though his boots snapped twigs, they did not give a sound.

"This isn't fair," Dirk laughed at the night.

"My love," came her voice echoed through the forest. "Fair doesn't exist. Have I taught you nothing?"

Dirk's senses gave warning, and he ducked back as Krentz's fist materialized and cut through the air. Dirk grabbed the arm, which turned to smoke in his hand. He defensively jumped back and was proven correct when Krentz materialized, coming down with a kick from on high. She charged him, and, as he moved to block, she disappeared and reemerged directly behind him in a heartbeat. She shifted in front of him, and Dirk threw a quick elbow behind him.

Krentz materialized behind him, caught his elbow, and tried to move into a hold. Dirk quickly shifted into the proper countermove, as she had anticipated. She brought up a foot to his face as he spun out of the arm lock, but he was yet a step ahead. Just as he loosened his arm from her grasp, he grabbed the foot flying for his head. He ducked between her legs and rolled backward, pulling the leg with her. Krentz shifted her leg to a wisp of smoke, and Dirk rolled to stand behind her.

They faced each other yet again. Krentz flinched a feint, and Dirk tensed. She grinned.

"Wait until you see what else I can do in this form," she laughed and disappeared.

Dirk was slammed to the ground as Krentz solidified, straddling him.

CHAPTER FOUR
The Coming Storm

The news came to Cerushia of the victory and taking of Fendora Island and the closing of the rift. Also came word of the three kings. Whill, Roakore, and Zerafin were now lost on the other side of the rift. Reports began to come in from the Ralliad scouts through the Looking Glass of Araveal that the rifts had been closed in the other kingdoms as well. The elves rejoiced at the news of the swift victory, but also lamented their losses.

Tarren and Helzendar remained within the dwarf quarters along with Lunara, who spent most of her time reassuring them both that Whill and Roakore would find a way. It had only been two days, she reminded them, but the boys remained fraught with worry and continued to think up some other possible obstacle they might face.

"What if they are stuck in Drindellia for good?" Tarren asked through a mouthful of bread.

The entire lunch was spent doing more speculating than eating. Helzendar nodded to Lunara, sharing Tarren's sentiment.

"Aye, took you elves better than three months to cross the oceans to Agora."

Lunara was young for an elf, and it showed in her lack of patience. She put her glass down a bit too hard and abruptly left the room. Tarren noticed a hint of tears in her eyes.

"Bah, what did we say?" Helzendar asked Tarren with a mouthful of goat cheese.

"I think she be as worried as us, and we ain't helping with all our questions, I bet," said Tarren, worrying after her. He got up from the table to seek her out.

"What, am I the only one who be hungry?" Helzendar complained as Tarren walked out of the room.

Tarren found Lunara up at the top of the dwarves' hill. She stood still as stone as her silver hair danced in the breeze. Her only movement came in the occasional tremor.

Tarren wasn't sure whether to approach her or leave her alone. The boy nervously shifted between turning back and staying a half a dozen times.

"Are you coming or going, love?" Lunara asked, wiping her eyes.

He walked to stand beside her. He didn't want to look in case she was embarrassed of crying. He wondered why she cried. Tarren dared not ask; he had learned from his mother that when it came to women, they sometimes wanted to be listened to rather than helped. And so, he simply stood by her and waited.

Lunara gave no indication she wanted to talk, so they simply stood in the afternoon sun, watching the strange-colored clouds thicken. Tales of Whill's feats in the battle of Fendora had been grand, and the remaining clouds of the destruction he wrought were proof. The city below was alive with activity as more elven armies arrived hourly from all parts of Agora. The rift on Fendora Island had been opened for days, and legions of dark elves and darker creatures had poured forth. The entire island had nearly been stripped bare to build the hundreds of ships that had ferried away Eadon's armies. Whill had closed the rift, but fleets of dark elf warships had taken to the seas–already reports came of an escalation in naval confrontations.

When Lunara finally spoke, it was of Whill. "I have dreamed of him for all of my life. He is the reason I insisted on joining the elven force that aided Isladon and the Ro'Sar dwarves. Then I heard of you, Whill's ward, and I thought, if I become close with the boy, I can get closer to Whill."

She turned to Tarren and put a hand to his on the balcony railing. "It was what drew me to you, but not what keeps me at your side. I have come to love you, Whill or no Whill."

"I know," he smiled. "He will be all right. You have to believe."

Lunara laughed and cried at the same time, and Tarren wondered how that was possible.

"I know," she said weakly and wiped her eyes, annoyed. "I know that he will be safe. I believe he is the chosen one and all shall come to pass. But I will never know him as...it shall never be. His heart belongs to Avriel. I am a poor subject to my princess and an egocentric mess."

Tarren suddenly understood and things got a bit more uncomfortable for him. What did a boy know of such things? What should he say? Luckily his mother's advice came to him again, and he simply listened. However, Lunara seemed to be done talking; instead, she stood and stared out over the city below, dim under the dark clouds of Whill's victory.

Tarren's mind returned to Whill and his own worry. He had waited for six long months for any word of him. The first weeks had been the worst, those spent within Kell-Torey. Everyone had been kind enough, though he had more than once overheard offhanded comments about Whill's frivolous claims of his lineage. Many simply didn't believe it, and others–King Mathus's son, namely–didn't want to. He viewed Whill as a direct threat, rather than a blessed, long-lost nephew, and his disdain he did not hide, no matter the king's wishes or proclamations regarding Whill and his ward. Tarren had made no friends with any of the children of the royal family, who saw him as little more than a lucky street urchin.

Tarren was glad when Abram had traveled to Kell-Torey to bring him to Roakore's mountain. There, his depression and loneliness were replaced by rigorous training and study, and he found fast friends in Roakore's son, Helzendar, and Lunara. Without the talented elf healer to tend to his many wounds, he would never have been able to train with the dwarves. She had bestowed upon him a great gift in the staff, Oakenheart, and he knew he could never truly repay her for all she had done. He looked to her with renewed gratitude and, to her surprise, suddenly hugged her.

Lunara laughed and bent to hug him full.

"It will all work out," Tarren told her with a smile.

"You are the bravest human I have ever known," she smiled back. "Thank you."

At the edge of the city, a deep bell tolled and echoed forth in a note of foreboding. Another bell answered its call, then another, and soon the city began to buzz with activity.

"What is it?" Tarren asked.

Lunara set her jaw and gave a determined sigh. "Cerushia will soon be under attack."

CHAPTER FIVE

Taming the Dogs

The Seven Tribes of Volnoss marched south with the Draggard army for two days. After the portal had suddenly closed, Eadon flew off toward Agora, leaving Aurora to lead. Five thousand Draggard had made it through the rift before it suddenly and violently disappeared. Aurora knew that the dark lord had not intended for the rift to close, for she had felt his fury. She could only guess that Whill had something to do with it.

The Draggard made the barbarians uneasy, and with all haste they traveled to the southern shore, eager to put the beasts far from their villages. They made camp only once, and few barbarians slept, so loud were the sounds of the Draggard horde in the darkness.

Led by the silent lich, Azzeal, they found the waters frozen as Eadon said they would. The channel between Volnoss and northern Shierdon was frozen thick with ice; the masts of marooned boats and fishing vessels that had been frozen solid jutted out in every direction. Aurora followed the elf lich and led her armies across the channel.

By nightfall, they had arrived upon the coast of Shierdon. Mounted scouts reported the coastal town deserted, and Aurora ordered camp be made. As the supply caravans drudged forth, Aurora stared sidelong at Zander. The elf sat upon a large barbarian horse akin to Aurora's and regarded her with a nod. "There is something on your mind, General?"

"Your Draggard army will march well beyond the town and wait while my people sleep. I would have them rested before we travel further," she ordered.

"The Draggard require no rest, General," Zander informed her.

"Humans do, and I will not have the beasts disturb them. Do as I say–we will join you at first light."

Zander nodded slowly, "As you wish, but I would stay at my lady's side, if it pleases you."

The barbarians made camp in the deserted village, and Aurora had her tent set up in the town square. She called for the Chiefs of the Seven, including the newly appointed Chief of Eagle Tribe. They heeded her call swiftly, and soon they sat before her at a long table within her tent. She regarded them all with a steely gaze as Zander stood by silently.

"How far are we from Shierdon's main force?" she asked the dark elf.

"The lich Azzeal shall lead us to them by nightfall tomorrow," said Zander.

"How do we know the human army can be trusted?"

Zander smirked. "My master has ensured their loyalty."

The Chief of Fox Tribe spoke up; he was a grizzled old barbarian named Moontooth, with knots of gray hair falling about his wide shoulders. He had nearly as many scars upon his face as lines, and Aurora knew many battle wounds hid beneath his heavy plate armor.

"Long have our people waited to reclaim our ancient lands. We extend our gratitude to your master," he said to Zander and his fellow chiefs; some nodded agreement.

"Our master sees great strength in your people. You choose wisely in your allegiance," said Zander.

"Once we meet with the Shierdon army, what then is our destination?" asked Goldenwing of Dragon Tribe.

"We are to march to the Uthen-Arden border and await instruction," Zander told them all. The seven chiefs shared glances.

"The ancient lands are to the southwest. We should march on Ky'Dren while they are weak," said the Chief of Bear Tribe, Beorin Sharpclaw.

"Patience, my friend. You will see those mountains soon enough," Zander replied.

Beorin was not placated; he scowled at the dark elf from behind a winter beard. "Do the Chiefs of the Seven follow you, or Aurora Snowfell?" he asked boldly.

Zander arched an eyebrow.

Beorin Sharpclaw's words seemed to help the other chiefs find their courage. They nodded in agreement and began to mutter to themselves.

"The Chiefs of the Seven Tribes of Volnoss follow Chieftain Snowfell, and she follows master Eadon," said Zander. He leaned forward to meet the chief's glare. "Why did you not express these concerns when your fellow chieftain was bleeding at the end of Aurora's lance?"

Beorin's eyes flashed, but he said no more. Aurora didn't like where his questions were coming from. If they thought she was not in control, she would not last long. Zander had made clear to them she was in charge, but the chiefs were not convinced. She could not allow the Seven to see weakness.

"I did not raise this army so we might wait like dogs for our master's orders," she told the Seven. "I will decide our course of action once we meet with the Shierdonian army."

Beorin scowled at her from across the table as she spoke. He had not taken his eyes off of her. "You will decide nothing but what you are told," Beorin laughed.

Aurora leaned forward on white knuckles and rose above them all. She was about to speak when Zander interrupted her and addressed Beorin.

"What she means is–,"he began, but Aurora's backhand caught him across the face, snapping his head to the side.

"You do not speak for me," she said calmly, and Zander grinned, licking the cut on his lip.

"Yes m'lady."

She turned on Beorin with a wide smile. "Do you think you can lead this army better than I?" she asked as she began to slowly walk around the table. Beorin eyed the others again, and Aurora wondered of a multi-tribal plot against her. She put a hand to his shoulder and whispered in his ear loud enough for all to hear.

"It is your right to challenge a chieftain you believe unfit," she reminded him and moved slowly to the other ear. "But, understand when I defeat you, as I shall, I will have you turned into a lich like the undead elf. Then you will heed my every word."

Aurora trailed his face with her fingertips and scraped across his beard. Beorin had lost his gusto to her promise. He turned his head from her sidelong gaze. "You have my loyalty Chieftain Snowfell...I am eager for glory, is all."

Aurora could tell it hurt his pride to utter the words, but he understood as well as the rest of them that, had he not, he would have died. She looked to the others and knew this was the time to gain true loyalty.

"I was raised on the ancient tales as you all were. Many of you passed the stories on to your own children and grandchildren. The songs of ancient glories and days past are taught to every child who survives three winters. We honor the deeds of our dead, and we celebrate their bravery."

She locked eyes with each chief in turn as she began pacing before them. "But what of our deeds, our bravery? We stand upon the brink of reclamation, and you would set us squabbling among ourselves?" she chastised Beorin, and he bowed his head in shame.

"This is our chance to make history! To take back, with devastating force, what is rightfully ours. We have slumbered long upon the frozen island, fighting to survive one more winter. No more, I say!" she slammed the table. "No more. I shall lead the Seven Tribes to the glories of old. I will not be stopped by man or elf, dwarf or dragon. If you would see the power of the Seven Tribes restored, then you are my brothers. If not, you have no place here."

She turned from them and regarded the fire at the center of the tent for a long time, letting her words echo in their minds. They would be staring at her arse, no doubt; she knew that, like her words, her figure stirred their passion. She turned on them suddenly and walked to the table. They regarded her with newfound respect; even Beorin seemed to be appeased.

"Give me your undying loyalty, and I shall carve your names in history!"

CHAPTER SIX

Infinite Consciousness

Whill drifted in and out of sleep for hours. Every time he awoke, he found himself still within the nightmare. The chains from which he hung sent a constant trickle of blood down his body, dripping into a puddle at his dangling toes. A large candle above him offered the only light. He stared at the flame while he prayed to the many gods, none of whom he had ever believed in. At the moment, he was ready to believe in any god who might release him from his prison.

A sudden sensation passed through him, and he realized he was not alone. A blurred figure stood before him in the dark cell. Whill thrashed and cursed, thinking that the torturer had returned. When his vision cleared, it was not a dark elf standing before him, but Abram.

Whill laughed until he coughed, sending blood-speckled spray dancing in the candlelight. Abram said nothing but waited patiently. He was as Whill remembered him in the best of days: broad and strong and seemingly taller than his six feet. He could go unseen if he wished with a hunch of the back and hooded cloak, but when Abram wanted to be seen, men and women alike could not help but notice him. People were drawn to Abram, and he to them. If ever a man possessed the ability to read others like an open book, it was he. Abram had risen to a position of influence and power within the kingdoms of men, dwarves, and elves, not because of lineage or title, but through character and deed.

"Why do you torture me so?" Whill sobbed, and Abram's stoic face broke into one of barely contained sorrow.

"Ah son, why do you torture yourself so?" he asked and walked forward to reach out to Whill.

In a thrashing of chains, Whill screamed to be left alone. He reeled from the outstretched hand as if it were a cleaver. Abram touched Whill's forehead and held firm. Blinding light flashed, and all pain left him. Whill found himself outside in a world of clear winter's night sky, and beside him stood Abram; the two of them stood upon the snow-covered Old Road.

"This is where everything began," said Abram. His words, like the steam that rolled from his mouth, dissipated in the chill wind.

Whill was bewildered; he spun a full circle like a dog chasing its tail and noticed he wore the clothes of a winter traveler.

"This is…" Whill began, but lost his words as over the hill came Abram and himself from long ago.

"Yes," said Abram, "last year on our way to Fendale for the Winter's End Celebration, just before the wolves attacked us. Our last journey before the world went mad."

He turned to Whill and laid a hand upon his shoulder. "You have learned much this last year. You have had to do things, had to make hard choices. You have endured pains I cannot imagine, and you are a bigger man than I. Now you face the toughest opponent, the most worthy adversary, and one who has laid many men low. Now, you face thyself."

Whill turned away from Abram to hide his wet eyes as the image of himself and Abram topped the hill. Whill remembered clearly now the boy he had been, quick to laugh and always filling people's ears with stories of elves, dwarves, knights and monsters. His years with Abram and Teera had given him every advantage, considering the destiny he would have to one day face, and he felt as though he had squandered it all.

The images of he and Abram stopped with the raising of memory-Abram's hand. Standing in the middle of the road, Whill thought for a moment they had been seen by his memory-self. But he soon remembered the moment.

"Ride, boy, ride!" memory-Abram hollered in the night, and both horses surged forward as a pack of wolves sprang from the cover of the dark, snow-laden forest. Whill found himself and Abram caught in between their charging selves and the attacking wolves. Arrows flew by to strike true, felling two of the beasts. Whill closed his eyes instinctively and flinched as the horses sped by, and a host of wolves followed. Before them, the entire battle played out until the two men emerged victorious. "Come on!" memory-Whill bellowed into the night, and the defeated wolves retreated.

"I knew then you were ready," Abram recalled in reverie.

Whill turned from the scene to Abram and studied him. "How can this be real?"

Abram smiled his same smile. "Does it matter? The fact remains you are in mortal danger of losing your-self to your inner demons. Eadon has fractured your mind and created the Other so you might bend to his will. You must face your demons once and for all, else become a slave to them eternally."

The memory of himself tending to Abram's wounds played out before them, and tears streamed down his face. "I wish none of this had ever happened. What have I ever done to deserve this…this hell?"

Abram gave Whill a sympathetic smile. "What have any of Eadon's victims done to deserve his cruelty? How many of them wish all of this had never happened? You are not alone in this. The essence of life is struggle; you either get back up, or you lie down and die. This is the choice we all must face every day."

Whill knew Abram's words to be true. He had a choice to make: hide from the pains of the world, curl up in a ball, and cower from the cruelty of life, or accept what was, and fight for survival.

Around him the world of snow and ice began to fade as a whirlwind of white circled them.

"My time has passed. I must go," said Abram, as the whirlwind of snow began to swallow him up.

"Wait!" yelled Whill, reaching out as Abram became like the snow.

"Acceptance, my friend…that is the way to peace," said Abram, and his voice faded with the world of memory.

Whill opened his eyes, and, below him, a desert unfolded. He found himself flying through the air at high speeds and did not know where he was. He realized the Other had been in control, even as he felt the struggle within him. The Other ripped himself out of Whill and turned to choke him. Whill's concentration wavered, and they fell through the sky, grappling.

"Clever of you to find a way out, but I tire of these games," said the Other in Whill's ear, as he choked him and caused them to fall like a rock. Whill struggled against the apparition of his ego and attempted to slow their descent. They hit the ground hard, sending a plume of dust into the air.

Whill unsheathed Adromida, as the Other shot his chains from his wrists. The glowing chains flew at Whill, and he parried them wide. The Other pulled back a glowing hand and shot a fireball at Whill, which exploded against his shield. Smoke and dust filled the air as the effects of the blast were taken by the wind. He whirled around looking for his doppelganger, but found only leveled trees, long dead.

"I am not your enemy!" Whill screamed into the wind as he turned in his search.

"You are your own worst enemy, Whill. Look at you, talking to yourself in the middle of Drindellia. You are insane and no longer fit to control our body."

Whill stopped looking for the Other, realizing there was nowhere to look but within. He turned his mind sight once again inward. The familiar web of lightning stretched out before him. He moved deeper into his mind, past thoughts that rode the lightning, farther than he knew existed.

Far into the depths of his own consciousness, he delved, past the organized chaos of his thoughts and mental impulses. He went to a place within himself beyond the fabric of his being. Here was only light, harmony, tranquility, and peace. Here, he realized his true identity, his true self, one that had nothing to do with either the body or its worries. With him, he dragged the Other, and in the presence of the spirit that was Whill, his ego was humbled.

"This is what I am: infinite consciousness," said Whill, as he floated with arms stretched, bathed in light. At his feet, the Other cowered from the brightness.

"This form, of which you are a part, that you call the self, is not your dominion. It is the host through which I experience this world. You seem to have forgotten your place, my friend."

The Other squinted up at the incarnation of Whill's spirit with spiteful, blood-streaming eyes. "Destroy me and have done with it!" he screamed.

The spirit of Whill raised a hand, and the Other was lifted to his feet. Before he was able to retaliate, Whill embraced him and held him still. The Other lashed out and struggled against the unmoving form of the spirit. The illusion of Whill melted away, and the Other floated up, arms outstretched, to be bathed in piercing light. The voice of Whill surrounded the Other.

"You carry a great burden my friend, and you must carry it no more."

The all-encompassing light hummed brighter with warmth, and the Other stopped his thrashing and began to glow with an inner light of his own. His chains shot out wide, only to be dissolved. His eyes cleared of blood, and his scars melted away. A smile that had never been worn crept across his face as he was born anew.

Light and sound melded as Whill's spirit spoke through the light coursing through the Other. "I release you, my friend, from all your earthly pain. No more shall the memories haunt you. Be at peace, and know you are loved."

Shimmering tears found smiling cheeks as the Other was bathed in light and love from the spirit of infinite consciousness. They shined brighter still, until the two were one.

CHAPTER SEVEN
Winterstar

Dirk awoke after a few hours of rest and eagerly called Krentz and Chief from the spirit plane. They danced around each other as wisps and materialized before him. Chief bounded over to Fyrfrost and playfully barked and nipped at the dragon-hawk. Krentz solidified and offered Dirk a smile as she gained her bearings.

The morning sun rose behind rolling clouds, causing them to glow with ambient light in the east. The mild day's breeze carried the reminder that winter was on its way. Krentz approached Dirk and gave him a long, slow kiss.

"I have been thinking while I waited to be summoned back," she said, taking Dirk's hands in hers. Reading her eyes, he knew she had come to a decision, and her resolve was strong.

"I must make this right. The world around us falls to my father. It is in my power to move against him."

She released Dirk and gazed upon her palms as she shifted to spirit form. "No matter your words, the truth remains unchanged. My hands are stained with the blood of the innocent. I will wash them in the blood of tyrants."

She stared at her hands as they glowed bright. Dirk understood little about the powers of spirits; only legends attempted to explain such matters, and they were seldom reliable. Aside from her new ghostly powers, it seemed she retained her ability to perform magic, as she still possessed her father's gifts of power.

"Krentz," said Dirk loud enough to reach her in her current state of concentration. She jerked her head as if she thought herself alone.

"These are times of war my love." She hummed and stroked his hair. "Together, we shall be a force to be reckoned with. I am done running and hiding. I have already given my life. What is left, but my very soul? I would see it redeemed."

"As would I," said Dirk, "as would I."

The remainder of the day was spent repairing the enchantments upon Dirk's cloak and gear. His darts she replaced to the best of her ability with materials gathered from the nearby forest, and, though she possessed no dragon's breath, there were other means with which one of knowledge and skill might create explosives.

Long into the small hours of night, she wove her spell work by firelight. Chief watched curiously for a while. He soon became disinterested, however, and seemingly disturbed by the occasional swirling light or sparks of enchantment. Krentz poured forth large amounts of energy into the embedded gems within Dirk and his gear; his cloak alone contained thirteen gems.

At some point in the night, Dirk fell asleep as he watched Krentz empty herself into her work. He was always fascinated by the elven craft, and though Krentz taught him enough to be able to use the enchanted weapons and trinkets, he showed no magical proficiency. Dirk Blackthorn's abilities lay in other areas, and they were many.

Due to Krentz's recent proclamations, Dirk understood he would not be getting a good night's sleep any time soon, so he took advantage of this last opportunity. All morning and early afternoon he slept soundly, knowing Chief was guarding the perimeter and Krentz was nearby. His dreams were haunted by the echoed exclamations of the drunkard from Helzenvargen. In the town, the strange fortune teller had called Krentz a harbinger of death. In his dreams, one word played over and over: *wraith.*

Dirk awoke with a start when an explosion ripped through the day. He quickly found its source in Krentz's guilty laughter.

"Apologies," she laughed, as she put the newly made wooden darts into their holsters on the bands Dirk wore around his legs.

"I needed to test one," said Krentz with a mischievous grin.

Dirk lay back on his bed of moss and leaves with a sigh. He was startled by the blast, but relieved to be awakened all the same. His dreams had shifted from the fortune teller's hissing accusations to images of the mother and child, the blood steadily dripping from the petals of a black rose. He was not afraid of her, but rather, afraid for her. He never possessed the faith of a religious man, but recent events caused him to rethink his beliefs. He, like everyone else within earshot of a town pub, had heard numerous stories of ghosts and spirits, but he never witnessed anything that convinced him either way. The wards he trapped Chief within had been learned out of the insistence of Krentz; Dirk had never taken them seriously until he saw the spirit wolf with his own eyes.

If spirits existed, then reason dictated that the gods and heavens were real also, as were the hells. He found no solace in the idea of gods and rules, nor heavens or hells. He liked the world wild and the afterlife a mystery.

He had contemplated dismissing Krentz to the spirit world for months, years even, until the wars ended and the dangers passed. But, he could not. If her time in the spirit world was like days to his hours, he would be condemning her for decades or centuries, and he did not have the heart. So, he would stand by her, he would fight beside her, and, together, they would do what they could to turn the tides in the coming battles.

He sat up and roused himself to the waking world laboriously. Sleep clung to him like a reluctantly-parting lover. Krentz had resumed her soft chanting and spell weaving, and Dirk knew enough to leave her to her work. Getting up, he called to Chief and took from his gear a dagger and a dart marked with a single elven rune. Chief sprang from the forest and over the lightly burning fire without disturbing the smoke and landed without making a sound nor leaving a track.

"Any game around?" Dirk asked. Chief dropped down on his front legs and barked soundlessly. He bounded up and turned back into the woods with Dirk close behind. A few hundred yards in, Chief slowed to a prowl. Dirk followed his lead and sniffed at the air as he crouched and scoured the forest. Many smells permeated the early afternoon air, and one was of man.

"Hold, Chief," said Dirk, and the wolf froze.

Calling upon the enchanted studs on his earlobes, he listened to the sounds of the forest. There came the faint noise of someone walking through the forest slowly, followed by a soft thump.

"Stand down, Chief, they are no enemy to us."

Soon, a man came into view, walking toward them through the forest. Dirk's suspicions were proven correct when an Eldonian tribesman, with spear in hand, waved to them from afar. During their time living on Eldon Island, Dirk and Krentz had often been the guests of the Eldonian tribe, who called themselves the Morenkara. They had been visited many centuries before by elven Morenka, and the monks found eager students in the tribesmen. The people of Eldon Island embraced the ways of the Morenka, and lived in peace ever since under the protection of the powerful kingdom of Eldalon to the north.

"Well met, Winterstar!" Dirk yelled in greeting as he walked toward the tribesman whom he now recognized as one of the elders.

The man raised his staff in greeting and offered a bright smile as he came to stand before Dirk.

"Blackthorn returns to Eldon. It is good to find you well during these dark days," said Winterstar with a small bow, causing his many leather necklaces to swing wide of his bare chest.

"And you, my friend," said Dirk with a similar bow.

Winterstar smiled at Chief as he fully solidified.

"You walk with powerful spirits, Blackthorn. The dark ones hunt you still?"

Dirk nodded with a scowl. "They are like sand fleas, always biting at the arse."

Winterstar gave a long laugh. "They give everyone trouble it seems. Come, I have food. We trade stories of the world, and we eat."

Dirk glanced back toward his camp. Krentz would be at her spell work for some time. He followed the tribesman the few miles to his camp and asked many questions of the villagers he and Krentz shared as neighbors. He was informed of a few deaths and many births in the years since he left. He was glad to learn life on Eldon Island remained seemingly unaffected by the evil of Eadon.

They arrived at the camp, and, upon his first glimpse, Dirk realized Winterstar was on a spirit quest. Dirk helped the tribesman stoke the fire and prepare the food. He had no meat, but there was an abundance of roots, nuts, vegetables, and fruit. Soon they were eating and talking like old friends.

Dirk told him much of what had happened over the years, and to hear the tale repeated made it seem like a much more grand adventure than it once seemed. Now that it was all behind him, Dirk was surprised he had lived through it all. He doubted that many swore fealty to the dark lord Eadon and lived to tell about it. When such talk as dark elves came up, Winterstar became sullen. Dirk did not miss the weight upon his friend's mind.

"Traders come many days ago with strange tales of war and death. Them stories have been bad for many seasons, but this news, these stories, them make it sound like end times," said Winterstar. His eyes studied the forest and the sky above as if gleaning meaning from the leaves and clouds.

"A change is coming, Blackthorn. Royal family of Eldalon has fallen; them kingdom is crumbling. Dark spirits cover Agora in darkness."

Dirk frowned at the tribesman as if perplexed. "Since when do Eldonian Morenkara care for the affairs of the mainland? Have you not embraced the teachings of your revered elven prophets?"

"I hear all voices, ask many questions, realities become many," he explained.

"Will you fight for your life, if need be?" Dirk asked, intrigued.

"I do for myself, and I do for the ones I love, they who are many. But, we are no warriors. We will weather this as we would any storm. I go on spirit quest in search of answers, and I have found you."

Winterstar watched Chief stalk a wide perimeter around the camp. In his old eyes was a helplessness that was uncharacteristic of the man.

"You've sent your people to the Burning Mountains?" Dirk asked.

"Yesterday, the move began. We have food for long winter," said Winterstar.

Dirk and Krentz had explored the small mountain range often and found a wealth of crystals within many of the deep chambers. Why dwarves had not settled the small range, he could only guess; likely, they had sent mining parties who came back empty-handed, having found only useless crystals. But, where the dwarves found the multicolored crystals worthless, Krentz found them suitable to be used in the practice of Orna Catorna.

"The Burning Mountains will be as good a place as any to make a stand. Besides, I doubt that the dark scourge will come here. They've no reason; you are not a threat," said Dirk.

Winterstar smiled. "We are free, so we are a threat to the dark one. We will not be taken; we will die free, as we lived."

Dirk respected the tribesman's courage. If the dark elves came for the Eldonians, none would survive. The Burning Mountains would become nothing more than a tomb for them. He would offer his help in their preparation, but this was one fight of many, and Dirk had eyes on bigger battles. Eventually, Whill would have to face Eadon, and he intended on being present.

"I seek the head of the dark one, my friend. I offer what help I can give, but I fear I cannot fight with you this time," said Dirk.

Winterstar shook his head in understanding. He gave a toothless smile and offered more seeds and berries. The trees gave a sudden rustle, and leaves were sent spiraling into the air as Fyrfrost landed close to the camp. A whirlwind sent the small fire leaping and sputtering hot coals, as the dragon-hawk turned its natural color of brilliant silver and landed fifteen feet away. Krentz slid off his back and landed gracefully. She offered Winterstar a smile and tossed Dirk his repaired cloak.

"Winterstar of the Morenkara, what do you know?" she asked, and gave a small bow.

Winterstar bowed so rapidly, the bones through his ears caused them to flap. "She-with-no-name, my heart smiles at your health," he said.

Krentz gave a brave, half-cheeked smile at the greeting, but Dirk knew her heart. She had yet to completely come to terms with the loss of her mortal life, no matter her words.

"It is good to see you, friend," she replied.

"Come, eat, fortune gave me a beehive. Honey water?" Winterstar asked, extending the hollowed wooden container.

Dirk was about to explain that Krentz had recently been ill, to help hide the truth of her condition, but his words were cut off by her acceptance. She brought the drink to her lips and drank greedily. Krentz offered him a wink and nodded as she swallowed.

Winterstar motioned to Fyrfrost, who sat perched in the midday sun, gleaming like a silver vein of dwarven lore. "I never seen that kind."

"If you ever do again, turn the other way and run," said Dirk.

Winterstar laughed. "You live a life of fireside stories, Blackthorn."

Dirk raised a glass to that as if to say "lucky me," and took a long drink of his honey water.

"What have you heard of the mainland war?" Krentz asked.

"Traders speak of darkness, armies of monsters, defiled lands, and kingdoms under siege. They call it the end."

"Many rifts were opened by Eadon, his armies invaded every country, and their numbers are many," said Krentz.

"Have you any news of one called Whill of Agora?" Dirk asked.

Winterstar's eyes answered before his mouth, and he nodded quickly. "Traders them coming from far waters, them speak his name. Say he shows himself again, he with the elves and dwarves. Nigh on a tenday, they stormed Fendora Island."

Dirk and Krentz shared a glance.

"They say Fendora is free of Draggard, waters now clear. Whill made fire rain on Draggard. He went through tear in sky, tear closed."

"He went through and it closed?" Dirk asked. He turned to Krentz. "He could be trapped there."

"Or, he is dead," she replied.

They supped with Winterstar, and Krentz offered to help with their defenses. He was glad of the offer, but worry etched his usually jovial face.

CHAPTER EIGHT
Wolves at the Door

From the balcony, Tarren, Helzendar, and Lunara watched as elves scrambled to and fro throughout the city preparing for the coming invasion. Thousands of elven soldiers poured out to face the threat. Horns blared, and a deep humming began that Tarren could feel in his teeth.

Lunara jerked her head as if alert to something. "We have visitors," she told Tarren and Helzendar.

Soon, two elves with shining armor embedded with many softly glowing gems joined them on the balcony.

"We have been sent by the queen to watch over the children," said one of the elves.

"Who you callin' children, elfie?" Helzendar said and spat over the balcony.

"My apologies, master dwarf," he said with a bow to Helzendar and Tarren, who lifted his chin to seem taller. "I am–"

"Good, she sent the fearless Geldian, and the silent, but deadly, Arzarath," said the Watcher as he joined them upon the balcony. "Geldian here was about to inform you three of two more guards waiting outside. Good, yes? Yes."

The ancient elf bent to regard Tarren and Helzendar long enough to make Tarren shift uncomfortably. "Yes, quite a pair you two will make. The oceans will part for you, queens will offer themselves, those of evil heart will quiver, and men of honor will rejoice in your deeds."

Tarren and Helzendar shared a glance.

"Master Watcher, your words? What do they mean?" Lunara asked.

"What is meant is heard, fair child," said the Watcher, gazing out over the city.

"Words plucked from a river of possibilities by a hand groping blindly, but the reaching hand still searches, does it not?" the Watcher seemed to ask himself. "This night will be one of darkness." He pointed out to the west. "And, so begins a Song of Swords." The Watcher sang as flashes of lightning erupted in the western sky. The thunder followed five seconds later.

"They've landed, the shores have been breached," Lunara gasped, as again lightning flashed and thunder rolled over them like the growl of an angry god.

Tarren thought that Helzendar looked eager for the approaching madness. But Tarren was hard-pressed to be anything but terrified of the storm heading their way.

"How many can they be?" he asked, as a violent bolt of lightning hit miles away. The thunder shook the stone beneath them.

"All of them," said the Watcher with a faraway stare. "Eadon unleashes his legions upon Agora. Drindellia has been emptied."

Tarren stared wide-eyed at the Watcher. The far off lightning and rumbling thunder was getting closer. His fear grew as the dark elf armies neared. A high pitched bell rose over the deep thunder, and the Watcher nodded.

"What does it mean?" Tarren asked, trying not to sound too worried.

"It is the warning bell; the queen has ordered the city's energy shield be erected," said Lunara in sorrow.

A deep rumbling began under the city, followed by a multi-octave humming. Light shot from the capstone of the closest pyramid to the next, until all were connected by the beams of light. The glow from the pyramids grew as the humming became more high-pitched by the second. The noise reminded Tarren of a whistling pot before the boil. The air was thick with energy and taut with anticipation. Without warning, the sound stopped, and time seemed to pause. Finally, a crack of lightning ripped through the city as the energy shield weaved into life. The shield stretched out and thickened as the webs joined ever faster to each other until a dome of pulsing energy as smooth as glass surrounded them. A moment later, a great fireball soared through the air from the outside and slammed into the shield. The city was shaken, but the shield held as the fireball exploded against it, and debris rained down like a river of fire. Another spell hit as the Draggard hordes poured through the eastern jungle. The voice of the queen boomed through the city as she gave a command in Elvish.

The jungle came alive around the advancing army and began to attack. Vines thrashed and whipped the beasts as the monsters hacked with spear and blade. The dark elves retaliated with destructive spells of fire and wind, scorching the earth in a wide breadth around their armies.

Tarren's fear grew as the spells battered the energy shield of Cerushia. The explosions sounded as if the city were under water as they began to become more frequent and spread out across the dome.

"Will it hold?" Tarren asked Lunara. She did not answer, but turned to the Watcher. The old elf ignored them as he watched the flying draquon slam into the shield violently. As they continued to stare at him, he regarded them as if unaware of their question.

Finally, with a sigh, he spoke. "Will it hold? Of course not."

Tarren slumped on the balcony rail.

"It is not meant to hold," said the Watcher, and the boy perked up.

"What you gettin' at, ye old crazy elf? Spit it out!" Helzendar groaned.

The Watcher regarded him with a growing smile and turned back to the shield shimmering above them.

"The shield will hold long enough for us to prepare, which I suggest you all do."

"Come." Lunara gestured to the two boys as she walked from the balcony.

Tarren and Helzendar followed her into the dwarven abode. Tarren's trepidation had not lessened in the least. He had always dreamed of helping in the fight against the dark elves, but in the face of such violence, he began to reconsider his imaginings of war and glory.

CHAPTER NINE
Kellallea's Offer

Whill opened his eyes and found himself float-ing three feet off the ground with his arms raised skyward. Before him, a dark elf stared in wonder. There was fear in his eyes. He raised a hand to the dark elf, who flinched and brought up a powerful energy shield.

"You are free," Whill said to him, and the dark elf dropped where he stood. With his mind sight, he watched as the dark elf's spirit separated from its vessel and was absorbed by infinite consciousness.

Whill looked around, not knowing where he was. The smell of sulfur permeated the warm breeze. The land was barren and covered with miles of odd rock formations jutting up to the sky like knotted fingers. He was nowhere in Agora that he had ever seen. The last thing he remembered was standing before the rift on Fendora Island.

Had the Other brought him through? He guessed as much as he scanned the landscape for any sign that he was still near the rift.

Seeing nothing, Whill rose up into the air until he was just below the clouds. He found he could now do so without consciously summoning the power of Adromida; the blade simply flowed with his thoughts. Even from this high vantage point, Whill could no longer see the rift he had likely come through. He worried for his friends back on Agora, assuming they had not come through as well.

Many miles to the east, a brightness shined for a fleeting moment, the kind made by a reflection of light from shining metal. Having nowhere else to go, he flew off in that direction. It was a little past morning here, but he had no real way of even knowing what day it was. He had no idea how long he had been under the influence of the Other, or what he had done. He had defeated his alter-ego somehow, but his memories since being overtaken by his other side were like a dream.

Whill flew over the strange landscape of gnarled stone in the direction of the reflection, but still he found no sign of life. When he reached the spot he believed the light came from, he found nothing. He turned to his mind sight and looked out over the terrain, but had no better luck than with his eyes.

He landed upon the crest of one of the large, gnarled stone formations sprouting from the earth. High above the world, he sat and began to meditate with the Sword of Power Given in his hands.

"Kellallea, oh ancient one, whose roots reach the edges of Drindellia, hear my words," he said to the wind. For a long time, nothing happened. But Whill was not deterred. Kellallea had said she became one with Keye, and as such, it stood to reason she would hear his call. He focused his will into the stone formation beneath him and spread his consciousness down deep into the roots of the world. He called to her with his mind and called upon his learned knowledge from the *Book of Krundar* to connect with Keye.

You have come far, young one, Kellallea said in his mind. Whill breathed a sigh and smiled to himself.

Ancient one, it gladdens my heart to hear your voice and know that you carry on, he said.

He sensed her struggle, and, also, her animosity toward him. She had asked for help, and he had refused; he was not sure if she would help him now.

What is it you seek? she finally asked.

I am lost…I was brought here by a cunning foe, but I finally defeated him. I must return to Agora so I might lead the people against Eadon. Will you help me?

Yes, I am aware. I have watched you since you and the others came through the rift, and I saw what you did, she said.

The others? Then they are here as well, and trapped as I am?

They search for the Gate of Arkron, as they assume you are doing, she confirmed.

Will you help us?

I offered my help, young one, but you refused reason. I've neither time nor strength to spare for one so young and fool-ish, she said as her voice trailed off, and the connection began to fade.

Wait! Whill commanded her as he forced more of Adromida's power into strengthening the connection.

You would dare command me? You, who are to me as a new-born to an elder? I waited millenniums for the one who might transfer the power of the blade, one who might be wise enough to see beyond the lie of the prophecy. But alas, you will not lis-ten to reason, and so you shall fail. Your only hope is to give to me the power of Adromida. Only then can this war be won, said Kellallea in a voice like an earthquake.

I believe your tale, for it has been repeated by one of the elder Council of Elladrindellia. Eadon wishes for me to transfer the power to him. The prophecy is a lie, said Whill.

You understand now your only chance is through me. You have come to reason?

Yes, I have come to reason, and discovered many things.

Then, you will give me the power so I might defeat Eadon and bring peace to our lands? she asked.

No, Whill answered, *I know your secret; all has become clear to me now.*

What do you think you know? she asked with a conde-scending sneer.

You remain stronger than Eadon, and you seek a place among the gods, as he does. You feign weakness and bide your time. You

allowed Eadon to put into motion his creation of the Sword of
Power Given, so that one day it might be given to you, by me.
With it, you will gain the power of a goddess, you who stripped
the elves of the knowledge of Orna Catorna, you who have pos-
sessed the greatest power taken since the time of the taking of
knowledge. You have allowed the destruction of Drindellia and
the rise of Eadon, if only as a pretext to influence my hand.
Eadon understands this, and he seeks ever to surpass your
strength so he might attain the greatest power taken.

A long pause followed, and Whill sensed Kellallea's rage. She had been discovered, and her anger was great. There came a rumbling deep within the depths of the earth, and the stone formation on which Whill sat cross-legged began to sway. Above, storm clouds suddenly swirled to life menacingly black and wreathed in lightning. The wind picked up and would have sent him flying from the stone, had he not used Adromida to secure him within a globe of energy. A flash of lightning struck the stone where he sat, and Kellallea suddenly appeared there on the rock. Her hair blew in the torrential winds as she stared down upon Whill with eyes of fury. Lightning struck again, this time hitting the center of the large rock formation. The stone formation was hewn in two and crumbled violently down to the ground below. Whill remained unmoved, floating as he had sat.

"You are clever, young one, perhaps too clever for your own good. Tell me, what is to stop me from destroying you here and now?" she bellowed with a voice like thunder.

Whill regarded her with a steady gaze as the storm gathered in strength and surged menacingly around him. "I alone can wield Adromida; you need me," he said.

Kellallea's anger grew, and she pulled back an arm as if to smite him then and there. Whill set his jaw and looked back at her defiantly. "Destroy me, and you have gained nothing."

The murder in her eyes slowly subsided, and the storm along with it. Whill blinked, and he was standing among the rubble of the fallen stone. Kellallea stood before him calmly, her glowing beauty had returned and gone was her rage.

"Eadon cannot be allowed to attain the Sword of Power Given," she said calmly.

"Instead, you should attain the power?" Whill asked. "You should ascend to the heavens and become like a god? You, who allowed your people and homeland to be defiled as a means to your power-hungry ends, would you make a better god?"

"Eadon would bring an end to all things." she said.

"You are no different."

Kellallea looked to Whill as she had not before. Her disdain melted away and her smile became warm. "The weight of the entire world sits upon your shoulders, yet how brave you are." He was aware she could destroy him with a thought, even with the sword of power in his possession. She was the oldest living thing in the world. She had seen the rise and fall of mountains, and, to her, the life of entire forests was but a season. She had pondered the mysteries of the universe for thousands of elven lifetimes; she was patient, and she was cunning. His only saving grace was that the Sword of Power Given needed to be given freely; it was the only reason he remained alive.

Through the contact of her hand to his cheek, Whill began to feel pleasure flood through his body, as her smile widened and her gaze locked him in place. He shuddered in ecstasy as bliss coursed through him. She leaned in to whisper in his ear, and her voice was like music, and her breath was the warmth of a spring breeze. She smelled of flowers after a spring rain. Whill arched uncontrollably, as a million prickles of pleasure danced down his spine and weakened his legs.

"You need bear your burden no longer, Whill of Agora. Give to me freely the Power of Adromida, and, together, we shall put an end to Eadon's reign of darkness. Together, we shall liberate Agora and build Drindellia anew. You need only say the words, and it will be so."

Whill lost himself in her eyes. Before his mind's eye, the beautiful new world she promised was rich with life and bursting with beauty, a place where war was a distant legend, sickness and disease a myth. Together, they would guard their world kingdom against evil, she, from her heavenly throne, and he, from his earthly. Together, the three races of man, dwarf, and elf would thrive. A new age of enlightenment would be born of their union and would live eternal. The beautiful new world she promised brought tears of joy to his eyes. She released him, and the pleasure subsided as did the vision, leaving him yearning for but a glimpse of what he had envisioned.

Kellallea stood before him with her intoxicating smile. Beyond her eyes, Whill sensed a knowledge unsurpassed by all but the gods, and he was humbled. Confused, he tried to remember why he had refused her, why he had fought the inevitable. Why didn't he just give her the power of Adromida? It could all end now if he only said the words...

"You need only say the words, and you shall deal the fatal blow against the dark one, you shall become legend. Your name will be spoken in celebration for time immeasurable."

Whill realized why he hesitated. It had been there at the back of his mind the whole time, wavering but somehow staying alit like a candle of reason against the winds of her persuasion.

"You allowed the rise of Eadon, and the destruction of your people," he said.

"It is a small price to pay for the world that we can create. Sacrifices must be made."

"No," said Whill. "You are no different than Eadon. You would leave a trail of destruction in the wake of your pursuit of power."

"I did not allow the rise of Eadon, or the destruction of Drindellia," she said with sorrow in her voice. "His crimes are the crimes of many. I once stripped the elves of their knowledge and power, because we almost destroyed ourselves over it. What began as a great enlightenment and enrichment of elven life, soon became its greatest danger. And for an age, there was peace in Drindellia. But the ancient knowledge and the pursuit of power began to grow once again within the hearts of my kin. The memory of magic held strong throughout the ages, and soon one came to me that had rediscovered the old ways. I thought to kill him, but something stayed my hand; now I know my mercy was a mistake. For now history has repeated itself once again, and my people have suffered at the hands of those that would seek infinite power."

"You seek infinite power," said Whill.

"I seek infinite peace!" she yelled, her brow bent with indignant anger. "Eadon must be stopped."

"Why did you not raise a hand against him when the Dark Elf Wars began?"

"I have not existed these thousands of years as you understand it. I took the form of a tree those many ages ago. I slept, and I grew. I became like the mountain and the forest. I became one with the spirit of all things, and

I knew peace. I was mildly aware of the struggles of my kin, but knew not the full extent of their plight until I was awakened, until I was attacked by Eadon. He came to me as I slept and attempted to steal from me all the power that I possessed. The battle nearly killed us both. What it did to the land is my deepest regret. He is my equal; I cannot defeat him without the power of Adromida."

Whill wasn't sure what to believe. He knew he could not defeat Eadon on his own, yet he did not trust Kellallea. He alone could wield Adromida, and he alone possessed the ability to transfer its power. He realized she had likely been the reason Eadon had made it so no elf could wield the blade.

"Will you help me? Surely, together, we can defeat Eadon, and then this business of the blade can be dealt with," said Whill.

"I offered my help young Whill, and my offer remains, with but a word this can all be over," she reminded him.

"I do not trust you enough to turn over a power such as this on faith! You tried to manipulate me with your words and visions. I will not hand over the power of Adromida. Kill me if you like, but neither of you shall possess it if you do."

Kellallea regarded him with slow smoldering fury hid well behind patient eyes. "What is it you would ask of me?" she asked.

"Help me to the last Gate of Arkron."

CHAPTER TEN

Veolindra

As the sun broke over the horizon illuminating the dull clouds hanging overhead, the barbarians broke camp, and, within the hour, they marched southwest once again. They followed in the footsteps of the Draggard down the once heavily used trade road. The beasts left the road behind them trampled and muddy, making the going slow and laborious for the wagon train. Soon, Aurora instructed Zander to order the Draggard to fall back behind the seven armies; better to break through the snow themselves than navigate the mud pits the Draggard left in their wake. The early winter weather was in a transition period when fat snow fell but quickly melted, leaving everything wet and slushy.

The barbarians stiffened and the horses whined nervously as the Draggard passed to take up the rear. The dwargon lumbered past by the hundreds, their heavy three-toed feet leaving wide puddles in the road. The beasts passed without incident, though they snarled and bit at the air if a barbarian stared too intently.

Beorin of Bear Tribe road up next to Aurora then, glaring at Zander as he took his place beside his chieftain. "This weather is shyte, and this mud is for the dogs," he spat.

"Unlike the dark elves, we cannot control the weather. Focus on what we can change, Bear Chief," said Aurora.

"Ah, but you are right," Beorin replied. She felt him staring sidelong at her, measuring. "You have impressed me, Chieftain," he said finally, and turned his hard gaze to the road. His eyes told of deep consideration, as if his words escaped him. His beard came together as he puckered his lips, his lack of teeth bringing his bottom lip up and out. His gray eyes sparked with resolution.

"Yes, I see clearly now our destiny."

"Save your arse kissing for one who gives a shyte, Beorin," said Aurora.

"You have me wrong, m'lady. I came only to tell you of my wishes should I die in battle. I ask to be raised by the dark elf. If I can be of further use dead, then I accept."

Aurora jerked her head to the side and took a new-found measure of the man. His eyes showed his sincerity. She was impressed and disturbed by his resolve.

"You do not know what you are saying," she told him.

"I speak with my heart of hearts, Aurora," said Beorin, and fell back, leaving her to her thoughts.

The conversation made her think of Azzeal. She had seen little of the lich, but more than she could stand. His milky white eyes made her skin crawl; they saw nothing and everything it seemed, and she always felt them staring at her, past her, into her very soul. She thought of the elf she had known for such a short time, how he had fought to free her and the others from the arena in Uthen-Arden, and how he had tried to save her. She knew he was inside, somewhere behind the crooked stance and downward stare. She had turned out to be a coward after all, unable to die doing the right thing. Instead, she had done something unimaginable. The memory of impaling Azzeal with the Dragonlance of Ashai came to her again. His eyes locked hers in place, and rather than outrage or shock, they conveyed sympathy. What if she had gone against Eadon, and ordered her armies against the Draggard?

Zander moved to ride beside her once more, his head craned back as he spied Beorin. "Hard to find one so dedicated, even among my kind. He is possessed of something beyond honor. Keep an eye on that one…he will be quite useful."

"Honor? Your kind cares for such a thing?" Aurora asked.

"You may think us monsters, but who claims such things? Humans? Dwarves? What have they to say of your people? As your people's names have been tarnished by fallacy, so too have the dark elves," said Zander, his voice carrying spiteful anger. "We did not start the War of Drindellia, 'twas the intolerance of the Elves of the Sun that drove us to defend ourselves. I was born without the gift of magic. Eadon used his power to give many of us the gift of Orna Catorna. But the sun elves did not approve. They came after us. They waged war. Yes, we know honor, but our shared enemies do not."

Aurora sensed a deep seeded anger within him, one born of oppression and injustice. She understood. Long her own people harbored such racial pains. But she did not trust the dark elf, and therefore his every word remained suspect.

"You do not believe me," said Zander.

"I believe those I trust, and you have yet to gain mine," said Aurora.

Zander laughed, his handsome smile doing more to disarm her than his words.

"I doubt many can lay claim to such a feat," said Zander.

"What feat?"

"Gaining your trust."

Aurora threw him a look.

They rode on in silence. It was near noon now she guessed. The thick, hazy cloud cover gave no clear indication of the sun's position. Many hundred yards ahead, the lich Azzeal steered them ever south. Aurora hoped soon they would be rid of the undead elf. She grew weary of his presence. He often stopped and looked back upon the armies; she imagined those milky white eyes staring through her even over such distance.

"You were not born with magic?" she asked Zander.

"No."

"And you were taught by Eadon?"

"He awakened dormant parts of my brain," Zander explained.

"Why did the Elves of the Sun find offense?" she asked.

"Are you familiar with the relationship between the practitioners and the Enta?"

"I have been told the Enta offer their power to the gifted ones. Theirs is a symbiotic union."

"Union," Zander scoffed. "It is slavery. The Elves of the Sun know the gift can be shared, and they are threatened. Eadon freed us from our bondage. He empowered us to be more than energy slaves, constantly being leached of our inner strength."

Aurora reminded herself to be weary of the dark elf, but she found herself believing him. An idea came to her then.

"If elves not born with the gift can be taught… can humans be taught also?"

Zander did not hide his pleasure. "Yes, you could be taught the ways of the Orna Catorna. The sun elves know this as well, yet they do not help any but themselves. In five hundred years, how much has their magic helped your people?" he asked.

Aurora did not have to search long for the answer. The elves remained strangers to the barbarians of Volnoss. From what she had gleaned from her time with the other races, they were strangers to all of Agora.

"Would you teach me?" she asked. Though she hated asking the dark elf for anything, she was tempted by the idea of wielding magic.

"I can awaken your mind, but the art does not come quickly. I have studied the arts for hundreds of years, and I have only mastered three of the schools."

"Could I live so long?" she asked.

"With the power to be gained through the practice, you might be Chieftain of the Seven for a thousand years."

Aurora's heart leapt at the prospect. She imagined the grand empire she might build with the power of the elves. She would have many daughters, the empresses of the Seven. The barbarians would grow strong once again, and never would they be defeated.

Many grand fantasies kept Aurora occupied the remainder of the journey. By nightfall, the city of Orenden rose beyond the distant valley. The many lights of the city illuminated the thick dark clouds that had blanketed the sky all day. In the valley before the city, a sea of tents emerged. Many banners hung in the still night air.

Azzeal stood like a statue looking out over the valley as Aurora and her armies arrived. She was loath to speak to the lich, and slowed enough so Zander led by half a horse length. As they reached Azzeal, he turned to regard them with a dead stare. His head sat perpetually cocked slightly to the side, and his gaze sent shivers through her body.

"Report, lich!" Zander ordered.

Azzeal turned his head slowly with jerky spasms, and his gaze captured Aurora. "Lady of the North," he said in a wet, rasping voice that gave her chills. "The Shierdon army awaits."

"Lead us on," she uttered, feeling sick.

Azzeal took many long moments to turn from her. He floated an inch from the ground and on down into the snow-covered valley. The glow from the clouds above the city cast the lich in an eerie light, but Aurora found herself unable to turn away. She realized Zander had been staring at her.

"That...thing, is never to address me again. Do you understand?" she ordered Zander.

"As you wish," he replied.

Ahead on the road leading to the valley and stretching fields, a horseman had stopped next to Azzeal. Soon, the lone figure came galloping toward them. Aurora ordered the armies to stop as he approached. As the horsemen drew near, she realized it was not a man at all, nor human. The dark elf female stopped a horse length from her and Zander and saluted them with an open palm over her heart and bowed.

"Zander, and...Aurora Snowfell, Chieftain of the Seven Tribes of Volnoss," she said, bowing once again.

"Veolindra," Zander greeted her in kind.

"What is your title?" Aurora asked.

Veolindra tossed her long, flowing hair over her right shoulder. Black armor, made of a multitude of overlapping bones, gleamed beneath a sleek flowing cloak. She raised her chin proudly.

"I am Lich Lord of the Western Shierdon Army," she proclaimed proudly. "I command three regiments of ten thousand."

"The human soldiers of Shierdon? They follow a dark elf?" Aurora asked, confused.

The smile of the necromancer stretched across her face and became a maniacal grin. "The armies of Shierdon are dead. They have been raised to better serve our master. They are now my death knights; they feel neither fear nor pain. Settle your army and join me for a meal. Many things shall be explained."

"Very well," said Aurora.

The dark elf put her hand to her heart once more; silver tattoos swirled and danced upon her dark skin. "Chieftain." she bowed.

"Lich Lord," said Aurora.

Camp was made, and soon fire pits sprouted up throughout, the firewood having been gathered from the nearby forest surrounding what had once been wheat fields. The city sat bordered by farmland on all sides but the eastern, where long rows of apple trees covered rolling hills leading to the forest. The Draggard armies kept a good distance away from the barbarians and horses, but still too close for Aurora's liking.

By the light of the small fire at the center of her tent, she rummaged through her old trunk. Her mother had seen to it that her personal items made it to her wagon. Aurora was grateful for the thought, but none of her old furs would do for the Chieftain of the Seven. She reminded herself to have a new wardrobe made, and armor would not hurt either. Frustrated, she flung a dark-red fox fur dress to the bed. The barbarians would view it as advocacy of Fox Tribe. She didn't need anything causing strife between the tribes now. She decided on wolf fur, being that she was from Wolf Tribe. The skirt sat low on her round hips, and though it reached her knees, it was slit nearly to the top. The shirt had only one sleeve, with a thick strap running over one shoulder. She fought her left breast under the fur and adjusted herself. She blew her hair out of her face and scowled at the foggy mirror in disgust.

"You look like shyte," she sighed, and grabbed her fur boots.

Outside, fluffy snowflakes fell lazily from the dimly illuminated clouds. What little wind remained danced around the heavy snowfall piling quickly upon the fields. If the snow didn't let up soon, the going would be slow tomorrow. Aurora's guards came to stand beside her. She ignored their presence and stiffened when she noticed the lich Azzeal standing before her.

"This way, Lady of the North," he croaked as he stared with unblinking eyes. Even after he turned, she could feel him watching her somehow. She looked around for Zander so that she might scold him, but he was nowhere to be seen. She reluctantly followed the lich through the barbarian camp.

Azzeal floated over the snow leaving a line of frozen ice behind him. Through the camp they went, across a short gap between armies, and into the Shierdon camp. The smell of rotting meat permeated the air. None of the regular chatter or activity filled the camp, and soon Aurora knew something was wrong. The cook fires burned low and none of the soldiers sat outside. Sentries stood guard, but even they seemed odd, standing eerily still at their posts, with none of the men conversing. The silence was haunting; not even the sparse wind made a sound. It was like walking through a graveyard. Following a lich only made it worse. To her relief, Azzeal stopped before a large black orb the size of a house, its surface reflecting the landscape around it like ice. Aurora soon forgot the lich as a door was formed and the ice melted away before her. She stepped through the threshold and turned to watch it reform behind her, sealing her inside. No fire burned within, but the strange orb was warm, and a soft orange glow cast evenly across the surface of the dome. At the center of the dome sat a large, four-poster bed made of what appeared to be dragon bones. Dark blue silk sheets folded over a blanket of white fur, and fat pillows of the same fur lay piled at the head. At the foot of the bed sat two beautiful chests, with identical inlay of pearl throughout panels of dark cherry wood. To Aurora's right, a long table stood with four chairs to a side, and upon the table a three-tiered candleholder, made with the bones of Draggard fingers, burned bright. Other odds and ends that would be found in a commander's tent were present. Maps on smaller tables, stacked books upon a writing desk, dressers, chests, and a liquor cabinet.

Veolindra greeted her at the center of the large dome, and to her utter surprise, the dark elf pulled her down and kissed her on the lips. They remained that way for a long moment in which Aurora's wide eyes stared at Veolindra's closed ones. When she released her, the lich lord kept her eyes closed and bit at her bottom lip, savoring the kiss.

"You have a fire in your soul that is seldom found, Aurora Snowfell," she said, holding Aurora's hands in hers.

"Come, sit, and let us drink."

She led Aurora to a heavily cushioned lounging chair and guided her to sit. Her hair spun in a flourish as she went to the liquor cabinet.

"What is your drink?" she asked as she eyed the contents.

"The road has been slow and uneventful. I want fire in my stomach."

Veolindra hummed hungrily and returned with two small crystal glasses and a dark red bottle. The dark elf poured them each a half glass and raised hers.

"To the Chieftain of the Seven: together, we shall conquer Northern Agora in the name of our master."

Aurora nodded as they clanged glasses. She had asked for fire, and fire she got. The liquor went down like lava, and she did all she could not to choke. The drink was stronger than any of the barbarian spirits, stronger still than any concoctions of the dwarves she had ever had. The drink hit her stomach and spread warmth throughout her body. Veolindra refilled her glass and sat in the large fur-covered chair beside her.

With a murmured word, a small cage of stone, set upon the low table, came alight with dancing flame. The lich lord sipped her drink and surveyed Aurora's long form. She was accustomed to being gawked at, but not often by women.

"What is it called?" Aurora asked, raising the glass.

"This drink is Kronosh. It is as old as my people."

"It is the strongest I have found," said Aurora, studying her glass in the light.

"And likely the strongest you will ever find. I would have offered something sweeter, but this seemed to be what you wanted," said Veolindra. "But enough of spirits; you had asked about my death knights," she said with a devilish grin.

The door melted open once again, and a soldier walked inside to stand before them both. He stood, heavily clad in silver plate mail, with a sash of purple over one shoulder. At his hip sat a long, thick sword sheath, and upon his helmet a plume of brilliant silver feathers, that of the silverhawk. He came to attention with a click of the heels and took off his helmet to address his mistress. Aurora expected the same milky white eyes as the lich Azzeal's; instead she found green, glowing orbs set deep in a sunken face.

"Mistress," he said in many voices, one deep and gravely, another unnaturally high but faint, and yet another, cold and menacing.

"They are much more useful in this form. Not long ago, the soldiers, and then captains and generals, began to ask too many questions. The humans became suspicious, and we would have soon lost control. Lord Eadon saw to the work himself. He is yet a master of arts unknown; his work is marvelous," said Veolindra. Aurora could only nod, disturbed by necromancy.

"Does anything of the person they once were survive?" Aurora asked quietly.

"Sometimes. Depends on how much fire they held in their hearts," replied Veolindra with a grin. "Their most primal emotions live on, scattered memories. Rarely do they rebel against their bondage, and, when they do, they are made example of."

"What is your name?" Aurora asked the death knight.

"Seven, of ten."

She turned from the death knight to Veolindra, confused.

"Seven of ten. Each of the ten command one thousand. I dictate to the ten, and they down to the others. They will do anything I say. Watch," she said, and pointed a long black fingernail at the knight's dagger.

"General Seven, remove your left glove and stab yourself in the hand."

Seven took off his glove, unsheathed his curved dagger, and buried it to the hilt through his hand. He stood unflinching and held out his hand; no blood fell to the ringed carpet at his feet.

"They feel not pain, they know not fear," said Veolindra.

"Leave us!" she ordered Seven.

The death knight commander saluted Veolindra and left them. Aurora was glad; she was no more comfortable around the death knight than the lich.

Veolindra seemed to sense her unease. "They take some getting used to."

"Indeed," said Aurora. "Though I am anxious to see them in battle."

The lich lord smiled at that. "Soon, my friend."

CHAPTER ELEVEN
General Mick Reeves

Krentz did what she could for the Eldonians. They had sent their women and children into the heart of the Burning Mountains and built defenses. Krentz laid wards inside the mountain, rather than out, as the dark elves would find any magical workings suspicious. Dirk would have stayed to help them defend, if not for Krentz's determination to move against her father. She would not be swayed, and Dirk let the argument go.

They left the next morning and flew north from Eldon Island toward the shores of Eldalon. The wind had picked up throughout the night, and now large waves distorted the waters below. Upon Fyrfrost, they would be all but invisible to anyone below. The channel between Eldon and Eldalon was quiet, with not a fishing boat nor Eldalonian naval vessel to be seen. This did not sit well with Dirk. Emptiness permeated the air, lending a foreboding quality to the blustering wind. The capital city of Kell-Torey had fallen, and the land was without a king. Dirk knew nothing but murder and mayhem awaited him in the kingdom.

"Do any of Whill's line survive? Is there an heir to the Eldalonian throne?" he asked Krentz over his shoulder. After a pause, she answered, her voice carrying the weight of sadness.

"I left none alive," she said in a low voice.

"The twins…was it just you three set to the task?" he asked.

"No. I was set with but one task: the King and his immediate family…I…It is likely the other assassins succeeded," said Krentz.

"No, the twins failed. I killed them both. Lord Carlsborough yet lives, or so I left him."

"Whill remains the heir, either way," said Krentz, her voice somehow unaffected by the wind as was Dirk's. "Unless Lord Carlsborough is of closer relation than the king's grandson."

"He is the late King's third cousin, or so he says," Dirk confirmed.

"Then, your Whill of Agora is heir to two falling kingdoms."

"May the Gods pity he who hath the world," said Dirk reciting an ancient elven proverb. Krentz finished it for him.

"For he has nothing more to gain, but loss."

The coast came into view before the noon sun, and soon, the ground was speeding past below them. The winds from the sea pushed them on for many miles during which Fyrfrost only glided. Dirk had long ago learned to keep his hood tight to his ears, lest the wind pound them deaf. The weather had turned colder since his last long flight. His cloak did much against the chill, but any exposed flesh felt the bite of the wind. Krentz sat behind him and often leaned forward to hold him tight, but she was not a source of heat in her spirit form. She possessed the ability to conjure such an inner warmth, and she would if asked, but Dirk did not want to remind her of her lack of warmth and, therefore, her condition.

"Fyrfrost tells me of movement ahead," said Krentz, and Fyrfrost growl-cooed the affirmative.

"Can't you teach him to speak?" Dirk asked.

"With time, but dragon speech at its best is nearly impossible to understand. The massive teeth tend to hamper pronunciation."

Fyrfrost turned into a spiraling descent to bring them closer. They were still too far for Dirk to make anything out, even with his enchanted hood.

"He says there are Draggard ahead."

"How many?"

"Twenty, twenty-five. A dark elf is among them, their handler," said Krentz.

"Handler? They usually command hundreds, thousands," Dirk replied, intrigued.

"Yes. Either they are on a mission of importance, or there are more dark elves within Agora now."

Dirk pondered the situation as the group finally came into view. Fyrfrost's color-changing feathers would not hide them from the dark elf's mind sight. He just hoped the elf didn't use it.

"They are a small enough group for a bit of practice. Shall we?" he asked over his shoulder. Krentz was not there. She had turned to a wisp and suddenly solidified, straddling his lap. Her hair blew rapidly, leaving them in its shelter. For a moment, only her eyes existed, and then her lips as she kissed him softly, and they were warm. For a fleeting moment, Dirk wondered if she had read his mind, and the moment was gone.

Krentz dissolved as Fyrfrost flew over the marching group and bathed their flanks in dragon fire. As screams of pain and warning rang out, the attackers banked left to circle around once more. Fireballs erupted from the Draggard ranks, but missed as Fyrfrost turned.

"Fly high, Fyrfrost. When she gets the caster's attention, bring me in low," said Dirk.

The Draggard began to spread out wide, increasing the target range. No barked orders rang out, however. Krentz once told him the dark elf handlers controlled their groups with but a thought.

At the southern edge of the group a noticeable disturbance began, and he knew it to be Krentz. From his pocket, he took the wolf figurine and yelled to Fyrfrost. "Fly me around to the left flank, keep well away from the caster, and get the runners."

Fyrfrost complied and banked left to the edge of the scattered group. Dirk leapt from the gliding dragon and landed in a roll.

"Come, Chief, battle awaits," said Dirk.

Swirling smoke drifted out of the figurine along with a howl. The nearest Draggard rushed them and soon wished it had disobeyed its master. Chief slammed into it, and, together, they rolled away in a tangle of thrashing claws and snarling maws. Dirk came in faster than the next Draggard's striking tail. A dart to the eye sent the beast reeling back in agony, and when its hands instinctively flew to its face, Dirk sliced open its belly with his enchanted sword. He sped along to the next, leaving the Draggard's steaming entrails spilling into its clawed hands.

They ambushed the group on an open road surrounded by nothing but rolling fields of wheat and corn. The fields had long been harvested and were now brown with the coming of winter. Chief moved through the dried and brittle husks like smoke and solidified upon the back of the Draggard in front of Dirk. He sliced the back of the Draggard's knees as he passed, and Chief rode it to the ground tearing at its neck. Across the road, flames erupted in the wheat field, and Dirk knew Fyrfrost had rejoined the fray.

Chief was at his side once more as Dirk kept low through the field of husks. He could have used his hood to locate the Draggard, but instead, he trusted

Chief to guide him true. They moved north, and Chief gave a low growl. His quarry came into view not far off through the gaps in the corn: three Draggard. Dirk threw an exploding dart up into the air that arched in its flight and came down in the midst of the small band. The explosion was followed by many shrieks.

"Finish them off!" said Dirk.

Chief charged toward the rising smoke, and Dirk continued north and east. Another explosion rang out among the tumult. He came out of the corn field and scanned the road to the south. Fyrfrost bathed it in flames from on high. Between him and the dragon-hawk, Krentz battled a dark elf handler and his minions. She moved with liquid grace and deadly precision, dancing around her opponents and turning to smoke before their blades landed. The dark elf knew his danger and kept his beasts after her as she advanced.

Dirk started toward them, and Chief came crashing through the field to join him. They ran down the road at the dark elf's back as he hurled spells frantically at Krentz. The wheat field to the left was littered with scorched bodies; none lived to attack from the side of the road. To the right was the cornfield they had just circled from. If any Draggard remained, they did not advance.

"Distract him, Chief!" Dirk called.

Chief took spirit form and shot toward the dark elf with a snarl. Dirk went wide of the elf as Chief took form and slammed into him. Beneath Chief, the elf vanished, leaving only a cloak to be pawed at curiously by the confused wolf. Dirk ran the outskirts of the group Krentz had engaged and, with his enchanted blade, cut two of the beasts' tails off. When they turned in a rage, Dirk went to work with sword and dagger. A spear came at him and was deflected wide, followed by a spiked ball and chain. Dirk spun away from the heavy ball and turned quickly as it hit the ground hard. The Draggard yanked back on the handle, and Dirk severed the chain and sent the beast flying backward. His dagger came up to catch a long spear blade as he engaged two others. He moved in a blur of motion, leaving the Draggard weaponless and bloody, even as their heads slid from bleeding necks and shock covered their hideous faces. He cut through another to find Krentz standing before him, holding her bloody curved blade.

"It's about time," she teased, and he wiped his blades with a smile.

Chief whined and pawed cautiously at the dark elf's cloak. Krentz knelt and felt the ground beneath her. She closed her eyes in concentration, and, after a time, stood, shaking her head.

"He is gone to the south."

Fyrfrost sat, gnawing on a Draggard head, trying to get to the brains. The road stretched on toward the coast between similar fields. Bare road and blue sky dominated the landscape.

Dirk moved to investigate the cloak, but was stopped by Krentz.

"Wait," she said with a hand to his chest. "He would not leave his cloak behind. Any practitioner of Ralliad or Krundar knows how to shift their effects along with themselves. It is likely a trap."

"Come, Chief," said Dirk, and then whistled to Fyrfrost.

"Men approach from the north, an army it seems," Krentz told him.

A hill in that direction obstructed Dirk's view. "How far?" he asked.

"A few miles," she said as if listening. She bent and once again felt the earth at their feet. "They are many hundreds. With cavalry and wagons."

"Shall we avoid them?" he asked.

Krentz shook her head slowly. "We should learn what we might."

"They will not take kindly to a dark elf," he reminded her.

"I can appear however I wish. They will see not a dark elf, but an elf of such beauty they will be compelled to cooperate," said Krentz.

"Chief, stay close, but stay hidden and wait for my word," said Dirk. It would be much easier on the horses.

They mounted Fyrfrost, and he flew them over the hill to the north. Large regiments of marching soldiers came into view. A cavalry, two horses wide and at least twenty long, followed. Long lances of silver and blue shone brilliant in the sunlight. Two knights rode ahead and behind the company, each flying large Eldalonian flags on long poles. The army of silver and blue stopped on command as the first cries of "dragon!" began to ring out.

Between the marching soldiers and cavalry were hundreds of men, women and children: the refugees of Kell-Torey.

Dirk urged Fyrfrost to land upon the road many hundred yards before the soldiers. He and Krentz dismounted as the company halted, and arrows were nocked by the soldiers as they took a knee. The cavalry split and charged past the soldiers and refugees to form a wide barrier. Dirk raised his empty hands to them and began to walk down the road to meet them. Krentz followed. The arrows did not fly. He considered that a good sign. A flag bearer and two knights on armored horses galloped out to meet them on the road.

"Ho!" one shouted as they approached. "Show your hands!" he yelled. The three knights circled them with lances pointed at their chests. The speaker, who was only distinguishable beyond the helmet by his large curled mustache, seemed to be the leader of the group. He eyed them both, but paid particular attention to Krentz.

"Drop your weapons and surrender," he ordered, shooting a wary glance at the dragon-hawk.

"We are not enemies of Eldalon," said Dirk as he tried not to think about the recently deceased Royal family. "Neither will we lay down our arms."

The knights tensed and held their spears a bit higher. Dirk stared down the shafts. The two looked to their general for guidance, but the mustached man only continued to take measure of Dirk and Krentz as the knights circled slowly.

"You would dare defy an order from an Eldalonian knight?" barked the general.

"No need for all this, good sir. We are not enemies to Eldalon, but allies. Our enemies are one and the same: Eadon and his dark elf minions."

"Lay down your arms. This is your last warning," said the general, unsheathing his sword.

Dirk opened wide his cloak, and the amazed knights regarded his small armory of weapons in amazement. "To do so would leave me standing before you naked." He closed his cloak around him once more. "If we were your enemy, we would not be having this conversation. No offense, but my dragon could destroy you all. Luckily, he prefers Draggard blood to human."

"Who are you?" asked the general with all authority, yet sheathing his blade.

"I am called Blackthorn, and my companion is Krentz," said Dirk. He pointed to the dragon-hawk as it shimmered silver in the sun like the mount of a god. "Would you like to meet Fyrfrost?"

The general scowled at the veiled threat and stopped circling to stare at Krentz. "What business does an elf have in Eldalon?"

"We were checking up on old friends, the Eldonians. They told us fantastical stories of a rift to another land opening up and swallowing all of Kell-Torey. Curiosity got the better of us," she explained with an exaggerated but delicious accent that the other two knights ate up. Their demeanor changed immediately. Tense shoulders dropped, the lances slowly sagged to safely point at the ground, and their eyes traveled over her lithe form wrapped in tight leather. The general too was intoxicated by her exotic beauty. The horses, however, were restless so near to her.

She tossed her long cloak back over her left shoulder to bundle at her side, and Dirk, knowing what she was up to, tried not to smirk. She turned, and all eyes were drawn to her statuesque backside and long legs as she pointed southeast.

"I am on a mission given me by the Queen of Elladrindellia. I elicited the help of Mr. Blackthorn as he is known to me to be a great warrior, and a legendary lover," said Krentz as she turned with a flourish of her cloak, and all eyes darted up guiltily.

"I apologize if you find my words too forward, we sometimes forget humans frown upon women speaking so," she added, as if concerned that she had made a slip as an ambassador of her people.

"Quite all right," said the general with a raised chin. "Eldalon is known for its tolerance of many things. However, dragons entering our lands is not one of them. The elves of Elladrindellia should know as much."

"Indeed," Krentz acknowledged. "As I explained, we received word your kingdom was in dire ways, and we decided to offer what aid we might. Do you not require help? Please tell us these crazy fishermen's stories are false."

The general seemed to search his mind as if mulling over a riddle. Dirk knew Krentz had played them perfectly, and he was not entirely sure that she had not bewitched them. The general was a stubborn one, however, and good for his post.

"The tales are true," he finally admitted. "The dark elves opened some sort of portal at Kell-Torey's doorstep. The city was destroyed. The King and his people murdered in their beds," he lied. Krentz had killed them all in their siege room, but neither she nor Dirk corrected the man. "A horde came out of the portal, the likes of which I have never seen. Must've been nearly twenty thousand by the time the damned thing closed."

"Closed?" asked Dirk.

"Days ago," the general confirmed.

"Now, you go to warn the next city?"

"Village…town…whoever is left."

"Where will you go?" Krentz asked.

The general caged his loose tongue and regarded her again with his wary eyes. "Knowing the tales are true, what will you do now? Report to your queen, who will do nothing to aid Eldalon?"

Krentz shook her head dramatically. "The elves will help. Even now, the call to arms rings out in my native land. The plight of Agora is the plight of the elves. We will help in any way we can," said Krentz.

"What help did the elves ever offer us?" he asked.

"The one called Whill of Agora allies himself with the elves and dwarves, and he has attained the legendary elven sword of power. He will soon face the dark elf lord himself. You would be wise to lead your people to the Ky'Dren Mountains. There you will find safety," said Dirk.

"Whill of Agora you say? The man is nothing more than myth and legend," the general scoffed.

"He is as real as you or I, and, given the loss of the king and his people, he may well be the heir to the Eldalonian crown," said Dirk.

The general considered for a moment, his thick mustaches twitching. "I am aware of the allegiance of the three races, but the fruit of that union remains to be seen. As for an heir, Eldalon has no king; he fell with the city."

He pulled his lance high to sit in its holster. "If you are here to help as you say, you will lend your dragon and your skills to our people. Otherwise, bar the road no longer. We tarry with the demons of the hells upon our heels."

Dirk knew Krentz's mind on the subject. He gave a small bow toward the general. "We offer what help we might to see your people to the Ky'Dren Mountains. Surely, it is your only haven."

"Indeed," the general said with a nod. "Eldalon and Ky'Dren have long been allies." With a glance to Krentz, he added, "They will help."

"Do you accept our offer?" Dirk pressed.

The general turned his horse to return to his people. "We need an airborne scout," he said, regarding Fyrfrost. "Just keep the dragon at a distance; it is likely to give the horses heart attacks, not to mention the people. We've enough worries without the dragon fear."

"Understood," said Dirk.

The general and his men turned to leave, but he suddenly stopped. As if in afterthought, he bent to offer his hand. Dirk took it and gave him a firm shake.

"General Mick Reeves."

"Well met," Dirk replied.

Reeves squeezed his hand and searched his eyes for a lingering moment. With a firm nod, he turned. He and his men rode back to the group and could faintly be heard bringing the soldiers up to speed. Dirk and Krentz returned to Fyrfrost and took to the sky as newly appointed Eldalonian scouts.

CHAPTER TWELVE
The Fall of Cerushia

Tarren was unable to sleep well with the constant pounding of explosions and spells, but at some point in the night the bombardment stopped. He woke for the hundredth time to find Lunara sitting beside his bed, while, on the other side of him, Helzendar snored away amid the rumbling. Lunara was in the midst of spell casting. She wove an invisible pattern, and her lips moved in silent chanting. She opened her eyes, smiled wordlessly at Tarren, and reached toward him. A tingling sensation danced down his spine as her enchantment covered him and Helzendar.

"What?" Helzendar said as he sat up with a start. He groggily eyed Lunara with suspicion. "What you about elf?" he asked through an angry yawn.

"Laying wards of protection, nothing more," she answered with a tired smile. "Come you two, and eat."

Helzendar grumbled and got up, and Tarren followed. Outside of their sleeping quarters, the two elven guards stood like statues overlooking the common room. The Watcher was at the stone fireplace humming a joyful tune over a pan of frying bacon. Helzendar purposefully stormed his way to the balcony, and Tarren followed, curious of what was happening outside.

Helzendar pushed wide the door, and Tarren gasped. The shield dome around the city was now cracked and sparking in hundreds of places. The dark elf army was gathered just outside the flickering energy shield. Tarren had seen draquon and Draggard before, but he now beheld the dwargon for the first time. The beasts bore an eerie resemblance to dwarves, and Tarren heard the sharp inhalation of his friend at his side.

"Those gods-damned devils!" Helzendar cursed as he beheld the dwarf-dragon crossbreeds. "They ain't right, I tell ye."

The dwargon slammed their hulking figures against the shield, as Draggard writhed and climbed over one another hungrily trying to get through. They clawed and repeatedly struck with their long, pointed tails, as the dwargon pounded. Smoldering land had replaced the lush jungle surrounding that side of Cerushia, opposite the Thousand Falls. Turning to the high ridge, Tarren was surprised to see Cerushia's rivers had stopped flowing. Where once had been large pools of water at the base of the falls, now, there were deep gorges. The riverbeds were dry, but for the occasional puddle where dozens of dying fish jumped and flipped. Tarren followed the arching wall with his eyes from its apex and down beyond the falls. He assumed the shield stopped the flow of water to the falls, but that did not explain why the water did not flow around the shield and, therefore, the city. The dark elves must have dammed the water.

"Yes, you are quite right lad," said the Watcher cheerfully, as he gnawed on a piece of bacon. "The dark elves have dammed the river as far back as the canyons. They will have collected a marvelous amount of water. I suspect any moment it will be released to rage against the shield wall."

Tarren swore the old elf sounded excited.

"Will the shield hold?" he asked, and realized the question had already been answered. The Watcher grinned down at him without answer.

"Let 'em take the damned thing down now! Me half-moon'll show 'em right quick the error of their ways," Helzendar promised.

The Watcher chuckled. "When your body catches up to your rage, you will be quite right," he mused.

Lunara joined them on the balcony, and she too noticed the dry falls. "How long?" she asked the Watcher.

"Just after the offer, and refusal, of surrender, I assume," he said and nodded to himself. "Yes, that seems right."

"Is help coming? The other elves of Elladrindellia, I mean," Tarren asked.

"Other elves?" the Watcher repeated, seemingly perplexed. "I would think not. They have problems of their own, I imagine."

Tarren wished for the hundredth time that Whill was there. He wondered what his mentor would do. Would he be scared? Possibly, but he would also be prepared. "C'mon Helz, let's eat."

They returned to the kitchen and ate under the watchful eyes of the elven guards. "You two hungry?" he asked. He was tired of their staring.

"We require no nourishment," one answered and fell back into his staring trance.

"What's with those two?" Tarren asked his friend as they ate. The bombardments had begun anew, and the city rumbled with each attack.

"Gods only know. Probably watchin' the siege through the walls with their weird elf ways," Helzendar replied with a mouthful of eggs. "Eat up till yer stuffed, Tare. Who's to say what the day be bringin ."

Helzendar was right. Tarren forced himself to finish his plate, even though he couldn't wait to be out on the balcony. Wondering what was going on drove him mad. The food went down slow and gave him no joy. He already felt good, if overly excitable. Whatever enchantments Lunara had laid on him covered him like an unseen sheet. Layers of magic prickled his skin, and the fine hairs on his arms stood on end within the energy field. It gave him some solace to know that he was protected, to what degree the wards would hold remained to be seen. Pushing his plate away, he swallowed the last of his breakfast and washed it down with elven sweetwater.

He went to his room and retrieved his staff. The feel of Oakenheart in his hands gave him a renewed sense of security. He had never called upon its power, but he knew it was there waiting for the time of need. Lunara said the staff would answer his call, and would grow with him in power and size.

Helzendar leaned on the archway, half-moon spear in hand. "Ready to kick some Draggard arse?" he asked with a quick flash of the eyes.

"You possess the strength of many men, even at your age. And you are the bravest kid I have ever met, but how can you be so relaxed, even eager?" Tarren asked.

"Bah, certain doom be waitin' for all o' us. It be the true test o' the warrior how he be actin' when that time comes. Ain't no dwarf in history quivered at the feet o' his enemy, and I ain't bein' the first."

"I guess you're right," said Tarren as he and Helzendar ventured once more to the balcony.

"Ain't no guessin'. You be a born warrior and don't ye be doubtin'. We'll live to laugh about this someday, you just watch."

Tarren doubted he would be laughing any time soon. He doubted many things, mostly himself. Sure, Lunara had laid wards of protection around him, and he was surrounded by powerful elves. But, if the city was breached, if the horde poured forth, what could he do? He was only a human boy of eleven.

"Ah, just in time, I believe," the Watcher nodded as they walked on the circling balcony. "Yes, seems so," he answered himself.

The bombardment of spells abruptly ceased, and silence filled the city. Outside of the spell shield, a voice rang out unnaturally loud, a voice of spiteful arrogance.

"Elves of Cerushia! Queen Araveal! Surrender yourself in the name of Eadon and spare your people!"

"Is that Eadon?" Tarren breathed and tried to hide the terror in his voice.

"No," the Watcher replied. "Eadon sends others for such deeds and waits for his feet to be kissed upon surrender."

"Surrender now, or be destroyed," the dark elf finished.

Minutes dragged by, and they waited in anticipation. No reply came from the queen. Tarren shifted nervously and watched the city. Movement down below caught his eye. Hundreds of elves were shifting to the outer edge of the city, closer to the spell shield. Above the city, hundreds of draquon flew circles like huge carrion birds, waiting to feast on the eyes of the dead. More quiet minutes passed, and still no word from the queen. The Draggard hurriedly scrambled across the blackened and scorched earth, away from the shield.

A rumbling began outside of the spell shield. Dull at first, it slowly grew until it sounded through the spell shield like an underwater explosion. The city shook, and the rumbling increased. Soon, the crashing waters poured forth.

"They have released the dam," said the Watcher.

From the balcony, Tarren watched in terrified awe as the unleashed river crashed over Thousand Falls and pounded on the spell shield. The dome rippled with shimmering webs of multicolored energy, but held the great weight of the water. Tarren assumed dark elf water weavers must have been behind the force of the water, for it came down upon the city with unnatural speed. The sun elves who had moved to the edges of the city began making patterns upon the spell shield with glowing hands. The shield glowed deep blue as the water continued to crash down. Ice began to form on the other side of the shield. Tarren did not know if it was the work of dark elves or sun elves. The shield disappeared to choruses of cracking ice, echoing throughout the city as the river's waters were frozen solid. For a moment, they were encapsulated in a dome of sheer ice, still smooth from solidifying against the spell shield.

Tarren jumped with a start as all the enchanting silence beneath the ice dome was shattered, and noise and violence once again found them. He realized the sun elves had frozen the flooding river. The gathered elves that circled the city gave a cry and outstretched their hands by the hundreds. The deafening blast broke the ice into a million jagged pieces shooting in all directions. Tarren found himself deaf and dazed as the world erupted into chaos.

The elves poured forth from the city blasting spells at the dazed and battered Draggard forces. Many of the beasts had been impaled by long, thin ice shards; they stood dead, held up by translucent lances. Spells and fireballs blasted through the air toward the city once again, a barrage coming from the dark elves lurking behind the hordes of monsters. Many of the spells were intercepted and destroyed harmlessly; some, however, could not be stopped. Explosions sounded all around them as Tarren was pulled by Lunara toward the shelter of the mock dwarven mountain. At the same time, the Watcher firmly held him on the balcony. Lunara's face showed her confusion.

"That way leads to sadness," said the Watcher with a grin. He acted as if he was not aware of the destruction around him. "Better we wait here a moment, and prepare to jump."

"Jump?" asked Lunara as she leaned closer to the old elf. "What do you see, master?"

"Yeah, w-what do you see?" Tarren echoed.

"Right then...everybody near the ledge," he bade them, even the two stoic elven guards.

Tarren moved to the ledge with the rest of them and peered down the side of the hill, he soon wished he hadn't. This hill was not a true dwarven mountain, but tall nonetheless. Next to the pyramids, the hill was the tallest structure in Cerushia. Tarren didn't like heights any more than he liked the Watcher's insinuations.

"Now?" the Watcher asked himself. "Oh no, not then, nor now. Maybe this one, or, no, no. Ah ha, yes, this one. In five, four," he counted off and turned to Tarren and the others. "Jump now." And he leapt.

Tarren was no coward, nor was he stupid. Back home at the inn in Fendale, he had often climbed to the rooftop of his family's tavern with his friends. He had walked the peak of the roof fearlessly. But this was something different altogether; he guessed they were at least two hundred feet high. There was no getting up from that fall. But, as the Watcher yelled jump, he found himself complying. From the corner of his eye, he noticed Helzendar leapt, with a war cry to boot.

Even as they leapt, a giant green fireball shrieked through the sky, defying all counter spells, and slammed into the side of one of the large pyramids. The capstone blew out, up, and to the side and hurtled through the air to collide with the peak of the dwarven hill. Tarren screamed as he fell rapidly toward the jutting rocks below. He found himself again screaming as an unseen force solidified under his feet, and guided him safely wide of the rocky hillside. He and Helzendar laughed hysterically together, Tarren's fright showing itself in his manic laughter.

The balcony upon which they had stood tumbled past them, and more debris followed in its wake. One large slab would have killed him, had it not been deflected by an unseen shield.

They soon reached the bottom, and found themselves on the cobblestone streets of war-torn Cerushia. The city had come alive. Monsters made of twisted and tangled vine lurched to life to intercept the incoming magical missiles. The fireballs blasted them to pieces or froze them solid, while still others withered them to dust. More vines rose up in their places. Elven druids rode upon the heads of the vine behemoths and shot spells and counter spells against the dark elves.

"Come," said the Watcher, and everyone listened.

"Ye think this ole crusty elf be knowin' where he be goin'?" Helzendar asked as he kept pace beside Tarren.

Tarren shot him a disappointed glare. "He be your captain, ain't he? You be following him. He got us off that hill afore it blew, and floated your fat arse down safely."

"When an elf be me captain, that'll be the day I kiss a dragon's arse," Helzendar replied.

The Watcher led them through the mostly deserted city streets. All around them, explosions sounded big and small. Dust and debris clouded their vision, and they were left to trust the Watcher's guidance.

"Left, now run!" he would say, and a moment after they had veered around a structure, an explosion would sound where they had been. He led them on this way through fire and ash and lurching vine-monsters until they reached scorched earth.

"This is the edge of the city!" Lunara protested. "You lead us out?"

The Watcher distracted himself from his pondering amid the dark smoke to regard her curiously. "Silly girl…does the city look safe to you? Come then," he said and dashed off to the north, and right into the battle upon the outskirts of the city.

Tarren and Helzendar shared a glance. Mad glee filled the dwarf's eyes; Tarren imagined his own looked petrified.

"Come on!" Helzendar yelled and ran after the mad elf.

"Stay close," Lunara urged Tarren as they followed the Watcher into the fray.

The small group ran toward the back line of advancing sun elves as they fought back the Draggard and dwargon. Some among them were not magic users, but plain soldiers endowed with gifts of strength and protection from their practitioner kin. Behind them, healers sent steady bolts and streams of writhing blue healing spells into them. Offensive spell casters bombarded the Draggard ranks with devastating blasts, while defensive casters shot bolts of light and streaming energy coils at incoming spells. The battle left Tarren humbled, and he thought no matter how much he had sparred with wooden weapons, or how many tournaments he had won, he was not ready for this. He wasn't sure if he ever would be.

"Stop! To the left! Go, go," the Watcher hollered over what sounded like the end of the world. The ground shook with a boom as two thousand pounds of headless dwargon landed where they had been.

They ran on past the healers and casters and the rear line of soldiers and devastating Gnenja. Tarren followed behind Helzendar, wanting nothing more than to be away from this madness. Beside him, a Draggard broke through the ranks, maimed and bleeding. He came at Tarren with wicked claws and drooling fangs. Lunara stopped the beast in its tracks with a glowing staff to the face. A flash blasted the Draggard back, its broken body landing twenty feet away.

"Tarren, count to three and duck," the Watcher yelled behind him.

Tarren's eyes searched for danger as he followed his friends.

*One, two, three...*he ducked as a spell flew over his head, singeing his hair.

The Watcher skidded to a stop as the dark elves breached the line of defenders before them. The sun elves fought to secure the line, but an explosion had greatly decreased their numbers. The healers worked franticly to keep the front line alive, but they were sent flying high and wide by the sweeping hammer of a monstrous dwargon. The Watcher slammed his staff into the earth, and, before him, a wall of vines grew to life from the blackened earth. The wall parted and drove earth and beast aside. The Watcher smiled at his creation and urged the others through the living pass. Tarren ran through the vine hall and watched above him as the vines came together creating a tunnel. The walls shook and rustled, emitting screams of agony from those Draggard attempting to get through. The Watcher leaned on his staff, and the rest soon caught up.

"What is it?" Tarren asked, concerned.

"Go on then, forward. Don't forget to hold your breath," he waved them on.

"Hold our breath?" Tarren asked Helzendar as they rushed on.

"The old elf is a nutter, that's what."

Behind them, an explosion sent smoke shooting through the tunnel. Tarren was suddenly blinded, and like Helzendar, he coughed and choked, having been too busy jesting to heed the old elf's words.

A swift wind blew the smoke far ahead of them down the tunnel, and a shove from Lunara urged them on as they sputtered and gasped for fresh air. All around them, the vine tunnel went up in flames. Finally, the end was near, and Tarren braced himself for whatever nightmare might await them beyond the green overgrowth. To Tarren's relief, they came out into a glade, far away from the dark elf blight.

"We are away, for now," said the Watcher, appearing among them as if he had never fallen behind.

"What be the meanin' o' rushin' a dwarf *away* from battle?" Helzendar yelled too loudly for Tarren's liking.

The Watcher seemed to study him for a moment. "No doubt your father told you that brave is not stupid, nor is dying from stupidity honorable."

Helzendar was left to boil, speechless.

CHAPTER THIRTEEN
The Lost Gate of Arkron

Roakore wiped his brow and gazed up to the sun. *Good enough*, he thought to himself, and took a much needed drink from his water flask. Below him, Drindellia rushed by as he and Silverwind scoured the horizon for any sign of Eadon's other portal.

He couldn't get the image of a rift inside one of his mountain cities out of his head. He remained convinced the other portals led to dwarven mountains, and he was fraught with worry for his people. The dwarves were fighting for control of the mountains, and he was helpless to do anything to help.

Roakore cursed himself; he should have listened to Nah'Zed. What kind of king left his mountain during a war? He heard his royal brain lecturing him on the responsibilities of a dwarf king. Maybe he wasn't cut out to be royalty.

Knowing the rifts had been closed did little to remedy his mood. For all he knew, they would be trapped here in Drindellia for months. They needed to find the portal, and fast. War was being waged in Agora, and he intended to take part.

Not even the strange stone formations below took his interest; he had too much on his mind. Next to everything was the problem of the *Book of Ky'Dren* and its implications. If indeed the elves taught Ky'Dren how to move stone, his religion was likely a lie, and the power to move stone was not gods-given.

"I shoulda left the damned book alone," he told Silverwind.

Roakore made one more turn around the lake and gave up. The sun would be setting soon, and he was anxious to find out what the others had learned.

"C'mon Silverwind, best we be headin' back to camp," he said, and turned his mount around.

He found nothing new on the way back to the group. They were easy to locate; the mushroom-like cloud left a scar in the sky that could be seen for miles. When he arrived, he noticed the elves and dwarves had made camp. Below, many small cook fires and tents were scattered near the face of a large cave. After landing, he dismounted Silverwind and soon found Zerafin among the elves. He was huddled with a small group, looking over a map of Drindellia.

"Ye failed to mention ye brought a bloody map," he said to Zerafin.

"Ah, Roakore, did you find anything?"

"That was gonna be me question," he replied with a sigh. "Where the bloody hells be Whill?"

An alarm rang out, and something streaked across the sky, coming in fast. Roakore and Zerafin squinted at the object.

"Well, what ye spyin' elf?"

"Whill," said Zerafin with a smile.

Whill came down fast and slowed at the last second; he floated to the ground and landed among the elves. Roakore pushed his way through the elves with Zerafin in tow.

"Well, Laddie, what do ye know?"

"Prepare to march. We make for the lost portal of Arkron," said Whill.

The elves and dwarves prepared to march. Whill, Roakore, Zerafin and Avriel met at the mouth of the cave. The sun sat low. Drindellia had become cold. Already, their breath came in plumes of vapor as they spoke.

"I have spoken with Kellallea," Whill told them.

"That old crazy lady? The words outta her mouth be suspect if any ever spoken. She's a nutter," said Roakore.

"She possesses great power, and she has agreed to help."

"Last we saw her, she struggled to keep the blight at bay. How can she be of help?" asked Avriel.

"She is stronger than she appeared," said Whill. "She has told me how to reach Eadon's stronghold."

"And you be believin' her? She what told you the prophecy was a lie and such? Bah!" Roakore spat.

"I believe her information is correct," said Whill

"How far?" Zerafin asked.

"It is a day's march southeast of this location."

"Well, then," said Roakore. "Let's be off, I for one wish to be back in Agora right quick."

The elves and dwarves prepared for the road. Whill had not been back for thirty minutes, and they were already heading out in the direction he had indicated. Avriel stayed behind with him, and they watched the small army of elves and dwarves start out over the rocky terrain.

"What happened?" he asked Avriel.

She regarded him with a small scowl. "You do not remember?"

Whill shook his head.

"What do you remember?" she asked concerned.

"We came through the portal, but then the Other gained control. I don't remember what I...what the Other did."

Avriel smiled. "You destroyed the rifts, and the entire Draggard army. I have never seen such a magnificent spell cast before."

"It was not my doing," said Whill.

"The Other then, is he...?"

"He is gone," Whill confirmed. He studied Avriel's reaction to the news and sensed more than a little disappointment. "You would see the tortured side of me endure?"

"I do not mean to be insensitive, Whill, but he struck a great blow against the dark elf forces. You do realize the two of you are one."

"And he has been put in his place, once and for all. Let us speak no more of him," said Whill.

"Of course, I apologize. I understand what great pain it must have cost you. I am glad you are well once more." She gazed at him intently.

"What?" Whill asked.

"I don't know, you are different. There is a peace about you."

Whill understood what she meant. There was a calm deep inside him, like soft lapping waves on a moonlit beach. He had discovered the essence of all life within him; he had become illuminated. The raging inner fires of the Other had been quenched.

"I spoke with Abram," he said.

Avriel perked her pointed ears at the mention of his oldest friend. "He yet lives?"

'No, he came to me inside the prison of my mind. He took me away to a memory," said Whill.

"Was it a good one?"

"Yes," Whill laughed. "As good a memory as a wolf attack can be, I suppose."

"Do you think that it was real?" Avriel asked with genuine curiosity.

"I do," he said, the memory bringing a wide smile to his face.

"What did he say?"

"He told me what I already knew."

"What?"

"I needed to let go, I had to accept…the Other."

Twilight came to the world, a time when shadows flirted with phantoms in the corner of the eye. The last of the army crested the far hill. Somewhere in Drindellia was Eadon's floating palace of crystal, or so Kellallea had said. Would he find Eadon as well? Would the final battle come tonight? He hoped not…he was not yet prepared to die; there was much work to be done. Whill had united the elves and dwarves, but had yet to unite Agora.

"We should catch up with the others," said Avriel, bringing her head to rest on his shoulder.

Whill hummed agreement, lost in his thoughts of facing Eadon. He found he was no longer afraid, no longer bitter because he was expected to face impossible odds. The scales were tipped against him, yet he did not care. He was no longer at odds with his reality.

"Come, fly with me upon Zorriaz. You have wielded incredible power this day; come and rest."

Mounting Zorriaz the White, they flew off to follow the two armies. A half-moon rose as the sun died away, and the clouds began to part. The further they got from the dark cloud that still hung over the battlefield, the clearer the sky became. Roakore flew with them, as well as a host of elven Ralliad. They came as eagles and hawks, owls and crows. Whill suspected the dwarves had been given energy from the elves, for the two armies ran at a fast pace and did not slow. The armies made good time over the mostly barren terrain, the lack of vegetation leaving them unhindered.

Although Whill could have stayed awake indefinitely with the power of Adromida, he fell asleep on the double saddle. He had faced his inner demons, and he had won. No longer did he fear his dreams.

Avriel came to his mind and gently woke him, and he stirred in the saddle stiffly. Morning had come. When he dismounted, Zerafin was there to greet him.

"The crystal fortress is beyond the ridge, as you said," Zerafin told him. "I have sent elves out wide to strike from the sides. The dwarves will do what they do best: charge straight in."

"You be gods damned right!" said Roakore, coming upon them. "I say we take 'em by storm."

The dwarf king cocked an eyebrow toward Whill. "Unless ye be wantin' to bomb 'em back to the hells as before."

Whill avoided the suggestion, having no idea how the Other had wrought such devastation down upon the Draggard horde.

"We cannot risk damaging the portal; it is our only way home," said Whill.

Walking to the crest of the hill, he peered over at Eadon's forces. When he realized the Draggard army numbered many times more than the dwarves and elves combined, he refused to let it affect his resolve. When he returned to the others, they waited in quiet anticipation of his words. He shook his head, at a loss.

"I don't know if Eadon is there. I cannot sense him," said Whill.

"If he be, then so be it, I ain't for hidin' out in this gods-forsaken land," Roakore proclaimed.

Zerafin scowled at such words against his homeland, and Roakore did not miss the expression. "Meanin' no offense," he said, slamming his chest.

The elf king nodded understanding and turned to Whill. "What do you suggest?" he asked.

"I would see a promise kept," said Whill.

He had asked Kellallea to help them against the dark elves, and meant to hold her to it. Closing his eyes, he focused his consciousness down into the hard-packed earth. He connected with the essence of Keye and called to the ancient one.

He knelt and put a hand to the ground. The dirt around his hand began to vibrate, causing small stones to jump sporadically. Whill stood and dusted his hands off.

"She will come," Whill said confidently, though he was not convinced entirely.

Roakore turned from Whill to Zerafin, and then to Avriel expectantly. "Who's *she?*" he asked.

"Kellallea, the ancient," said Whill.

Roakore threw up his hands with a huff, turned a circle as he shook his head, and squared back on Whill. "That crazy old elf ain't gonna be o' no help. She be thinkin' the prophecy be a lie, she ain't right that one."

"The prophecy *is* a lie," Whill told him. "She spoke the truth, though she has motives of her own. I have discovered the truth about her. There is no need for her to feign weakness."

"Why have you not spoken of this until now?" asked Zerafin.

"We have come to an understanding. It is between her and I." said Whill.

"She best not be takin' all day then," said Roakore, resting an elbow and leaning upon his axe.

A low rumbling began deep within the earth. The spot where Whill had touched the ground began to vibrate and heave. They backed from the spot and watched expectantly as the heaving subsided. A flash of light caused them to turn their heads away, and, when they looked again, she stood before them.

"Kellallea," Zerafin gasped, and fell to his knees. Every other elf nearby fell to their knees. Avriel, however, did not greet her as she had before. She, like Roakore and Whill, remained standing.

The ancient elf gazed out on the elven army with eyes of bright green. Her short hair grew into long tubers resembling reaching roots. She wore a garment of moss and leaf, flower and vine, which left much of her dark skin bare in the sunlight. Around her bare feet, grass and vine grew and radiated with life.

"Zerafin, son of Verelas," she said, laying a hand upon his bowed head. She cocked her head, and a smile crept across her face. "Rise, first King of Elladrindellia."

Her gaze fell upon Avriel, who still refused to kneel. Avriel averted the powerful elf's gaze, and stood her ground stubbornly.

"Do you sense Eadon?" Whill asked.

Kellallea lingered long on Avriel. "No," she finally answered. "He is not here in Drindellia."

"He must've gone through one o' the rifts," said Roakore.

Whill hummed agreement. "And he knows they have been closed. He is likely making all haste to reach the last portal's twin in Del'Oradon."

"Or, he be waiting just on the other side," Roakore suggested as he stroked his beard the way he often did when pondering.

"Perhaps," said Whill, looking to Kellallea.

"Surely, it matters not!" Zerafin proclaimed. "We have Whill of Agora and Kellallea the ancient one. None shall stand before us!"

Zerafin's voice boomed for all to hear. The elves pumped their fists in a cheer, and the dwarves began to dance on their toes. Kellallea, who had spent so much time in seclusion, seemed moved by the excitement around her, for a wild look came to her, one of mischievous excitement.

"Lead the way, good king," she said with a small bow. Zerafin straightened and seemed to gain strength from the gesture from one such as her.

"Elves and dwarves, to arms!" he called.

"Formations, lads!" Roakore bellowed and leapt atop Silverwind.

Avriel and Whill mounted Zorriaz and took to the sky behind Roakore. Many Ralliad joined them in their various bird forms. Below, Zerafin and his small cavalry crested the hill. Kellallea too had changed into such a bird as Whill had never seen. He wondered if such a creature even existed. Her wingspan rivaled a dragon's, and her feathers were like dancing flame.

Ahead, a horn rang out, signaling they had been discovered, and many draquon took to the sky. The Draggard army surrounding the crystal fortress, fanned out, and took up defensive positions. Whill guessed they numbered a few thousand, but what caught his attention was the sheer size of the crystal palace. Dominating the landscape, it cast a shadow that seemed to stretch on forever. He wondered what might await him inside the fortress.

Kellallea's voice came to his mind then. *Follow me to the Fortress.*

"What is it?" Avriel asked from the saddle in front of him.

"She calls to me to follow her."

"Be wary of that one. I do not trust her."

"Nor do I," he said, and leaned forward to kiss her. He laid a hand upon her chest and transferred a surge of power from Adromida. He kissed her again as she shuddered, unable to speak. "Be safe."

Whill leapt from Zorriaz and flew off after Kellallea as she glided swiftly toward the fortress. Dozens of draquon descended upon her, meaning to intercept. They soon fell from the sky, dead.

Spells shot forth from the Draggard ranks and slammed into the elves' energy shields. The charging dwarves sang the "Call o' Ky'Dren" at the top of their lungs, as their boots echoed like thunder upon the land.

Whill reached the fortress and approached Kellallea as she blasted a hole in the side of the floating monolith and disappeared within. Whill prepared himself with a calming breath, and followed her inside.

Within the floating crystal monolith, no sound bled through from the outside world. A soft humming reverberated steadily with the pulsing of the multicolored crystal walls within. He had entered a long hall with a floor like polished glass. No uniformity was found in the shape or cut of the walls, which arched up and melded smoothly into the ceiling. Kellallea stood before him in elven form, concentrating on something. She opened her eyes as he approached.

"Arkron's gate is this way," she said, beckoning him to follow her.

Whill walked after her down the hall despite his growing unease. She had gotten into the supposed fortress quite easily. How she knew the location remained a mystery. But he had no choice; he had to get back to Agora, and this seemed the only way.

A small explosion shook him alert, and he reached Kellallea in time to see a dark elf fall dead at her feet. Another came around the corner, and she raised a hand, stopping him. A surge of lightning shot from the elf's body into her palm. At first, Whill thought he had attacked her with a spell, but he soon realized she had drained him of all power. The dark elf stared at his hand in horror as he tried to cast a spell. A sword took his head as Kellallea passed. Whill stepped wide of the body and caught up to her.

"You take not only their power, but also the memory of magic?"

She did not answer, but walked on.

"It is the very spell that ended the first age of enlightenment?"

Still she did not answer.

"Teach it to me," he said, raising his voice and causing the crystal around them to sing. Kellallea wheeled around to glare at him.

"What would you do with such a spell? Disarm your enemies? Would you dictate who is worthy to wield Orna Catorna?"

"Seems as though someone should."

"And that someone should be you?" she asked. "When I stripped the elves of all knowledge of Orna Catorna, I left none with the ability. None."

"You left one with the ability...yourself," said Whill.

Kellallea did not reply. She turned from him and continued down the hall. They passed many rooms and wide corridors as they made their way steadily down deeper into the fortress. No call of alarm rang out, though the ancient elf left a line of dead in her wake. Whill jumped as they turned a corner, and Eadon stood before them. Kellallea raised a hand, and the dark elf went rigid.

"It is not him," said Kellallea as she drained the doppelganger, and he fell to a pile of ash. Whill's heart hammered in his chest as adrenaline coursed through his veins.

"If not Eadon, then who?" he asked.

"Eadon has made copies of himself to do his bidding. When I made a connection with this one, I sensed the dark one. Now he knows we are here, and he will come. We have little time," she said and sped off down a corridor.

Whill followed, eager to find the portal and be done with it. His mind drifted often to his friends outside fighting for their lives. They traveled down many winding crystal stairs and finally came to a landing off which many halls led. A strange mewling came to Whill from the hall to his right, the opposite direction Kellallea had veered.

"Come, we've no time," she bade him.

"That noise, it comes from just past the threshold," he said as he moved forward to investigate.

The strange sound came again, clearer this time, and equally more disturbing. Something was in pain. He followed the sound down the hall and came to a wide open chamber of soft glowing light. He stepped through yet another threshold and came out on a wide balcony. He moved to the edge and discovered the source of the sound. Below, surrounded by what must have been thousands of Draggard eggs, was a Draggard queen. She moaned in apparent ecstasy as an egg slowly oozed from the long birthing canal behind her.

"Come, we are close," Kellallea said behind him.

Whill tore his eyes away from the hellish image and followed her the way he had come. When they had again reached the landing, she indicated the many halls branching off in every direction.

"These other halls lead to more birthing chambers. I can feel the portal below the chambers; great power surrounds it," said Kellallea. "Come, this way."

They took the hall leading to a short staircase that wound down to a wide chamber below the birthing chambers. Spears, swords, axes, and massive war hammers hung by the thousands, and ramps led up and into the walls every few feet. Whill assumed these led to the birthing chambers. When the Draggard were hatched, they would be led here to the armory before going through the gate of Arkron and into Del'Oradon. He followed Kellallea to the end of the chamber, where they found the lost gate of Arkron. It was identical to the one they had found on Drakkar, only much bigger. Ten men could walk through it side by side, and it was high enough to easily allow a dwargon to pass through.

"What awaits us on the other side?" Whill asked.

"Let us find out," Kellallea answered with a wry grin.

CHAPTER FOURTEEN

A Way Out

Aurora awoke with a throbbing headache. A lot of the dark liquor had passed between her and Veolindra. Zander would be able to alleviate it easy enough. With a groan, she sat up in her bed and gave a stretch exposing her bare skin to the cold winter air.

"Lady of the North," said a voice, and she jumped to discover Azzeal standing at her tent door. His head hung lazily to the side, and a steady line of drool hung from the corner of his mouth. His haunting eyes looked at nothing.

"How did you get in here?" she demanded, as she pulled the fur blanket up to her chin.

Rather than answer, Azzeal jerked his head to the other side, as if looking at her more closely. A shiver danced up the small of her back.

"What do you want?" she asked, wishing he would just go away.

Again, he refused to answer.

"Get out!" she ordered, pointing at the door.

Azzeal rushed forward until his milky-white eyes stared inches from her face.

"I have seen into your heart," he croaked with a twitch.

Aurora was horrified, though she wasn't a woman who scared easily. The rugged and unforgiving tundra had made her as strong as any barbarian. But the lich petrified her. He was the embodiment of her sin, a walking testament to her cowardice. In those white eyes, her reflection stared back, putrid and rotten like her soul.

"Never speak to me again!" she screamed in a rage born of guilt and self-loathing.

"I have–"

Aurora backhanded Azzeal to shut him up. His head snapped to the side from the powerful blow, but he did not waver.

"You!" yelled Zander from the door. He stalked over to Azzeal, grabbed him by the hair, and bent his head back to face him.

"You have orders to stay away from the Lady! Why are you here?" Zander searched the dead white orbs and pushed the lich away with a disgusted snarl. Clumps of dark-green tinted hair fell from his hand. He raised a fist to Azzeal, and a ring set with a brilliant emerald began to glow. The milky-white eyes mirrored the glow.

"Why are you here?" Zander insisted, and the inner fire of the ring glowed with his will.

Azzeal's head snapped up, and, for the first time, he seemed alert. "I wanted to see her."

"You *wanted?*" Zander repeated, as though he did not understand the word. "You do not *want* anything. You do not *feel* anything. Do you understand?"

"Do I understand? It is a feeling…I believe," Azzeal cocked his head toward Zander. "Can I believe?"

Zander sneered at the lich and punched out with the ring. Azzeal bent at the waist as if he had been struck and shot upright again with such force that he bent back unnaturally far, his bones cracking. A howl of pain in many voices sang out in agony as he fell sideways to the bearskin rug in convulsions. Aurora found herself fighting the urge to cry as she watched the tortured form of her friend. She sensed him still, and knew a part of the elf remained.

"Stop this!" she screamed, and Zander complied at once. He turned and frowned at her. Conscious of his probing mind, she wiped away at her tears urgently and tried not to sniffle in front of the dark elf.

"Send him away," she waved toward the door.

"Report to the whipping post at once!" Zander yelled, and, with a lifting motion of his ring hand, Azzeal was pulled to his feet like a puppet. Guided by the ring, he was shown to the door promptly.

"I want that thing destroyed. Do you understand me?" exclaimed Aurora, fighting to hold back tears that she feared might never end should they fall again.

Zander regarded her with what might have been pity; she could not be sure. What she did recognize, however, was the hint of disgust playing at the corners of his eyes. "Apologies, Chieftain, but that will not happen until our master releases him."

"Master? What does Eadon care for the fate of Azzeal?" Aurora asked, unable to bear the thought of having to see him anymore, pained as he was. She had never meant for any of this to happen.

"Azzeal is Eadon's Risen; only he may dictate such an action. It is also personal to him: Azzeal interfered in our master's plans. He does not forget, and he does not forgive. His retribution is swift, and his punishments...inventive."

"Then, send him far from here," she said in a voice more pleading than she liked.

"Perhaps," Zander nodded, and walked to sit at the foot of the bed. He gazed upon her with searching eyes.

"No matter how far you go from the lich, there you will be," he said.

Aurora knew his words to be true. It wouldn't matter; Azzeal's dying eyes would haunt her dreams and waking hours forever, as her guilt over Abram still did. No respite would be found, not even in death. Sorrow took her breath away and wracked her body. Her mind spun in maddening circles as she tried to think of a way out. Her tears came in uncontrollable sobs, and she hid her head in shame.

Zander's hand touched her shoulder and squeezed softly. "You suffer needlessly," he said in a soft, melodic voice.

She wasn't comfortable exposing such feelings to the dark elf; she hoped he would just go away and leave her to her misery. Every tear she shed would be seen as yet another sign of weakness, and likely her behavior would get her killed. To think the Chieftain of the Seven–the commander of the Seven Armies–was crying, naked in her tent. She felt pathetic.

"There is but one way out for you," he went on, gripping her shoulder firmly, even adding a small jolt to focus her attention. She listened, but she dared not admit anything to him.

"Embrace thyself. Embrace thy nature. Cast away your selflessness, your guilt. Azzeal offered you death, and for what? Honor? Eadon offers you power, freedom, and eternal life."

"What I did was for my people," she said, looking at him finally. Tears streamed down her face, but she no longer cared.

"No," Zander said, as if they both knew the truth. "You did it for yourself. The sooner you admit your actions were guided by your lust for power, the sooner you can begin to become whole."

"That is selfish, it's–"

"Wrong?" Zander laughed. "Is it wrong for the wolf to eat the doe? Is it selfish? Is selfishness not simply survival instinct? You fight your own instinct, and so you suffer."

Aurora stared at him, fixated; she clung to his every word, wanting to be convinced. He offered her a way out, and she wanted to take it. But, a voice inside her head warned of evil, its insistent whispers reminding her Zander was a monster. She was a monster.

"You are a hunter; do you not forsake thought and embrace instinct while on the hunt?"

She nodded affirmation.

"Life is no different. Those who claim to be civilized, to be above animal instinct…where does it lead them? All civilizations fall…a testament to their obsolescence."

When Aurora looked away, Zander grabbed her firmly by the chin and forced her to face him.

"You stand upon a precipice, Aurora Snowfell. You can become the greatest barbarian chieftain Agora has ever known. Or, you can follow your guilt into the depths of the hells, and wallow there forever, forgotten and alone."

He left her then at the precipice, clutching her fur blanket. She understood what she had to do, what she must become. Her cheeks itched with the memory of tears, and her eyes were swollen. The burning in her throat from her choking sorrow faded, and she smiled. There was a way out.

CHAPTER FIFTEEN
Trouble on the Road

Heavy snow fell in the early morning hours, blanketing southern Eldalon with white dunes where wheat and corn once grew. Such heavy snow was early in these parts, and the refugees viewed it as yet another bad omen.

Dirk and Krentz had been patrolling the skies since well before dawn. Circling the civilian wagons, they had seen nothing to cause alarm. Camp was made close to the sheer coastline where the refugees would be protected by the cliffs. The humans found much needed rest. The coast would protect them only so much, however, and by noon they would reach the first of many coastal towns. Dirk assumed Reeves would steer clear of the harbors and beaches, where invading dark elves might lie in wait.

He wondered if the city of Fendale and the majestic Light of the North had fallen. He had been to the grand lighthouse once before, when Krentz used the Everfire within to enchant Dirk's sword. Reason dictated that if Kell-Torey had been destroyed, so too had Fendale.

"How many rifts did Eadon open?" Dirk asked Krentz as they flew above the snow-covered world.

"I cannot be sure. They were strategically placed throughout Agora. At least one for every kingdom."

"Including Uthen-Arden?"

"Yes," said Krentz.

Dirk pondered the implications. "The dwarf kingdoms as well?"

"I am not certain, but I believe so. No doubt he saved the majority of his new dwargon for the dwarves."

Dirk gave a mirthless laugh. "That would be a bad move on his part. From what I know of the dwarves, it will only infuriate them further."

"The one you fought beside, Roakore—what was your impression of him?" asked Krentz.

Now Dirk's laugh was real. "I have met a few dwarves in my time; they are a tough lot, as you know. Roakore was chiseled from the mountainside itself. He is a descendent of Ky'Dren, as all the kings are, and his power over stone is incredible. He once killed a black dragon by weaving molten lava and pouring it down the beast's throat. He is a formidable opponent, he that cast me from the back of the red dragon, Zhola. The dwarf bested me in battle, a feat no human can claim."

"You sound as if you admire him," Krentz noted.

"Indeed," he agreed.

Fyrfrost gave a low growl, and Dirk wondered what had caught his interest. Below in a snow covered field, near the edge of a thin forest of yellow birch and ash, was a small herd of deer.

Fyrfrost dove as Dirk gripped the saddle horn and tucked in low. He yelled to Krentz behind him. "We take them all. There are many mouths to feed."

They leveled out and skimmed the tree line at a swooping angle as they came upon the herd. It darted deeper into the field, bounding away from Fyrfrost and the tree line.

Krentz leapt from her saddle and disappeared below Fyrfrost in a wisp of smoke. Dirk unstrapped himself and crouched in his saddle, waiting for Fyrfrost to strike. They quickly gained on a buck and three does. Fyrfrost came down among them and pounced on one of the does with a hooked claw, stabbing it through. Dirk leapt from the saddle before the dragon-hawk kicked off with his other foot and went after the two does who veered to the left.

Dirk did not want to spoil the meat with any poison, so rather than a dart, he threw a dagger. The weapon left his hand before he hit the ground and rolled. Springing up into a run, he saw the dagger was buried to the hilt in the buck's rear left flank. The deer faltered for a moment, but quickly sprang back into a leap. Dirk hit a patch of field blown bare–the field was covered in such patches, like islands amid frozen waves in an ocean of snow. At the edge of his vision, like a phantom of ice, Fyrfrost descended upon another doe. The buck Dirk injured left a crimson trail of dark blood behind. He kept pace with the slowing deer, knowing that the initial adrenaline would wear off, and he would have his kill.

He was not surprised when the buck landed badly and stopped. With one last surge of energy, the deer turned and reared on Dirk with its broad crown of antlers. Dirk unsheathed his short sword on the run and charged. When the buck struck with a sideways sweep of the antlers, Dirk shifted into the blow and spun with his strike as the antlers grazed his cloak. He skidded to a stop, and spun as the buck wavered and collapsed into a low drift.

Dirk wiped the blood from his blade and walked to the dying animal. Its breath came in slow, steady plumes of mist in the cold air. A long, thin line was cut across its neck, and the deer's lifeblood pooled around its spiked crown. Soon, the frosty breath came no more.

Krentz returned to him then, showing no sign of her exertion.

"I downed two: a buck and a doe," she said, looking around, as if searching for Dirk's other kills.

"Fyrfrost beat us both," he said with a chuckle, as the dragon-hawk dropped three does at Dirk's feet and flew off to gather Krentz's kills.

Soon Fyrfrost returned, and they mounted once more. He leapt into the air and pumped his large wings until he could hover and scoop up all six deer.

They flew back to the refugees just as the wagon train was heading out. Reeves had asked that Fyrfrost be kept at a good distance from the civilians, and Dirk respected his request. They flew over the long line of soldiers and villagers and dropped the deer on the road just ahead. Dirk dismounted and remained behind, as Krentz and Fyrfrost took to the air once more to scout ahead. Soon, they would veer northeast to avoid the coast, and by nightfall, they would reach the city of Orington, if indeed it remained.

Dirk waited in the blizzard for the first horseman to approach. The wind had picked up from the coast, and though Dirk was protected from the storm by his enchanted cloak, he knew many of the refugees suffered the cold. The soldiers were used to bad conditions; their job was to brave the elements and the greater dangers of the world. But many of the refugees were city folk, used to comfortable lives away from the worst weather and protected by the city walls. He doubted half of them would survive the trek to Ky'Dren, if this weather kept up. He wondered if Eadon had anything to do with the storm.

Dirk was pleased to see the first horseman to arrive was General Reeves. He nodded at Dirk and looked to the slain deer with a smile.

"It seems you have been busy."

"Indeed, it is a beautiful day for hunting," Dirk joked.

Reeves gave a laugh and dismounted deftly. Behind him, the cavalry could just be seen through the blustering sheets of snow.

"This might lift the people's spirits," Dirk offered.

"Much appreciated, Blackthorn. Did you see any Draggard upon the road ahead?"

"None. We started out early, before the storm came in. We flew many miles down the road and saw nothing," said Dirk.

Mick Reeves nodded absently as he stared ahead down the road, though visibility was limited to a dozen feet. Dirk recognized the stare as a seasoned veteran's.

"If this weather keeps up, the wagons will be buried before nightfall. Already the road is undistinguishable," said Dirk.

"It cannot be helped. If our enemy would wait out the storm, then I would trudge on. The soldiers will clear the road with their marching feet. They understand what is at stake here," said Reeves with a raised chin.

A soldier came into view, and Reeves ordered the deer brought to the butcher's wagon to be chopped and spread throughout as much stew as possible. Dirk knew that, while five deer was a grand catch for a day's hunt, among the thousands of refugees, the meat would go quickly. But, it would add flavor and fat to a hot meal, and do much for the group's morale.

Reeves also ordered a horse be made available, and soon, Dirk was riding next to him on a fine mount. Morning was well past, and midday brought an end to the furious winds and snow. Dense, gray clouds with no end blocked out the sun but for a steady haze permeating the thick blankets. Warmth came to the world, and though a chill remained, the wind no longer forced the cold between seams and under hoods.

Behind them, Dirk could barely make out the long stretching line of soldiers beyond the cavalry. They were followed by the wagons and civilians. Marching soldiers and a regiment of horseman took up the rear.

"You seem like a well-traveled man," said Reeves with a sidelong glance at Dirk and his attire. "What do you know of the larger battle?"

Dirk thought for a moment on how best to respond. His words would bring questions, and many he could not answer without rousing suspicion. He was happy when his answer was interrupted as Fyrfrost gave a roar and flew over them.

"They have spotted something," said Dirk, and leapt from his horse. The animal likely would not remain calm around the dragon.

Reeves joined him, and together they ran to Fyrfrost as Krentz leapt down from the saddle.

"What is it?" Dirk asked.

Krentz pointed beyond the next valley before them. "Draggard on the road, coming this way. Maybe a hundred, with two dark elf handlers."

"A hundred, you say," said Reeves. Deep concern shone in his eyes.

"Beyond them?" asked Dirk.

"Nothing for the few miles we searched," said Krentz.

"Are they aware of us?" Reeves asked, already looking ahead for a choke point.

"Not that I can tell. They march steady, but with no haste."

"How long?"

Krentz looked from Reeves to the road in thought. "Half an hour, at best."

"If I remember this road clearly, a bridge isn't far from here, with steep banks on either side."

"Yes, perhaps ten minutes from here," Krentz confirmed.

"Then, we will set an ambush. Come, we have precious little time," said Reeves, turning toward his men.

"Wait for us?" Dirk asked Fyrfrost.

The dragon-hawk let out a small puff of smoke and pawed at the ground in anticipation, digging up the road. His feathers turned white like the snow. Dirk and Krentz followed Reeves as he approached his forward cavalry. Many of the men, captains and lieutenants, dismounted and came to the beckoning of the general.

A plan of attack was made and set to action. The rear cavalry stayed behind to guard the civilians, and the remainder of the small army made all haste to the ambush point. Dirk and Krentz flew ahead of the soldiers and landed near the bridge.

"Come, Chief," said Dirk.

A howl and mist swirled out of the trinket.

"Chief, Draggard approach from the east. They will have sent out scouts to look ahead. Find the scouts, and do not let them get this far. Once the Draggard army passes, follow them to this bridge. When you hear the first cries of battle, attack,"

The spirit-wolf perked at the word Draggard, and he began sniffing at the air, his ears moving independently of one another, and his bushy tail swaying back and forth slowly. He dropped his chest to the ground and growled low as Dirk spoke, his excitement for the hunt showing. When Dirk gave the word, Chief shot across the bridge and darted into the woods.

Krentz studied the river; it was twenty feet wide, and shallow enough for a man to wade across.

"Will it do?" Dirk asked.

"It will have to," she said, looking upriver. "On your signal."

Dirk confirmed the plan. "I will wait until they have gathered to gawk at the empty river. The stupid beasts won't know what hit them."

"Good hunting," she said, kissing him deep and long. She pulled away abruptly and slapped him across the face. "Stay alert!" she laughed, and, like Chief, turned to a wisp and moved swiftly among the low pines and bent birches, over jutting rocks along the shallows edged with thin ice. Dirk took to the sky with Fyrfrost and flew downriver, before turning to the east to spy the road from a safe distance. He knew the dark elves could see him, camouflaged as he was. So, he kept low to the trees and flew adjacent to the road. Soon, the Draggard came into view. They didn't so much as march, but stalked down the road four abreast. Luckily for the humans, the wind came from the east. Dirk came around behind the beasts. He knew the human soldiers were now taking positions, and the cavalry behind, hidden just out of sight and waiting for the right moment. Somewhere in the snow covered forest, Chief was likely stalking the scouts. The time for battle drew near.

The old, familiar rush of anticipation filled Dirk, as Fyrfrost weaved back and forth above the road, so as to not overtake the horde. He scoured the sky and was a bit disappointed the group had no draquon; he had become quite fond of aerial battle. Since his defeat to Roakore atop the back of Zhola the Red, he had vowed to master the art. It was also the reason he had asked Krentz to enchant his cloak to allow him to glide upon the wind, should he find himself falling to his death once more. She hadn't time as of yet to formulate a spell to do exactly what he envisioned, but the cloak would slow him considerably now.

The horde drew closer to the bridge, and Dirk smiled to hear the first shrieks of discovery. It was time. He kicked Fyrfrost's sides and pushed forward the horn of the saddle.

"Light 'em up!" he urged his mount.

The dragon-hawk surged upward and arched downward, quickly gaining momentum as his wings sent up a wall of snow behind them. The Draggard never saw them coming as flame burst forth in thick streams. Those caught in the initial blast were laid to waste. Dozens shrieked and howled as they scrambled frantically and dove for the deep snow. Fyrfrost's second attack was deflected high by a dark elf energy shield, and Dirk steered him out wide. The dark elves lifted their shields as the flames subsided and on cue, the arrows of Eldalon rained down upon the disorganized horde of frothing beasts.

The Eldalonian soldiers taunted the Draggard from across the bridge, screaming obscenities and slamming sword to shield. Dirk flew upstream even as the first of the Draggard rushed toward the bridge. Three small bends in the river brought him to Krentz. She stood upon the riverbank, arms stretched out wide, a look of deep concentration etched across her face. The riverbed was bare; fish slapped and flipped in the shallow channels left among the once submerged weeds.

Krentz held the river at bay, surging within her bowl-shaped energy shield, waiting to be released.

"Now!" he yelled, and she dropped her shield. The water floated unmoving for a still second, and, with a violent crash, reclaimed its passageway. Dirk steered Fyrfrost to bank hard and together they flew behind the raging river as it breached the banks and bore down upon the bridge. The soldiers had taunted the Draggard to the bridge, and many of the beasts were pressing their ranks.

The water rolled over the land and grew to a height of twenty feet before slamming into the bridge. Wood buckled and moaned, and ropes snapped under the weight. The bridge and dozens of Draggard were swept away by the water rushing down the empty channel, leaving a muddy bank of jagged ice in its wake. Fyrfrost bathed the Draggard with dragonsbreath once again, but was forced to pull up and bank quickly to avoid a fireball coming at them from the middle of the horde. The dark elf hurled another, and a third, forcing Dirk and Fyrfrost to sail beyond the trees. They flew back around to cross the river once more, and Dirk leapt from his mount to land on the side of the soldiers. Many dead littered the ground, but those Draggard who made it across lay among them. Dirk noticed the archers had pulled back and waited for word.

"Hold your arrows, the dark elves!" Dirk warned.

"Fall back!" General Reeves ordered.

Dirk turned at the wet sound of a Draggard landing upon the steep bank as more came leaping across the river. Some fell into the still rushing waters, and others clawed their way up to be met with Dirk's enchanted blade. He fell upon one and twirled along the bank, deftly avoiding the reaching claws of his victim. The Eldalonian soldiers retreated around the bend in the road as dozens of Draggard attempted the great leap. Dirk threw two explosive darts on either side of him and sprinted away from the advancing horde. The howl of Chief rang out in the cold air, and was soon followed by the cry of a dying Draggard. The spirit-wolf came leaping out of the woods to Dirk's right and intercepted a Draggard that flew at his back. They tumbled in a blur of thrashing tails and snarling teeth over the bank and into the river. Dirk noticed two forms, smaller than Draggard, soared over the water to land upon his side of the river. They shot spells in unison, and Dirk leapt to the side as the explosions shook the earth and sent him whirling into the trees. He crashed through the low branches and was buried in falling snow from higher bows. Knowing another spell was likely headed his way, he dove behind a large boulder as its edge was shorn by lightning. Swords clanged, and curses echoed from the road. He recognized Krentz's voice and dared peek around the boulder.

Krentz danced around the two dark elves as their swords sparked off of one another and the Draggard came rushing at them from the riverbank. Fyrfrost appeared out of the gray sky, pouring fire down among the three dark elves. Krentz turned to smoke as the flames were deflected harmlessly around her opponents. With an ear piercing shriek, Fyrfrost doused the Draggard yet again in dragonsbreath, causing fog to roll up in plumes from the river as he passed.

Draggard charged past the fighting dark elves in pursuit of the soldiers. Dirk whistled the signal, and the blaring trumpets of the forward cavalry marked their charge. They came fast around the bend and met the Draggard charge with long, gleaming lances leading the way.

Across the water, Fyrfrost descended upon those Draggard yet to make the leap. The dragon-hawk ravaged with tooth and claw and sent Draggard flying with sweeps of his long tail. Chief joined him in the fight, flying from one beast to the next, and violently snapping necks with his powerful jaws.

Dirk bolted from his place behind the boulder to aid Krentz, as she exchanged blows with the dark elves. One broke from the fight and blasted a bolt of lightning that hit the cavalry and Draggard alike, sending man and beast flying limply through the air. The Draggard had absorbed the initial charge, and now engaged the knights at the bend in the road. From behind them came the charge of the remaining soldiers, as they poured forth by the hundreds to take on the nightmarish beasts. In their eyes shone the pain of their losses and the promise of vengeance.

Dirk whirled as a spell sped by. He came down upon the dark elf with a flurry of sword and dagger, forcing his foe to take up his own blade. Their swords met, and sparks exploded from the contact angrily. The dark elf's speed was incredible, and Dirk soon found himself on the defensive. His sword parried the enemy blade high and to the left as he bided his time, waiting for the dark elf to cast. He felt a pressure in his head and knew his opponent was attempting a mental assault. Dirk landed a blow to the dark elf's side, and, though it was deflected by the energy shield, he saw surprise in the elf's eyes.

Behind them, the knights of Eldalon fought bravely against the towering Draggard, and though many fell to the beasts, they held their ground and even began to push the horde back. Krentz flew as a wisp around her enemy, solidifying only long enough to land a sparking blow against his energy shield. The dark elf gave a frustrated scream of rage, and with an outstretched hand, shot writhing black tendrils that wrapped around Krentz, binding her, even in spirit form.

Dirk was distracted for a moment by her baleful scream, and his dagger was sent flying by the dark elf sword. His attacker sneered and slashed at Dirk's face, forcing him to parry high. A spell erupted from his free hand, and lightning hit Dirk square in the chest. He was jolted painfully, though his cloak absorbed much of the blast. Still, he was shaken enough to be slow in his next parry, and the dark elf blade tore through the cloak's enchantments, and those of the armor beneath. Pain shot through his shoulder, and he lost all feeling in his left arm. He parried desperately as the dark elf came at him, sensing victory. Another blast of lightning erupted from the dark elf's hand, but Dirk quickly intercepted it with his sword, which absorbed the spell and glowed white hot with pent-up energy. With a cry of rage, Dirk released the energy in a powerful strike that the dark elf parried. The blades collided, and an explosion ripped through the air, sending them both flying backward. Chief came to Dirk's aid then, and collided with the dark elf in a flurry of snapping jaws and raking claws.

Krentz cried out again, and her form wavered as the dark elf bore down upon her with a maniacal grin, pulsing black tendrils tightening around her spirit form, causing it to waver. Before Dirk could move to help her, Fyrfrost swept over the river and pounced upon the dark elf. Krentz fell to the ground in spasms, as her body flickered in and out of existence.

"Back to the spirit realm, Krentz," Dirk commanded.

She looked up at him from the ground with a pained expression which was not the result of the assault. She turned into a wisp that swirled around and around, as she fought the pull of the trinket in his pocket.

Chief cried out as the same dark tendrils held him fast. Dirk threw a dart at the dark elf as he bore down on Chief; it hit the energy shield and exploded in a ball of fire.

"Back to the spirit realm, Chief!" Dirk yelled.

Through the thick black smoke and rolling fire, Chief came as a wisp into the trinket. The dark elf attacking him disappeared. Dirk looked quickly to Fyrfrost, who leapt into the sky clutching the other dark elf bleeding in his massive talons. The dragon-hawk's powerful wings lifted them high into the gray sky. With a slash of his curved blade, the dark elf was free of Fyrfrost's grip and fell. Dirk followed his descent and groaned when the dark elf changed into a large crow and flew up to meet Fyrfrost in battle once more.

Behind him, the Eldalonian soldiers battled the last of the Draggard horde. Dirk scoured the woods once more, and, seeing no trace of the dark elf with his eyes nor through his hood, he joined in the fray. He tucked his useless arm in his belt and sped toward the three Draggard who held back the circling soldiers with spear and tail.

A soldier saw Dirk speeding directly at him. "Down!" Dirk yelled at the man. The soldier dropped to his hands and knees, and Dirk took a leaping step off his armored back. Up and over the group of soldiers he went. He flipped four times as his cloak engulfed him in his flight. He felt spear and claws hit his cloak harmlessly and planted his feet firmly when he knew the ground to be near. Dirk landed in a crouch in between the three hissing and snapping Draggard, and his enchanted blade sliced through all of their legs as he spun in a full circle. Tails came at him but were sliced in half before they could connect, and their limbs flew in all directions as claws reached out to throttle him. The Draggard screamed in anguish, and tried to get away from the death dealer. They found their escape at the ends of Eldalonian spears.

Dirk whirled his head to find the dark elf and Fyrfrost, but they were nowhere to be seen. The soldiers hooted, and cheered their victory, but Dirk swiftly brought his sword up and screamed for silence.

The soldiers fell silent and listened as he did. After a time, they began to relax their still postures, but Dirk cocked his head and jerked his sword. Again, they listened to the silence, but then a baleful cry echoed from the road behind the, and an explosion followed. The soldiers stirred angrily.

"That blast came from the wagon train!"

"They are under attack!"

"Hold!" General Reeves ordered and followed Dirk as he moved swiftly back to where he had bombed the dark elf. Soon, he found what he sought. He showed Reeves the footprints heading west, the direction they had come.

"The other dark elf?" Reeves asked, even as another explosion sounded in the distance.

Dirk nodded agreement as he scoured the sky. At last, he spied Fyrfrost and the large crow far off to the north. They circled each other and exchanged blows, but soon dipped beyond the horizon once again.

"Can you defeat him?" Reeves asked with a glance at Dirk's badly bleeding shoulder. Dirk followed his eyes. He had nearly forgotten about the wound in his worry for Fyrfrost. He worried too for Krentz and Chief. He had no idea if they were well or not; he did not know what the dark elves had done. He had his suspicions, however, and knew them to be necromancers.

From the forearm band of his useless arm, he extracted a glowing dart whose vial was full of swirling blue tendrils. He jabbed it into the deep gash. Through the cut in his leather armor, the wound glowed blue, and soon the gash closed and the bleeding stopped. He still did not have much use of his arm, as the magic would take some time without the guidance of a healer, and, if not properly tended to, it would never be the same. But, for now, it would have to do.

He rotated his shoulder gingerly with his good hand over the wound. Another explosion sounded, and Reeves moved to give an order, likely for the cavalry. Dirk stopped his words with a hand to the general's arm.

"Give me a fearless horse, and I will do what I can. And please, send scouts to search for my mount. I would know his fate."

"Of course," said Reeves with a strong hand of his own over Dirk's.

"Gelhamond, your steed!"

The horse was brought to him in short order, and Gelhamond, a tall knight with fierce green eyes and a winter beard of red, patted the mane of his mount.

"His name is Shadow; he will not falter," he said with pride.

"Nor shall I," Dirk promised him.

He mounted and reared Shadow to his hind legs before speeding off down the road. He soon sensed someone following him, and turned to see General Reeves pacing him not far off. He slowed Shadow enough for the man to catch up and spurred his mount to pace his.

"What are you doing?" he yelled over the biting wind.

"If these devils can be killed, I would see how it is done!" Reeves hollered back.

"So be it, but stay clear."

They rode the few miles back to the wagon train at a brisk pace that Dirk slowed as they approached the last bend. He wanted Shadow to have something left for the charge. Reeves slowed with him, his eyes staring expectantly as a glimpse of the valley in which he had left his people inched closer. A voice came then, full of authority and malice. It echoed over the land and seemed to speak to any who could hear. It was not so much threatening as promising.

"You Round Ears, with your numbered years, your time has passed. The end is nigh. Your kind have no place in the new world; your ways are obsolete, your bodies, weak."

Dirk and General Reeves came around the bend and spied the valley below through weighted brows. The dark sky above hung still as if upon the spoken words, and the wind died to a whispering breath. Below in the valley, many wagons burned, and many dead littered the ground. The lone dark elf stood defiantly before the hundreds of villagers who huddled among wagons guarded by soldiers.

"Behold!" his voice commanded and clapped like thunder. Even from their vantage point of a quarter of a mile, the far spreading spell of crackling green tendrils could be seen. The snaking spell engulfed all the dead it found and lifted them to their feet. The dark elf's voice roared as he chanted his spell. Women shrieked, and a man charged forth. The brave soldier came in screaming, his sword arched back for the kill. But he never made it. The green tendrils engulfed him, and he froze where he stood. He too soon joined the raised dead. The spell ended, and the dead soldiers and villagers stood limply before their kin. Cries of blasphemy sounded, but were quickly silenced, as any who spoke was pulled from the crowd by an unseen force and torn apart by the Eldalonian undead.

"My master offers life eternal, yet you balk at such gifts?"

Dirk and Reeves charged toward the dark elf as he stood before the people. They sped past wagons, and any cowering nearby were forced to scramble out of the way. Reeves had not heeded Dirk's warning. He paced his charge and unsheathed his blade with a war cry. Dirk could not help but smile and do the same. As he had expected, the dark elf turned toward them and, with a clutching fist, pulled them from their mounts to fly the hundred yards toward him. Dirk flipped through the air once, and, as he came about, threw three darts in rapid succession. They, too, were pulled by the dark elf's force like arrows and collided with his outstretched hand. An explosion blasted snow and ice in all directions as the flames shot into the sky. Dirk and Reeves fell fast to the ground and hit the snow-covered field hard. When he had rolled to a stop, Dirk looked from the ground as the second dart's spell took effect. A deafening hum sounded from the flames, and the explosion was pulled backward into itself, engulfing the dark elf in a churning fireball. Dirk leapt to his feet and charged the blazing elf as his third dart took effect. The fire subsided, and the dark elf stood before them, covered in searching blue tendrils of healing energy.

The ground below him heaved and buckled, and the snow was pulled toward the dark elf from all sides.

"Go!" Dirk yelled at the dumbfounded humans as they breathlessly watched the incredible show of magic. They seemed to snap to attention with his bellowing, and quickly, they began to scramble away from the dark elf and his undead.

The third dart was one of Krentz's newest creations, enchanted to release a spell that would attract all nearby water. Around the dark elf, a small blizzard had begun to form as more snow piled around him. He blasted at the snow with a multitude of different spells; some slowed the wind but not the snow, and others slowed the snow but not the wind. Soon, his enraged voice added to the chaotic whirlwind Dirk and Reeves charged into. Dirk timed his charge as he counted down to the spell's end, and, when he reached zero, the snow dropped and the winds subsided. Furious by the attack, the dark elf shot his hands out wide in a rage. Before the spell was released, Dirk slammed his dagger, Krone, through the hole in the dark elf's energy shield.

"Stop your casting and drop your shield!" Dirk yelled in his face.

The dark elf's face twisted in rage as he shuddered and convulsed, fighting against the effects of Krone. He panted and wheezed, sweat beginning to dot his face. Reeves wasted no time in engaging the undead. He cried out with each strike in a keening voice of horror and sorrow as he struck down many he had once known by name. His living soldiers soon joined him and took down their undead kin.

A cry of alarm rang out, and Dirk looked to the sky. Against the gray clouds, to the east, a large bird came quick and low.

"Your friend has returned," said Dirk, standing before the dark elf. Dirk bent the dark elf's hand and stabbed Krone into his chest.

"Hit the bird with everything you've got. Destroy him!" he ordered, and the dark elf screamed in pain at his resistance. He raised his other hand, staring at it, horrified, and his cries of protest became frantically-chanted spell casting.

The crow flew low and changed to elf form as a spell slammed into his energy shield. Red fiery tendrils pulsed brighter as the screaming dark elf was forced to pour all of his stored power into the defense. The other elf was pushed back as he strengthened his energy shield against the attack. Spells shot out at Dirk from the opposing dark elf, and he took cover behind the one he controlled. The force of the spells intensified, and, with a final, ground-quaking blast, the dark elf's power was spent.

The one Dirk controlled wavered and fell to his knees, as everyone looked up hopefully from the ground. Many of the wagons blazed from the battle, but none moved to put them out. Dirk rose first and investigated the charred remains of the shape shifting dark elf. He kicked the smoldering bones and turned back to the kneeling elf.

"How many are you?" he insisted.

"We…" the elf coughed up blood and spat into the snow, leaving a long line of red spittle trailing down his chin. "We are legion!"

"What are your master's plans?" Dirk shook the dark elf as his eyes fluttered and rolled back, showing blood-shot whites.

"My master will destroy the world of man," the dark elf sneered.

Dirk shoved the dark elf to the ground in disgust.

"Reeves, send this one to the hells where he belongs."

General Reeves strode forth and placed his blade across the back of the dark elf's neck. "Gladly," he said and raised it high over his head. The sword fell and the head rolled across the snow to stop at Dirk's feet. The eyes blinked and looked around frantically; Dirk lifted the head by the hair and stared into the dying eyes of the dark elf.

"We shall not go easily," he said, and tossed the head out over the field. With a flick of his wrist, he sent a dart sailing, and the head exploded in a fine red mist.

CHAPTER SIXTEEN

Open Waters

Tarren and the group followed the Watcher through the thick jungle for what seemed hours. The dull roar of the attack still sounded far away. The idea of the beautiful elven city being destroyed saddened Tarren deeply. Lunara seemed to share his sentiment, as she followed behind them quietly.

The jungle thinned, and the crash of the ocean began to drown out the thunderous battle they had escaped from. The Watcher stopped and motioned for all to do the same. Tarren followed his gaze and was surprised by the steep cliff overlooking Cerushia's harbor. Black smoke rose from the many destroyed ships and buildings within the bay. Hundreds of dark warships littered the harbor, anchored among the jutting masts of sunken vessels. The bay was a graveyard of torn fin sails and splintered wood. The bodies of both beast and elf floated among the wreckage.

Tarren shivered as he lost count of the bodies in the water. He had seen such things before, but he doubted he would ever get used to it.

"Come," said the Watcher, and began along the cliff.

The Watcher stopped many times on the way down to the shore, and, every time, Tarren froze, held his breath, and waited, but they remained undiscovered. After a particularly long wait, the Watcher ushered them down a stairway of stone leading to a dock. Tarren had no idea where the Watcher led them, but he trusted the old elf. Helzendar, it seemed, was not so keen on the idea, and did not keep it a secret.

"Where the bloody hells ye takin us, ye crazy elf?" he said, but quiet enough as to not gain attention.

The Watcher turned on him with one cocked eyebrow fluttering high upon his brow. He leaned in past Tarren and squared on the dwarf prince. "Good dwarf, why ask questions that will be known to you, but shortly? Hmm?"

"Why ye be answerin' questions with questions? Eh, elf?" Helzendar retorted.

The Watcher cocked his head and let out a chuckle. "Yes, indeed, we are leaving, of course," he finally said.

"Leaving?" Lunara asked, concerned.

"Yes, this is the path. Come, there will be plenty of time for chatter," said the Watcher, dashing to the beach leading off the stone stair.

Tarren and Helzendar shared a glance and ran after the elf. The two elven guards followed without a word.

The Watcher led them away from the harbor and around an outcropping of land. Soon, they were well hidden from any prying eyes that may find them from the bay. Just when Tarren allowed himself to relax, the Watcher hissed, "Faces to the sand, and do not move!"

Everyone complied without question and flattened on the beach. They were covered in heavy sand and sunk deep. Holding his breath, Tarren tried not to panic. His heart hammered in his ears, and the smallest of movements sounded to him like loud rustling. The dull sound of someone approaching reached him through the sand. The sound stopped, and Tarren felt pressure in the sand all around him. The hole was filling with water. Panic welled in him as the pressure mounted, and the water crept over his buried face. He knew that he was doomed. The weight of the sand left him unable to move. It crushed his chest, and his lungs burned with the pressure. Tarren felt himself begin to slip; he was spent from the struggle with panic, and he was tired. Sleep called to him, and he happily followed her soft song.

Cold, salty water jolted Tarren, and he sucked in a mouthful of sweet, salty ocean air. Gasping and panting, he greedily choked down as much air as he could get. In the corners of his blurred vision, stars danced. Then came swirling blue light that he knew well, that of Lunara. His dizziness left him, and his mind calmed. His breathing became steady, and his vision cleared.

Helzendar reached down and pulled Tarren up by the arm.

"Are you all right, Tarren?" Lunara asked in a voice laced with concern and a dash of panic.

"Is that really the best you could do?" Tarren asked the Watcher as he got to his feet. The ancient elf did not respond. He stood covered in wet sand, arms outstretched as if bathing in the sun.

"You almost killed me," Tarren continued, as he walked to stand before the elf.

"Enough o' this shyte," said Helzendar, throwing up his arms. "I'll take me chances in the woods."

Tarren was ready to join him, when, behind them, the water began to churn and bubble. The Watcher raised his hands, and, from the frothing ocean, an elven ship arose high above the water. The ocean fell away, and the Watcher began to weave his hands back and forth, up and down, in and out. The sails of the ship wavered and straightened, its holes closed up, and the tears closed. A big breach in the side of the ship was reshaped in an instant.

Tarren looked in awe from the Watcher to the ship. The serenity with which the old elf cast his spells was enchanting. His closed eyes fluttered as if dreaming, and his hands seemed to compose a symphony. The boat descended slowly and drifted forward to stop before him, and he dropped his arms. The Watcher turned to the others with a smile. "Let us be off!" he said, but soon realized the scowls of Tarren, Helzendar, and Lunara.

"What?" he asked.

"You nearly drowned me!" said Tarren, exasperated and a little hurt.

"*Nearly* drowned? Rain nearly drowns us," said the Watcher.

"I don't care how old and respectable you are, Watcher. That was foolish," said Lunara.

"Perhaps…indeed, possibly." He looked around at them all. "And yet, I say nay, here we all are, alive and well. And we had averted the attention of many Draggard."

The guards leapt and floated over the side of the ship, and soon set the ladder over rail. The Watcher stood in knee high water, his robes hung from one shoulder, and his eyes twinkled with life and the promise of adventure.

"You want to hunt pirates, might as well get used to the sea," he said to Tarren.

"Where are you taking us?" he asked.

"Me?" The Watcher scowled, as if confused. "I take you nowhere, but the road, my boy, takes us all," his voice drifted off and he stared to the horizon.

"This elf be smokin' somethin', and I be gone," said Helzendar, and turned from the beach.

"You will want to come where we are going," the Watcher told them from the ship.

Lunara raised a hand for Helzendar to stop. "Wait!"

A Draggard patrol stalked around the small peninsula; one of the two beasts gave a screeching cry. Lunara urged Tarren to the rope ladder, as the two elven guards sped past the dwarf as he brought his half-moon spear to bear. Tarren scrambled up the ladder and tried to watch his friend at the same time.

"Helzendar!" he yelled, as his fearless friend charged right after the elves, intent on spilling blood.

"Hah, there he goes," the Watcher laughed.

"Get on the boat, you crazy fool!" Lunara screamed as she ran after Helzendar.

The two elven guards engaged the Draggard with blade and spell, and soon the beasts bled at their feet. Lunara caught up to Helzendar and whirled him around. Dozens of Draggard and one giant dwargon charged around the corner and down the beach. Though outnumbered, the two elves sprinted to meet them.

Helzendar struggled against Lunara's clutches as one of the beasts broke through the guards and leapt at them. A spell from Lunara's hand stopped the beast in midair, and Helzendar's half-moon spear sliced through its neck.

"Ha-ha!" he yelled triumphantly, and tried once again to join the elves, but Lunara held him firm.

"Let me go, ye damned elf!" he yelled, and pulled his arm away hard.

Lunara hit him over the head with her staff. A quick spark of light flashed, and Helzendar fell to the sand, sound asleep. She picked him up with a heave, and no doubt called upon her stored power for strength. The guards held their ground and let none pass, but more came.

Lunara splashed into the water and made for the rope ladder quickly, all the while the Watcher only grinned. Tarren looked at him dumbfounded.

"Are you gonna help?"

"Huh? Ah yes," said the old elf with some reluctance, as if he had been thoroughly enjoying himself simply watching.

"All right then," the Watcher began, and turned to Tarren. "What is it they say? Ah yes," he smiled and straightened. "All aboard!"

In an instant, both Lunara and Helzendar were sprawled out on the deck, along with the two soldiers who had been in mid-swing. The ship began to pull out of the small lagoon as the Draggard chased after it into the water.

"Incoming!" Tarren called as the dozens of Draggard began throwing spears. The ship was yet only a hundred yards out, and many of the spears found the ship. Lunara got to her feet, and, with a lifted hand and uttered spell, she raised an energy shield. The boat surged forward with the Watcher's steady wind-weaving and soon found deeper waters.

The land remained to their right, and Tarren knew they traveled south. He sat with Helzendar as the dwarf boy snored loudly. He wasn't looking forward to his friend waking; likely, he would be angrier than a wet sack of bees.

"Don't worry, he isn't injured," said Lunara as she watched for pursuers.

"When will he wake?" Tarren asked.

"He could be awakened now, but I prefer silence when I am sneaking away from a dark elf armada."

Tarren chuckled. "He is gonna be pissed."

"Mind your tongue," she said, taking her eyes off the horizon to accentuate her point with a glare.

"Yes, ma'am," he laughed.

They sailed through to the afternoon, and still no ship came for them. They had steered south long after the land turned west, and were now far out to sea with no land in sight. Lunara determined they would be safe with Helzendar screaming, and, with a touch of her hand to his forehead, his eyes shot open.

"What, what happened?" he demanded as he looked around wild-eyed.

"Whoa, pal, you–"

Helzendar pushed Tarren away and shot to his feet. "What? Where?" he ran from end to end of the ship, sputtering with his every word. When nothing could be seen but the constant blue of the ocean, he returned and squared on Lunara. "You!"

"Yes, me, you dolt! You trying to get yourself killed?" she asked, annoyed.

"Ye got no right knockin' me unconscious and takin me prisoner on this here vessel," Helzendar protested and began to lurch. He wavered and grabbed the rail for support.

"I am under the authority of your father and king, Roakore, to do whatever I deem fit to keep you safe. And I intend to, whether you like it or not."

Helzendar meant to argue, but was overcome with sickness. He bent over the rail and vomited. Once again, he turned as if to argue, but urgently went back to the rail.

"Ah, Helz, how you gonna hunt down pirates with me if you be gettin seasick?" Tarren asked with disappointment. But his friend was in no shape for conversation.

"Bring him below. I've a tea called Roz that will help settle his stomach," said Lunara.

"C'mon, Helz." Tarren ducked under his arm and pulled his sick friend along. Helzendar's head lulled weakly from side to side, and his usually rosy cheeks were a light green shade. With much coaxing and two quick shuffles back to the rail, Tarren got his sick friend below deck.

Having traveled on a similar boat to Cerushia, Tarren was familiar enough with the design to find his way below deck easily. The elven ships, with their interwoven vines, reminded him nothing of human ships of wood. The elves used vines in all of their structures, and boats were no exception. The boat's shell was wood, but, below deck, vines made up the many dividing walls. To Tarren, it seemed like floating in a huge tree stump.

After laying Helzendar on a cot in the first room on the left, Tarren went about finding a bucket. Though it seemed the dwarf had nothing left to throw up, Tarren would rather be safe than sorry when it came to dealing with vomit. He found a bowl in the cooking area to set beside the cot. Helzendar groaned and babbled about being kidnapped, and Tarren set out to make the Roz tea.

The small storeroom contained a variety of food and drink, and Tarren wasted no time fetching himself a smoked flounder and a loaf of dark bread. In his rummaging, he nearly forgot the tea. He lit the small wick below the elven teapot with a fire stone he had been given by the elf girl, Zuree, who he had danced with at Zerafin's coronation party. He wondered about her now, as he waited for the water to boil. Was she all right? Had she and her family got out? He vowed to himself he would find her, and, one day, marry her.

As proof of the old saying, "absence of mind causes a pot to boil faster," the soft whistle of the boiling tea water shook him from his pondering of Zuree's fate. He steeped the leaves and set the tea to cool. Helzendar seemed no worse for wear when Tarren pulled a chair up beside the cot.

"Here, Lunara says this will help," said Tarren through a mouthful of bread.

"Bah," Helzendar swatted at the drink, nearly spilling it. "Forget that traitorous wench–"

"Hey!" Tarren yelled, scowling down at him. "Best be watchin your tongue, she be my godsmother."

"Elven godsmothers, vine cities, bloody rockin' boats. Give me cold hard stone and steady ground, ye can keep yer elves, may they ro–" A dry heave wracked him, and left the dwarf panting and clutching his sides.

"Bah, yourself," said Tarren, "You ain't right. If you had your head about you, we would have a row."

"Boy," Helzendar laughed sickly, "I be whoopin' your arse with one hand tied behind me baa–"

Tarren shook his head as his friend strained against another heave, leaving his eyes bloodshot. "Drink the damned tea…who knows how long we will be out here. We got better things to worry about than your silly pride. A bloody war be wagin' around us, and the enemy ain't Lunara. So stop your pissin'…"

Tarren spit out his last bite of fish with disgust. "What in the hells? Ugh," he scraped at his tongue. He couldn't quite place the flavor, and he didn't want to. It was like dead fish and dog crap.

"What ye fussin' about?" Helzendar asked, amused.

"The taste, ugh–disgusting. Don't eat the fish."

"Why?" Helzendar asked with a chuckle and a look of anticipation for a punch line.

Tarren frowned at his friend. "It be like eating shyte… ugh!"

Helzendar laughed as Tarren again spit and scraped at his tongue. His laughter mixed with dry heaves once more, which only made matters worse. Helzendar grabbed a disgusted Tarren by the sleeve.

"Seems yer elven godsmother be serious when she said to watch your tongue, baha! Ye can't even swear like a man round that one."

Revelation came to Tarren, and he realized that Helzendar was right. "Shyte…ugh!"

—

CHAPTER SEVENTEEN
Revelations

Roakore watched as Whill followed the ancient elf into the crystal fortress. He didn't trust her, and thought about trailing them. But he had his dwarves to worry over. Whirling his stone bird above his head, he gave a toss as he and the elven Ralliad flew to meet the draquon. His twirling weapon spun like the seed of a maple, speeding out before him to clip the wing of the closest draquon. The beast gave a shriek and flailed to the ground below.

The Ralliad force tore through the advancing draquon with gleaming beaks and slashing talons. Roakore steered Silverwind into a dive, bringing them flying low over the dwarven ranks. His stone bird came whirling down the front line, breaking in two the leading spears of the Draggard.

Holdagozz and Philo led the charge, their voices singing the war song of Ky'Dren in unison. The dwarves of both Ky'Dren and Elgar barreled into their enemies, unleashing the pent up energy of Whill's enchantment. Picks and axes–gripped by hands made strong from days untold in the ancient mines–fell on the front line with devastating effect. The sun elves came over the ridge casting spells into the center of the Draggard horde. The dark elves attacked from the jagged outcroppings of the crystal fortress.

The sky streaked with dozens of spells and counter spells, some so bright the sunlight seemed dim in comparison. Explosions shook the ground, adding to the steady rumbling of the armies' footfalls. The dwarves took many casualties when a fireball got through the elves' defenses and hit their rear left flank.

Roakore surveyed the battle from above and gauged where the dwarven line was weakest. He steered Silverwind down, and mentally pulled his stone bird along with them.

"Give 'em hell, Silverwind!" he yelled as she flew him low over the heads of his kin.

He leapt from the saddle and gave a roar, cocking his axe high over his head. The momentum of the jump sent him flying into three Draggard that had engaged a wounded dwarf. They saw him coming and turned, bringing their long spears to bear. Black eyes gleamed and skin peeled back from hungry maws as the dwarf king attacked his foe. The stone bird whirled in at the command of Roakore, catching two of the Draggard upside their heads. He kicked aside a spear and sunk his axe into the shoulder of the third beast. Yanking the blade free, he ducked under a swipe meant for his head and came up under the attack, burying his axe in the Draggard's armpit. The beast reeled, its arm dangling, and a hatchet thrown from behind Roakore silenced the screams. A war hammer came sailing past to take the remaining Draggard in the head. Roakore turned to the wounded dwarf as his soldiers poured around them as if they were an island. The king's attack had stirred the already manic dwarves, and now they pushed the front line forward many feet.

"How bad?" Roakore asked the prone dwarf, who was trying but failing to prop himself up on an elbow.

"Bah, me king, it be nothin' o' yer worry," he groaned with a pained smile and a hand over his left chest.

"Ain't what I asked ye, soldier," said Roakore, pushing the dwarf's hand away to spy free-flowing blood. He grabbed a passing dwarf by the collar. "Get this one to the back, to the elven healers."

"Yes, me king," said the dwarf, and hoisted up his comrade.

Roakore turned and joined his dwarves in the charge. Spells continued to sing overhead, many coming down at them. Seemingly at the last second, the magical missiles would be intercepted by counter spells. Few spells made it through the elven defenses, but those that did caused incredible damage, the likes of which could not have been withstood by the dwarves without the protection of the elves.

They reached the front line, and Roakore took up the shield of an injured dwarf and shouldered his way to the front. The dwarves at the front dug in their heels and raised their shields against the ocean of Draggard. The battle had stopped, it seemed. A line of dwarves with shields low protected the row from low attacks, and for each of them, a dwarf stood with a shield above. Still behind their crouching forms, a third dwarf completed the formation, this one raising the shield wall even higher.

Roakore took up the rear shield station abandoned by the injured dwarf. He shouldered the tall shield against the spears that darted through the gap.

"Hatchets at the ready!" Roakore bellowed. The line of shield bearers echoed the command to the ranks behind them.

"Down!" he cried, and dropped low over the back of the dwarf before him. Those of the same station did the same, exposing the ranks behind them to the Draggard for a moment. A hatchet for every dwarf in range flew into the Draggard front line, sending it back.

"Up and over!" Roakore bellowed.

He was pleased when the shield bearing dwarves all moved seamlessly to create a ramp. Roakore braced himself as the hatchet wielders charged toward the front line and ran up the shield ramp. They poured over the ramps by the hundreds, using the momentum to push the Draggard back farther still. Soon, he was up and charging with his men.

Above them, the crystal fortress loomed like a mountain, blocking out the sun and casting a long shadow over the land. Whill was inside somewhere, searching for their only way home.

The elven battles raged on all around them, and Roakore knew one loose spell could take out dozens of his fearless dwarves. He hated magic for that reason. A dwarf might train for decades, and more than hold his own against the likes of dragons. But an elf could learn one spell and wreak havoc on an entire army. It just wasn't right.

He scoured the aerial battles above, but did not spot Silverwind, which was neither a good nor bad sign. He trusted his mount's fighting instinct, and Lunara's and Whill's enchantments.

A flash of light caught his eye close by, and three dwarves flew by overhead, on fire. Another explosion sounded, and still more dwarves sailed through the air spinning. Roakore's anger grew as he shoved forward through the unmoving crowd. A wide gap had been made by the explosions, and at the center of a smoldering crater stood a dark elf. Roakore stepped forward through the flames burning dull in a ring around the shallow crater.

"You," said the dark elf, "King Roakore of the Mountains Ro'Sar."

The elf strode forward confidently, his arms crossing and hands resting upon twin sword hilts. His voice came muffled from behind a large, horned helmet, yet it reverberated like a bell. Large pauldrons set with wicked spikes sat a layer above thick plate mail. The armor was copper red with dents and scorch marks. A darker red cloak trailed out behind the elf.

"Lad, I don't be knowing who you be," said Roakore.

"I am–"

"And I don't be right givin' a steamin' shyte who you be, hear? All you be to me be dead!" Roakore charged across the crater. He could feel the stone beneath his feet and began to touch on it with his mind. The dark elf didn't move, but rather, watched amused as Roakore barreled toward him. Roakore summoned his inner rage, and his heart leapt, lending strength to mind and body. He focused his will into the stone before him and pushed at the air with his calloused hands. The ground in front of him heaved and exploded forward toward the dark elf. A cascade of pebbles, stones, and boulders arched up and buried the dark elf where he stood.

In the shadow of the crystal fortress, the dwarves held a collective breath before cheering the victory, many eyeing the stone pile as they fought off the nearby Draggard. Roakore knew better than to think he had yet won. He set his stone bird whirling and prepared for retaliation.

"Get ye back! Press the lines, we be taking the fortress!" Roakore ordered his dwarves and the Elgar dwarves as well.

The dwarves moved back, and none too soon. The stone pile exploded in every direction, but soon conformed and came together to swirl above the dark elf's helmet.

"I have waited anxiously to test the earth-weaving powers of the legendary descendant of Ky'Dren," said the elf.

"May his name become poison on your tongue," Roakore spat.

The dark elf laughed and raised his arms to the swirling stones. They split into two groups, which spiraled downward, encasing his raised arms. He slammed his stone fists together and stalked toward Roakore. A dwarf charged in from the right, only to be swatted away like a bug by a stone fist.

Roakore roared in anger, and gathered loose stone to his arms as well. He surged forward, even as the swirling swarms of rock and crushed stone converged to form massive fists of his own. The dark elf leapt high into the air, bringing his massive appendages high above his head. Roakore leapt to meet him, forcing the collection of stone under his control to fly at the dark elf. They were as high as treetops when they collided above the battlefield. Silverwind appeared then, as if out of nowhere, crashing into the stone hands just as they shifted to strike Roakore. The quick deflection sent the blow wide, and Roakore came in hard, swinging down from on high as if splitting wood. His stone fists slammed the dark elf and shattered, sending sparks webbing across a yet unseen shield wall. Silverwind swooped away quickly, as the dark elf was rocked hard by the blow and whirled out of control for a moment. Roakore's arms flailed as he fell through the air. He saw his faithful mount circling in a dive to catch him, and prepared himself for a rough landing upon the saddle. He hit with a thud and groaned a thanks to Silverwind.

The dark elf landed and rolled to stand, the swirling stone in his control once again. He weaved his hands in and out in a peculiar dance, which the stone responded to by melding to form a large, writhing serpent. It rose up and quickly lashed out as Silverwind circled. The silverhawk reared, and the stone snake struck. An explosion knocked Roakore and his mount off course.

"Steady now, girl," he urged Silverwind as she righted herself and steered away from the dark elf and his stone serpent. The enchantments had saved them from serious damage, but Roakore didn't think they would withstand many blasts of that magnitude.

"Bring me down, girl. Do what ye can to distract the devil, but don't be doin' nothin' stupid."

Silverwind banked and glided, nearly colliding with a draquon as it dropped from the sky ablaze with blue flame. Roakore leapt and rolled to stand before his men at the edge of the shallow crater. He once again poured his consciousness into the earth, but was shaken from his concentration by a firm hand on his shoulder. He turned to regard Philo.

"Let me at the dark son o' a demon's arse!" Philo pleaded, slurring arse into a long hiss.

"This one be mine, soldier," Roakore replied, and walked to meet the dark elf.

The stone snake waited, coiled next to its master. About its neck, a hood formed as it slowly weaved back and forth. The dark elf extended a hand and blasted a spell toward Roakore. The dwarf connected to a sheet of stone below him, and brought it shooting up out of the ground. He ran wide of the stone as the spell slammed into it, turning it to rubble. He brought up another such slab, and another as he charged on. The two slabs were joined by a third, and, together, the three circled Roakore, slowly at first, but swiftly gaining momentum as Roakore growled with determination. Spells flew at him, but each hit stone instead. The slabs were blasted to rubble, as smoke and fire and a million jagged pieces of rock swirled around Roakore. To those dwarves who witnessed the charge of their fearless king, he looked like the revered Ky'Dren himself.

The stone serpent reared to strike, and Silverwind swooped down to peck at its eyes. The dark elf hit her with a fireball, leaving her engulfed in flames for a long moment during which Roakore's heart stopped. Finally, she could be seen spiraling out of control, trailing black smoke and scattered feathers of silver.

"Silverwind!" Roakore screamed in a rage that was not long contained.

He growled and bellowed a curse at the dark elf, shooting his palms forward, sending the millions of stones flying straight at him. His opponent raised a palm, stopping the assault mid-flight. Roakore roared and redoubled his push on the stone, and the dark elf was visibly taxed to hold it still. The stone serpent struck quickly then, as the two were fixed in their deadlock. Roakore sent an open palm out as it lunged at him with stone teeth leading.

All around them, the battle raged on, but not a Draggard nor dwarf entered the crater. Nothing existed, but him and the dark elf. The sounds of battle were muffled, a faint sound at the back of his mind. Time slowed, and Roakore reached out for the serpent. He felt instead the slithering presence of the dark elf's mental control. He fought for the serpent as he fought for control of the floating missiles. The serpent began to writhe and buckle, rearing its head to strike first Roakore, and then the dark elf. It fell to the ground with a crash and heaved once again, raining stone as it began to fall apart. Roakore found himself screaming with the exertion. He dug deep, summoning the strength of his line.

"O Ky'Dren, king o' the mountain, give me the strength to smite me foe!" he cried. Strength found him then, and his eyes beheld a part in the clouds above. A single beam of light pierced the thick cloud cover and set its edges aglow with silver light. Tears came to the dwarf king's eyes as power flooded his body.

"Ky'Dren!" he bellowed, and sent the newfound energy surging through the stone, overtaking his enemy and burying him. The stone serpent too descended on the elf.

The dwarves cheered their king once more as the dark elf was buried. Roakore wavered and fell to one knee, panting with the effort. He did not know the extent of the dark elf's power, nor did he dare hope that he had killed him. He gathered his strength and watched the pile of rubble. The dust had settled, and the pile remained still. Roakore stood once again and dared a few steps toward the debris. The ground began to shake; loose stones and pebbles nearby bounced and began to float into the air slowly.

"Down!" Roakore yelled to the nearby dwarves.

The ground shook violently, and the heaping pile of stone exploded. Roakore did not try to take control of the flying debris, rather, he conserved his energy and waited for the dark elf's next move. Dwarves and flying draquon alike were hit by the missiles, as the dark elf rose once again and guided the flying stone. Roakore ground his teeth and summoned his strength. He squared on the dark elf as the stone fragments began to swirl once again.

The cry of a bird caught his attention. He looked to the sky expecting Silverwind, but instead saw a sun elf shifting out of bird form and descending through the center of the debris-ridden whirlwind. The sun elf drew his blade, and the two battled within the eye of the conjured storm. Roakore reached out and felt the dark elf's hold still strong on the stone. He began once again to wrestle for mental control while the dark elf was distracted by his newest foe. But Roakore was tired, and he would need the strength of his kin if he was to continue.

Roakore had learned how to use the strength of his fellows from his father, and he from his, and so on down the line all the way to Ky'Dren. A thought occurred to him then as he reached out with his will and summoned the strength of his dwarves. This practice was very similar to the elves', who used the power of others—even stored it in gems. He was reminded once more of the *Book of Ky'Dren,* and the possibility he could control other elements. His anger rose as he chastised himself for such blasphemous thoughts. Together, with his new-found energy and his burning rage, he charged into the deadly whirlwind with a howl.

Roakore barreled into the fray, unconcerned by the swirling stone; it would not touch him. He brought his axe to bear, and the dark elf was there, twirling away from deflecting the sun elf's blade. Roakore saw only gleaming eyes within the horned helmet, and was suddenly spinning through the air. He landed hard outside of the spinning debris field and tumbled to a stop at Philo's feet.

"Me king!" Philo cried, and bent to scoop him up.

Roakore went deaf and blind as a sudden explosion ripped Philo away from him, and he was tumbling through the air once again. Dust and smoke hung like curtains; all around him, he could hear the groans and coughs of his kin. The smell of burnt flesh found him, and anger roused him from his stupor. He shook his head and rose to his feet, looking for his axe. Stumbling blindly, he finally found it in the dirt, with a severed hand clutching it…his hand. Roakore looked down and found a bloody stump cut off at the wrist.

"Me king!" Philo's voice called to him.

Roakore turned to find the dwarf lying on the ground, a jagged shard of stone protruding from his belly. A shaking hand pointed behind Roakore.

"Boulder," Philo wheezed.

Roakore turned as a shadow fell through the sky at them. He summoned everything left within and lifted his remaining hand to the projectile. Roakore screamed with the exertion as he caught hold of the rock with his mind and slowed its descent. The great shadow hovered above him, turning slowly on an invisible axis. Roakore heaved the slab away and fell to his knees with exhaustion. As he watched, the slab sailed through the air, spinning, and stuck in the ground like a spear. He reached out and took Philo's hand. The dwarf's grip was weak, though in his eyes burned the same wild energy as before.

"Pull this cursed shard out o' me gut, and lets…" Philo coughed blood that sprayed from his dirty mouth in heavy clumps. "Kill us some Draggard."

"Nah," Roakore shook his head drunkenly. "It be keepin' yer gut in. Sit tight, lad," he said, getting to his feet. He took his own severed hand and tucked it in his belt. He then retrieved his axe and turned to face the dark elf as he strode forward through the settling dust.

"Let me take care o' this bastard, and we'll find ye some help," said Roakore over his shoulder. When no response came, he looked back. Philo's head was slumped over on his chest, which barely rose with his breathing.

Roakore screamed a curse and staggered toward his friend, but the words of the dark elf held him fast.

"He is as good dead, as are you all. Shall we have a last dance?" the voice behind the horned helmet asked.

The dark elf stood tall in his thick plate armor, blood dripping slowly from the end of his lowered blade. Roakore took up his axe, closed his eyes, and prayed to the gods for the strength to defeat his enemy. When he opened them, a blur of white scales flew through the air and slammed into the dark elf. Avriel leapt from Zorriaz as the dragon mauled the dark elf. Sparks flew from her maw as her teeth struck the energy shield surrounding the warrior. A spell sent the dragon reeling; the enchantments laid upon her by Avriel shimmered as they absorbed the blow. Avriel sped forth and swords clanged. Something caught Roakore's eye and held it fast. Disbelief, dread, even anger coursed through him as he stared, shocked. The stone slab that he had sent back was not stone at all, but rather a large piece of lumber that had been the shaft of a destroyed catapult. Roakore stared at the wooden beam, transfixed. He dropped his axe and fell to his knees as if defeated. The reality he had known all his life was shattered in that moment.

He had moved something other than stone with his mind.

CHAPTER EIGHTEEN

Warcrown

Whill walked through the portal blindly, his hand on the cold hilt of Adromida and his shield humming around him. It might be a trap, but he had no choice; this was the only way home. The chamber within the crystal fortress was replaced by darkness as he followed Kellallea. He used mind sight and quickly regretted his stupidity, as he beheld the piercing light of Kellallea's power. He cried out and held his head, feeling as though it might explode.

After a time the pain subsided, and he was able to open his eyes. Kellallea watched him with a knowing grin. Torches on walls of stone had been lit, and Whill guessed they were in Agora, inside his family's ancient mausoleum. On the other side of the stone walls stood Del'Oradon Castle, and somewhere deep below were the dungeons and torture chambers where the Other had been born.

"Do you feel him near?" Whill asked.

"I do not," said Kellallea.

"Then I must hasten to get the others through," he said, and turned back through the portal.

Kellallea followed him into the crystal chamber; they were not alone. A half dozen of Eadon's doppelgangers stood, barring the way out. As one, they spoke in Eadon's voice.

"Ancient one," they said with a small bow. "Still your power and beauty shame the sun and the moon. What an honor to find you in my fortress."

The many Eadons regarded Whill with a familiar smirk. "And, young Whill. I assume you have surrendered to reason?"

"I have," said Whill, with s smirk of his own. He unsheathed his father's blade and held out a hand. A writhing shadow like a serpent of darkness grew in his palm and lashed out at the doppelgangers. The black serpent stretched from his hand, branching out and surrounding them. The many Eadons were lifted into the air and disintegrated as Whill stole their power. They fell to the floor in ashes, and Whill shuddered as he stored the power within his father's blade. Kellallea stared at him.

"How did you do that?" she asked, putting space between them.

"It seems my greatest gift is that of a mimic. I can cast any spell used against me," he said. A brief flash of intrigue flashed in her eyes.

"And you find nothing wrong with the taking of power?" she asked.

"Not from a maniacal dictator," he answered with a laugh.

"Do you not recognize your own hypocrisy? You so eagerly judge my actions, yet you do the same," said Kellallea.

Whill ignored her argument and went about inspecting the portal, which seemed to be fused to the crystal. Somehow, he needed to get it out of the fortress; there was no time for the two small armies to file through. He studied the crystal walls and put a hand to the closest. Power hummed gently within; he could sense the life force of every egg and Draggard queen. Many spells had been woven throughout the fortress; they spread before his mind's eye as webs of light, not unlike those the Watcher had shown him. Energy emanating from the core rode the light and pulsed throughout the crystal. Whill was transfixed by its brilliance, and he wanted the power within.

"Protect the portal," said Whill, and left the chamber and Kellallea.

He moved toward the center of the fortress. Guided by his mind sight, he soon found the room that housed the core, and, standing before the door, a dark elf.

"It is you," said the elf.

Whill raised a hand, and the dark elf stiffened and screamed in defiance as his energy shield dissipated in a shower of sparks around him. Black tendrils wrapped the dark elf in a sweeping embrace, stealing his energy.

Whill stepped over the dry corpse and blasted the crystal door with focused energy. It shattered inward, resonating like broken glass on ice. At the center of the room, a lone diamond the size of an apple hovered in place between two points. Energy rotated in the form of a helix, a pattern revered by the elves, both dark and sun. Whill unsheathed his father's sword, Sinomara, and stabbed forth through the many spells. He used the power of Adromida to clear the way, but the energy taken was not stored there. He drew out the power of the diamond slowly, pulling it to Sinomara. An arc of lightning shot from the diamond and danced along his blade as he pulled harder, shaking with the power coursing into the sword.

The humming of the crystal fortress grew quieter by the second as Whill drained the diamond of its power, Eadon's power. The soft light illuminating the crystal walls began to flicker and die. The fortress shifted, and Whill knew whatever spells kept it levitated were failing. The last of the diamond's power poured into the blade, and the fortress began to fall.

Roakore sat on his knees on the scorched battlefield, staring at the broken lumber protruding from the ground. All around him the battle continued, but Roakore saw only the wood he had moved, heard only the words from the *Book of Ky'Dren*. The elves, not the gods, had bestowed the power to move stone on Ky'Dren. He was tormented by nagging doubt about his religion; if the reason behind his power was a lie, then what of the dwarf gods and their promised mountain?

An explosion tore him from his disturbed pondering. Sunlight shone down on him as the crystal fortress fell into itself. Its point shattered against the ground, and the monolith toppled with an ear-piercing report. Another explosion sounded deep within the crystal, followed by a concussion that shattered the walls and reduced the fortress to a pile of jagged shards. Out of the rubble rose Whill, surrounded by a pulsing energy shield.

Seeing his friend roused him to his feet. He wiped dirty tears from his swollen eyes and took up his axe. Avriel had been joined by her brother, and, together, she and the elf king were driving back the heavily-clad dark elf. Roakore forgot his grief and set aside his doubts. There would be time for such things later; now, there was a victory to secure. With a heavy heart, Roakore began the war song of Ky'Dren and charged with his dwarves into the wavering lines of Draggard.

After the fall of the crystal fortress, Eadon's dark elves quickly fled, leaving the Draggard to their fate. The two armies overtook the beasts with renewed vigor, scattering the lines and laying them low. Many dark elves escaped, but the dwarf and elven armies did not pursue.

Whill rose above the wreckage of the crystal fortress as if floating upon the cheers of the armies below. Kellallea had protected the portal from the destruction, and guided it to the ground within a glowing force field. The power taken from the diamond hummed within his father's blade, and he set his sights upon the band of fleeing dark elves more than a mile off.

Whill quickly flew past the dark elves and landed among them. None moved to meet him, and Whill was excited by their fear. He sped toward the closest and stabbed the female dark elf through the chest. Sinomara hummed with energy as Whill sapped the dark elf of her energy. A bombardment of spells came at him as he unsheathed Adromida and strengthened his energy shield. With the two glowing swords, he made short work of the dark elves.

Panting with exhilaration, he stood over the crumpled corpses of his enemies. The dark elves he once feared now feared him, and rightly so, for he wielded the ancient blade of legend, and none could stand in his way.

Whill flew back to the armies and landed before the portal. The elves were busy tending to the wounded, one of whom was Roakore. He sheathed his blades and went to kneel beside his friend as Avriel tended to him.

"Be but a hand, there be others in need o' yer healin'!" he yelled at Avriel as she prepared to reattach his hand.

"Find me dwarf, Philo, he be dyin'!" he added.

"Your friend will live," Avriel promised him. "Other healers tend to him as we speak–now sit still."

The dwarves and elves alike had taken many casualties. The dead were laid out and covered in vines that grew around the corpses at the command of the elves. The Draggard, however, were left to rot. The bodies of the fallen dark elves were incinerated, lest their spells of preservation regenerate their corpses.

All of the dead had been gathered in two rows, and the elves and dwarves shared a short service for their fallen. Words were spoken for comrades and brothers, and tears were shed. The occasion was a solemn affair in light of the victory. Whill took heart that such a loss–though grave–had unified the two races like few things could. The elves and dwarves bled and died together, and they were now brothers-in-arms.

"Come!" Whill said as he stood beside the portal with Roakore and Zerafin. "Agora waits!"

Whill went through the portal expecting to find Kellallea. She was not within the mausoleum, nor was she anywhere to be found outside of the stone structure.

He came out into a gated cemetery full of old gravestones. A light snow fell, adding to the thin sheet covering the old tombstones. Some were grand and others modest, but beneath every one laid the dead. Whill wondered how many of his relations were buried here. Some of the grave markers had broken with age, the centuries leaving the engravings unrecognizable.

Every marker, whether the statue of a king, or the simple slab of a stillborn child, showed its age, and every one reminded Whill that time takes all things in the end.

A ruckus came from the mausoleum behind him. Silverwind exploded through the heavy stone doors with Roakore trying to hold on. When she passed the threshold in a rage of flying feathers and angry squawking, Roakore slammed his head on the arch and was thrown off. The silverhawk took a leaping step and launched into flight. Roakore got to his feet and staggered after the bird, cursing all the while.

"Bah, ye bloody bane! We ain't got time for yer games, we gotta get back to Ro'Sar!" he called after her in vain.

Whill ignored him for the figure approaching across the cemetery gate. He was short, but walked with the weighted steps of purpose. A hood was drawn low leaving only the end of a white beard to be seen. Roakore followed Whill's eyes, and straightened in the presence of the stranger. The man stopped many gravestones from them, and stared for a long moment before slowly proceeding. Ignoring Roakore, the hooded man walked up to Whill and brought back his hood slowly, as if in a trance. When Whill met his eyes, he was held by a haunted gaze. Dark rings cradled the old man's wild eyes, and deep lines beyond his years sharpened his dour expression. A short gray beard flecked with dark gray strands bent under his high collar.

"I near the end. I am tired," said the man in a broken voice. "If this is my final test, then I shall fail, but I would do so looking upon the face of my king, be he real or nay."

The old man reached forward slowly with a shaking hand. His cracked lips parted slowly with anticipation of the contact. When his cold hand touched Whill's warm cheek, the old man bent with a quiet sob.

"Tell me you are real, you have come home to us, and I will die a happy man," the old man begged with a hopeful smile.

"I am Whill...of Agora, and I have come home," said Whill, taking the man's hand in his. A smile grew beneath streaming tears. The old man fell to his knees and bowed at Whill's feet.

"Whillhelm Mathus Warcrown, as I once served your father, I offer my life to thee," the old man pledged.

"Please, please stand," Whill urged him and helped him to his feet. "To whom do I owe the honor?"

"Alrick Dupree, and the honor is mine. Damned if you aren't the spitting image of your father, 'cept for the long hair," Alrick mused.

"Mathus you said? Whillhelm Mathus Warcrown?" Whill asked.

Alrick was taken aback. "You don't know your middle name? No, I guess you wouldn't. Your mother told of it the night before they left...to visit her family."

Alrick seemed lost to a distant time; Whill's introduction of Roakore broke him from his thoughts.

"Alrick, this is Roakore, King of the Mountains Ro'Sar."

"Honored," said Alrick as they shook hands. Roakore only grunted; his mind and eyes were on the sky and Silverwind, and getting home. Dwarves and elves alike began filing through the doors of the mausoleum; Alrick looked delighted as he beheld the growing army.

"What magic is this?" he asked with a wide smile.

"I will explain later," Whill promised. "But, for now, I must know about Addakon. Where is he?"

Alrick's smile soured at the mention of the name. "The imposter Eadon you mean."

"You are aware of Eadon?" asked Whill. "Is it common knowledge here in the city?"

"Common, no, not at all. The older staff know the truth, but it is not spoken of," said Alrick, looking to the castle looming behind them, past the cemetery gates. "The dark one has eyes and ears all over the castle; our thoughts are not even safe from him. But whether he knows our minds matters little. What will we do with the knowledge?"

"The lad asked if he be about, out with it," said Roakore impatiently. Whill had noticed the dwarf king's growing agitation. Roakore worried for his mountain, but something more bothered him.

"He's not been here in a tenday, and good riddance! Would that he never returned, our city might find peace," Alrick spat.

Whill considered the old man's words, but they shed no light on the question of Eadon's whereabouts. Eadon knew where Whill was, for he had a link to the crystal fortress. Eadon had either gone through one of the rifts, and was trapped somewhere in Agora when the Other destroyed them, or he was still somewhere in Drindellia. Whill could not be sure. Either way, the gate of Arkron needed to be destroyed.

"This way. Follow Alrick through to the castle grounds," Whill urged the elves and dwarves.

Many of the elven Ralliad had taken to the sky in bird form to scour the city for dark elves. Whill walked past the steady tide of outgoing warriors. Avriel and Zerafin were there, ushering in the new arrivals. When Avriel noticed Whill, she took him aside.

"Look," she said, indicating a thin groove in the marble wall. As she pushed hard on its center, it clicked and swung open. Beyond the door, long stairs descended down into darkness.

"Must lead to the castle, likely to Eadon's quarters," said Whill, though he knew where it led. Somewhere down there, within the deep, dark depths of the castle, the torture chambers waited.

"We should search it out," said Avriel beside him.

"Not yet, the portal must be destroyed before anything else is done. It is too dangerous."

Soon, the last of the elves and dwarves had made their way through the portal. Avriel went through once again and came out with Zorriaz. The gate allowed her room to spare; the mausoleum doors, however, would not. A krundar master had remained behind for that reason. He grazed the walls with a hand and an ear to the cold stone. When it was time, he moved between the white dragon and the doorway, raised his hands, and began to chant.

"The eastern tower is large enough to house her," Whill told Avriel.

She shook her head reluctantly. "She fears the castle. She will not stay here."

Whill understood how she felt.

He looked to the elven Ralliad and listened to his steady chanting. He understood the words, and saw with mind sight as the spell formed.

The stone began to vibrate with a soft humming. Cracks appeared in the corners, and the wall opened wide. When Zorriaz had finally gotten through the space, the krundar returned the stone to its place and fused the seam.

The others left Whill to the portal; he didn't want anyone getting hurt. The last time he destroyed a portal, the resulting explosion had been significant. He unsheathed Adromida and called up an energy shield.

He was disappointed to have to destroy such an amazing and useful invention, but he had no choice. He could not allow a portal to Drindellia to remain in his castle. With a quick slash of Adromida, he cut through the enchantments and stone of the thick arch. There was a quick explosion as the spell of the gate escaped its containment. He watched from behind his pulsing shield as it flashed bright and dissipated. The last gate of Arkron was destroyed.

Whill walked out into the cemetery and instantly heard the clamor in the courtyard. He followed the path through the shining gates, past the hedge, and came out into the courtyard where the two armies had gathered. The castle guard had raised the alarm. They stood at arms before the castle door. Zerafin and Alrick stood closest, assuring the guards they meant no ill will. The elves stood calm throughout the entire affair, while the dwarves danced on their toes, weapons ready.

Whill walked to the front of the two armies and stood with Alrick and Zerafin. Many of the older guards shared the same expression of recognition Alrick had shown upon first seeing Whill. They remained in their defensive stance, however, and more soldiers filed out of the castle.

"Hold!" the captain of the guard ordered, striding forward to meet Whill. "What is the meaning of this, Alrick?" he asked, eyeing the elves and dwarves wearily.

Alrick moved between the captain and Whill. "Our lost prince has returned home. I give you Whillhelm

Mathus Warcrown, son of Aramonis Warcrown, and rightful king of Uthen-Arden."

The captain scowled with disdain. "Have you gone mad, Bishop? Step aside and allow me to deal with these intruders."

"He has returned to us!" Alrick proclaimed for all to hear. He ignored the captain and spoke to the soldiers at the man's back. "From the Warcrown Cemetery he came; as it was written, so shall it be!"

"Move aside, this is not your concern," the captain of the guard hissed.

Whill had a flash of something odd just then–something from the corner of his eye. He gave the captain a closer look, and the man's eyes darted to his. The captain was unable to turn away; Whill sensed the struggle within. He summoned power from Adromida and began applying pressure. A secret hidden just beneath the surface whispered in the man's thoughts. Whill heard them as muffled and distant. For a human, this man was putting up a good fight. Whill found his answers when he gazed upon the captain with his mind's eye.

Whill released the captain's mind and extended a hand in greeting. "I am Whill of Agora."

The captain stared at the offered hand and began to shake. He looked around at all of the watching faces and seemed to waver. A thick sweat began at his brow and pooled below his brown locks. He licked his lips and began to shift his weight nervously. The soldiers behind him looked on perplexed, and even the elves gave him a puzzled look. All the while, Whill smiled and held out his hand.

Whill snapped his hand back, and, in a blur of motion, his other hand was turning the captain by the shoulder. A faint whimper escaped the man as he was turned to face the human soldiers.

"This man is a puppet of the dark elf Eadon!" Whill announced, and thrust him to the end of his reach. He held the quivering man by the collar. The soldiers looked to their captain for an answer, and found it in his eyes.

"He lies! He is the enemy. He has invaded the castle grounds with an army!" the captain desperately pleaded.

"If I search you for dark elf trinkets, what will I find?" Whill asked, but the guard would not answer.

"If you are innocent, this should be quite painless," said Whill, and extended a hand forward. The captain screamed and convulsed as Whill began to pull the many dark elf gems to him. When the captain's legs failed him, Whill held him firm by the collar and stopped.

"Confess your guilt to your brethren. Save what is left of your honor," said Whill, and threw the captain forward into the soldiers.

The captain was shoved back by his men, and he reared on them angrily. "I saved your lives! The dark elves wanted to have you all killed and replaced! My words alone stayed their hands."

One of the soldiers, a man of years with hard eyes and chiseled features, unsheathed a blade. "Traitor!"

"Hold!" Whill yelled. "He is not to be harmed. He and the other traitors among your ranks shall be questioned. Take him to the dungeon."

Two of the guards took the captain by his arms and led him away. Whill extended a hand to the soldier who had drawn his weapon; he sheathed his blade and shook Whill's hand.

"Justice Walker," he said in greeting.

"Well met," said Whill, and quickly searched the man's mind. He found no secrets, no hidden guilt; instead he sensed elation and hope. "You are now the new captain of the guard, for the time being," Whill told him. He turned from the man and regarded the other soldiers...his soldiers.

"I *am* Whillhelm Warcrown, and I now rightly claim the kingship of Uthen-Arden."

CHAPTER NINETEEN

Say My Name

The wind moaned through the timber, bending branch and bow, and howled in many voices across the field. Whirlwinds of snow danced in the frozen chaos of the night, and the cold, piercing silver beams of the moonlight swept across the landscape. Aurora peered at the dancing snow through her open tent flap. Cold had come to northern Agora, but to the barbarians, the first snows meant little. It was still a time of rigorous work and preparation for true winter.

Lavish furs from the Seven Tribes had been brought to her as gifts. Once, she shunned the idea of wearing the other tribes' furs, but she now embraced the honor. Veolindra had noticed the furs and taken them, and the next day she returned with armor made to include them all. The armor itself was the same make as Veolindra's: smooth and dark, like black ice. Black leather was woven into the armor, twisting its way around the legs and arms. The many furs puffed out through the seams, in an ascending color scheme. The red fur of the fox covered most of the boots, and continued up along the calf. At the knee, the black fur of the bear replaced the fox's red, which in turn gave way at the hip to a coat of wolf and snow cat fur that fell below the knee. Eagle and hawk feathers formed a diamond pattern upon a dragon-scale cloak. Many precious stones were set about the armor. "Those are gifts, for your ongoing fealty," Veolindra had told her. The gems stored many spells; Aurora could only guess their power. Veolindra said they would protect her from attacks of the body and mind, heal her wounds, and lend her strength.

Aurora eyed her most valued gift and spun the ring around on her finger. The emerald within burned with a dull light: no undead were about. The ring was given to her by Zander. With the ring, Aurora would be able to control the Lich Azzeal and other undead given to her command.

She rose from her desk and strode out into the camp. The night was cold, but also a good one for drinking. Zander found her quickly, and she welcomed his company.

The Seven Tribes had been on the road for a week now, and Aurora had begun to recognize the telltale signs of their weary hearts. They had all left their children and elders to the coming winter, and, though their own absence would increase rations, the winter would be hard. The soldiers needed drink and song and tale, lest they lose their drive.

Aurora led Zander to a large tent at the center of the camp. Bonfires had been built and stumps set about in rings around them, though few sat. Tales were being shared, and songs were being sung. At one fire, heavy drums and moaning horns accompanied songs of loss and remorse, while, at another, fast rabbit steps and quick strings told tales of glorious spring in the Valley of the Elk. The tribes celebrated mostly separate from each other, as they always did, but they were in good spirits. If fights broke out, they were brotherly, with no weapons drawn.

At the center of the many fires, one was left in honor of the Chieftain of the Seven. Aurora strode through the crowds, acknowledging no one. When she reached the long-back wooden chair, she turned with a flourish and sat. Beorin of Bear Tribe strutted over to her and offered up a pint of dark beer. Aurora took the drink with a nod and downed it in a single gulp. The watching barbarians cheered, and the music continued. Zander sat to her right as the long table, set in her honor, began to fill up fast. Bread and beer was set upon the table, along with the day's kill. A flask of grog made its way down the line, and Aurora did not pause before drinking also. The rum burned well on the way down, and set a small fire in her guts.

"Give us a tale, Chieftain!" a woman yelled down the table. The hundreds of barbarians yelled their agreement.

"Settle in, settle in. For I have traveled far these years passed," Aurora sang out to the crowd, and they leaned forward in anticipation of the telling.

She told them of her journey from Volnoss to the shores of Shierdon and beyond. She spoke of the many men who had regarded her with fear, and, the women, a quiet respect. Her journey brought her along the seemingly endless Elgar mountains, to the borders of the elf land Elladrindellia, and finally to Del'Oradon. She made her capture sound planned, just a way to get close to the fabled Whill of Agora. The story ended with her glorious return, after escaping Cerushia.

The crowd listened, engrossed in the tale laid out before them. Aurora, like her father, had a gift for storytelling. Her voice rang loud and clear above the howling wind, while at the same time, it was melodic. She wove such a tale that the listeners became enthralled. Her father had told her that the best stories were those you never wanted to end. Her tale ended–to the barbarians' regret–with her glorious defeat of the Chieftain of the Seven. The crowd clapped, stomped, and cheered her tale. The Seven Tribes had crowded together for the telling, and the lines of division faded.

The morning came quickly for Aurora and many other barbarians. The merrymaking had gone long into the night, and, though she understood the last thing a traveling army needed was a hangover, she did not regret it. Many tales and imaginings of future glories had been shared the night before. The tribes' people had spoken of reclamation and conquest as Aurora had never heard before. They had found again a passion once lost to their people, pounded out of them by centuries of toil and the unforgiving cold of the north. The barbarians of Volnoss had rediscovered pride, and dared to hope for a better future.

Aurora lay in her bed, laughing to herself as memories of the night played in her mind. The ruffled spot beside her was still warm; stroking it, she smiled at the memories. She had invited one of the tribesmen to her bed last night, Shadow Darktail, son of Chieftain Gnash of Wolf Tribe. When she rolled over to the pillow, his smell remained.

She rose for the day, feeling refreshed and in good spirits. Her dreams had been pleasant, and though she slept for only a few hours, she was rested. As soon as she left her tent, the tribes' people went to work dismantling it. By the time she had gotten herself a hot bowl of whale-fat soup and a hunk of bread, her tent was down and stowed in a wagon.

The Seven Tribes of Volnoss took up the rear as the Draggard and Shierdon armies started out for the day. Veolindra fell back, as she often did during travels, and taught Aurora the language of the undead. When dealing with the creatures, there was a way of wording things; the wrong phrasing would have disastrous consequences.

Aurora had not seen much of Azzeal, and when she did, he displayed none of the peculiar behavior he had previously. Aurora had abandoned her guilt, and shed her fear and self-loathing. Veolindra and Zander had shown her a new way, one that would lead to glory, wealth, and power. Embracing their words as one would a new lover, she forgot all else, and focused on her lessons. Aurora became accustomed to the power of the emerald ring. In only a few days, she learned to command an undead soldier with but a thought. Her new-found power was exhilarating; she watched Veolindra's demonstrations, and her lust for knowledge grew. The lich lord commanded entire battalions with her mind. In battle, she could unleash swarms of the unfeeling, undead soldiers upon her enemies; they were but cannon fodder to her.

"Soon our master will announce himself to Agora," said Veolindra, with a wide smile as Aurora caught up to her.

"Is there any doubt he is here?" Aurora asked with a laugh.

"The humans and dwarves know nothing. How much can one trust the news of the world passed on from mouths to ears a dozen times? The kingdoms have been divided; as we speak, the cities of humans, dwarves, and elves burn. As of yet, Eadon has been a rumored whisper, a myth cloaked in shadow. Soon, all shall know him, and all shall bow."

Veolindra turned her head quickly, as though some-one had called her name. A wide smile spread across her face as a low rumbling began deep in the earth. The armies stopped in their march as the rumbling grew. Horses whined and shifted nervously, their fear-ful eyes darting.

"The time has come," said Veolindra with a shudder and wide-eyed laughter. "He speaks!"

Eadon stood before the long, white expanse of the Thendor Plains. Deep beneath the surface, the cours-ing power of Agora's crossing ley lines waited to be tapped. He raised a single, dark crystal shard before him, and began to chant.

Twelve other dark elves stood in a circle around him, more than two miles wide. They too began the chant. The crystal shard began to vibrate in Eadon's hand, gaining power. The steady chanting of the elves lent to his power, and solidified the connection between the crystal and the deep ley lines. Eadon planted the crystal shard into the ground and floated into the sky.

A deep rumbling began in the earth as the rivers of energy beneath the ground triggered the spells within the shard. The crystal pulsed with blinding light and began to grow. A quake shuddered through the land, followed by another, stronger jolt. The frantic chant-ing of the dark elves rose into the air as the shard grew downward into the earth. The roots of the crystal shard connected with the flowing energy of Agora's ley lines, and a cascade of light shot forth, piercing the heavens. Eadon floated high, bathing in coursing power.

The vibrating crystal began to steadily grow as the elves continued their chant. Earthquakes rumbled through the earth, and the ground heaved and split. Soon the crystal towered thousands of feet above the Thendor Plains. Large mounds of dirt crashed down like rolling waves as the crystal grew into a monolithic spire reaching steadily for the thin clouds and digging its roots deep into the earth.

The spire grew high and wide, fed by the energy of the ley lines; it pierced the clouds and continued to grow. The flat plains were torn asunder, leaving gaping canyons in the wake of the spell. Lava from rivers deep within the earth spewed forth, filling the widening canyons.

The rumbling subsided, and the dark elves fell dead at the edges of the spire. Eadon flew to the highest peak of jutting crystal and landed upon the smooth surface. He extended his consciousness down through the spire and into the coursing rivers of energy below. As the connection was solidified, Eadon spoke, his words traveling through the spire, into the rivers of energy, and throughout all of Agora.

Whill stood tall before Alrick and the soldiers as they knelt before him with heads bowed. Before, he felt uncomfortable to receive such treatment, but now it bothered him not. He was rightful king of Uthen-Arden, and he had claimed his birthright. His choice was made, and there would be no turning back now.

He raised his hands and bade them all stand.

"Long live King Whillhelm!" Alrick cheered, and the soldiers answered in kind.

Whill began to address them, but a deep rumbling stole his words. The rumbling grew so violent it seemed the world might be torn asunder. Men, elves, and dwarves alike fought to keep their balance as cracks formed in the courtyard, and the ground split. Whill shot into the sky and hovered high above the city. The oldest and tallest buildings swayed with the earthquake. The highest towers cracked and fell to the streets below sending people scurrying for cover. Below him, the castle buckled and moaned, and the two towers crumbled in a heap of dust. The elves extended their shields throughout the courtyard, blocking chunks of falling rock from crashing down upon the armies.

Just when he thought that the city could take no more, the rumbling subsided. He looked out over the horizon in every direction, but could find no cause for the disturbance. It was not until he looked with his mind sight upon the city below that he found the cause. Deep below the city, the surging power of the ley lines converged upon the castle from different directions; the brightest of them flowed north. Whill rose higher into the sky, until the air became thin and his breath came laboriously. With his mind sight, he followed the thin ley line north. Far away, a jutting spire glowed brightly. Whill unsheathed Adromida and prepared himself, but no attack came.

"People of Agora: human, dwarf, and elf. Hear my words!" Eadon's voice bellowed forth from all directions, scattering birds from the treetops. Whill flew swiftly down and landed in the courtyard as Eadon's words echoed throughout the land. He saw fear in the faces of the soldiers, anger in the dwarves, and in the eyes of the elves, a quiet foreboding. Silence followed in the wake of Eadon's command, and all of Agora waited.

"You know my name, for it is whispered by warriors and cowards alike. My armies are legion; my reach is infinite; and my power, absolute. My brethren of old have put you all in danger. These elves of Elladrindellia, who you revere and hold in such high regard, have included Agora in a war that should have ended five centuries ago, and far from here. These sun elves you call allies; they are your greatest enemy. They have refused to surrender and pay for their war crimes. Instead, they hide behind humans far weaker, but braver, than they."

Eadon paused, and Whill stood beside Zerafin and Avriel. Zerafin's face was void of expression, but his eyes darted anxiously as he waited for Eadon to go on. Avriel hid neither her anger, nor her fear. Whill noticed many of the dwarves had been nodding, or sharing glances, testing each other's resolve.

"The dwarves of Agora have lost much for these elves, and for what? Have they shared with you their great secrets, their power? Have your lives been enriched by their presence? I would end this war, before any more blood is shed."

"Lyin' son o' bitch!" Roakore screamed into the sky. His face was beet red, and his hands wrung his axe handle so hard it seemed his white knuckles might pop. Many of the men and dwarves jumped at the exclamation, having been pulled from the effects of Eadon's voice; more than a few of their faces reddened with the guilt of their thoughts.

Far away, upon the southern oceans of Agora, Tarren and the others heard Eadon's words. Helzendar mumbled profanities as he clenched the rail facing north. Lunara held a hand over her mouth as deep tears pooled in her eyes. The Watcher however simply stood and listened; his face shone neither fear nor anger. Tarren wondered if this was the end of all things.

"I have come to Agora seeking only my brethren," Eadon continued, "I have no fight with dwarves or humans. I want only what was stolen from me long ago. I seek only the ancient blade. One among you is in possession of this blade; one among you can end this war: Whill of Agora! Your name remains the last secret hope of the masses, and you are my last hope as well. The Elves of the Sun would let Agora burn out of sheer stubbornness. They have done nothing to stop this war. You can. You can end it all."

Humans, dwarves, and even elves looked to Whill then. In some of their eyes was accusation; in others, hope. The Uthen-Arden soldiers glanced at the blade in wonder. The legend of Whill of Agora had suddenly come to blazing life before their eyes. A small, rumbling shudder coursed through the earth once more, and cries rang out in the city as everyone prepared for another series of violent earthquakes, but they never came. Once again, Eadon's voice echoed from all directions.

"As a show of faith to all of Agora, I shall give you seven days of peace. If Whill does not come to Felspire with the ancient blade by the seventh sunset, I will be forced to destroy you all."

Eadon's last word echoed throughout the land, through every tunnel in every dwarf mountain. It was heard by every man, woman, and child, every dwarf, and every elf in Agora.

The Del-Oradon Castle courtyard was utterly silent. All eyes were on Whill, waiting for him to do something, anything. He avoided the waiting gazes and turned to Alrick.

"Bring me to the castle war room," he told the bishop, and with a nod to them, Roakore, Zerafin, Avriel, and Justice Walker followed him.

Whill had imagined his glorious return to his family's castle many times; reality held none of the romantic luster of his daydreams. He had solved one problem, only to find another waiting for him. Seven days. Whill's mind raced as he tried for the thousandth time to think of a way he might actually defeat the dark elf. To his surprise, Eadon's ultimatum came as a bit of a relief to him. In only a week, it would be over. For better or worse, it would be over.

Alrick led them from the bailey and through the thick double doors of the castle. He ushered them swiftly into the great hall. Whill felt a pang of sorrow upon seeing the beauty of his family's castle. The great hall was twice as long as wide, with a long, dark table of highly polished wood that could seat more than a hundred. The long table, however, was dwarfed by the room's high wooden arches of dark red and gold that seemed to grow like webs from the walls. Banners and flags hung all around, along with paintings of kings of old and artwork depicting battles won and beauties sought. Axes, swords, daggers, and war hammers ornamented the walls as well. A large map of Agora hung on the southern wall. At the middle of the eastern and western walls, twin stone fireplaces burned low fires; their chimneys towered to the ceilings and became lost in the web of arches. The floor was a highly-polished dark wood that hid well the heavy footfalls as Whill and the others moved through. Curved molding along the walls led to lighter brown, recessed panels, curving out from the center in an X-pattern. The wooden panels gave way to walls of mineral-rich, rough-surfaced stone. Light from the tall and narrow windows–which reminded Whill of long talons–sent the walls dancing with fractured light as he moved through it.

Many doors led off from the great hall, but the group took none of them. At the end of the hall, Alrick led them to the left and behind a wall that had been hidden from view until now. Behind it, a wide staircase brought them to a set of large double doors. Alrick opened the doors and bowed before Whill as he entered. Many of the elven masters had come with their king; likewise, Holdagozz and Philo came with Roakore. Walker had brought one man with him. Whill took a moment to search the man's mind, and he found nothing of import.

The war room looked as though it had not been used in decades. Cobwebs draped chandeliers like curtains, and a fine layer of dust had settled upon everything. Alrick swiftly went to lighting the many torches, but, with a lazy wave of Krundar Master Arngil's hand, all of the torches blazed to life.

"This room ain't been used in an age!" Roakore grumbled.

"No, it has not been used since the days of King Aramonis. Addakon took what items he found useful, and moved them to one of his underground chambers. He seemed always to be down in those dark chambers," said Alrick.

"Food and drink please, Alrick. We have had a long journey," said Whill, sitting down at the round table.

"Of course," Alrick bowed, and swiftly left the room.

Whill blew the dust off of the table, and began wiping at it with his cloak. Walker joined him, and soon a map of Agora–with a large, blown-up map of Uthen-Arden within it–shone brightly beneath the table's clear surface.

"Please, join me," Whill bade them all with open arms.

When everyone was seated, Whill looked to each of them in turn. He was not striving for dramatic flair; he simply did not know where to begin.

"We have seven days," said Whill, "and I am at a loss."

"I says we march our arses right to this…Felspire, and kill the dark bastard right now," said Roakore, jabbing his stubby finger with the last four words.

"I couldn't agree more my friend, but how do you suggest we accomplish the feat?" Whill asked.

"Ye got the damned sword o' power, ain't ye? It be time to quit the lollygaggin', and lay that devil low."

"It isn't that easy," said Whill.

"It be written in the prophecy o' old that you be the one doin it, with the bloody blade at your hip. Me damned mountain, and the mountains o' me kin been invaded!" Roakore suddenly exploded with rage and slammed the table as he stood from his chair. "It be time for you to be fulfillin' the prophecy."

"Writings of old are oft as lies of old," Whill said calmly.

Roakore heard the words from the *Book of Ky'Dren* once more, and in his mind's eye he saw the massive timber that he had moved. He became so angry that he began to shake; his words came forth, tinged by restraint, as if a hurricane was building inside the dwarf king.

"I have no time for idle talk," said Roakore, and pointed a shaking hand at the elven masters. "Agora shall burn thrice over before you lot get off your tree huggin' arses and do anything useful. I…Bah, I be wastin' me breath! Come on!" he said to Philo, and stormed to the door.

"Roakore!" Avriel begged.

"King!" Zerafin yelled, and Roakore stopped at the door.

"We need you," Whill told him.

"Me people be needin' me, and I be needin' them," said Roakore over his shoulder. After a time in which it seemed he might talk himself into staying, he stormed out of the room with Philo in tow.

"Excuse me," said Whill to his guests, and got up from the table.

"Give this to the dwarf king, so that you may contact him…should he leave," said Avolarra En'Kayen, a master seer. She handed him a large circular crystal, chiseled with so many edges that Whill saw dozens of reflections. He pocketed the trinket and left the room. In his haste, Roakore was nearly across the great hall when Whill came down the stairs.

"Roakore!" he called, but the stubborn dwarf king did not stop.

Whill sped across the great hall in a blur of motion and stood before his friend, causing him to stop abruptly.

"Please, speak with me for a moment," Whill asked.

Roakore took a deep breath and his rigid shoulders sagged. He looked tired, and haunted. He nodded to Philo, and the dwarf took the cue. When Philo was well out of earshot, Whill regarded his friend with concern.

"What is it?"

"What be what? Roakore replied.

"Cut the shyte, Roakore. Something has been eating at you since the fall of the crystal fortress. I know that you are anxious to learn of your mountain's fate, but there is something else."

Roakore puffed up as if to make an argument, but he deflated with a long sigh. Looking around suspiciously, he pulled Whill to the corner where they might have more privacy.

"During the battle in Drindellia," Roakore began, but paused as if searching for the words or the courage to speak them. He licked his dry lips and continued.

"One o' them blasted dark elves sent a large stone sailing through the air. I didn't see it right well, but Philo yelled something about a boulder. I thought it was a slab o' stone, and I sent it flying back at the devil. But…when the dust settled, I saw that it was no stone at all, but a piece o' lumber broken off a catapult arm."

Roakore had begun to shake, not with rage, but as if he were very cold. The deep curve of his brow spoke of loss and regret. Whill had never seen the light in his friend's eyes shine more dimly. The dwarf king's haunted eyes searched Whill's, asking if he understood the severity of what he had said.

"I moved wood with me mind, as though it was stone!" said Roakore in a strained whisper. "The *Book o' Ky'Dren* be true. The elves didn't help Ky'Dren's dwarves in Drindellia, and there ain't no help to be found from them now. The stories o' the dwarf gods be a lie as well."

"You don't know that for sure," Whill interjected reassuringly, but Roakore would not hear it.

"Our religion be based on the fact that me line can move stone! It be a gift from the gods and proof of their existence. And it be a lie! It be nothing but an elf trick."

"That does not disprove the existence of the dwarven gods."

"It ain't provin' they be real either," Roakore argued.

"You told me yourself that you saw your father's spirit float free of his bones when you reclaimed the mountain," said Whill.

"That proves that there be some sort o' life after death; it says nothing o' gods and the like. Besides, I could have been hallucinatin'."

"Do not cheapen that moment with your doubts, you know as well as I do that what you saw was real. I saw... hell, I spoke with my father, and saved the infant life of my mother's reincarnated soul. What you saw was real; there is some kind of life after death."

"That ain't changing the fact that me ability ain't comin' from the gods. And, if there be no gods, there be no mountain o' the gods," Roakore insisted.

Whill sighed and patted the distraught dwarf on the shoulder.

"The truth of the past, the answers of the grave, these things cannot be known with surety. All that we know for certain is that we know nothing for certain."

"One thing I be knowin' for certain be that me dwarves need me, and me mountain needs me. This battle be one o' powerful casters and magic trinkets. It ain't no place for a dwarf."

"You have a magic inside of you too Roakore. If you can control wood, you can learn other-"

"I ain't wantin to be learnin' no elf magic; it ain't right, nor be it rightly natural. A warrior be as good as his heart, his mind, his brawn, and his skill. Spells and magic be devil's work, don't ye be doubtin."

"Devil's work or not, it exists, and it can only be defended against by like force," Whill told him.

"Bah, ye fight a devil with devil tools, ye best be fightin yerself. You humans got such a sayin' ain't ye? Best ye heed the works o' yer people. But, for me, I'll be havin' none o' it."

Whill had never seen Roakore like this. Sure, the temperamental dwarf had his moods, but detached resignation had never been one of them. Whill could feel Roakore's emotions emanating from him, so powerful were they that he could not help but sense them. The more Whill wielded the ancient elven blade, the more in tune they had become. As a result of the constant connection, his senses had been quite keen as of late. Had he not been so tested by the Other, he didn't think that he would be able to control all of the strange new sensations that bombarded him. He felt Roakore's anger, his fear, and his resolve; Whill knew then that his mind would not be changed.

"I don't know if I can do this without you, Roakore," Whill told him.

It was Roakore's turn to pat a shoulder. "Bah, Laddie, ye done grown into a powerful warrior this last year from that whinny bitch I met atop Ky'Dren Mountain."

Whill could not help but laugh, and, though Roakore fought it hard, he too erupted into rolling laughter. Their laughter became contagious to one another, and, soon, they were leaning on each other, holding their sore sides. Whill was overcome then by fear at the thought of going forward without Roakore. Their laughter ebbed, and a smart silence filled the great hall.

Again, Roakore gave Whill a pat on the back and a brotherly hug. With a sniff and a nod, he quickly looked away. "You be doing just fine, Laddie. You be a god among men with that blade," said Roakore, and looked to him once more. "Mind what kind o' god ye become."

Roakore turned on his heel and marched through the great hall. Whill meant to say something to him, but 'good luck' sounded to cryptic, and 'farewell' too final.

He said nothing, and Roakore slipped through the sliver of light at the end of the great hall, and was gone.

CHAPTER TWENTY
To the Ky'Dren Pass

Eadon's words faded, but the weight of them remained long after. The earthquakes subsided, though no one moved from under cover. They waited and listened, but Eadon's words came no more. Dirk did not doubt Eadon's ultimatum had been heard by all of Agora. The dark elf's power seemed to have no limits. Dirk put Eadon's every word to memory. The speech spurred many questions in Dirk's mind: What and where was Felspire, and why was Eadon attempting to lure Whill?

Hours had passed since the battle by the river, and the wagon train was slowed by the destruction of the bridge. They soon found a narrow expanse to cross, and got back on the road quickly. Even at their slow pace, Orington was less than an hour away.

Scouts had searched for any sign of Fyrfrost, but to no avail. Chief and Krentz would be able to find the dragon-hawk, but he did not dare summon them yet;

he wanted to give them time to recover from the dark elf necromancers' attack.

Reeves ordered the wagon train moving again. Slowly, they started out once more northeast. Many of the wagons had been ruined beyond quick repair, and many of the sparse supplies had been destroyed. The refugees were weary, having been on the road the better part of a week. The attack of the dark elves and the raising of their dead had shaken them all. Eadon's claim of a seven day respite did nothing to quell the mounting despair. Even if the dark elf forces stood down for a week, there was still cold and hunger to deal with.

Dirk rode ahead with the forward scouts to spy the road to Orington. The clouds had begun to part, but little warmth was gained from the sun which set fast behind them. Judging by the day's weather, the night would be below freezing. No matter what condition they found the village in, at least shelter would be found. He hoped the rift he had seen outside of Kell-Torey had been the only one. If so, it was possible the dark elf armies had not made their way this far east.

The forest stood tall and thick in these parts, and the road often ventured beneath heavy bows of everpine trees, creating a tunnel of sorts. *Good place for an ambush*, Dirk reminded himself as he scoured the quiet forest. The thick forest abruptly ended, and he looked out over a wide valley of rolling hills lined with snaking streams and rivers. The waters ventured from the high hills to the east that began the vast expanse of the Ky'Dren Mountains.

Orington was found intact, its stacked-log walls standing high, and the smoke from hundreds of cottage chimneys hung in the twilight promising warmth. The small city was alight with the glow of lanterns, torches, and scattered bonfires. Dirk noted the watch was out in force; many men stood guard upon the walls, and no doubt the towers were likewise full of watching eyes.

Dirk raced back and informed Reeves of his discovery. Word spread quickly, and the mood and pace improved dramatically. The last stretch of mile seemed the longest to the hundreds of cold and starving refugees. Together, Reeves and Dirk rode ahead to the city's western gate, and were met by two Eldalonian soldiers and two members of the city guard. When they noticed the general, the four men stood at attention and saluted their superior.

General Reeves was the highest ranking member of the Eldalonian army in the city, and therefore, the command was his whilst he remained. The gates opened wide, and the city began to prepare for the influx of refugees. Every inn and tavern on every street was ordered to ready their empty rooms and spare cots, to the annoyance of more than a few innkeepers. Hot tea and bread was brought to the refugees as they continued to pile in, and, after nearly an hour, the city gates swung closed.

Dirk remained outside when the gates closed; the time had come to summon Chief and Krentz. He rode his borrowed horse back to the edge of the forest from which he had first eyed the city, and drew the wolf carving from his pocket.

"Come forth, Chief, I summon thee!"

Silver mist swirled out of the trinket and solidified into the spirit-wolf Chief. Dirk patted his leg, and Chief strode over to stand at his side. He lifted his chin and accepted a vigorous scratching behind the ears.

"Now, there's a good fellow, how you feeling boy?" Dirk asked.

Chief gave a single bark.

"What of Krentz, is she ready?"

Again, Chief barked. Dirk stood and summoned Krentz to his side. To his relief, she solidified before him looking as good as she ever had. She glanced around searchingly, as if expecting trouble to be afoot. When she saw nothing, she turned her gaze to Dirk.

"What happened?"

"The dark elves are dead, as is the Draggard horde. The people are safe for the time being in Orington, just west of here," said Dirk, pointing in the direction of the city. "However, Fyrfrost is lost to me. One of the elves turned out to be a shifter. The last I saw of him, Fyrfrost was fighting an aerial battle. He might have gone down anywhere between here and the bridge."

"I will find him," Krentz assured him.

"What of you? What were the dark elves doing to the two of you?"

Krentz gave Chief a scratch on the ribs, and his back leg kicked the air. "They were necromancers," she said with disgust. "Attempting to take control of our spirits. If you hadn't dismissed us when you did, I don't know how much longer we would have lasted."

"One of them raised a dozen dead soldiers'" Dirk told her.

"Yes, they are quite powerful," Krentz nearly whispered. Her distant gaze told Dirk she was deeply troubled.

"You've told me little of such sorcery."

"Had little to tell until now," said Krentz, looking out over the city of Orington. "Eadon has unleashed his most powerful weapon: the undead."

"How does it work?" Dirk asked.

"That is a long tale, and we've precious time to find Fyrfrost if he is injured," she said abruptly.

"You are right. Are you sure you've recovered? You may need to travel far from the trinket in your search."

"I will be fine," said Krentz as she bent to Chief's level and petted his head. "We search for Fyrfrost; he may be injured, so we must be swift."

Chief barked, and together they turned to mist and flew off in separate directions. Dirk began down the road, leaving the city behind him. He was not sure if he would return. If the dark elf armies came this way,

Orington would surely burn. It seemed to matter little now, since Eadon's ultimatum. In seven days, Whill
would be forced to face Eadon. Dirk had little faith that
Whill could defeat him. If he had his way, he and Krentz
would leave this land forever. Agora was doomed.
However, Krentz had a mind of her own on the matter,
and she wanted to help in the fight against her father

More than an hour passed before either of them
returned to the road. Dirk had not seen any sign of the
dragon-hawk, as he had expected. He could only see so
far through his enchanted hood, and nowhere did he
see any sign of Fyrfrost.

Chief came flying out of the forest in spirit form. The
horse reared, startled, and nearly threw Dirk from his
saddle.

"Whoa, boy, whoa!" he said, calming the beast. "Chief,
have you found him?"

Chief barked and spun in a circle.

"Lead me to him."

Chief leapt into the forest and turned, waiting for
Dirk to follow. Dirk knew the horse would only slow
him in such dense woods. He tied his mount off on a
birch and trailed Chief through the heavy snow.

He followed Chief for what felt like hours. The going
was slow. A lot of snow had fallen in these parts the
last few days. Even where there were no drifts, the snow
came up to Dirk's knees. Chief avoided the worst of it

however, keeping under the weighted bows that caught much of the snowfall.

Chief danced a circle and barked as they neared Fyrfrost in a large clearing. Dirk quickened his pace and caught up with Chief. As he got closer, he realized this was not a natural clearing. Many trees had been snapped in half and lay strewn about, while others laid on their sides, their roots having pulled with them large clumps of earth. Beyond the initial destruction, lying on his side amid the felled lumber, was Fyrfrost. Krentz knelt beside him.

Fyrfrost's breathing was slow and labored. Blood pooled around him, turning his silver feathers red. Many deep cuts and gashes riddled his still body. One wing lay mangled and broken, splayed out across the snow; the other was simply gone. His left hind leg was broken; jagged bone protruded from his thigh, leaving the leg dangling awkwardly. All along his slowly heaving chest, feathers had been burned away, and the scorch marks from spells marred his once beautiful scales. The gravest injury however, was a thick piece of broken tree branch that had impaled him during the crash landing.

Dirk walked a slow circle around his mount, his foreboding growing with every injury he found. He turned to face the dying dragon-hawk and saw tired resignation in his large eyes.

"Can you heal him?" he asked Krentz.

"Yes, but his injuries are extensive. I was weakened more than I first thought by the dark elves; it will take some time before he is in any condition to fly."

"You told me you would be fine," said Dirk, concerned. He and Krentz didn't keep things from one another.

Following his train of thought, she waved a dismissive hand his way. "I said I would be fine, and I shall."

"Chief, set a wide perimeter; let none pass through," said Dirk. Chief whined for Fyrfrost and reluctantly left his side to keep watch.

"I will collect what deadwood I can find. If the last few nights have been any indication of the weather to come, tonight will be a cold one."

Krentz only nodded at him, having already begun her inspection of Fyrfrost's injuries beyond the surface of his flesh.

Dirk went to gathering the deadwood. The work was slow and tedious, having to dig through the forest for the frozen branches. The fallen and broken trees around the crash site would come in useful, though they were still green. Krentz could use spell work to force the wood to burn. In an hour's time, Dirk had procured enough for a fire, and Krentz set the wood ablaze with a spoken word.

"I am ready to begin," Krentz announced as she stood from her kneeling position beside the dragon-hawk.

"First we must remove this branch from his belly. I need you to keep him calm."

"Keep him calm?" Dirk laughed. "You are the one who can speak to his mind, and hear his thoughts."

"Yes, but he trusts you. I must focus on stopping the bleeding."

Dirk went to stand before Fyrfrost's large head, which, when lying on the ground, came up to Dirk's shoulder. The dragon-hawk's breath still came quick and shallow, and his heavy eyes seemed to float at the threshold of death.

"It's all right Fyr. Krentz is going to fix you up. But this is going to hurt...a lot," said Dirk as he stroked Fyrfrost's long, beak-like snout.

"He understands your words," Krentz informed him. "Best you take his mind off of the pain."

"Best he knows what's coming, don't you think?" Dirk retorted.

"He will soon enough," she said as she summoned a ball of healing energy to her palm. Closing her eyes, she began to chant.

Dirk leaned toward Fyrfrost as if imparting a secret. "Buddy, when this is over, we're going to go hunting, just you and me. We'll find us long-stretching fields of green with no end, fat with cattle and deer. Maybe a clear stream of mountain water filled with all the fish you can eat."

Fyrfrost's eyes shot wide open, and he let out a roar of pain.

"Hold him down!" Krentz hollered over the cries.

"You're joking, right?" Dirk yelled, backing away from the thrashing dragon-hawk.

"Got it!" Krentz cried victoriously, and Fyrfrost let out an ear-piercing roar once again.

The bloody shaft was tossed to the side as Krentz set to work to staunch the bleeding. Blue healing energy was sent weaving through the air and into the deep wound. Fyrfrost gave one last cry, and his head dropped heavily. His tired eyes found Dirk and closed with a flutter.

"Did my fearless dragon-hawk just pass out?" Dirk asked with mock disbelief.

Krentz settled in for a long healing session. She understood far less about the dragon anatomy than she did elves or even humans, and she knew nothing of the anatomy of a dragon-hawk crossbreed. Dirk went about once more gathering wood. By the time midnight came, three separate fires blazed around Fyrfrost. Dragons withstood colder conditions more comfortably than people, but he thought the extra warmth couldn't hurt. Fyrfrost gave no indication of his preference. The dragon-hawk slept so soundly during Krentz's spell work, Dirk would have mistaken him for dead if not for the slight wisps of smoke from his nostrils.

Dirk found what comfort he could on the cold ground, and slept until the morning sun woke him.

Krentz was still by Fyrfrost's side, the puncture wound from the large branch was gone, along with many of his lesser wounds. She now worked on his broken wing.

"Good morning," she said as she weaved her spell work. There was a crunch of bone and Fyrfrost stirred weakly with a growl.

"He seems better already," Dirk remarked, as he surveyed her work.

"I managed to close his wound and repair the damage within," she said wearily. "Once I heal his wing properly, I shall begin building the other."

Dirk noticed Krentz's physical form was slipping. She had become slightly translucent; she needed to return to the spirit realm soon. Chief came out of the woods then, two limp rabbits hanging from his mouth. He laid them next to Fyrfrost's beak-like maw and nudged them closer. Fyrfrost's nostrils widened and his eyelids fluttered. His tired eyes focused on the offerings, and with his long tongue he scooped them up into his mouth.

"It is hard enough to keep him unconscious without a fresh kill rousing him," said Krentz, annoyed.

Fyrfrost stirred and rolled from his side to sit up on his hind legs. The wing that had been broken was still torn in a few spots, but it mattered not, as he still had only the one wing. Krentz sighed, frustrated, and slumped down to the ground.

"You have done enough for now. He is no danger of dying. You should rest. I will take him hunting while you are away; we can resume tomorrow."

"Tonight," Krentz argued. "I need only a few hours to gain my strength."

"Very well," said Dirk. He went to her side and reached to touch her face, but she could no longer hold a physical form in this plane. His hand went through her as it would smoke, and Krentz regarded him with a shy smile. Dirk held up the trinket, and she became a wisp and was gone.

"How about you, do you need a break?" Dirk asked Chief, as he held the figurine out to the wolf. Chief snorted and shook his head, and then snorted again and pawed at his snout.

"What, you smell something Chief?" The wolf spun a quick circle and barked once. His behavior told Dirk something was about, but it was not an enemy.

"Is it game?

Chief shook his head and let out a quick, fake sneeze.

"A man."

Chief dropped to his chest, his tail high, as a puppy might during play.

"Show me."

Chief led Dirk through the forest to the east, leading to the road they had taken to Orington. He soon came upon General Reeves, and three of his soldiers, trudging through the woods.

"Easy Chief, they are friend, one and all," said Dirk. Chief fake-sneezed as if the warning was insulting.

"Aye, there you are. Have any luck finding your dragon?" Reeves asked with a friendly smile. Dirk had not seen the man smile so easily in the short time he had known him. The man had a new spring in his step; a weight had been lifted from his shoulders since finding Orington intact. Had the city been destroyed, the civilians would have had to travel another week to the Ky'Dren pass.

"Yes, he is resting, his injuries were great," said Dirk, shaking the general's hand. "You found me easily."

"Yes, well, the horse next to the road was my first clue," Reeves admitted with a wry grin.

"Of course," said Dirk with a small laugh of his own. "Take it with you back to Orington. I am no longer in need, and thank you once again for the loan."

"Think nothing of it, my friend. We are in your debt."

"You have come all this way, might as well sit through some tea," said Dirk. "That is, if you can stomach closeness to Fyrfrost. He is still recovering and does not need the distraction of human fear."

"I will be fine," said Reeves, looking to his three men who had lost a bit of color at the mention. "How about you three get the horse to stable?" Reeves suggested, and the men eagerly agreed. Dirk didn't miss the apprehensive looks they gave Chief; they seemed transfixed. The spirit-wolf was showing off. Dirk noticed that his paws left no footprints in the snow, to the curiosity of the soldiers.

The three soldiers left for the road, and Reeves followed Dirk the short distance to his makeshift camp. Reeves saw the crash site and stopped in his tracks to study the felled trees. He regarded Fyrfrost with wonder.

"That there is one tough dragon!" he said, searching the dragon-hawk for an injury, aside from the obviously missing wing.

"Sure is," Dirk agreed, searching out the makings for tea in his saddlebags.

Soon, he had found the kettle and had snow melting over the fire. Reeves sat upon one of the fallen logs and took out his pipe and tobacco pouch. He sat first, and Dirk smiled to himself when the general chose the log that would leave him facing Fyrfrost. Dirk sat across from him, his back to the dragon-hawk.

"You smoke?" asked Reeves.

"Only opium, and rarely," Dirk answered as he always did; he enjoyed the varied reactions that followed. However, Reeves showed neither comical nor quizzical reactions.

"Well, you are in luck, good sir. I happen to be of the same taste, and I have some with me," Reeves announced, cheerily.

Dirk could not help but laugh. "You carry opium with you?"

"Of course, 'tis the best way to have it at the ready, nay? Besides, I do not partake often. When the fancy strikes me, I would rather have no bother about procuring it. A little bit of a good thing never hurt nobody, but a lot of anything will kill you, as my pappy used to say," said Reeves as he dropped a small, black ball in a pipe. Before Dirk could refuse the offer, the general had the opium hissing and bubbling with the fire from a small branch. He coughed and handed off to Dirk.

"A little, then," said Dirk. He whistled to Chief who was sniffing about. "Best you keep an eye on things boy, I'll be back in a bit."

Chief cocked his head to the side, and his ears perked curiously. Reeves began to laugh then, and did not soon stop.

The tea came to a boil, and Dirk poured two cups. Reeves slowly accepted his with a happy grin. He slumped to sit on the ground so he might lean back upon the log.

"Relax friend, these woods are guarded, and you have the ghost wolf to keep watch. Even if foul beasts are about, a man such as yourself need not fear much, whether he be up on an opium cloud or not."

"You speak of the spirit-wolf as if he is nothing of concern; you are familiar with such magic?" Dirk asked.

"These are strange times, friend. Draggard and dwargon and all manner of nightmarish creatures walk the land, and dark elves wielding such power as to make a man feel like a child in their presence. Dark proclamations by a dark lord ride on the wind and are heard by all…no, a spirit-wolf is of little concern to me these days. Though, I am curious as to how you obtained such a hunting partner."

"I came across him in my travels," said Dirk.

Seeing Dirk was not about to elaborate, Reeves let it go. He lit up his tobacco pipe and lazily blew rings into the cold, still air.

"Is your destination still the Ky'Dren Pass?" Dirk asked.

"Nay, Orington has adequate lodging, and their food stores will last the winter," Reeves answered. "You think we should travel on?" he asked, seeing Dirk's thoughts on his face.

"'Tis a miracle the city still stands. Should a horde the likes of which we saw yesterday come this way, the city will be destroyed, and everyone in it."

"We can hold our own," Reeves replied with a raised chin.

"I've no doubt," Dirk assured him. "However, against the magic of the dark elves, your swords are as feathers before flame."

"If you are right, then a mountain will give us no reprieve from our fate. Nay, we shall die beside our kin if that be the will of the gods."

"The gods are silent, my friend."

Reeves laughed. "Is the ocean silent because you do not hear it?"

"I do not hear the ocean because it is far from me."

"Ah," Reeves shot up his brow with a wide smile, "but, unlike the oceans, the gods are always near."

"I surrender. I have many weapons, but against the words of the devout, I have none. Nor would I wish to weaken your beliefs, as you wish to strengthen mine."

Reeves nodded with a victorious grin. The steam had left his tea, but he drank all the same. The sun remained bright in the cloudless sky. The day was the warmest he had seen since leaving Eldon Island. The snow would become even heavier now, and the rivers would be stressing their banks. Dirk wondered if Eadon had anything to do with it. Many of the people would believe it. The dark elf promised a week-long cease-fire, and the next day the sun shone brightly in a sky of blue. He wondered if Eadon would honor his cease-fire. Armistice or not, the dwarves would not stop in their advancements. Dirk assumed the humans had received the worst of the attacks, being that they occupied the largest majority of Agora. They would be glad for the peace, and would use the reprieve to fortify what strongholds remained. Dirk could not guess what the sun elves might do next.

Dirk and Reeves shared another cup of tea, and had a small lunch of smoked meat and goat cheese. The General's gaze lingered on Fyrfrost. His eyes showed not fear, but wonderment. Fyrfrost had not stirred, and slept soundly as he recuperated.

"A spirit-wolf for a pet, an elf for a woman, and a dragon-hawk for a mount," Reeves mused. "I bet a man like you has more than a few stories to tell."

"No more than a general of Eldalon," said Dirk, raising the last of his tea.

Reeves looked to the sky with a hand at his brow to block the sun. "Looks to be near midday," he said, and retrieved a curved flask from a hidden pocket within the folds of his winter armor. He popped a small cork and handed the flask to Dirk. His eyes asked Reeves what it was.

"Eldalonian Spiced Rum," the general answered.

Dirk tossed back a gulp and passed the flask back to Reeves with a grateful nod. The general drank deeply and wiped his mouth with the back of his hand. Dirk could see a question behind his eyes. Reeves knew that he had given himself away and chuckled.

"You are a man of many talents, yes? I would ask a favor."

"Go on."

"Take me with you," said Reeves.

Dirk sighed, but before he answered, Reeves raised a hand that told Dirk he had not finished.

"I know you are headed to the Ky'Dren pass and beyond. You and Krentz will reach it by the end of the week. And then to Felspire?" he guessed correctly.

Dirk got up to stretch his legs and threw a few pieces of wood on the fire. The general was adamant, and Dirk wouldn't mind having him along. However, the general had nothing to offer Dirk, and he saw no logic in it.

"My road is one of constant dangers," said Dirk, stirring the coals with a short stick. "All respect friend, but what occurred yesterday is commonplace in my cursed life. You have your duties, you are now the highest ranking soldier in Orington. You will be more useful there."

"You travel to the Ky'Dren Pass, with a dragon-hawk, no less," said Reeves with a nod to Fyrfrost. "If I am there to speak for you, your journey through the mountains will be much easier, and important information might be gained, for both of us."

Dirk considered for a moment. He doubted the dwarves would allow Fyrfrost anywhere near the pass, whether General Reeves spoke for him or not. Should Dirk travel through the Pass, it would have to be in secret. Krentz had made it through without trouble, and she could do so again.

"Perhaps my road does not lead to the Pass. It's not the only route by which to fly into Uthen-Arden," said Dirk.

"No, you might fly south around the mountains. What information will you find there? The route would take you over Turrell, if the city still stands. You seek information, and the Ky'Dren Pass is sure to hold your answers, not the endless empty miles of western Uthen-Arden," Reeves replied.

"True," Dirk acknowledged. He moved from the fire and sat back down on the stump across from Reeves. "What do you seek, that you would abandon your responsibilities to the people of Eldalon?"

"I abandon nothing," Reeves growled. "My responsibility to Eldalon would be served well should I go to the Pass, where, surely, our soldiers have gathered."

"But, you wish to travel beyond the pass, to the lair of the beast," Dirk reminded him.

Reeves' eyes lingered long on nothing and turned to the burning fire. In them stirred sadness, and a deep anger.

"My king is dead," whispered Reeves, the words coming out as a hiss of contained rage. "His line has been slaughtered. Kell-Torey lies in waste, the city that stood for centuries...is gone. This dark elf, Eadon, has destroyed my country. I would bear witness to his end."

"You believe he will be defeated by Whill?" Dirk asked.

"I believe the gods will not suffer him to destroy what they have created. There will be a reckoning," said Reeves with shimmering eyes of dancing flame.

"Very well," Dirk said at length. "You will accompany us to the Ky'Dren Pass and beyond. Perhaps, together, we shall witness this reckoning you speak of.

Reeves nodded his thanks and offered a hand. Dirk took hold, and they shook. "Have faith, my friend. In these dark times, it may be all we have."

"I will drink to that," said Dirk.

Reeves gave a much needed laugh and produced his flask; the two men drank and sat in silence.

Midday had come and gone, and the sky remained cloudless as the day progressed. The temperature had risen noticeably; no longer did the men's words produce such dense plumes of mist in the cold air.

"The elf, where is she?" Reeves asked. The question had been on his mind for a while.

"Resting," Dirk replied. The general was a man of honor, and likely trustworthy, but Dirk kept the secret of Krentz and Chief to himself. "She will be along shortly, and will resume Fyrfrost's healing."

Reeves only nodded and did not press the issue. His eyes lingered on Fyrfrost, likely on the missing wing.

The effects of the opium had worn off, having been mild to begin with due to Dirk's high tolerance to such drugs and poisons. He rose from his seat and stretched; his body was restless from inactivity. He unsheathed his short sword and ran a gloved finger down its length.

"Care to spar?" he asked Reeves. "My muscles grow tight, and we have a long flight ahead of us."

Mick Reeves stood with a growing grin and unsheathed his own blade. "No magic," he said, eyeing Dirk's large array of weaponry.

"No magic," Dirk agreed.

They moved to the first of the fallen trees strewn about the crash site. There was not much room to move about in the heavy snow between the fallen timbers, so Dirk climbed atop one of the many large logs and walked its length, breaking branches where they would hinder movement. Reeves set aside his heavy fur cloak and followed; his footing was sure upon the rough, bare bark.

Dirk came at Reeves as soon as the general squatted into a ready stance. Reeves' heavy long sword cut through the air with impressive speed, and, when the two blades met with a spark, Dirk felt great strength behind the blow. Reeves was strong, and he wielded his comfortable blade with confidence. His speed was lacking, but against any other man it would be formidable.

The general did not back down, but met Dirk blow for blow. Dirk slowly began to put on the pressure as Reeves sparred cautiously. Dirk had more power and speed, and so Reeves remained on the defensive, always expecting a faster blow to follow the last.

After nearly an hour they stopped; both men were panting, and sweat covered their bodies beneath their armor. They had not remained on the fallen tree, but had covered a large area in their sparring. Notches had been chopped along many of the logs, and the heavy snow had been trampled flat in many areas when the fighting went to ground.

Reeves patted Dirk on the back as they caught their breath. "Good session," he managed to gasp between panting breaths.

"Likewise," said Dirk. "The blade suits you well."

"Was my grandfather's. He served the Eldalon army for thirty years," said Reeves.

"And your father?"

"No, he was already raised with a father in the military. He wanted to be around more for me, and he was content with the life of a farmer…much to the disappointment of my grandfather."

"You followed in the footsteps that he would not. Must've caused strife," Dirk surmised.

Reeves chuckled. "Indeed, but once I graduated, my father gave me the blade, and his blessing. He did not want to make the same mistake his father had."

"Your father sounds like a wise man. Not many can forget their anger, especially for those closest them," said Dirk.

"Indeed, often those closest to us stir the greatest passion, be it anger or love."

Dirk thought of his own father, a man who had seen it fit to teach a child the ways of a thieving highwayman. A man who was drunk more than not. Dirk's skill at pickpocketing fed them both from the time he was seven. They stayed for weeks at a time in various cities, until suspicion inevitably began to arise around Dirk's father.

Dirk shook his head from past ponderings and sheathed his polished blade. "I go to find what food I might for the road."

"I shall procure rations from Orington; I need to inform my second of my intentions," said Reeves.

"Very well," said Dirk. "We leave just before the setting sun, don't be late."

"Wouldn't miss it for anything," Reeves replied, and began walking back through the forest.

Dirk had no intentions of hunting; he had plenty of rations from Eldalon Island left in Fyrfrost's saddlebags. He had needed an excuse to go to the woods to summon Krentz in privacy.

From the opposite side of Fyrfrost came a rustling in the woods, followed by a heavy dragging noise. Dirk walked around the huge dragon-hawk, and Chief came, pulling behind him Fyrfrost's missing wing. He could not help but laugh at the sight of the wolf, hauling along a wing ten times his size. The drooling grin upon his pet's face didn't help matters.

"Well, I'll be damned if you aren't the best wolf a man could ask for," said Dirk, bending to give him a scratch behind the ears.

Chief released the wing to enjoy his reward. He quickly dropped and rolled on his back for a belly rub, and Dirk was glad to comply. Fyrfrost's wing was tattered and broken, but the healing would be much easier now for Krentz, as she would no longer have to force one to regrow.

Dirk gave Chief his due and summoned Krentz from the spirit realm. She came to form before him, and soon noticed the large, severed wing. She gave Chief a wide smile and a few more scratches below the ears.

Reeves arrived just before the setting of the sun as Dirk had said. He carried with him two bags over his shoulder, one of which, Dirk assumed, held the rations he had promised.

"Ah, the wing has healed," he said nonchalantly, as if it was of no import that the previously severed wing had somehow appeared again, whole and new. "And the beautiful Krentz has returned from her rest," he added, with a chivalrous bow.

Krentz gave the general a smiling curtsy. "General Reeves, it is good to see you again. I hear you will be joining us in our travels."

"I would, if it pleases you, of course."

"It pleases me," she assured him with a smile.

Reeves' bags were added to the gear strapped to the saddle, and the three mounted Fyrfrost.

As the sun set over the horizon behind them, they set off northeast toward the Ky'Dren Pass, and, possibly, the end of the world.

CHAPTER TWENTY-ONE

Two Brothers and the Elven Blade

Whill returned to the war room and apologized to those waiting. Alrick had brought beer, wine, and liquor. Even the elves found occasion for spirits. Food there was also, but it seemed that none had much appetite for it at the moment. Whill returned to his seat and nodded his thanks when Alrick handed him a mug of beer.

"The dwarves are not needed. Your friend's departure is of no consequence," said Zionar Master Ornarell, the storms in his eyes gleaming.

"Mind what you say about King Roakore. His friendship has proven invaluable, as well as his council," said Whill.

"I mean no disrespect," said Ornarell with the smallest of bows. "I simply speak the truth. Eadon shall not be defeated by dwarves; they've enough work clearing their mountains."

Whill turned away from Ornarell, ignoring him. He was in no mood to debate at the moment. Seven days…the words replayed in his head over and over again, reminding him of his dilemma. He had spent weeks with the elves, yet he was no closer to an answer than he had been.

"What do you think Eadon will do if he attains the power of the two swords?" he asked the elves. The two humans, Alrick and Walker, were lost in the conversation.

"He will gain the power of a god," said Master Libratus, and many of the others nodded agreement.

"Will the gods respond?" Whill asked.

The elves seemed to ponder the question for the first time.

"Haven't any of you considered the gods may have something to say about all this?" he asked.

"We cannot rely upon the gods to defeat Eadon." Master Arngil argued, as he sought confirmation from his brethren.

"That cannot be known," said Avriel.

"The god of peace can be relied upon," Morenka Master Myrramus assured them. "If all would simply stop fighting for peace, peace they would have."

"We are not here to debate dogma," Zerafin reminded them all.

"Many religions exist, and, though you may not be devout, your culture speaks of the gods. So what of them? When Eadon ascends to their level of power, will they answer?" Whill asked them all.

"*Our* gods do not meddle in the affairs of mortals," Captain Walker put in.

"Nor, the elven gods," said Master Arngil.

"This will cease to be a mortal affair if Eadon becomes godlike," said Whill. "Should he continue this war after that point, he will be a meddling god and they will be forced to intervene."

"You would give Eadon what he seeks, and have faith that the gods will deal with him?" Ornarell asked, amusement lacing his words.

"Enough of this. The man is simply trying to weigh every possibility," Zerafin interjected, annoyed. "Cerushia was been attacked; many of our kin are dead! This is not the time for your condescension, Master Ornarell."

The Zionar master nodded curtly to his king, and then to Whill in turn. "Apologies," he said dryly.

Zerafin went on. "If we do not succeed in stopping Eadon, we will find out what the gods intend to do. As for now, I suggest we focus on the task at hand." He looked to Aklenar Master Avolarra En'Kayen. "What does your sight show you?"

Avolarra jerked as if from a trance; it did not appear she had been listening. Her eyes settled upon Whill, and long they remained, until finally she answered. "Many paths...they change with every turn of events... every word of this conversation."

"Do any of them end with me defeating Eadon?" Whill asked. His words came out more forcefully than he had intended.

The thin smile she had worn disappeared completely, and was replaced by a disturbed expression. "Many rivers in the timeline," she said in a near whisper. The others waited for her to go on, but she fell silent, head bowed and gazing upon the table. Her wide eyes stared, as if unable to turn from a disturbing vision. Whill's gaze lingered long upon her, but was never met.

Nearly an hour later, the group still had gotten nowhere, and Whill began to think the elven masters had no answers. Though he had the full support of the elves, when it came to defeating Eadon, they still looked to him. Would that he could give away the power within the blade; the elves could deal with their own mess. He was about to call an end to the meeting when the doors swung inward and an elven Ralliad strode into the room.

"My king," he said with a bow to Zerafin. "We have been in contact with the queen's scouts."

"Report," said Zerafin, and Whill perked up to the news.

"Kell-Torey has fallen; Eldalon has no king."

Whill's heart dropped, and his throat tightened. "Who is the next in line for the throne?" he asked Alrick.

He began to answer, but the messenger interrupted him with a raised hand. "It is believed his entire line was wiped out," he said. "All, but one."

"Then you, my king, are also heir to the Eldalonian throne," Alrick said to Whill with a glorious smile.

Whill ignored the man; Kell-Torey had fallen. King Mathus, his grandfather, had been murdered, and his mother's family had been wiped out. He felt his outrage and anger well inside of him, the sword responded with a high-pitched hum and began to glow.

The messenger backed away from the table a step and stared at Adromida on Whill's hip. He had more to say, and he looked to be searching for the courage to speak.

"Out with it!" Whill yelled, trembling with the effort of keeping his rage at bay.

"Fendale was destroyed; the Light of the North has been taken. Also, a portal opened on Belldon Island in Shierdon. We are estimating nearly ten thousand Draggard came through that rift alone. The capital of Isladon, Del'Harred, has fallen to a rift as well. A rift was reported in Volnoss, and a barbarian army moves toward the Ky'Dren Pass as we speak."

"How many rifts in all?" Zerafin asked.

Whill tightened his closed eyes at the answer.

"Seven."

"There were more than seven in Drindellia," said Avriel.

"The Dwarven Mountains," Whill said, thinking of Roakore.

"A portal opened upon the eastern shore of Elladrindellia…Cerushia has fallen," said the messanger with a bow.

Zerafin, who had stood for the report, now fell to his seat slowly. "The queen?" he asked.

"She is alive." The druid was happy to report; it was the only news spoken with a smile.

"He's already won," said Master Flouren En Fen looking crestfallen.

"Not quite," said Zerafin with determination.

Whill thought of the countless dead; human, dwarf, and elf. While he had been wasting his time dealing with his inner demons, Eadon had been planning a full-scale invasion, and the assassination of his entire line. Eadon had made him heir to the Eldalonian throne as well, but why?

"What of this Felspire?" Whill asked.

"Eadon tapped into Agora's ley lines; he used the power to create a crystal spire that reaches to the veil between earth and heaven," said the messenger.

"He seeks to reach the gods, one way or another," Avriel surmised.

"Can we utilize the energy of these…ley lines?" Whill asked. The elven masters looked at him as if he spoke blasphemy.

"That is not our way," said Zerafin.

"How are we to defeat Eadon if we are bound by rules that he does not obey?" Whill asked, his annoyance growing with every obstacle set before him.

"To do as the dark lord does, is to become the dark lord," said Master Myrramus.

"Still, it is preferable to his tyranny," Whill pressed. He was met with no argument, only the stares of the masters. He turned to Zerafin, but the elf king's face was unreadable. Avriel seemed concerned by his words. He wished Roakore was still with him; he would have a thing or two to say on the topic. Whill thought for a moment as Roakore might. To the dwarf king, things were black or white, right or wrong.

"We've learned much," Zerafin said after a long silence. "Let us learn what else we might, and take the time to analyze what we know."

"I agree," said Whill, with a nod to the seated elves.

He left the room with Alrick and Captain Walker following him briskly. Avriel pushed past them on the stairs to the great room and came to walk beside Whill.

What do you hide in the back of your mind? She asked, meeting his brisk pace.

Whill stopped abruptly and faced Alrick and Walker. "Gather everyone to the castle gates, I would address my people."

"Yes, my king," they answered in unison.

They hurried off to the task, and Avriel stepped to block Whill's view. Her face told him she would not be ignored. He took her face in his hand and kissed her lips. Whill allowed himself to become lost in the kiss, and he was freed of his worries. She ended the kiss, and Whill opened his eyes to her patient smile.

"Where is Kellallea?" he asked, but she would not answer whilst her own question hung unanswered.

They stubbornly stared at each other for many long moments. Finally, Whill gave in, but could not bring himself to reveal what was on his mind.

"I hide nothing; it is just the beginnings of a thought, a whisper…"

"You need hide nothing from me," she reminded him, as she stroked his broad shoulders. Her hands felt their way across his armor and down his chest.

"I can only defeat Eadon…if I attain what he seeks," he said finally.

Avriel did not seem offended by the idea as the masters had been. She kissed him again and smiled, leaving Whill feeling silly for having been hesitant to admit he was considering the possibility. She dotted kisses across his cheek to his ears.

"I believe whatever you do will be the right thing, and you will indeed be victorious."

"You would set no boundaries to what I must do?" he asked.

"I trust you will choose what is right," said Avriel.

Whill kissed her once more, happy to have her at his side. Together, they walked out of the castle and made their way to the gates, where the call to hear the king was being sung by the criers.

"The King addresses the city at the castle gates! To the castle gates!" and many other such proclamations echoed throughout.

People came from all over to hear the king speak, for they thought Eadon had summoned them; it was not so much curiosity driving them, as fear. Whill and Avriel made their way through the courtyard, which was full of elves and human soldiers. The dwarves had already left the castle grounds.

At the castle gate, Alrick led Whill up a stair running along the high wall of the grounds. Thirty feet above the gathered crowd, Whill and Avriel looked down upon thousands of Uthen-Arden citizens, all waiting for the word of the king. Whill strode forth and raised his hands to the crowd, and many questioning whispers and murmurs issued from them. He gazed out over the city of his forefathers, a city unfamiliar to him.

"Good people of Uthen-Arden! I've a story to tell you this day!" Whill said with open arms; Adromida lent power to his voice.

"A tale of two brothers, and an elven sword. A tale known to only a few humans," he said, gaining the attention of everyone. He let the silence thicken as they waited for his words. When the moment was right, he went on with his tale.

"Long ago, the elves came to our shores seeking shelter, and the good king of Uthen-Arden gave them Elladrindellia. In return, and unbeknownst to all, the queen of the elves taught the human king her magic. Since that day, every prince of Uthen-Arden has gone to the elves, and has learned their ways. King Aramonis and his brother Addakon were no different; they went to the elves, and they too learned their magic. But Addakon wanted more, and so, he killed his brother and took from him the crown of Uthen-Arden!"

There were quick, sharp screams of disbelief; men looked at each other wide-eyed, and some women even fainted to hear the words that had been rumored for twenty years, now spoken loud from the castle wall. Supporters of Addakon–those few there were, mostly nobles–booed and grumbled.

"Addakon himself ambushed him with a horde of fifty Draggard at his command… his command! King Aramonis was killed. But, he took every one of the Draggard bastards with him!" he cried with a raised fist, and the crowd cheered and raised their fists alike.

"Your good Queen Celestra was with child when a Draggard arrow took her life. That child was cut from her dying womb…by the king's guard Abram. He raised the boy, and kept him hidden in the wilds and mountains of Agora. Addakon took the throne in his brother's stead, and slowly he turned this once great kingdom into one of war, poverty, and squalor."

The crowd had begun to nod in agreement of his words. Where once they had seemed timid and on guard, now life began to find them again. The shackles of fear had been thrown off by Whill's words, and he was now seeing an oppressed people that had found their voices once again. Whill waited until the cheering settled down. He reached into Adromida until his whispered voice came out loud and clear to all nearby, as if Whill was standing beside them each.

"Addakon wanted the throne, this is true. But, more so, he wanted the ancient elven blade Adromida. The blade was said to be made by a powerful elven Seer. The elven Aklenar saw the rise of the dark lord Eadon, the very one that has brought darkness to Agora. And so, he created a weapon that would one day destroy Eadon. The blade cannot be wielded by elves; only humans with the knowledge of elven magic might. Aramonis and Addakon had such knowledge, and could have wielded the greatest power ever given. It is for this very reason that Addakon killed his brother, and tried to kill the child."

The people looked on, waiting for the words to come. For they had all heard the legend of Whill of Agora; the recent incident in the gladiator arena had only strengthened the people's hope.

"I have been hidden from you for twenty years," he said, and many women wept with hands over open mouths. Men looked on with strong set jaws, shoulders pulled back, and necks straight, as if Whill's words lifted them from where they stood.

"The lost prince of Uthen-Arden has found his way home. I defeated my murderous uncle six months ago; he has since been replaced by the dark elf Eadon. For the dark one can wear the skin of another, to the knowledge of none. After months of torture, I was sentenced to death; many of you saw me fight in the arena," he said, raising a hand toward the burnt out coliseum at the center of the city.

"I have since been across the ocean in Drindellia. It was there that I found this."

Whill unsheathed Adromida and held it high for all to see. It shone with a bright, white light that forced all to cover their eyes. Whill finally willed it to dim. When the crowd looked again, the sword had found its sheath.

"I, Whillhelm Mathus Warcrown, son of Aramonis Warcrown, wielder of the ancient elven blade Adromida, claim by birthright, the thrown of Uthen-Arden!"

"Long Live King Whillhelm!" Alrick cried, and the call was taken up by all. Seven times it was cheered. On the faces of his people, Whill saw victory. That he had dared lay such claim in the midst of the booming voice of the devil Eadon, helped the people find their own courage.

"I shall meet the dark one at Felspire in seven days…" Silence filled the air once more as everyone hung on his last word. Even Avriel looked on in anticipation.

"And I shall lay him low!" he finally growled. The crowd erupted into growls of their own, and, for the first time in many years, the streets of Del'Oradon were alive with happy faces and cheering crowds.

CHAPTER TWENTY-TWO
Elven Stones and Dwarf Kings

Roakore led his mounted dwarves through the city, passing droves of people heading in the opposite direction toward the echoing voice. All the way out, Roakore listened to Whill's speech, and he could not help but tear up a bit. More than once, he almost turned around, but the images of Draggard inside of mountain halls stayed his course. When Roakore went out of the city gates, he and his men stopped to listen to the rest. When Whill's proclamation had finally echoed away, Roakore slammed his fist to his chest and bowed low; his dwarves followed suit.

"Give him hell, Laddie," Roakore said to himself, and tears found his eyes.

The gruff dwarf king wiped at his eyes and hid it by cupping his hands to yell to Silverwind. He scanned the sky, calling out all the while, but to no avail; the silverhawk was nowhere to be seen. Philo stayed at his side, even after Roakore had waved his dwarves off.

"What ye thinkin we be findin' when we get home?" Philo asked as he too scoured the sky for Silverwind.

"I ain't for knowin," Roakore mumbled, his gaze still upon the low clouds.

"Silverwind!" he bellowed to the heavens. He motioned for Philo to follow, and they spurred the dwarven horses on.

"Blasted bird be pickin' the worst times to be rebellious," he told Philo.

They caught up to the dwarves, and Roakore pushed them into a quick gallop down the road leading out of the city. The Ro'Sar-Arden road connected their namesakes, and had been used for centuries as a trade route between them. No trade had moved between the two kingdoms in twenty years, but the road was still well-worn with other uses. They hadn't gotten much snow yet in those parts, just a light coating that didn't hinder the horses. Roakore was happy enough that mounts had been brought through the rift. The march back to the Ro'Sar Mountains would take them the better part of a week on foot. To Roakore, the days it took on horseback were still too many. He spent more time looking to the sky than he did the road; he needed Silverwind now more than ever. He needed to know what was happening inside his mountain.

An idea occurred to him then, and he cursed his stupidity. He had communicated with King Du'Krell of the

Elgar Mountains with the speaking stone the elves had given him. If he could get ahold of the dwarf again, he could at least know the fate of Elgar. If a rift was not within those mountains, the Ro'Sar Mountains were likely safe.

He fell back and urged his dwarves on. Philo slowed with him. Soon, the mounted dwarves had passed. From a deep pocket, he took the apple sized speaking stone and held it near his lips. "I wish to speak to Du'Krell o' the Mountains Elgar."

Philo gave him a curious sideways glance. "What that be for?" he asked, reaching for the smooth crystal.

Roakore waved him away dismissively and commanded the stone once again. As before, nothing happened. If the other dwarf king was not near his speaking stone, he would not hear it to answer. After a long wait, Roakore tried again.

"Roakore to Du'Krell, Roakore to Du'Krell, you be 'round, king?"

Ky'Ell, Dwarf King of the Ky'Dren Mountains, held his breath as he listened. No sound came from the tunnel, but he knew the Draggard were about. Their scent rode on the air: a stench that burned his nose and turned his stomach. Behind him, filling the city of Tsu'Dar was an army of five thousand dwarves. The rift had opened inside of Northern Ky'Dren, and the estimation of invading Draggard grew daily. The two mountain ranges of the Ky'Dren Mountain Kingdom had been cut off from each other, and fighting over the Pass raged. Ky'Ell had found himself cut off in the far-northern reaches of the mountains, and, for two days, he and his growing army had been fighting their way south toward the pass.

Tsu'Dar had seen many casualties; it was the third such city Ky'Ell helped to liberate. The Draggard, dra-quon, and hulking dwargon had been driven steadily south since the dwarves had regrouped from the initial invasion. The beasts still controlled the northern mountains from the Pass to Tsu'Dar, which was located at the center of the northern range. The city had held its own, but to great loss. Those dwarves still able to fight joined the main force, which grew by the minute as dwarves from all over found their way there.

He grumbled to himself as he looked upon the evidence of dark elves; a massive carved stalactite had been dislodged by a spell and dropped on the buildings below, destroying dozens of them. But, like their chambers and halls—which had been carved by ancestors over the centuries–the dwarves endured.

Ky'Ell accepted a mug of dark ale from Fior, allowing his gaze to leave the distant tunnel for only long enough to down the drink. He and Fior stood upon a high balcony overlooking the southern entrance to the city; below him, the army rested.

"We be ready for another advancement within the hour," the dwarven priest informed him.

"Aye," Ky'Ell nodded, wiping his mouth with his long beard.

The booming voice of Eadon had sounded even in the Ky'Dren deeps, and Ky'Ell replayed every word in his mind for hours. Felspire…given the name, and the great earthquake that preceded Eadon's speech, he guessed it was created by the dark elf. At the mention of Whill of Agora, the king smiled. He was glad to hear the lad still lived, and was apparently giving the dark elf hell. He had heard news of Whill's capture, and his glorious escape with the help of Roakore. Ky'Ell knew whatever happened at Felspire would determine the fate of Agora. Reports had come in from the eastern lookout towers along northern Ky'Dren; a large contingent of barbarian and Shierdon soldiers, and a horde of Draggard led by dark elves, were moving south toward the Pass. Ky'Ell knew he was in a race against time, a race he was determined to win.

"Roakore to Ky'Ell…Roakore to Ky'Ell…ye be hearin' me King?" said a voice that made Fior jump and look every which way.

Ky'Ell hastily discarded his ale and fumbled in his pockets for the speaking stone. He found it in one of his inner pockets and nearly dropped it over the balcony in his haste to answer.

"Aye, this be Ky'Ell," he answered.

"See, you dolt. It be a speaking stone, and it be working," said Roakore.

"Excuse me?" Ky'Ell huffed.

"Not you king, was talkin' to someone else. I tried to contact King Du'Krell, with no success. Must be he ain't got the stone on him."

"Well, I have answered. What news?" Ky'Ell asked, eager for any information of the wider world.

"I was about to ask you the same thing," said Roakore. "I ain't heard from me mountain in days...were you attacked?"

"Ye ain't been home for days? Where in the hells else would ye be at a time like this?" Ky'Ell asked.

"I be explainin' later. Have you been invaded or nay?"

"Aye, a bloody rift opened up deep within the northern mines. Northern and Southern Ky'Dren be cut off at the Pass. I ain't for knowin if there be another one to the south."

A long silence, and Ky'Ell wondered if the connection had been lost. Finally, Roakore's strained voice came again.

"Then, me mountain has been invaded as well."

Roakore told Ky'Ell why he had been away from his mountain. He had been escorting the human boy, Tarren, and an elven ambassador to Elladrindellia. The elves and Elgar mountain dwarves had planned an attack on Fendora Island, and he and his dwarves had taken part. Ky'Ell was glad to learn the rifts had been destroyed for good; at least the numbers they faced would not increase.

"And what of this Felspire?" Ky'Ell asked. Beside him, Fior noticeably leaned forward in silent anticipation.

"I ain't for knowing nothing but the name. But, I be guessin it be just what the name be saying: another filthy abomination o' the dark elves, rising up so high to be stinkin' up the heavens."

Ky'Ell grunted agreement, and was about to ask about Whill's presence in Del'Oradon, when an explosion rocked the tunnel. The cavern shook, and many loose stones–shaken from their place of eons by the earlier earthquake–came down, crashing into the city. A fire-ball slowly grew in the depths of the dark tunnel, and a shockwave blasted through the cavern, raising dust and debris. Braid and beard were blown back by the hot blast, and the call to arms rang out in many voices.

"Keep me posted. Ky'Ell out!" he yelled into the stone amid the rumbling and clamor of a city being shaken to its roots.

"To your station!" Ky'Ell ordered Fior, and leapt over the balcony.

"Father!" yelled one of his sons, Dwellan, as he came running with two of his brothers in tow. The boys, ranging from fifty years to two hundred, came to their father's side, bearing shield and arms.

"They block the way!" Kelgar, the eldest of the three yelled, pointing at movement beyond the dust and smoke before the mouth of the tunnel.

The tunnel began to cave in; large chunks of stone rained down from above, scrambling any dwarves stationed too close, and killing those who were not fast enough. When the dust began to settle, the tunnel was no longer there. Among the broken slabs of stone, one of the pillars that held the curved arch jutted out like a broken bone. Many fallen dwarves lay among the rubble, their blood pooling with the dust.

Ky'Ell marched forth and began bellowing commands. His sons followed, seconding the orders. When they reached the pile of rubble, Ky'Ell kicked the nearest stone with a growl.

"What o' the secret passages 'round this choke point?" he asked any who would answer.

"Six tunnels lead 'round to the south, and a few narrower ones." said Ky'Ro. "Tsu'Dar had to close 'em' up. They ain't no secret no more, me King."

"We ain't needin' to be goin' around, we need to be going through it," said Raene, and Ky'Ell turned to regard his daughter.

Raene stood behind her brothers in full plate armor; two dark-red braids shot out of the top of her silver helm and fell over her heavy pauldrons. Her sixty years were not apparent on her delicately-featured face, but her fierce green eyes showed the knowledge of her age.

"Raene! I ain't for tellin' ye again, the battle-"

"Battlegrounds be no place for a lass. Yes, o' course father," she said dismissively. "But I see no battle, only a heap o' rubble need be moved, and right quick. Best we gather the priesthood, we five be needin' the blessin' o' the gods to be movin' that much stone."

Ky'Ell stammered over his own words at his daughter's disregard. Raene smiled brightly and, on tiptoes, kissed her father's cheek, disarming him in an instant. "It's all right, Papa. I be a mover o' stone right well as me brothers. Ain't no harm in a little stone movin'."

"Bah, c'mon then, you four," Ky'Ell said to his children.

Dwellan sent Raene a mirthless glare as he turned to follow the king. Her twin brother Ky'Ro, whose braided beard and hair was the same red as hers, shook his head, chuckling at his sister. "You gonna be givin' Pa a heart attack."

"I can't help if his outdated sensibilities cause him grief," she said with a mischievous grin.

"Bah, outdated or no, yer one o' the best stone movers the family got. We be needin ye for this," Ky'Ro admitted.

"One o' the best?" she teased, and her brother's raised eyebrow told her not to push it.

Fior had gathered his priests, nearly two dozen of them; they stood before the rubble, bent in prayer. Behind them, dwarves had begun to gather for the prayer ritual. Ky'Ell and his kin moved to stand between the priests and the destroyed tunnel. The three sons and Raene spread out beside their father, and each nodded that they were ready and took a knee, their backs to the priests.

"Begin!" Ky'Ell yelled to his dwarves, and hundreds of them dropped to their knees. Each dwarf reached forward and placed a hand on the shoulders of the two in front of them, and began to chant. The gathering of kneeling dwarves narrowed toward the priests, and hands were laid upon their shoulders, as they in turn laid hands upon the shoulders of Ky'Ell and his children. A chanting began and rose steadily as the deep voices of the praying dwarves hummed throughout the chamber and vibrated in their bones. Pebbles began to dance on the floor, and small stones jostled among the rubble.

"O' Ky'Dren, great and powerful king of kings, lend us your strength in this task before us," Fior began.

"On my mark," Ky'Ell reminded them.

Raene felt the surge of energy coursing through the group. For a moment, she was overwhelmed by the power, and the instinctual thought to release built in her quickly. But she fought the urge as she shook, waiting for her father's command. She tried to forget the struggle within her, and focused only on her intent, picturing the broken stone and rubble being blasted back through the caved-in tunnel. When it was too much to bear, her father's words came to her through the over-whelming humming sound.

"Release!" he bellowed, and his children were eager to comply.

The five descendants of Ky'Dren unleashed the pent-up energy into the stone, and, with their minds, they willed it back. Raene's legs wobbled and nearly faltered as the power coursing through her threatened to over-whelm her control. To her dismay, nothing happened.

"Focus!" Ky'Ell yelled at them all, and every dwarf redoubled their efforts. The stones began to shift as the energy given by their kin flowed through them. The king raised his hands to the ceiling as he chanted furi-ously, his voice rising with every word. Raene felt the power building within him, and waited for the moment of release. When it finally came, Raene and her broth-ers lent all they had. Ky'Ell shot his open palms out toward the rubble, and the heavy slabs of stone began to slide noisily across the floor. The seconds it took for the rubble to be forced into the next chamber seemed like hours, but, soon, the way was clear.

Raene and her brothers remained on one knee, pant-ing; her head swam and she felt as though she might throw up. But she stubbornly stood before either of her brothers, although not before her father.

"Got to be a showoff, ain't ye? Oh! There she goes," said her twin brother, Ky'Ro, as Raene stumbled three steps one way and two the other. She held her ground and gained her senses with a force of obstinate will.

Laughing, Ky'Ro rose as well and walked drunkenly toward her. Dwellan was up then too; he hefted his massive war hammer over a shoulder and scowled as he stopped beside the twins. "You two best be getting your shyte together. This ain't no game; this be an invasion."

"Shove it up your arse, Dwellan," Raene said and walked as straight as she could to the side of her father.

Ky'Ell was giving the dwarves a few minutes to recuperate from the ritual; they had each lent large amounts of energy to it. The king looked sidelong at his daughter with a happy smile, and, to Raene, he looked like a god.

"Thank you for helping with the ritual, Eeny. I need you to help the mothers secure the-"

"You need me to fight," she said. "I be too good at killin' Draggard to be helpin' the wives with menial tasks."

"No task is menia–"

"You know what I mean," she interrupted him for the third time.

"Listen lass, ye cut me off again, and I be putting ye on yer arse like I would yer brothers, whether ye be a lass or nay," he warned her.

"I be glad you be treatin' me no different than me brothers," she said with the smile that disarmed his heart, again.

"No different," he agreed.

"Ain't no different," Raene went on, and Ky'Ell's eyes squinted with suspicion. "And just like me brothers, I be raisin me blade to our invaders."

Ky'Ell's nostrils flared as he realized the trick. "Ye ain't fightin with the boys, that be final!"

Without warning, three hulking dwargon came barreling through the newly cleared tunnel. Their massive, scaled shoulders sparked against the walls as they pushed each other to be the first at the dwarves.

"Barrage!" Ky'Ell commanded, and instinctively moved between the beasts and Raene.

She looked around him as hatchets rained down upon the smashing hulks like locusts. Hundreds of hatchets fell on each dwargon, and they were stopped dead in their tracks by the initial attack. The dwarves' aim was impeccable, their strength was legend, and, thus, their hatchets had flown true. The dwargon reeled and clawed at the hundreds of hatchets that had been embedded all along their heads and necks, leaving them looking as though they might have porcupine in their blood.

Kelgar, the eldest of Raene's brothers, rushed toward the dwargon with his wide, double-headed halberd held high. A battle cry escaped him and was joined by those of his kin. The other dwarves were already on their feet; they cheered on their prince and fell in behind him. Kelgar's long, leather-wrapped braid reminded Raene of the tail of a swimming eel as her brother pumped his legs harder in his charge. The lead dwargon carried a tree in his right hand. The roots shot out in every direction, and red blood shown on those jagged roots. The tree was thick enough for two dwarves to wrap their arms around, but the dwargon handled it easily. The club came swinging at Kelgar, but he was quicker. As the tree-sized club swung by, he leapt on and clung to one of the many bloodied branches. The strong-but-brainless dwargon followed through with the swing, and looked shocked to find Kelgar was gone. He looked up stupidly, and it was too late for the dwargon. Kelgar came down with the spear-tipped end of the halberd and thrust it into the beast's left eye. When his boots landed upon the dwargon's shoulders, the spear had been sunk two feet straight down into its body.

Kelgar rode the dwargon as it fell back toward the other two, dead. The other dwarves and Raene's brothers charged forth to meet the beasts, and, all the while, Ky'Ell held her back with a firm arm across her shoulders.

"Ye ain't no warrior, Eeny. Ye gots to know yer place among yer people."

Raene knew he didn't mean to cause her pain, but his words hurt. Even at her age, she had not stopped trying to catch his attention, to prove herself. She met her father's eyes and stubbornly stared back at him, refusing to blink. Another dwargon coming through the tunnel caught her eye. In her anger, she reached out with her mind and took hold of a twelve foot high stalagmite. With a cry of effort and rage, she snapped the formation free from its flowstone perch and sent it flying with an extended hand. She guided the projectile with her mind into the chest of the dwargon. The stalagmite went straight through, leaving a gaping hole of dripping gore larger than the creature's head.

"Yes, Father!" she yelled at him. "You be right, this be no place for a delicate lass like meself."

"Ky'Ell! Ky'Ell!" Roakore yelled at the stone, but the connection had been severed.

"There be Draggard in our mountain," said Philo with uncharacteristic gloom.

Roakore shared his sentiment; he cursed himself for the hundredth time for ever leaving his mountain.

"Silverwind! Come to me now, or never again!" he screamed.

He and Philo looked to the sky for an answer, but none came. Philo's head returned to the road long before Roakore's did, but the king finally gave up hope. Beside him, Philo tossed back a shot from his flask. He wiped his mouth with a burp and handed off to Roakore; the king 'tipped her long.'

The road led them into farmland where the only trees were fruit trees, and the only bushes were berry bushes. Pastures abounded here, being home to the precious cattle. As such, many camps of soldiers guarded these lands, for they fed the city. Huge farms, run by four-generation families, dotted the landscape. The houses had been made as the land had been cleared, and the long wooden lodges were a marvel to behold, even for one of such craftsmanship as a dwarf king. Some of the houses were as high as four stories, with many large stone chimneys. Some looked like nothing less than castles of lumber. The barns too had been built to a grand scale. In the cold of the day, steam could be seen escaping the doors at the ends of the barns. The livestock of these parts was as varied as any, but they primarily raised cattle and horses.

As they crested a high bluff, Roakore's eyes followed the road that wound down and danced off into the horizon with a long lazy river. Far, far off to the northwest, a lone peak of the Ro'Sar Mountains was a hazy bump. Once again, Roakore cursed Silverwind and turned in his saddle to impotently scowl off in the direction they had come. To his sudden delight, she was there.

Roakore reared in his horse and climbed down. Philo did the same, and together they watched her come in. She gave her telltale squawk and circled them before descending. When she landed, Roakore stalked up to her, about to give her a good right-for, but when he saw the dark Draggard blood dripping from her beak, he lost some of his fury.

"Where in the hells ye been?" he asked as might a parent to a road-running child.

The bird regarded Roakore for a moment and quickly seemed to forget him as she set to grooming beneath her right wing. Roakore watched with slight trepidation, thinking that she had been injured. He soon discovered that she had not, and was just being herself, stubborn and indifferent.

"This blasted bird gots to be the most stubborn creature ever did exist," he said to Philo.

Philo's brow shot up. "Hah! Then ye be makin' a good pair, don't ye be?"

Roakore's scowl wiped the smile from Philo's face, but it could not be held, and soon the two were laughing at each other.

"C'mon then," said Roakore, as he mounted Silverwind. Philo grinned up at him and gave a laughing cheer.

They took to the sky and quickly flew the few hundred yards to the front of the dwarven line. They landed before the dwarves, and none too soon. Philo scrambled off the saddle and puked before his feet touched the ground. He fell to his knees and hugged the earth as if he had not set foot upon the ground in ages. Roakore too dismounted and chuckled at the prone dwarf.

"Takes a little getting used to," he said.

Philo could only groan.

Holdagozz came to meet them; he stroked Silverwind's neck high above him. "I see the silver-winged one has returned."

"Aye," Roakore said loudly for the benefit of all near. "An' I be hatin' to leave ye all on the road, but I need be gettin' to Ro'Sar, and right quick. Holdagozz, you be comin' with."

"Aye, me king."

"The rest o' ye ride as fast as ye can push them horses and get home. And kill every Draggard along the way. Once home, secure the mountain's eastern and western doors if they need securin'."

Roakore and Holdagozz soon left. Silverwind took them high, and rode a current down into the valley below. In the distance, the lone peak grew as they ascended, and Roakore set his thoughts to clearing his mountain. He thought of his father, whose spirit had lingered within those halls, as was the curse of a king who lost his mountain. Roakore wondered if he would face the same fate, then he wondered if it was even real, and he cursed himself for wondering at all. His thoughts soon turned to Helzendar and Tarren. Cerushia had been attacked as well. Roakore could only have faith Lunara would keep them safe.

He flew with Holdagozz toward Ro'Sar with uncertainty weighing heavily on his heart.

CHAPTER
TWENTY-THREE

Dark Places

Whill returned to the mausoleum alone and took the hidden passage down the dark stairs and into the depths of the castle. Memories returned to him in the dark depths, and, though he lit the torches with a fire spell as he went, he could do nothing to light the dark recesses of his mind. The memories of the Other came rushing back to him, those six long months in which Whill had been torn apart: mind, body, and soul. He refused to linger on those thoughts and be drawn into the endless pain to which they led.

Whill explored the depths for nearly an hour. He found the dungeons, but did not linger there long, lest the cries of his memory overwhelm him. He found many rooms where Eadon conducted experiments and dark magic. Vials of different colored liquids abounded, and jars of all sizes held various body parts of various creatures, including human, dwarf, and elf. Many of

the jars–some large enough to contain a small child–
housed hideously deformed creatures. One seemed
to be a failed attempt at crossing a dog with a pig,
while another seemed to be half-cat and half-goat. Yet
another creature floating in murky blue liquid had the
body of a spider and the curved tail of a scorpion. Whill
shivered as he found other, more disturbing creatures.
He was reminded of his first encounter with the dark
elf lord after he was freed from the dungeons. Eadon
had been performing a powerful spell, and Whill had
watched, horrified, as he put the fetus of a dwarf inside
of a dragon egg.

There were no limits to what the dark lord might
attempt. He had no respect for the laws of nature,
and, to him, nothing was sacred. Whill had an urge
to destroy the contents of the many laboratories, to
incinerate them all with a fire spell, but he did not.
Something of value might be found among the various
tomes and scrolls; even within the floating atrocities,
clues to Eadon's defeat might be found.

"The last of the dark elves are gone," Kellallea said
behind him, and Whill jumped, startled.

"I wondered where you had gone off to," Whill said
as he regarded her.

"Where I go is not your concern," she reminded him.
"Come, I've something to show you."

Whill followed Kellallea through a tunnel leading
from the laboratories and dungeons and into a large

library. Books adorned every wall of the large room, the volumes stretching all the way to the fifteen-foot ceiling. At the center of the room, she waited beside a large table. Every torch upon the walls flared to life. The dancing light fell on a large map at the center of the table. He recognized Agora, and the landmass far to the east: Drindellia. West of Agora, Whill was surprised by another continent and a long string of islands that seemed to have once belonged to the mainland.

"What is this place?" he asked, peering closer at the foreign land.

"Many such lands are scattered across the ocean. This, like all others, is called by the elves the outer lands."

"The elves have traveled to these lands?" Whill asked, intrigued.

"Long ago, the world was mapped by elven explorers. The elders banned any contact with the outside world beyond the borders of Drindellia."

"Who lives there? Humans, dwarves, other elves?"

"There are a variety of creatures, including humans and dwarves. We had never settled in a foreign land until five hundred years ago, when your ancestor gave them Elladrindellia," said Kellallea as she too studied the large map.

"You seem to know much about Elladrindellian history, although this is your first time here," said Whill.

Kellallea ignored the probe and pointed to the many markers about Agora on the map. "Those are the locations of the rifts," she said, and brought another marker to Whill's attention. This one was hard to miss, for it jutted out of the center of the Thendor Plains, a twisted crystal spire higher than the nearby mountains.

"Felspire," Whill breathed.

"Yes," Kellallea acknowledged. "Eadon has chosen it for his ascension."

"Then, that is where I must go," said Whill, staring at the spire.

"That is where you will die."

"Then help me! Help your people."

"I have helped you," she reminded him. "My offer still stands; I would free you of your burden."

"And become a goddess," said Whill with a snide laugh.

Kellallea found no humor in the conversation; she moved from her distracted study of the map and squared on him. "You will soon realize I am your only hope. The prophecy is a lie; you cannot hope to defeat Eadon. Should you bring this weapon to Felspire, Agora will burn."

"Agora will burn regardless," he reminded her.

"You know nothing. Wise that Eadon made the sword to be wielded only by humans. You are a weak-minded race! He will never see an opponent in you, only a puppet to be toyed with."

Whill turned from her, annoyed. She would not help him in the way he wanted her to. She would make sure he thought he had no chance so that he would turn to her to destroy Eadon. Whill had escaped from his imprisonment, had found the sword Adromida, and had taken his rightful place as king of Uthen-Arden, but he was no closer to an answer to his dilemma. Perhaps she was in league with Eadon, sent to confuse and disorient Whill to the truth. A thought had begun to grow in his mind; it seemed the only solution. Zerafin would not approve, and Whill did not know if he should even mention it to Kellallea. But if he was to learn the spell, only she could teach it.

"What about the taking of power?" he asked.

Kellallea's head snapped toward him, and her eyes burned. With much effort, he held her gaze.

"You think you can just take from Eadon? I can teach you a few lines of a spell, and your happy ending will play out? You understand nothing of magic."

"And if I die? You will do nothing to stop him, will you?"

"Should he attain Adromida, there will be nothing to be done against him," she said.

Whill stared at the sword at his hip, wondering if it was powerful enough to defeat Kellallea. He had not thought so before, but he had been overwhelmed and intimidated by her display of power. Whill had no way of knowing what power he possessed in the blade. He dared not delve too far. Kellallea seemed to read his every thought, for she too glanced at the sword. Her eyes moved to Whill, and the air became tense. Any thoughts he had about challenging her quickly fled him.

"Lend me your strength. Surely I would possess more power than Eadon," he offered.

"Lend?" she asked with a condescending laugh. "If between us enough power to defeat Eadon exists, you truly think that you should wield it?'

"What is to stop me from taking what I want from you?" he asked, and her levity vanished.

Kellallea circled Whill, her warm breath on his neck as she passed behind him. When she came into view, she was wearing a smile, though her eyes did not smile. They bore into Whill's mind like daggers. She attacked, and Whill was caught unprepared, distracted by the light from her blinding eyes. Kellallea brought Whill to his knees with a mental assault, scrambling his thoughts and sending torrents of pain coursing through his body. For a moment, he forgot everything, even his own name. Only one thing came to him clearly: a spell of revocation in the pages of the Zionar tome. With a massive sap of Adromida's power, Whill brought up a mental wall of such magnitude and strength Kellallea's mind was forced out.

His thoughts returned to him, but before he recovered, Kellallea spun a spell in the palm of her circling hands and released it with a scream of rage. The blast hit Whill's energy shield and threw him backward into the wall. Whill retaliated with a scream of his own, as he unsheathed Adromida and recklessly pulled power equal to his fury. A blinding spell erupted from his hand as the power coursed through him unchecked. Whill thought for a moment he might not be able to maintain control, and all of the power contained within the blade might explode from him and tear the world asunder. Whill fought for control. Only after he thought of love–and not rage–did he gain the control he sought.

Whill scoured the smoky room, ready for Kellallea's counter-attack, but none came; she was nowhere to be seen. Instead, he found a large cylindrical hole in the wall straight through to the surface. Whill flew through it and came out into the sunlight behind the castle. Kellallea's voice came to him then from all directions.

"Your only hope is to give me the power within the sword."

"We can work together to defeat him," said Whill, circling as he tried to spot her.

"Give me the blade, it is the only way," she said, ignoring his plea.

"Never. You would see the world burn in your pursuit of power. You and Eadon are the same."

Kellallea rose from the earth before him, her eyes aglow. She regarded Whill as one might an insect. "I will not allow you to bring the blade to him. You shall fail, and he shall ascend."

"You once stood for good…once walked in the light. You fought and defeated the dark elves of old. What happened to you? You abandoned your kin. You allowed the rise of Eadon, even when you knew his intentions," he reminded her.

"I endured," she roared, and the earth shook with her wrath. "I did what I could against the dark one, and the battle ravaged the land, nearly destroying us both."

Whill did not know what to believe; he had no reason to trust the ancient elf. She strode forward, and he backed a step, holding Adromida out before him. The blade of Power Given glowed white-hot and hummed in his grip. Kellallea eyed the blade and stopped her advancement. The rumbling in the ground subsided, and the fury of her eyes died out.

"Do you wish to make me your enemy, as well?" she asked calmly.

"You attacked me," he reminded her.

"You cannot fool me child, I hear your mind. You are confused, afraid, and overwhelmed. You cannot defeat Eadon. I offer you the only hope, and you turn from my help with scorn. The power of the blade calls to you, corrupting your reasoning."

She regarded his father's sword. "You've broken the laws of the Elves of the Sun: you have taken power by force." She closed her eyes for a moment as if in a trance, and Whill felt her at the edges of his mind.

"The dark elves, you took their power so easily, and you had a mind to attempt the very same with me."

Whill turned from her, not able to meet her gaze. He had an urge to lash out at her with Adromida, to take her power, to take all power. He was tired of being a pawn of those more powerful.

"Even now your inner mind tells you to strike me down," she said calmly. "Abram tried to raise you to be good, to walk in the light. So one day, you might be able to deny the temptations the sword's power would whisper to your heart, but it seems he failed."

"Do not speak of him!" Whill seethed.

"He was quite efficacious in that regard. You have been able to fight the calling of power so far. But, it is only a matter of time before you give in. Already your resolve is failing, as is evident of your recent acquisition of power taken."

"You are guilty of the same, you want only power," he said, not wanting to believe her.

"Perhaps," she conceded with a shrug. "The fact remains, only I can help you."

"I will take my chances," he said, raising Adromida as she began to move toward him once again.

"Indeed, you shall," said Kellallea, and to Whill she seemed troubled.

"You have seven days to decide. I pray you choose wisely. I do not want to kill you, but I will not see the power of Adromida fall into his hands."

With that, she was gone. She did not meld into the earth, nor did she fly off into the sky; she simply disappeared. Whill sheathed Adromida with trembling hands, and stood staring at where she had been. What if she was right?

CHAPTER TWENTY-FOUR

Adimorda's Vision

Eadon sat on his perch below the ceiling of clouds like a god looking down upon the mortals. He stole away from his focus on Del'Oradon Castle, his consciousness coursing through the many miles of underground rivers of energy in an instant. A smile crept across his face as he opened his eyes to the world.

Everything was coming to pass as he had seen in visions those millennia ago. His pride swelled as he considered his paramount patience, the thousands of years of waiting, watching, and learning. He had come far since those days so long ago, when he had gone by the name Adimorda, and began trading predictions and prophecy for power. He had used the gifted energy to watch his long life unfold, unable to deny the curiosity plaguing him. When he first looked years into the future, he was startled by what he discovered. He witnessed himself creating a temple so grand, as to gain adoration from elves far and wide. He created the Order of Adromida, and set in motion the creation of the greatest weapon ever made, one that could never be wielded by an elf.

Adimorda was left shaken. He knew not why his future-self had set to creating the blade, for only visions came to him, and none of the other senses. He bided his time, refreshing his energy supply, and when he had gained enough offered power, he looked once more. This vision brought him some years beyond, to a time when he faked his own death, wrote "Whill of Agora" in blood, and disappeared from the world of sun elves.

For thousands of years, he spent his time in faraway lands, mastering every school of Orna Catorna, and taking power from the land and its inhabitants. Into a new blade, he stored the taken power, and, for centuries at a time, he slept, waiting.

He returned to the world of sun elves and established himself once again within the city of his birth. Much had changed in his time away. He saw firsthand the grand institution his temple had become. Worshipping elves came from distant lands to give what they might to the blade of Adimorda, and always there were a number of monks offering up energy gained in rest and meditation.

He wondered about the sword that could be wielded by no elf, not even he. Now he understood why he had made it so; any practitioner who touched it would have been able to sense his binding. There was some opposition to the creation of Adromida, those who pleaded with the elders that the sword would one day be used against them, but they soon disappeared. The Order of Adromida would allow none to get in the way of the prophecy. Their word became akin to that of the gods.

Eadon began meddling with the creations of nature, dissecting and recreating what only the gods had. He began with wolves, cultivating their nature to his will. He bred stronger and faster horses and livestock, and the elves were pleased. Soon, he become bored with altering existing creatures and began to make his own. Animals he crossed with fish and bird, and soon began tampering with dragon eggs. Finally, he built his idea of the perfect soldier, by melding an elven fetus with a dragon egg and seeing it to term; he created his first Draggard queen, Velloria. She was the first of his Draggard wives, mother of his first army of Draggard children. Soon, the Elves of the Sun discovered what he had done, and they did not welcome his magnificent creations as they had the others. Instead, they set out to destroy them.

Adimorda witnessed the Draggard Wars of Drindellia play out and end with the sojourn of the Elves of the Sun. The ancient one, Kellallea, the Lady-Tree, rose up against him. The battle left a thousand-mile scar across the land, nearly destroying them both. In the end, he stood victorious, though she escaped with her life. Over the next five hundred years, Eadon reigned over the surviving elves. He allowed them to live out their lives for generations, but taking from them nearly all of their energy daily. He created many Draggard queens, and they gave him thousands of Draggard soldiers, and soon the time came, and the invasion of Agora began.

The vision moved to Agora, and the invasion of the Draggard over the years. In only a few short decades, he took control of the most powerful kingdom. He waited patiently for the One to be born, the one that would give him the power of the blade. He watched the creation of Felspire, and the final battle for Agora upon the Plains of Uthen-Arden. In his final vision, he stood atop the summit of Felspire, a shining sword of power in each hand, and ascended to the heavens.

Adimorda nearly died during the vision in which he witnessed his ascension, and needed the help of many healers to bring him back from the brink of death. When he was well enough to do so, he sought out to discover the truth of the two blades. His search took him years, but he finally found a prophecy of the gods, which spoke of two blades of power, and the way one might ascend and attain the power of the gods. Shortly thereafter, he set the plan into motion.

Now, many years later, looking out over Agora, Eadon knew his rise to godhood was only days away. Whill would come, and he would hand over the power of the ancient blade, else watch his beloved friends die. As it had been witnessed, so it would come to pass.

CHAPTER TWENTY-FIVE
The Eastern Door

Many platoons of the Shierdon undead joined with the barbarian and Draggard armies. Although Eadon had promised a seven day armistice, Veolindra assured Aurora they would still bring war to the dwarves of the Ky'Dren Pass.

"You shall lead the charge against the thieving dwarves. You shall have your revenge," the dark elf lich lord promised her. "When the dwarven dead begin to pile high, I will raise them up to fight for our lord."

Aurora thought of Roakore then, and knew the outrage that would be shared by the dwarves should their fallen kin be raised from the dead, but she cared not. She had taken the only way out, and, as such, she no longer had to worry or feel bad about such things. She was single-mindedly focused on only one thing: conquering the barbarian homelands. She would accept whatever means were necessary to accomplish her goal, even if that meant raising dwarves from the dead. They had helped drive her ancestors from the Agoran mainland. The barbarians had no place for mercy for such enemies as they.

The armies marched on steadily toward the Ky'Dren pass, their numbers collectively now in the tens of thousands. They had passed the border into Uthen-Arden only hours ago, but had yet to be met by any resistance. Veolindra assured Aurora that any they might encounter, be they dwarf, elf, or man, would soon be added to their undead ranks.

To the right, Aurora could begin to make out the majestic Northern Ky'Dren Mountains, which had–according to Veolindra–been invaded by a rift akin to the one through which she and Zander, and the Draggard hordes, had come. Snow capped the faraway peaks, and Aurora wondered if the white crown of the mountain ever lifted. Those mountains had once been home to her people, before the dwarves–with the help of the humans of Eldalon–had banished them to Volnoss, splitting among themselves the ancient homeland.

Aurora was in good spirits that day, as were the barbarian tribes. She knew they had begun to get restless, and, though they had gotten used to the Draggard being near, she doubted if they would ever get used to the undead armies who followed silently behind them. The barbarians of Volnoss were no strangers to the magic of the spirit world, but they had never seen the strange art used to such a degree as this. Many cursed the soldiers, and would not tolerate them being too close.

Since Eadon's proclamation to the world, the armies had not stopped in their march. Veolindra and the other dark elves had cast spells upon the armies, and now the barbarians ran with the haste of the Draggard. Tirelessly they marched forward, energized not only by the spells of the dark elves, but also by the promise of war and glory to come.

Ky'Ell and his army of dwarves steadily cleared the many chambers, halls, and tunnels on their way to the Ky'Dren pass. The horde that had poured through the rift within the depths of the mountain had left destruction in their wake, and as much as his heart broke to behold the ruined cities they came upon, he was gladdened to find many dead Draggard bodies amid those of his kin. The Draggard seemed to be moving to the Pass, for the dwarves oft came upon the beasts traveling south. He suspected the Ky'Dren Pass was under siege from Uthen-Arden as well. Eadon was likely trying to strategically cut off Eldalon from the rest of Agora, being that it was one of most–if not *the* most–powerful kingdoms of man.

Ky'Ell needed not push his dwarves, for they pursued the Draggard at a vehement pace, stopping to rest only when they would have fallen from exhaustion should they continue. But, as the pass grew nearer, Ky'Ell ordered a watch and had to force the dwarves to rest, lest they dive exhausted into the fray. The king too forced himself to take a respite, though it seemed his mind and body would never succumb to slumber, so anxious was he to discover the extent of the invasion. He had no way to know if there had been another rift within Southern Ky'Dren, and his dread was great.

"Me King." A voice came to him in his dreams, and he woke with a start. His daughter, Raene, stood before him.

"What be it, lass?" he asked, rubbing his bleary eyes of slumber.

"The scouts be reportin' the way ahead be clear for miles: the Draggard have gone."

Ky'Ell raised himself from the stone floor of the cavern, his bones reminding him of his age. "Then, we best be after the devils."

The dwarves were roused from their slumber, and, after a large meal, headed out once again. They had taken their rest in the city of Dy'Orinshald, which, like the others they had traveled through, had been sacked by the Draggard and dark elves. Evidence of the dark elves was apparent here as well. Explosions had rocked the cavern in which the city was built long ago, and now only rubble remained.

They traveled south for a full day, but they did not take the main route through the mountain range.

Instead, they traversed secret tunnels and passageways. Ever higher did they climb, up the Everstairs to the very peak of Mt. Vizzorus. Upon the peak, Ky'Ell got a view of the wide world around them. From the ancient observation tower, a three hundred and sixty degree view was enjoyed, but the dwarf king was not there for the sightseeing pleasures it provided. He arrived well before midday and had the fortune to find the day clear and bright. Snow covered everything in every direction, but rather than hinder his view, the snow let things stand out all the better.

The tower had not been built by the dwarves. Rather, it was the natural mountain peak carved out by dwarven tools. At the center of the tower, upon three legs of thick iron, stood a round, three-foot-long seeing-scope. The scope had been set upon a swivel, allowing for the entire panorama to be viewed through it. A round catwalk circled the scope–accessible by stair–that made it possible to point the scope at a sharp downward angle. But, Ky'Ell did not need the seeing-scope to see the thin, black, snaking army spreading from horizon to horizon.

Ky'Ell brought his eye to the scope and settled on the dark army that traveled adjacent to the mountain range. He focused until he could make out the marching army better. He could not see sharp details from this distance, but he counted ten to twenty abreast, and Draggard. Moving down the line, he was surprised to see humans marching behind them, and given their armor and proportion to the Draggard, he could tell that they were barbarians. To his further astonishment, he spied the banners of Shierdon among soldiers of the same.

"Whatcha spying, Pa?" Raene asked from behind him, and he did a startled dance upon the catwalk.

"By the tip o' Ky'Dren's bloody axe, don't be comin' up on an old dwarf unannounced. Ye got them braids too tight, or ye be tryin' to kill me?" he grumbled.

"Must be the braids," said Raene, ignoring his glares and moving past him to look through the scope.

"By Ky'Dren's beard, Pa! The army be headin' for the Pass!"

"Aye," groaned the king. "An' we be headin' 'em' off."

"Aye, me king," Raene nodded with a glimmer in her eye and turned to descend the stairs from the tower. Ky'Ell held fast his daughter by the arm.

"By *we,* I be meanin' we menfolk, ain't no place fo-"

"We got no time for this argument!"

"This ain't no argument, lass! This be the damned word o' yer king. Daughter or no, I ain't for havin' me orders questioned. And that's the last o' it, or Ky'Dren help me, I'll have ye in iron!"

Raene stood before him defiantly, but was compelled by her sense of dogma and duty to obey. "Aye, me king," she said with a bow. Her glares went unnoticed as Ky'Ell shoved past her and descended the stairs, and for the hundredth time she cursed the pigheadedness of dwarven men, and the acquiescence of dwarven women. She refused to let a single tear fall. Men didn't cry outright, and neither would she. She knew the truth even if they did not, and, one day, they would show her the respect a great warrior deserved. One day, the name Raene would mean *dwarven female warrior.*

Dirk, Krentz, and an exuberant General Reeves sailed over the forests of Eldalon upon the back of Fyrfrost. The night had been mild, in stark contrast to the days past. They made good time with the help of Krentz's spells that kept the dragon-hawk tireless, as well as her constant wind-weaving. They flew at breakneck speeds upon torrents of warm air, and, more than once, Reeves gave a whoop and cheer. He moved in his saddle to counter Fyrfrost's lunges and dives without having to be told. When finally they saw the Ky'Dren pass begin to grow from the horizon, Reeves cursed that they needed to land so soon.

As they drew closer to the Pass, they began to see the rivers of refugees flooding in from all roads leading north, south, and west. As Dirk had predicted, the Ky'Dren Pass, and therefore the mountains, was overwhelmed. But the dwarves would not allow chaos to break out within their realm, and, as such, receiving-tents blanketed the miles-wide expanse that was the western mouth of the Mountain Pass. The incoming Eldalonian refugees would be recorded and assigned quarters, rations, and duties, and the sick and dying would be tended to. The Eldalonian army was in force as well, and, though they had become greater in number in and around the pass as of late with the escalation of conflict between them and Uthen-Arden, now it seemed as though rightly half the army had turned out. This fact did not sit well with General Reeves, as it meant more cities had fallen to the dark elves.

"Bring us in low under cover of Fyrfrost's camouflage, if they see him before I can order them to hold fire, someone might get the wrong idea," said Reeves from the back.

"You met many dwarves, General? They aren't going to stand for a dragon anywhere near their mountain," said Dirk. "No, we are going to have to put down and walk in if we are going to learn anything."

They circled around and set down in a clearing surrounded by dense forest well off the road. It took the three an hour to walk to the mouth of the pass, but it was preferable to trying to rationalize with the dwarves. General Reeves led them into the Pass, making it clear he led the strange-looking group. People turned heads as they approached, and many hushed conversations sprouted in their wake. The refugees being herded into the tent-city looked ragged and weary. Many wore bloody bandages or slings, their faces slack and eyes ever down. No celebration greeted their arrival, for all had lost someone during the dark days behind them, and it was with the lost that their hearts remained.

Soldiers saluted with a smart click of the heels when General Reeves approached. He returned the salute to three soldiers.

"At ease," he said.

The three soldiers swung their hands from their sides to clasp them behind the back, and set their feet apart. To Dirk, they looked the farthest thing from at ease'.

"I need one of you to lead me to General Steeley," he ordered, and all three stepped forward.

"You," he pointed to the center man, a young soldier with high cheeks and hazel eyes.

"Yes, sir! This way," he said and, turning on his heel, began marching west at a brisk pace.

They followed the soldier through the maze of tents. Inside the first line of tents, Ky'Dren dwarves and Eldalonians were recording and instructing the refugee families. The names would be cross-referenced, and, if reunions could be made, the families would be informed promptly. The next line of tents fed the refugees who were hungry. Huge cauldrons boiled and bubbled within, and dwarves stood over them stirring with what might have been canoe paddles. Beyond, tents stood as crowded infirmaries.

They walked beyond the tents full of injured, and the moans of the dying followed them long after. They made their way to General Steeley's tent, and the soldier announced General Reeves to the standing guard.

"We will wait outside; I have a…history with Steeley. Though he likely no longer remembers, I would rather not test the theory," said Dirk, so only the general would hear.

Reeves's questioning eyes surveyed Dirk's; no elaboration was required–at the moment.

"Very well," said Reeves, and followed the soldier into the tent.

Dirk and Krentz waited for Reeves outside the tent with the awkwardly silent soldier. He looked as though it was torturous for him not to turn and take in a full measure of Krentz's long legs, lithe-yet-muscular form, and scanty armor. Dirk laughed to himself, aware that none of the men–or women–in the immediate vicinity could help keep their eyes from wandering to her, as if she was true north, and their eyes were compass needles. She met the stares of her admirers boldly, nearly giggling to herself when their startled eyes turned from hers in embarrassment of being caught.

Knowing the urgency of the situation, Reeves remained in the tent for little more than ten minutes. When he emerged, he shot a glance toward Dirk that bade him follow. He headed immediately in the direction they had come from. When the soldier moved to accompany them, Reeves waved him off and told him it would not be necessary. Once they were out of the pass and on their way back to the clearing, Reeves filled them in.

"Steeley informed me the pass has been under attack for days now. A rift like the one outside of Kell-Torey opened somewhere inside of Northern Ky'Dren. And even now, the dwarves fight the hordes that threaten to break through."

"What of Felspire?" Krentz put in.

"Eadon has somehow built a crystal tower within the Thendor Plains. Steeley said that it reaches so high as to split the clouds, and even then no end can be seen of it."

"Are the sources sound? That is a tall claim," said Dirk.

"As sound as any," Reeves replied, worry setting his brow low. "It has been reported by many Eldalonian spies, and the dwarves can see it from the peaks of Southern Ky'Dren."

Dirk considered what he had heard, but Reeves had more to tell.

"They are also reporting a massive advancement from Shierdon."

"So much for Eadon's armistice," said Dirk.

"They will bolster the Uthen-Arden numbers, and block the way through to prevent an attack from Eldalon by land," Krentz surmised.

"With them marches an army of Draggard, and barbarians," said Reeves.

Dirk thought of Aurora then, and wondered if the feisty barbarian had indeed avenged her father and taken the mantle of chief. The news that the barbarians marched with the enemy was worse news for the dwarves than hearing of the Draggard. The barbarians were fierce fighters, and much smarter than the dark elf creations. The dark elves who would surely accompany them, however, were worse than the two combined. Without sun elves to counter the powerful foes, the dark elves would rain destruction upon the dwarves.

They reached the clearing, quickly mounted, and took to the air. It seemed a battle was brewing in the eastern door of the pass, and none of the three meant to miss it.

CHAPTER TWENTY-SIX
The Way of the Peaceful Monk

Roakore and Holdagozz flew the entire day and well into night ever northwest toward the Ro'Sar Mountains. The dwarf king's anxiety grew with every beat of Silverwind's wings, and he spurred his mount on to maintain a brisk pace and find the quickest currents on which to fly home. The hour was well past midnight when a shimmering light, just over the horizon and below the moon, soared through the sky toward them. The light approached them rapidly and blinked out.

"I ain't likin the looks o' that," Roakore admitted. Behind him in the saddle, Holdagozz agreed.

"Ye thinkin it be best to take to ground for a bit? Lest it o' ill intent," Holdagozz asked.

"Bah," Roakore scoffed and spat, the spittle nearly hitting Holdagozz's beard blowing in the wind. "I ain't stopping for nothin', and ain't nothing stopping me getting home. If it be o' ill intent, it be dead."

Holdagozz maneuvered in the saddle to watch their back. Roakore scoured the sky before them as Silverwind rose higher. The light remained hidden, or had burnt out; Roakore did not know. He thought it nothing more than a shooting star.

No sooner had he thrown it from his mind, than a silver dragon-hawk uncloaked in front of them. With a squawk, it angled to intercept with wicked talons leading the way. Silverwind instinctively banked to avoid a collision, and Roakore instinctively lashed out with his axe. The talons missed, as did the blade, and, in the moments before the near-collision, Roakore recognized the rider.

"Be a dark elf on the beast!" Holdagozz yelled over the wind, as Silverwind went into a dive, lifting the two from their saddles to float weightless, bound only by the thick leather straps about the saddle.

"It be Eadon! Hold on!" Roakore yelled, and sent Silverwind into another dive. Behind them, the dragon-hawk reared to follow.

"We ain't for out flyin' that one!" Holdagozz warned.

Just then, the crackle of lightning ripped through the sky and a bolt came at them from the dark elf rider. Roakore banked hard, but the lightning followed and hit Holdagozz. The forking bolts branched off, jolting Roakore and Silverwind as well. Silverwind gave a keening cry and faltered in flight. Another blast hit them square, and Roakore pulled Silverwind's reins, attempting to gain control as the seemingly unconscious hawk fell limply.

"Wake up, ye bloody bird!" he screamed, as the world spun round and round in his vision. The ground was coming up fast to meet them. Holdagozz lolled in his saddle as they fell. Roakore kicked and pulled at feathers, trying to jolt Silverwind awake. As they spun, he spied the dragon-hawk in fast pursuit.

"Wake up, Silverwind, I ain't for dyin today!" he screamed, shaking the bird's neck.

Silverwind came to with an angry squawk. With a flutter of flailing wings, she righted herself and pulled up at the last moment. Their momentum brought them in fast as she leveled out and grazed the treetops below, clipping many of the higher branches. She barely kept them aloft. Another bolt of lightning hit them, and Roakore's vision went black.

When he regained consciousness, he realized the dragon-hawk had landed in a clearing made by its own dragon breath. Embers burned beneath the beast's large talons, and the smoke from the ring of burnt trees lingered lazily in the still air. Through the smoke, a dark elf strode toward them. Roakore fumbled with the leather strap that bound him, as he lay in a tangled mess with the unconscious Silverwind and Holdagozz. With a scream of rage, Roakore snapped the strap freeing him, and took up his mighty battle axe. Holdagozz moaned something inaudible as Roakore unstrapped him as well.

"Up and at 'em laddy, we got company," said Roakore as he walked to stand between the dark elf and his mount.

The dark elf strode forth boldly, the sword at his hip was sheathed, and an air of power surrounded him. Roakore had only ever seen the dark elf from a distance, but he knew this one to be Eadon.

"You!" Roakore bellowed as rage consumed him.

He took up one of the hatchets strapped to his thighs and let fly. Eadon didn't bother to deflect the weapon; instead, it bounced harmlessly off of his energy shield. Roakore growled with determination and charged with his axe held high. Eadon smirked as Roakore approached with a war cry, and brought his blade down with a powerful strike aimed at the dark elf's head. Eadon lifted but a hand and grabbed the blade as it descended toward him, stopping it dead. He tore it from Roakore's grip as if the dwarf king's strength was no greater than that of a child. With his other hand, he backhanded Roakore and sent him whirling to land hard among the burning embers.

"Me King!" Holdagozz yelled, getting to his feet and making a charge of his own. Two hatchets flew from him in rapid succession, but these too where deflected harmlessly. From Eadon's hand flew a fireball, and

Roakore grimaced, seeing his friend's fate. The fireball hit Holdagozz, and flames burst forth, covering the brave dwarf as he was thrown back twenty feet.

Roakore found many large, charred stones about the forest floor. Summoning his strength and focusing his mind, he willed the stones into the air. All around him, stones, rocks, and boulders rose up and churned. Roakore cried the name of the god of war, and sent the group of floating stones flying toward Eadon. The dark elf bellowed a spell, and the stones all turned to dust in their flight. Unrelenting, Roakore barreled in again, determined to have the dark lord's head.

Eadon was upon him before Roakore could react. The dark elf grabbed him by the throat and held him high. Roakore beat at the iron grip and kicked furiously, but it was no use. Eadon cocked his head, intrigued, taking a measure of the dwarf king.

"Your people are brave, good king. Your ferocity is admirable. I think I shall spare the dwarves, your strength and courage make the dwargon one of my most formidable creations."

"Eat shyte, ye dark stain!" Roakore croaked.

Eadon laughed. "Ferocious to the last." Roakore spat in his face, but the spittle sizzled against the energy shield and disappeared in smoke.

"You be a coward, hiding behind your fancy magic! If you was elf enough to fight me face-to-face, you would die where you stand," said Roakore, trying to taunt him into dropping his energy shield. Eadon punched him in the ribs, breaking many. Roakore grimaced, but refused to make a pained sound.

"I have not survived thousands of years by letting my opponents coax me into fair fights," Eadon laughed, and flung Roakore high into the air toward the dragon-hawk. Roakore landed hard, but ignored the pain. He sprang to his feet and charged again, wielding his hatchets. Behind Eadon, Holdagozz had gotten to his feet once again, and despite the small flames that still burned upon his armor and person, the brave dwarf charged Eadon as well.

Roakore was blasted back by an energy spell that knocked the wind from his lungs and slammed him against the dragon-hawk. He watched helplessly as Eadon turned toward the charging Holdagozz and punched his hand through his chest. The dark lord pulled back quickly, and a surprised Holdagozz stared at his own beating heart.

"Holdagozz!" Roakore screamed.

As his friend's body fell to its knees, and slowly toppled over, Roakore charged once again, hatchets in hand. Eadon met the charge, blocking the blades with his hands. Roakore screamed all the while, cursing and frothing at the mouth, consumed by grief and rage. Eadon sent the hatchets flying as he blocked, but Roakore came on with his strong fists. Punches strong enough to drop an ox were absorbed by Eadon's energy shield. Eadon caught Roakore's right arm in a block and snapped it like a twig. Unfazed in the least, Roakore continued screaming and slamming blows against Eadon's shield. The dark elf caught the other arm and broke that as well. He hit Roakore with a punch to the jaw that shattered molars and sent him flying once more.

Roakore landed with a thud, and the world spun. A few feet away, he met the dead eyes of his friend Holdagozz. Despite Roakore's rage, his vision went black at the edges. Fighting the daze, he tried to lift himself up to attack again. His arms useless, he sat up and stood on shaky legs.

"Your determination is commendable, good king, but I grow tired of these games," said Eadon. From his hand, a black writhing spell shot forth and hit Roakore in the chest, and the dwarf fell to the ground in a heap.

Lunara clutched her chest and fell to her knees. "Holdagozz," she breathed.

"What's wrong?" Tarren came to her, concerned. Lunara did not answer; she could not. She shook with grief, and tears welled in her eyes.

"What is wrong with her?" Tarren begged of the Watcher, but the old elf seemed not to hear. His head was turned to the north, and foreboding spread across his face.

"I have been mistaken," he said to himself.

Tarren comforted Lunara, and looked to Helzendar helplessly. The dwarf boy had no answers for him. Even the two elven guards had begun to act strange. They stopped in their water weaving, and they too stared toward the north. Tarren scanned the ocean, but he saw nothing.

"Holdagozz…has fallen," Lunara sobbed.

"How can you know?" Tarren asked, his tone assuring her she was mistaken.

"He comes," the Watcher said hypnotically. "He comes for you," he said to Tarren. The calm demeanor that the Watcher always wore withered away, leaving a frown in its place.

"Who comes? What do you mean?" said Tarren, frightened by the Watcher's uncharacteristic concern.

"What you elves talkin' about?" Helzendar began, but soon his attention was drawn to the north as well.

The air became thick, and Tarren's ears popped with the pressure change. Off in the distance, to the north, a swirling disturbance began high above the water. Darkened clouds swirled, spewing bolts of lightning. The wind picked up and blew Tarren's hair forward. The boat lurched as well, its bow pulled in the direction of the growing rift.

"This was inevitable," said the Watcher, staring not at the rift like the others, but the deck of the boat, as if pondering something of importance.

"What was inevitable?" Tarren asked him, but he was ignored.

A swift sucking noise came, and Tarren felt the boat pulled forward. But then, just as suddenly, there came an explosion of sound and the shockwave filled the ship's sails from the opposite direction. The noise came not from an explosion of fire and debris, but with the opening of a small rift floating high above the ocean waters.

"What was inevitable?" Tarren asked again, spurred by the promise of violence. When he was not answered a second time, he got in front of the Watcher and shook his shoulders.

"Answer me!" he begged.

The Watcher seemed to notice him then for the first time, dazed, as if he had just woken up. He raised his hands to take Tarren's and smiled upon the boy.

"The rivers of time flow as they may, all possibilities exist at once and not at all. I see all possibilities, but not this one. I am sorry. He will take you now."

"Who?"

Just then, a blood curdling cry issued from the rift, and from it flew a feathered dragon the likes of which Tarren had never seen. Its feathers turned from the blue of the sky to brilliant silver.

"Eadon," Tarren answered himself.

"Eadon," Lunara breathed, moving instinctively to guard Tarren.

"Does this end well in any of the futures you see?" Tarren asked. He was as scared as he had ever been in his life, but showing it would get him nowhere. The adults were scared as well, which made it worse. Helzendar showed not fear, but anger. For all he knew it was the truth, perhaps his dwarven friend was truly not scared. If so, Tarren was jealous of his strength.

"Yes, one of them," the Watcher answered, smiling at him. The old elf regarded Helzendar strangely and laughed. "Oh, no, dear boy, you shouldn't say that to Eadon." He waved a hand in the air and the dwarf fell to the deck snoring.

"What do we do?" Lunara asked the Watcher, as Eadon soared toward them.

The Watcher did not respond, but stared into Tarren's eyes. Tarren panicked, but the old elf called to his mind, and his soft voice soothed all fears.

"Trust in me, and you shall live," said the Watcher.

Tarren did trust him, he would trust in anything that would help him now. He felt a strange sensation of falling, and then being caught by warm, swift currents like hands ushering his soul. Vast, stretching fields of golden wheat and a sun bright and clear shone before him. Yellow streaks of golden light mingled, twirled and danced with bright white, silver, and orange. Another flash of light followed by another, and yet another, until only streaking lights existed. In his mind, Tarren flew through a field of fireflies...and opened his eyes.

Eadon' dragon-hawk splashed down amid a torrent of flying ocean spray. The wings, thick and muscled, extended twice the length of the boat. Its maw was wide and spear-toothed, so large that it could snap the boat in two easily. Eadon stood from his saddle, high atop the floating dragon's back.

Tarren turned to the Watcher, and, shocked, he saw himself standing there. His-self offered him a wink, and Tarren had to rub his eyes; still he did not believe it. He stared at himself and stumbled a bit but was caught by Lunara. When he saw his own arm he nearly screamed.

"Do something," she said to Tarren. "We must try. It is impossible, but we must try," she pleaded, staring into Tarren's eyes, which were not his eyes, but the Watcher's.

"It's all right," said the Watcher as Tarren. "The Watcher and I have a plan, please trust us."

Lunara looked to Tarren in the Watcher's body, her eyes asked many questions, but she remained silent.

Eadon strode down the long scales of his dragon-hawk as if down the stairs of his highest tower. Tarren would have trembled had he not been in someone else's body. The two guards moved to intercept Eadon as he stepped on the boat's rail, but from each side of the ship came serpents of water that wrapped themselves around the elves and yanked them off the deck and into the depths below. Eadon walked onto the boat as if nothing had happened. He stopped when he saw the Watcher.

"You?" he laughed. "I had not thought you alive after all these years."

Tarren didn't know what to say, what if he gave away the ruse? A power emanated from Eadon, and though unseen, it was surely felt, the way that a furious person darkens an entire room without word or gesture. He had the air of a thunderhead about him, and a silent hurricane was in his gaze.

"I must amuse the gods." Tarren heard the Watcher's voice and spoke the words, but not on his own accord. It seemed that the Watcher had left some of himself inside his body.

"Indeed, you must," Eadon squared on him. He felt the Watcher take control of his eyes. To Tarren's relief, he did not raise them to meet Eadon's, but settled upon the dark elf's chin.

"Do you still practice The Way of the Morenka?" Eadon asked.

"I do."

Eadon eyed him up and down, and Tarren felt the silent battle between the two elves; Eadon probing the Watcher's mind, and the old elf diverting Eadon's attention and leading him through circles of thought and imagery. When Eadon attacked more forcefully, the Watcher flooded his mind with the purest love that he could summon. Tarren was bathed in peace and love and the feeling of home, of friends and laughter and family. Eadon recoiled from the intensity of the Watcher's love for him with a pained expression.

"I would show you the way to peace, if you would only ask."

Eadon seemed at first furious, but soon he gained control of himself. Tarren thought that he would be struck down on the spot. The Watcher had pushed him too far. Eadon had recoiled from the light he was shown as if burned by fire.

"I am afraid that I never mastered your school. But, I find it fascinating," said Eadon with a mirthless grin. He turned his attention to Lunara, and Tarren recognized the hungry eyes that men used to give his sisters back home.

"She has nothing to offer you," said the Watcher. "Nor do any of us. It is the boy you want."

Eadon's eyes moved from Lunara to the Watcher, and then to Tarren's body. The Watcher played the part.

"No, no!" Tarren-Watcher screamed. "You have to do something," he clawed at the Watcher's robes.

Whether Lunara was playing along or not, she began to cry.

"You will do nothing to stop me?" Eadon asked, as he pulled Tarren's body to himself and held him by the collar as Tarren's body kicked and screamed.

"What is there to be done?" said the Watcher. "But pray that you will find the light?"

Eadon smirked at that. He seemed to ponder for a moment, waiting for Lunara or the Watcher to retaliate. He attempted to search their minds, but found only the Watcher's love surrounding them. Anger flashed behind Eadon's eyes, and Tarren was sure that he would kill them all.

"If you insist on shedding blood, I would offer mine. For with it would go my death-spell, and its power would consume even you Eadon, and you would know love," Tarren felt himself say through the Watcher.

Eadon sent them each a reproachful look, turned swiftly, and bore Tarren's body away. He mounted the dragon-hawk, and it took off across the ocean like a duck, flapping its wings to gain momentum and quickly running atop the water to finally soar high into the sky. He circled twice, flew into the rift, and was gone.

Tarren was amazed that they were all still alive. Off to the side of the boat, he spied a sleeping Helzendar. Lunara peered into his eyes, and it was strange to be taller than her.

"Tarren? Is that you?" she asked.

"Yes," he said with the Watcher's voice.

A pang of sadness tightened his throat as he stared after the rift.

Eadon left The Watcher in a barred room high in Felspire and opened another rift. He soared through it astride his dragon-hawk, Akrazza, and came out above the city of Del'Oradon. His mind-meld with the beast allowed him to control its every movement, and through the mind-meld he spewed forth fire into the city he had previously ruled. Thatch roofs went up like so much tinder, and people scrambled like ants from a burning twig. Through Akrazza, he roared, pulling strength from The Sword of Power Taken, Nodae. The dragon-hawk's roar shattered windows and bled eardrums, and any too near to the sound died where they stood, the dragon-fear shattering their minds and quieting their hearts. Arrows flew from below, and were snapped as twigs underfoot as they collided with the energy shield that surrounded Akrazza and Eadon.

He flew on toward the castle, leaving fire and death in his wake. In the courtyard of the castle, a gathering of elves and Uthen-Arden soldiers awaited him. The elves took no time in attacking, their spells shot forth through the air and exploded against the energy shield. Below, he quickly found Zerafin and his sister, Avriel. With a force of will, he connected with the energy of her form and pulled her through the air to him, as Akrazza swooped down and blanketed the courtyard in flames.

In minutes it was over, and just as quickly as he had flown from the rift to the castle, he returned. Through the rift they went, and into Felspire they flew. He flung Avriel to the stone floor. He had drained her of her stored energy as they flew, and she was no more magical now than a human sheep herder.

"Avriel, the one that got away," he mused, as he slid from the saddle and down the sparkling silver scales of Akrazza.

CHAPTER
TWENTY-SEVEN

Taken

The alarm sounded in the courtyard and city beyond. Screams and calls of "dragon!" rang out, but were soon drowned out by the ear-piercing cry of the beast. From his vantage point behind the castle, Whill saw nothing. He unsheathed Adromida, flew high above the castle, and found the courtyard in flames. The city beyond had been devastated, and many buildings were on fire. Off in the distance, a rift had been torn in the sky, and a large dragon-hawk flew toward the rift and disappeared. The rift folded in on itself until nothing remained. Whill flew to the courtyard and found it in chaos. The entire area had been doused in dragonsbreath. The elves had shielded themselves and the Uthen-Arden soldiers from the worst of the flames. He spotted Zerafin amid the chaos and flew down to land near him.

"What has happened?" Whill asked.

Zerafin was distraught, and his face told Whill what his words did not.

"Avriel," Whill said in realization, and Zerafin nodded grimly.

"Where is she?" Whill demanded.

"Eadon, he has taken her," Zerafin grit his teeth and stared to where the rift had been.

"What do you mean, taken her? How could that happen?" he asked desperately.

"He absorbed everything we threw at him and turned the spells back upon us," said Zerafin.

Whill was furious, and did nothing to hide it. He felt the old anger, the rage, and the fury of the Other well up inside him. But he did not lose control, and did not need the Other to bear the feelings of loss. He and the Other were one, which meant that Whill would not hide from such things any longer.

Aklenar Master, Avolarra En'Kayen strode to stand next to Whill and laid a hand upon his shoulder. "I see not her fate," she told him with a sympathetic smile.

"Is that supposed to make me feel better?" Whill asked.

"Not if you do not want it to. I meant that hers is not certain, for good or ill."

Whill turned from the elven masters with anger in his heart. They were some of the most powerful elven masters that Elladrindellia had to offer, and they had not been able to hinder Eadon in the least, let alone stop him. He couldn't tear his eyes away from the ravaged city and the dead soldiers, his soldiers. Beyond the castle, thick smoke billowed up into the pink sky. The sun was setting behind the castle, but Whill saw no beauty in the heavens that night.

"I must tend to my people," Whill said with a small bow to the gathered elves.

He walked to the castle gates and beyond. The city had suffered incredible damage considering that a single dragon had made only one pass. The intensity and breadth of the dragonsbreath had been great; a wide swath had been burned through the center of the city. In some places, the liquid fire had melted the very brick.

Captain Walker saw Whill and quickly came to stand before him.

"Report!" Whill ordered.

"Sire. The dragon destroyed over thirty buildings."

"How many dead?"

"The current count is forty-three, sire, and hundreds injured, mostly burns."

"Forty-three," Whill said to himself. His anger grew by the second. Where had Kellallea been? Had she been distracting him? Eadon attacked only moments after she left…were they working together? Whill felt sick to his stomach.

"Where have the injured been gathered?" he asked.

"At the Saw Horse, sire," Captain Walker told him. When Whill showed no recognition, he added. "A tavern, that way," he pointed behind him. "It wasn't touched by the flames. The elves have offered their help, but the people are suspicious and afraid. They turn to the gods with prayer for help."

"Take me there," said Whill.

Captain Walker led Whill through the streets. Rubble and bodies littered the roads and walkways. Few buildings were still on fire, however; the elves had put out many, and were assisting with rescuing those trapped in the ruins. A cry caught Whill's ear, and he told Walker to wait. The sound had come from a building to his right. It looked to have been a leather shop, for burnt saddles and a variety of leather clothing spilled out on the street. The tower of a larger building had come crashing down atop the shop, caving in the roof and busting the front wall. Broken glass and fused brick lay strewn about, and there was no clear way in.

"Momma!" the muffled voice cried again.

"Do you hear that?" he asked Walker.

"Sounds like a child," the captain replied and began manually moving chunks of fused stone aside.

"Allow me," Whill bade him with a hand to the chest, moving him away.

Whill scoured the rubble for the child. With his mind sight he spotted a little girl deep within the rubble, trapped between two slabs resting at an angle against each other. Through his mind sight, Whill saw her clearly, and her blood.

"When the stone lifts, bring her out," Whill instructed Walker.

"Sire?"

"Do you understand?"

"Yes, sire."

Whill unsheathed Adromida, which lit the street as if it were daylight. Walker blocked the brilliant light with one arm and stepped aside. Whill reached out with his mind and set his will upon the stone and splintered wood. With his free hand, he reached out and carefully created an energy barrier between the girl and the rubble. Tapping into Adromida, he raised the debris. Walker stared, awestruck, and Whill had to say his name twice to get him moving. On the second call, Captain Walker snapped to, ducked under the rubble, and shuffled to the girl. He scooped her up quickly, brought her back, and laid her down in the street. Whill dropped the rubble at once and turned to see her.

The little girl was bruised and broken. Her left cheek had a deep gash in it, so deep that the whites of her teeth showed. Both of her legs were broken and set at unnatural angles. Her left arm was broken at the fore-arm, and many other small wounds covered her small body. Tears burned hot in Whill's eyes. No matter how much he saw of battle, he would never get used to this. He bent to his knees and stroked the child's dirty forehead.

"Momma? Momma! Momma!" the girl cried. Her eyes searched all about Whill, and he realized that she did not see him.

"I am your king," he told her as he stroked her head, "And I have come to help."

Whill tapped into Adromida as he surveyed her wounds with his mind sight. He sent a surge of energy into her body, and she heaved up with a moan. He searched her mind and caused natural pain-killing chemicals to be released. Adromida's power coursed through him, sharpening his senses. He drew more from the blade, enhancing his mental capacity as he set to the task of mapping her injuries and planning their healing. He saw every muscle, bone, and fiber clearly in his mind, he was ready. With a surge from Adromida he sent blue tendrils of healing energy winding from her head to her toes. The light moved around and through-out her body, lifting her from the dirty street and heal-ing her many wounds. When Whill lowered her into his arms, all of her injuries were healed, and she was smiling up at him.

"Melody!" a women cried and came running through the gathered crowd.

"Momma!" the girl replied as Whill put her down.

Mother and daughter came together in a desperate embrace. People fell to their knees before Whill, some in adoration, others begging him to help their trapped loved ones.

"Lead me to them," Whill said to a battered old man with a bandaged head. The man had begged Whill to help his family who were trapped in a burning house.

Whill spent the night and most of the next day freeing the trapped and healing the injured. Word of his miracles spread throughout the city, and the people came in droves to witness the magic of their lost prince. In seeing Whill's healing, the people became more comfortable around the elves and allowed the healers to help their kin. When those close to death had been pulled from the brink and cared for, Whill returned to the castle to confer with Zerafin. The elven masters had gathered once more in the war room when Whill arrived, and they seemed to be in the midst of a lively debate.

"The time to strike Felspire is now! Cerushia has been destroyed," said Gnenja Master, Thryn De'Gregeth.

Master Myrramus shook his head and opened his arms wide to his brethren. "To attack is to contribute to the violence of the world. We must embrace peace."

Thryn moved his hand across his bald head. His frustration was apparent in his ice-blue eyes. "Your cowardice is shameful!" he finally erupted.

"Silence!" Zerafin bellowed. "Infighting will get us nowhere."

Whill took his seat and accepted a glass of wine from Alrick.

"Are you in contact with the elves of Elladrindellia?" he asked Zerafin, and sipped of his wine.

"Yes, they move toward Felspire as we speak," said Zerafin.

"We debate an offensive and you have already set into action the attack?" asked Myrramus.

"We debate nothing, your thoughts have been noted, and I have taken action," said Zerafin. He pointed to the map, "Our forces are already on the move. They shall converge on this Felspire before Eadon's deadline arrives. We are here to devise a plan of attack."

"This is unnecessary," said Whill. "I must face Eadon alone."

"You are not alone in this," said Zerafin.

"I appreciate the gesture, good King, but what is the point? All due respect, but the lot of you could do nothing against him yesterday. What will you do against him at Felspire?"

A few of the elves nodded, namely the Morenka.

"If nothing else, we shall try. My sister, Princess of Elladrindellia, has been taken. I shall not sit idly by and wait to see the outcome of this battle. I have vowed to lead the elves against the dark one, and I shall."

"How can they make the journey in time?" Whill asked.

"They are aware this may be the end. No use in holding back stored power, they will use whatever means necessary to travel there in time."

The doors swung wide and banged against the walls, gaining the attention of all. Through the door strode Lunara, Helzendar, and the Watcher.

"Master Watcher," said Myrramus, standing to bow.

"Lunara?" asked Whill, looking past them to the doorway. "Where is Tarren?"

"I am here," said the Watcher to Whill's confusion.

"We were attacked by Eadon. He came for Tarren," said Lunara.

Whill's heart skipped. Lunara put a hand so his shoulder.

"The Watcher…somehow switched bodies with the boy. Eadon was fooled. He took Tarren's body, not knowing the deception," she explained.

"Impossible, the Watcher would never meddle in such…such dark magic," Master Myrramus insisted.

"The Watcher gave himself to save Tarren. I would not call such a sacrifice dark magic," Lunara argued.

"But, we left you in Cerushia," said Whill.

"Yes. When the attack came, the Watcher led us away to the safety of the ocean. We have traveled here by boat. He somehow knew you and our king would be here."

"What the old crazy elf did was kidnap me! Where in the hells be me pa?" Helzendar chimed in.

"He may be in danger," Zerafin said to Whill, but he barely registered the words.

"Tarren?" he said, amazed, laying a hand upon the shoulder of the Watcher.

"Heya, Whill," the Watcher said, his inflections and mannerisms those of the boy.

Whill laughed despite himself. "He was deceived!" Whill said to them all.

He turned and paced around the table, his mind racing. "The Watcher has deceived Eadon, perhaps there is a way."

"There is always a way," said Aklenar Master, Avolarra.

"What ye be meanin', elf? Me father be in danger ye say?" Helzendar pressed.

"You will address him as King, or King Zerafin," Lunara berated him. "Your father would be embarrassed to hear such disrespect uttered by his son."

Helzendar lowered his head in shame. "What danger be me father in? King Zerafin."

Whill turned to his friend as well. In his excitement at the news of the Watcher's deception, he had forgotten the warning.

"Eadon opened a rift above the city and laid waste to many buildings. He also took Avriel," said Zerafin. "He meant to take Tarren as well. Stands to reason that Eadon would try to capture Roakore as well. Surely, he knows of your friendship. This is a game to him, and he is collecting his pieces. He will use them as hostages to convince you to give him the power of Adromida," he said to Whill.

Whill pondered this, and his anger grew. Not because of the lengths Eadon would go, but because, once again, his friends were in danger due to him, and that, even now, with the incredible power of Adromida, he was unable to help them.

"I must discover the fate of Roakore," Whill told them all.

"I would go with you," said Lunara, coming to him.

Whill saw clearly the love in her eyes, but thought of nothing but Avriel and Roakore. He put a hand to her soft cheek and offered her a thankful smile.

"I need you to watch over Tarren and Helzendar," he said.

"If you be ridin' the path to me mountain, I be going with ye. We be at war, me place be in Ro'Sar," Helzendar insisted.

"You will remain, and that is the last of it," Whill retorted.

"Take care of them both," Whill said to Lunara. He moved to the door and turned to the elves. "I go to learn of the fate of Roakore. I shall not return. If you go with your king to Felspire, I will see you on the battlefield."

Whill left them and made his way out of the castle with Alrick and Captain Walker in tow.

"Whill!" Zerafin yelled from the stairs. Whill waited for him at the door to the Great Room.

"Alrick, see to it the repairs to the city continue, we've still a long winter ahead of us, no matter the outcome of the days ahead," said Whill with a firm hand upon the older man's shoulder.

"Yes, sire," said Alrick with a bow. His proud eyes shimmered and lingered on his king. "Thank you."

"Captain Walker, close off the city, but do not turn away any refugees. Prepare the city for attack. Be ready for anything."

"Yes, sire," Captain Walker bowed.

The two took their leave as Zerafin approached. Together, he and Whill walked out to the courtyard.

"Do not attempt anything before we arrive at Felspire," said Zerafin.

"I shall wait for you, and, together, we will face the dark lord," Whill told his friend.

"Together," Zerafin repeated, his eyes showing a hint of skepticism. He extended his hand in the common human greeting. Whill took it and was pulled into a one-armed hug.

"Go with the blessing of the Elves, Whillhelm Warcrown."

Without another word, Whill summoned the power within Adromida and shot up into the sky heading north.

CHAPTER TWENTY-EIGHT

The Fate of a Friend

Whill flew in the direction of the Ro'Sar Mountains so fast a clap of thunder sounded. His egg-shaped energy shield formed at the tip of his sword and set the air aflame. The energy of Adromida coursed through him as he flew through the sky like an arrow.

He soon overtook the marching dwarves, and his heart leapt. He slowed and quickly descended to land before them. The dwarf Philo approached cautiously, but on seeing Whill, he relaxed his grip on his weapon.

"Aye, Whill," he said in greeting.

"Where is Roakore?" Whill asked, scouring the dwarves as they approached.

"He and Holdagozz left us yesterday. His crazy silverhawk returned, and me king wasted no time in flying to Ro'Sar."

Whill gave a disappointed sigh and looked again to the north. "Have you seen anything strange in the north?" he asked Philo.

"Ain't seen nothing strange," said Philo, turning to gauge the response of the dwarves. When no one spoke up, he looked to Whill. "What this be about?"

"Eadon attacked Del'Oradon and took Princess Avriel. He also appeared through a rift out to sea and attempted to kidnap Tarren," Whill told him and turned to leave.

"Where ye headed?"

"Ro'Sar, I believe Eadon went after Roakore as well."

"Then take us with you, we be needin' to be in Ro'Sar yesterday!" Philo insisted.

"I cannot, but I can lend you the strength to spur you on without rest."

"Well, then let's have it," said the gruff dwarf.

Whill extended his right hand and his left settled on Adromida's hilt. Philo cringed in anticipation of the energy offering. He had not approved of the offering outside of the city the day before, but the energy had turned out to be valuable. The dwarves had run all through the night and day without the need for rest, but they had not been impervious to the blisters that came with such haste.

Tendrils of blue-yellow energy shot forth from Whill's extended hand and surrounded the gathered dwarves. He healed their sore feet and replenished what energy they had used. Philo hooted and hollered when it was done, barely able to contain the vigor within him.

"I must be off, good luck to you all," Whill told them, and shot into the sky once more.

"And to you, Whill o' Agora!" Philo yelled after him.

Within the hour, he arrived at the Ro'Sar mountain range. He flew to the peak Roakore had said Silverwind's high perch was located. He found the arched entrance to the cave and flew into the opening, landing within the chamber. Silverwind cooed from the center of the room, but Whill's hope was short-lived when he noticed the bandages set against the bird's bloody, silver feathers.

"Who you be?" a dwarven woman insisted, holding a long dagger out before her.

"My name is Whill, I am a friend of Roakore," said Whill, holding his empty hands out to the sides.

The dwarf woman lowered her dagger and eyed him over suspiciously. "You be Whill o' Agora?"

"I be," Whill assured her.

"I be Roakore's assistant, Nah'Zed."

"Well met, Nah'Zed. I have heard a lot about you."

"And I, you," she said, unimpressed. "You be the one Roakore thinkin' he need be leavin' his mountain for."

"Is he here?" Whill asked.

"No. I was hopin' you brought word with you. Silverwind showed up this morning all bloody and beat up. I ain't for knowin' how she made it in her condition," said Nah'Zed.

"What of the invasion? Was a rift found within the mountain?"

"Aye. Hell-born devils invaded not a week ago, been all we could do to hold 'em back. Had a few dark elves with 'em they did, two o' Roakore's sons died takin' 'em out, but they got the devils, they did. Told Roakore not to go; his place be here with his people. When he finds out about his kin…he ain't gonna be forgivin' his self soon."

"I am sorry for clan Ro'Sar's losses," said Whill. He agreed with her as well. Roakore already felt bad about being away during such an important time. When he learned of his sons, he would be crushed.

"You said you had held back the Draggard. Have they been defeated?" Whill asked.

"Nay, they be trapped in Whar'Rok cavern. We sealed off every way into and outta there. The sittin' king be formulatin' plans as how to kill 'em all. Drown 'em out I say. Others say gas 'em, others beg to be let in to kill 'em. Some o' them men 'r crazy. Others say let 'em starve and eat each other. Any o' them's fine by me. Can still hear the scratchin' and clawin' at the stone, ye can."

"How many lives were lost in the initial invasion?" Whill asked.

Nah'Zed looked away to the side in thought for a moment. "Two hun'red seventy-two, and thrice more injured. A few die every day from their wounds. The ones who make it a week will make it a year, they say."

"Do you think they will accept my help?" asked Whill.

"I ain't for seein' why not. They be knowin' ye be a good friend o' Roakore's. I can lead ye down. First though, ye mind takin' care o' Silverwind? The king be right fond o' the bird."

"Of course," said Whill, and began inspecting Silverwind's injuries with his mind sight. Seeing the extent of her internal injuries, he was also surprised the bird had made it home.

Whill finished Silverwind's healing, and Nah'Zed led Whill down the many stairs, tunnels, and hallways leading to the injured dwarves. Few protested, and those who did were soon convinced to accept the healing. Roakore's son, Ror'Den, who had been left in charge of Ro'Sar in his father's absence, came to the cavern in which the healing was being performed.

"Aye, Whill o' Agora, I done heard a lot 'bout ye from me pa. Welcome to Ro'Sar, once again," said Ror'Den, slamming his fist to his chest. Whill returned the gesture in kind.

"Thank you. I hope you do not mind my healing of your dwarves. Nah'Zed told me about the injured, and I offered," said Whill.

"Bah, we be takin' all the help we can be gettin'. If me father be callin' ye dwarf friend, then dwarf friend ye be."

"About your father," Whill began, and Nah'Zed perked up instantly. She lingered off to the right, acting busy with the recently healed dwarves, but Whill knew where her attentions lie. "I believe Roakore has been taken by the dark elf Eadon."

Ror'Den's brow furled in anger, and his cheeks reddened as he looked around at the crowded chamber. "Come, we will find a place with fewer ears."

He led Whill through a tunnel that opened into a large natural cavern of stalactites and stalagmites, shimmering mineral rich walls, and waterfalls large and small feeding a massive underground lake. The crashing of the water would hide their voices from any curious ears.

"Eadon, ye say?" said Ror'Den, looking out over the lake. Torches illuminated the wide expanse in a ring about the still waters.

"Yes, he has kidnapped the Elven Princess Avriel as well, and meant to take Tarren, but was thwarted by a clever old elf."

"Hah! Well then, that be a bit o' good news then, ain't it? I grew to know Tarren well while he was livin' here…good to hear he got away from the scoundrel," said Ror'Den, stroking his long beard.

Ror'Den was the same age as Whill, though one wouldn't guess by his appearance. He was tall, taller than Roakore and most other dwarves. At only 20, he had a beard that reached the floor, braided in fat knots and set with silver rings every few inches. Ror'Den had wisdom beyond his age in his eyes. In those deep, dark pools, Whill sensed a high intellect, and the stubbornness of Roakore; also pain and worry, though no dwarf would admit as much. Whill did not have to read Ror'Den's mind to know he feared for his father's fate. Should Roakore not return, Ror'Den would be king of all of Ro'Sar. Whill knew the dwarf would rather see his father's return than accept his throne at such an early age.

"What ye thinkin he be wantin' with me Pa?" Ror'Den asked.

"Eadon is baiting me to Felspire," said Whill.

"Seems he wants you there and right badly."

"It would seem," Whill replied.

"Why there?" Ror'Den asked, his eyes still locked on the faraway shore of the cavern's lake.

"Sorry?" Whill asked.

"Why Felspire? Seems a right stupid move to follow a wolf into his den. He be baitin' ye, but why that place?"

Whill thought about the question, but the answer eluded him. Eadon had tapped into the convergence of energy within Agora's ley lines, and was more powerful than ever–likely more powerful than Whill and Adromida. Eadon would use Roakore and Avriel against him, and would likely kill them if Whill did not hand over the power of Adromida. But Whill would not give him what he wanted, no matter the cost. Avriel and Roakore would not want Whill to hand over such power on their behalf, and therefore, he would not.

"There are rivers of energy below the earth, ley lines they are called. Seems Eadon has bonded to those rivers of energy, and, with them, he created Felspire," Whill explained.

"He be luring you to where he be most powerful. The cowardly piece o' Draggard shyte," Ror'Den spat. "And he be usin' me pa as bait."

"If I know anything about Roakore, Eadon will wish he hadn't," said Whill.

Ror'Den gave a hearty laugh that echoed across the lake and was lost in the crashing of the waterfalls. Whill recognized genuine mirth in the laughter, but also a hint of nervous apprehension. One could say that at twenty years old–which was quite young for a dwarf who could live to be 400–Ror'Den was quite over his head. But, then, so too was Whill, who only a year ago had no more problems than those brought on by the weather. However, like Whill, Ror'Den would do his duty.

"You be goin' after him eh?" Ror'Den surmised.

"I be," said Whill.

A long silence followed, one of tumultuous pondering on the part of the young dwarf prince. Whill did not read his mind; he didn't have to, Ror'Den was projecting. He wanted to go with Whill; wanted more than anything to be part of the final battle. His sense of duty was too great, however. A part of him was angry with his father for ever leaving his post to help in human and elf affairs, but another part of him felt ashamed for such thoughts.

"When you see me pa, tell him Ror'Den crushed the Draggard invasion, and that he be keepin' the throne warm for him. Ye bring him back now, ye hear?"

"I will tell him," Whill promised.

Nah'Zed appeared then behind them, and the two turned to regard Roakore's teary-eyed assistant.

"You bring him back to where he belongs," she demanded, "say it, on your word, you be bringin' him back."

Nah'Zed walked determinedly toward Whill, her big red cheeks streaming with tears, two shaking fists gripping her thick braids, as if holding herself down from exploding with anger.

"You are a loyal subject and a good friend Nah'Zed," said Whill, with a hand to her shoulder.

"Promise!" she insisted through stifled sobs.

"I will try," said Whill; it was the only promise he could make.

By the time Whill returned to the surface, it was morning, and the sun rose behind a gray blanket of storm clouds setting the heavenly ceiling aglow. He had five days in which to respond to Eadon.

He had offered his help in exterminating the trapped Draggard, but Ror'Den declined, saying that Whill had already helped in the reclamation, and if the dwarves needed help a second time to hold their mountain, then they didn't deserve the mountain. Whill respected the wish.

Whill left Ro'Sar and flew north toward the Ky'Dren Mountain Pass. If his Eldalonian kin had been slaughtered, and he was now the rightful heir to the Eldalonian throne, he would be needed there as well. Eldalon and Ky'Dren had been allies for centuries. They would be working together to protect the pass.

CHAPTER TWENTY-NINE

The Pass

Aurora rode between Zander and Veolindra as they approached the Ky'Dren Pass. The mountain range, which spread for hundreds of miles to the north and south, ended dramatically in sheer cliffs to the Pass floor, as if the mountain range had been cleaved in two by the axe of a god. They had surely been spotted, but it mattered not; their goal was not stealth, but conquest. They had been joined by more bands of Draggard and their dark elf handlers, as well as one thousand more of the un-dead Shierdon soldiers.

As they approached the pass, a large crow came flying to them from the east. At first, Aurora dismissed the bird. But, when Veolindra stopped their advance and the crow landed before them, Aurora knew this was no regular crow. The bird grew to the height of an

elf and changed into one before her eyes. The trans-
formation was not completed however, and what stood
before them was a strange, feathered cross between
elf and crow. The dark elf's eyes remained the endless black of the crow, and where his nose and mouth
would have been, a strange combination of beak and
flesh remained.

"My Lord," he bowed before Veolindra. He did not
acknowledge Aurora whatsoever.

"Report!" Veolindra.

"A regiment of Uthen-Arden soldiers comes from the
east; they will arrive within the hour."

Veolindra looked out over the wide expanse that was
the beginnings of the Thendor Plains. "How many?"
she asked.

"Nearly five hundred," said the scout.

"Very well," said Veolindra. "See they are left unhindered. They shall add nicely to our undead human
ranks.

"Yes, my Lord," the dark elf bowed once more. He
leapt into the air and, with a flurry of feathers, turned
once more into a large crow.

"Zander, send the Shierdon ranks just over the
ridge to the east," said Veolindra. "Notify me when the
humans are through killing each other."

"As you wish," he responded, and rode off to carry
out her orders.

Veolindra offered Aurora a wide, mischievous smile. "The time for war draws near. Ready your barbarians to strike at the heart of the pass."

"Yes, my Lord," said Aurora with a grin to match.

They flew all night across the wide expanse of the Ky'Dren Pass. Dirk had dismissed Krentz to the spirit world during the night while General Reeves slept, tilted in his saddle. He did so as quietly as possible, aware the seasoned general would wake at the slightest disturbance. When asked about her absence, Dirk would attribute it to the elves' mysterious magic.

They glided over the mountains unseen, Silverwind taking on the color of the night sky above. Lookout towers loomed on both sides of the Pass, and the Pass itself was flooded with dwarves in gleaming armor. By morning, they had reached the eastern mouth of the Pass, and Reeves had awakened, stiff from sleeping sitting up. He had accepted Dirk's vague explanation of Krentz's absence however, more interested in breakfast than the comings and goings of elves.

When they crested the peak of Bharak Mountain and the pass could be seen, Dirk and Reeves realized the dwarves' peril. Camped beyond the mouth of the Pass was an army of Draggard, barbarians, and human soldiers. Dirk recognized the banners of both

Uthen-Arden, and Shierdon. He circled the mouth of the Pass and set down upon a high ridge overlooking it. From there they would be able to watch unseen.

"Uthen-Arden and Shierdon are in league with the Draggard! This is an outrage!" Reeves fumed in a hushed whisper as he peered over the ledge beside Dirk.

"Those soldiers are not quite themselves," said Dirk as he spied the armies through his spyglass. He handed it to General Reeves and showed him how to focus the instrument. Dirk's spyglass was of elven make, and quite unlike human or dwarven counterparts. Reeves' eyes widened as he saw the soldiers miles away as clearly as if he were standing among them.

"What in the name of the gods is wrong with them? Their eyes...they glow with a green light," said Reeves, taken aback.

"Turn the end ring to the left for a wider view. There, on the black horse, do you see him?" asked Dirk.

"The dark elf?"

"Yes, he will have on his person some sort of staff, or necklace, or glowing green gem," said Dirk.

"A ring, yes, glowing like the eyes of the human soldiers," Reeves reported.

"That, my friend, is a dark elf lich lord."

"Lich?" Reeves asked, taking his eye from the spyglass to regard Dirk curiously.

"Lich...necromancer...they have many names. They raise the corpses of the dead to do their bidding," said Dirk.

Reeves was disgusted, he went back to his spying and scanned the armies below. "So any who fall to the creatures…"

"Are raised once again to fight their brethren," Dirk finished for him.

"Such blasphemy. Is there no limit to the dark elves' evil?"

"It seems not," Dirk replied. "May I?"

Reeves handed him back the spyglass, and Dirk took in a wide view of the vast army at the mountain's doorstep. He guessed the combined armies to number in the tens of thousands. The undead made up the majority, but there were enough Draggard and barbarians alone to create a serious threat to the dwarves. Dirk's slow scanning stopped abruptly, and an exclamation escaped his lips. A few miles east of the Ky'Dren Pass, Aurora Snowfell stood before the vast barbarian army. She looked to be giving a speech, for every now and again, the barbarians would raise their weapons to the sky.

"Well, I'll be damned," Dirk mumbled to himself, amused. "Seems as though she has chosen."

"What's that?" Reeves asked.

"The barbarian leader, her name is Aurora Snowfell. She infiltrated and betrayed our group," Dirk lied.

"Your group?"

"Yes, when Whill of Agora fought in the Del'Oradon Arena. Aurora and I fought beside him, and escaped as well. She is a powerful warrior and, no doubt, made stronger now by the dark elves."

To their right, the dwarves had begun to pour out of the Southern Ky'Dren Mountains, filling the Pass. Huge catapults and war machines went with them, and those machines set about the cliffs along the pass were loaded and cocked back. The usually open Pass had been barricaded the entire length of its mouth by boulders and smaller stones, to help hinder the enemy's advancement. A steady stream of dwarves–looking to Dirk like worker ants from his vantage point–added boulders to the piles. Dirk spied a few dwarves raising giant slabs with nothing more than a wave of the hand; likely, they were Roakore's kin, and like he, were able to control stone with their minds.

"The dwarves won't have a chance against this army," said Reeves, still surveying the armies.

"They have the benefit of the bottlenecking Pass. The dwarves could hold out indefinitely against the barbarians, even the Draggard. However, many dark elves and undead are among them."

Reeves put down the spyglass to regard Dirk to his left. "Those who fall to this army, they will be raised by the dark elf lich lords?"

Dirk nodded in the affirmative. Reeves shook his head in disgust and went back to his spying. Dirk retreated to where Fyrfrost sat farther back on the ledge, her feathers had taken on the color of the surrounding stone, and had Dirk not known what to look for he wouldn't have seen her. He went to the opposite side of her and pulled the trinket from his pocket.

"Krentz, come to me," he whispered. She came in a swirl of mist and took form before him.

"We have reached the eastern mouth of the Pass," he said to her and motioned to the vast dark elf army before them.

Raene followed her father's warriors at a far enough distance as to not be seen by the rear scouts. She had been ordered to return to one of the secure cities and help the womenfolk; she had no intention of doing any such thing. She didn't like disobeying her father and king, but she was a warrior whether he would admit so or not, and, right now, Ky'Dren needed as many as it could muster. She followed her kin steadily south through secret tunnels that would lead them to the eastern mouth of the Pass. After many hours of constant marching, they stopped, and remained waiting for a long time; they had arrived. She would wait until the army began their charge, and she would follow them into battle. She had tucked her braids beneath her helmet and brought them around across her face to look like a beard. She hoped she would go unseen.

Ky'Ell moved to the front line and peered through the murder hole at the eastern mouth of the Ky'Dren Pass; what he saw took his breath away. Outside, his dwarves had begun to barricade the mouth of the pass, and beyond them loomed the dark elf army.

"What do you see, me King?" asked Dwellan at his side.

"We be under attack from the east: Draggard, human soldiers, and barbarians," spat Ky'Ell. "Prepare to charge on me mark. I go to speak to me generals. Keep the army hidden until me mark, we can be usin' the element o' surprise."

"Yes, me King," said Dwellan as he slammed his fist to his chest.

CHAPTER THIRTY

Captives

The guard tossed Roakore into the cell, and he slammed against the far wall with a thud. Staggering to his feet, he glared at the two dark elf guards through bruised and bloody eyes.

"That all ye got, ye sons o' bi-"

One of the guards hit Roakore with a blast of energy, pinning him to the wall. With a wave of his hand he shackled the dwarf king to the wall with red, glowing chains. Roakore hung from his chains with his head down, and blood dripping from the tip of his nose.

Avriel struggled helplessly against her shackles as the two guards beat Roakore, fighting against her chains desperately, screaming curses at the dark elves. One of them moved to stand before her, his long, thin fingers tracing the curve of her chin down to her chest. He squeezed her violently and grinned. "Wait your turn," he sneered, and licked her from neck to chin.

"Enough, Leowren," said Eadon from the door. "Leave us."

Leowren gave Avriel a final once-over, lingering long upon her supple form. He offered her a lewd wink and left with the other guard.

Eadon walked from the door to stand before Roakore. He lifted the dwarf's chin, inspecting his facial wounds. Roakore was unconscious, but he still grumbled obscenities and curses.

"A tough lot they are, wouldn't you agree?" Eadon asked Avriel.

"Why do you torture him so? You could read his mind to gain the answers you seek," yelled Avriel.

Eadon regarded her as if perplexed. "But what would be the fun in that?"

She did not honor the question with a reply. Eadon stalked toward her, his hands clasped behind his back, the ends of his dragon hide cloak shimmering at his heels, and his eyes locked upon hers. He reached a hand out and grabbed her by the hair. She tried to turn away from his gaze but could not.

"This will only hurt if you let it," he whispered into her ear like a lover, all the while boring into her with his gaze.

Avriel let out a cry of anguish as Eadon forced himself into her mind, into every memory since she had escaped him. Avriel fled from him, but could find no corner of her mind he did not occupy.

From the other side of the cell, the Watcher watched through Tarren's eyes. He refused to look at Avriel, lest she see some difference in Tarren, a difference that Eadon would perceive instantly through his link to her mind. The Watcher turned away, and his faith in non-violence was tested as it had not been in centuries.

Eadon flew through Avriel's memories and witnessed all that had occurred since she escaped him. In the first, she possessed the magnificent white dragon Zorriaz. He watched the escape from the gladiator arena in Del'Oradon, and their flight from the city. Then they landed, and Zhola the Red told them all to leave him and Whill. Avriel and the dragon were swimming now, hunting the deep waters off the shore. Eadon moved forward and saw Drakkar Island before them, he witnessed the battle between Roakore and the dragons and instantly gained newfound respect for the warrior. He was a master of only one element, but how he wielded it. Into the volcano they went, and through the rift. Now, they were in Drindellia, searching the ruins of a library. Flying once again, flying for days. A large mountain loomed before them, Kellallea's mountain. They fly down into its depths, and there, beside a river of clearest water, was the ancient one.

Eadon watched the entire encounter play out, and he studied his greatest enemy, one who had gained power to match his own, but had yet to move against him in this, the new age.

Whill flew over the coastal city of Turrell, a city within his kingdom he had only traveled to once, when he was fifteen. Turrell sat nestled in the shadow of the Southern Ky'Dren Mountains, and enjoyed booming trade with the Ky'Dren dwarves. Thus, Turrel was a rich and decorated city, known not only for its dwarven wares, but its decadent culture as well. It was a known stomping ground for pirates, who had their grubby fingers in every business, and roots in the city's history as well.

From his vantage point among the clouds, the Ky'Dren Mountains could be seen. Soon he would arrive at the Pass, and he would learn if the rumors of his kin's death were true. He knew in his heart it was, but he had other reasons for going. He was stalling. Eadon had given him seven days, and four remained. He had the elven sword of power at his hip, but he was afraid, as afraid as he had been in his life. He was not afraid for himself—he had come to terms with the idea that he would likely not make it out of all of this alive—rather, he feared for the fate of Agora and its people. He feared for the dwarves, elves, and humans. If he failed, if he was unable to defeat Eadon, the dark elf would become a dark god, and those that survived the final battle would wish that they had not.

But how could he win? He had never really thought he could. When the elves had told him who he was and what he was supposed to do, he had thought them mad, and he still did.

Whill felt quite alone then as he flew through the air with the combined effort of his will and the power of Adromida. Avriel and Roakore had been taken because of him, Tarren was trapped in the body of the Watcher, and all of his mother's relations had been slaughtered. All because of him. Whill was a death sentence to his family and his friends. He had once toyed with the idea that legend followed him, but now he knew the truth of it: death followed him everywhere he went, and those that called him friend became targets of his enemies. It was for that very reason he traveled alone now, and it was the reason he would face Eadon alone.

CHAPTER THIRTY-ONE
We Go to War

The last of the Uthen-Arden soldiers fell to the swords of their undead brethren. Veolindra strode to a battlefield littered with bodies and began the ritual that would raise them from the dead. Her arms shot toward the heavens, and her booming voice chanted in a sort of ritual song. High above, storm clouds began to churn violently, small flashes of lightning from deep within the clouds illuminated the battlefield and sent fleeting shadows darting across the corpses. Aurora imagined those shadows to be the souls of the departed, frantically trying to ascend to the heavens, but trapped by the lich lord's powerful spell. Veolindra's voice rose high as her spell gained power, and the storm churned faster with her every word. With one last bellowed phrase, Veolindra brought her arms down, and with them came crackling, green lightning that struck the dead where they lay.

The bodies of the Uthen-Arden soldiers rose slowly. Their eyes became dim green lights floating inside hollowed sockets. The lightning had left the battlefield smoldering with the smoke of burnt flesh and hair. The green lanterns within the undead skulls caused the smoke to glow like a green fog, and, from the fog, the new army marched to fall in line with their undead brethren.

Veolindra returned to Aurora and Zander with twenty undead limping, shuffling, and dragging their battered bodies behind her. Aurora's heart pounded in her chest; she was left speechless by the lich lord's incredible display of power. What a curse she was to her enemies, who were not free of her far-reaching power even in death.

"These shall be your personal guards," Veolindra told her, as she gestured to the undead soldiers. "With the Ring of the Dead, you will control them easily. You remember what I have taught you?"

"Yes," said Aurora. "Through the ring, my thoughts become their commands."

"Are you ready to command such a large group?" Veolindra asked.

"I am."

The lich lord nodded her approval and set her sight upon the Ky'Dren Pass. The stone wall stood nearly ten feet high, and large catapults had been set about the sides of the entrance.

"Send the dwargon to destroy their pathetic wall," Veolindra ordered Zander.

"Yes, my lord," he said with a malicious grin and closed his eyes for a moment. Aurora knew he was mentally relaying the orders to the dark elf handlers who controlled the hordes of dwargon, Draggard, and draquon.

"Are your barbarians ready?" Veolindra asked Aurora.

"They are."

"Good." Veolindra smiled as the dwargon began their charge. "I will send the Draggard up the sides of the mountain to descend upon the inner ranks of the dwarves. Another horde waits just within the northern range."

"They have come through a rift within the mountain?" Aurora asked.

"Yes, they will attack the eastern and western mouths of the Pass. The draquon will infiltrate the Pass as well. Go now to your people. You shall come in behind the undead. Leave none alive in your wake."

"Yes, my lord," said Aurora with a grin.

From the high ledge of the northern mountain, high above the Ky'Dren Pass, Dirk, Krentz, and General Reeves watched as the undead humans slaughtered the Uthen-Arden army. Though there were no Eldalonian soldiers among them, General Reeves nonetheless seethed with brimming anger at witnessing the slaughter.

"How does one defeat such wicked magic...such unrestrained evil?" Reeves asked.

"When you have found the answer to that question, you have won a war," Krentz replied.

They moved away from the ledge and prepared for battle, and, though Dirk urged Reeves to remain upon the ledge, the general would hear none of it.

"This is not a place for valor, my good man," Dirk explained. "This enemy has power beyond any human."

"Then, help to even the odds," Reeves argued, his glance moving to Krentz.

Krentz smiled at the brave general. "We've no time to teach you the finer points of magical weapon wielding, but I can strengthen your armor and weapons. Lay down your arms and stand aside."

Reeves unsheathed his sword and dagger, and laid them upon the stone next to his shield. Krentz first took up the sword and held it before her with closed eyes. She chanted words in Elvish and set the sword to glowing red until it finally burst into flames. Laying it down, she took up his dagger and similarly enchanted it as well, followed by his shield. When she was done with the weapons, she stood before Reeves and laid a hand upon his plate armor. A humming vibrated through the armor, and a strange, tingling sensation resonated throughout his entire body.

"Done," said Krentz, taking back her hand. Reeves felt as if he had been struck by lightning. "Your armor will protect you from heavy blows and some spells, but I suggest you steer clear of dark elves. Your blades have been imbued with fire and will pierce through armor and scale as if through cloth. And your shield shall absorb the most powerful of strikes."

Reeves fell to one knee, shaking with the energy within him. "Thank you, m'lady."

Krentz only nodded.

"Chief, come!" said Dirk as he held out the figurine. "We go to war."

Ky'Ell ventured to a door in one of the tunnels leading to the Ky'Dren Pass. He pushed, but found it stuck, a greater shove proved the door had been barricaded on the other side. Ky'Ell summoned his strength and blasted the door open spilling the sun's gloomy light into the tunnel.

"Northern Wall breach!" he heard a cry of alarm ring out.

He stepped out and squinted into the sunlight. "It is I, King Ky'Ell! Hold your fire!" he bade the dwarves. Upon seeing their king, all nearby dwarves slammed their fists to their chests and bowed low.

"I would speak to the nearest general!" he bellowed, and more than one dwarf went running off with a quick "Aye, sire!"

Soon, the dwarven general, Dar'Kwar, came rushing to stand before his King. "Me King," he said with a slam and a bow.

"Report," Ky'Ell ordered.

"The Southern Mountains be secure and sealed. We got five thousand warriors inside and along the Pass. The Eldalonian side be digging in, and they be reportin' a large advancement o' Draggard headin their way from inside Eldalon. Here at the eastern mouth be an army o' Draggard, barbarians, and human soldiers with some sort o' witchery about them."

Ky'Ell nodded as he contemplated the situation. "Two thousand warriors await me orders in the northern chambers. Have the Draggard come through from the north yet?"

"Nay, me King, we sealed off the northern mountains when the beasts began slaughterin' our search parties. We'd cleared the way for twenty miles north, but were overwhelmed by the beasts. Then, this army arrived at the foot o' the mountain from the north, and we ordered all arms to the Pass."

"Very well," said the King.

Ky'Ell surveyed the mouth of the Pass; too many dwarves were out in the open. He had seen what the dark elf spells did to an army packed too tightly.

"Order half of the dwarves back into the southern mountain chambers. This ain't gonna be no straight on fight. These be dark elves. The mountain doors be the first priority," said the king. "The Draggard that came through the rift in the northern mountains be coming out soon, I be bettin'. See it ain't no surprise attack. I want all soldiers against the southern side o' the Pass, and the catapults aimin' north. When the beasts come out, let it rain stone."

A dwarven horn blared a warning, and a dull rumbling shook the ground. Ky'Ell and Dar'Kwar looked to the east. The hulking dwargon charged with the Draggard close behind. The battle for the Ky'Dren Pass had begun.

Raene felt the disturbance in the stone below her feet; a dull vibration told her of marching feet. The charge had begun. She waited patiently for the dwarves before her to charge out through the secret doors leading to the pass. She waited for what seemed like an eternity, though she knew only minutes had passed. The rumbling in the stone had become stronger, and, where once she thought the vibration to have come from many feet, she soon discerned that it came from large feet. Through the stone below her hand, they seemed like giants.

She was nervous and exhilarated…and afraid. She was loath to admit it; she had never heard a dwarven man say such a thing. Did they feel fear? Were men truly different from women in that regard? Were they really tougher? She knew what they would say. A woman's place was at home tendin' to children, cookin' and cleanin', sewin' and fixin'. A woman's place was doing what the men could not, as the men were doing what the women could not. She understood the harmony it lent dwarven society, and she understood many women–most women–thought the traditions true and good, but, for her, they were not. Raene longed to train with the men in the vast arenas and battle chambers, rather than in secret against the only one who knew the full extent of her secret, her twin brother Ky'Ro. If the gods had wanted her to be a cooker or a cleaner or a tender of children, then they would have made her better at it. That was her way of thinking. Where she failed at those tasks, she excelled in armed and unarmed combat. She had surpassed her brother years before, and was skilled in stone moving, just as good as her brothers, she thought. But her father would hear none of it. He had tolerated her armor, and her helping move the stone from the tunnel, but, beyond that, he was as stubborn as a child at bedtime.

From the chamber and tunnels ahead, the call for the charge rang out, and Raene perked. The moment had come.

After a time the rear of the dwarven lines began to move as the dwarves went running out the doors screaming battle cries as they charged. Raene took up the battle cry and dared join the ranks as the last of them charged through the doors to the Ky'Dren Pass.

When Raene came through the door, she was not prepared for what awaited her. The brightness of the silver clouds blinded her momentarily as she followed the sound of the shuffling dwarven feet in front of her. When her vision returned, she realized they were running into chaos. Draggard climbed the walls in droves, springing from the stone to land among the dwarven ranks. Their vicious claws, teeth, and tails sent blood spraying in their wake. Overhead, draquon circled and dove down into the battle, and while some did not come back up, others returned to the sky with a thrashing dwarf in its claws. The ground shook with the heavy footsteps of fifteen and twenty-foot dwargon, as they stomped, thrashed, and crushed dwarves and Draggard alike. Heavy clubs the size of trees sent dwarves flying and destroyed catapults with a single blow. Human soldiers unlike any Raene had ever seen attacked like rabid animals, disregarding wounds as if they felt no pain. She watched horrified and perplexed as one lost its arm to a dwarven axe and never flinched, but single-mindedly continued in its attack.

The group of dwarves she was following thinned and began to slow. She soon realized this was not a head-on clash. A Draggard leapt from the southern wall and landed upon the dwarf behind her. Raene reeled as the Draggard latched its maw on the dwarf's face. Blood flew from his head, yet the injured dwarf found the strength to reach up and snap the beasts head completely backward, raking his own face with sharp teeth in the process. Raene froze, and more beasts leapt from the walls to attack the dwarves. A dwargon came barreling along the southern wall, dragging and scraping a dwarf against the stone. Dwarves had climbed its back and embedded axe and hatchet into the thick skin. The dwargon was trying to shake them loose, but they stubbornly held on for the ride. A Draggard came rushing through the dwarven lines at Raene, its spear held high and its bloody grin mocking. The spear went gliding toward her stomach, and Raene knew then she would die if she did not act. She blocked the blow with her heavy shield and came across with the ball of her large, spiked mace. The mace imploded the Draggard's head, sending gore flying in her face. The beast dropped like stone and lay twitching upon the ground. The dwarf whose face was mangled by the leaping Draggard patted her on the shoulder as he passed.

"Good to see ye stop acting like a girl," he said, and stormed off, howling obscenities into the chaotic fracas.

Raene smeared the gore upon her face and reminded herself why she was here: she was a warrior, and, right now, Ky'Dren needed warriors.

Dirk surveyed the battlegrounds as the dwargon began their charge of the pass with legions of Draggard in tow. Dark elves rode atop the lumbering beasts, casting spells of destruction upon the hastily made wall. Beside him, General Mick Reeves shook with the rush of battle and the energy he had been gifted by Krentz.

The dwargon crashed through the stone wall, and the Draggard poured forth. A dwarven horn bellowed a deep report, and hundreds of wooded spikes shot up at an angle just inside the breached wall. The charging Draggard were impaled and hung bleeding where they had stood. A few dwargon were felled by the trap, but most brought their long legs up to crush their way through the field of spears as though they were crashing through thistles. Dark elf spells of fire and ice blazed forth, burning the wooden spines to ash or freezing them solid to soon shatter among the reverberations of the thumping dwargon feet. The dwarves stood in the path of the dwargon bravely, and Dirk winced as they were mowed down by the hulking monsters. No retreat sounded, no command to fall back. The dwarves held their ground, and they paid dearly for their bravery.

"I have seen enough, let us help where we can," said Krentz.

"You and Chief must stay clear of the lich lords," Dirk reminded her.

General Reeves turned to them and gave a small bow. "I shall see you when the battle is won," he said, shaking with energy as if the weather were frigid.

Without another word, he turned and began to sprint for the ledge. He ran the length, tracking a flying draquon, and leapt like a madman from the cliff. Dirk and

Krentz rushed to the edge as he landed upon the beast's back and drove his blade through its neck. The draquon went limp and faltered and began to fall. Reeves leapt from the crashing beast to land upon the back of a twenty-foot tall dwargon. With his enchanted sword aflame, he sunk it through the back of the beast's head to the hilt. The beast lurched and swatted at him drunkenly before falling on its face. Reeves rolled with the landing and charged on.

Dirk was given an idea by Reeves's incredible display. Krentz's enchantments had turned a good warrior into a great one, it reasoned the greatest good she could do in this fight was to lend such power to the mighty dwarves. And he knew it was the best way to keep her away from the lich lords.

"I have a plan!" he said as he recognized the one dwarf from Ky'Dren he knew: Dar'Kwar.

"Trust me?" he asked Krentz.

"Always," she purred.

Dirk and Krentz flew under the cover of Fyrfrost's camouflage. Chief flew after them as a faint mist. When they were over Dar'Kwar's location, he and Krentz leapt from Fyrfrost and landed just behind the dwarf, who at the moment was conferring with his king. Krentz surrounded her and Dirk in an energy shield as the dwarves inevitably attacked, thinking they were the enemy.

"Hold! We are not your enemy!" Dirk yelled with raised hands as hatchets and axes sparked and ricocheted off the energy shield.

"Dar'Kwar, you know me to be your ally!" he pleaded with the dwarf as Krentz held back the attacks.

"Hold!" Dar'Kwar bellowed, having shouldered the king behind him and his men.

"Do you know this man, and this…elf?" Ky'Ell asked.

"Aye," Dar'Kwar confirmed. "He be an ally."

In her spirit form, Krentz was able to mask her swirling, tell-tale tattoos. Otherwise they both knew no amount of talking would gain them audience. Chief solidified at Dirk's side and stood at attention defensively. The dwarves took a collective step back, and suspicious eyes glared from all sides.

"Dar'Kwar, we are here to help. The dark elves have the advantage of their magic, we would offer ours to even those odds," Dirk explained.

King Ky'Ell stepped forward past his general, and many dwarves took a step as well, ready to pounce at the first sign of trickery.

"I be the bloody King of Ky'Dren, you will address me about such matters," said Ky'Ell.

"Sire," Dirk replied as he slammed his fist to his chest.

Ky'Ell gave a nod of approval at Dirk's gesture. "What do you propose?" he asked, looking not to Dirk, but Krentz.

She stepped forward bravely with her chin raised high. "I can offer your soldiers strength beyond their wildest dreams, and help them to fight on when they have received mortal wounds."

"We ain't for needin' no help from elves in protectin' our own mountain pass," said Ky'Ell, and his dwarves inched closer to them.

"Sire, King Roakore finds no wrong in the races fighting together against a common enemy. It is no sign of weakness to accept such an offering, but a great show of wisdom. With such power at his disposal, I have seen Roakore pour molten lava down the throat of a dragon," Dirk dared to say.

Far in the distance the mouth of the pass was being overrun. Dwargon laid the dwarven ranks to waste, and destructive spells blasted the pass unchecked. The barbarians had joined in the attack, and the pass was being lost. Ky'Ell took another step forward and the bluster left his demeanor.

"I would not ask my dwarves to accept such magic, if I have not tested it meself, first."

"Me King!" Dar'Kwar protested. But a raised hand by his king silenced his argument.

"Show me," he said to Krentz.

Krentz nodded and reached out a hand. The dwarves visibly tensed, but none acted upon their screaming instincts. Ky'Ell looked to the hand warily and slowly reached out to press his against hers. Krentz closed her eyes in concentration and through their connection, a surge of energy pulsed. Ky'Ell was jolted stiff as he received the influx of power, and Dar'Kwar instinctively reached for him. He too shot rigid as the energy coursed through him as well. Krentz released them both and all eyes watched what might happen next.

King Ky'Ell shook with coursing power and frantically looked around for an outlet for his energy; a few feet away, a boulder half the size of a man sat upon the ground. With a wave of his shaking hands, he shooed the dwarves to move away. He reached out to the stone and it immediately shot into the air one hundred feet. With wide-eyed excitement, he hurled the boulder through the air hundreds of yards to crash into the advancing horde at the mouth of the Pass. He turned his gaze from the boulder to Krentz with wild eyed excitement.

"Prepare to charge!" he bellowed to his dwarves. "We accept your offering o' power, lady elf," he said, slamming his fist to his chest.

Krentz closed her eyes and outstretched her hands to the nearby dwarves. Her lips moved frantically in a silent spell. The dwarves gave a collective gasp as she turned to mist and began flying from one to the next and touching them all with her spell. The dwarves became electrified as she passed, and a great roar echoed from the fierce dwarves. The "Battle Song O' Ky'Dren" rose among the ranks, and they charged the invading hordes with renewed vigor.

CHAPTER THIRTY-TWO
Sea of Shields

Aurora and her barbarians stormed over the rubble of the dwarven wall and into the Ky'Dren Pass. The Draggard and undead soldiers pushed the dwarves back steadily, but began to slow as the pass became narrower and the armies pressed into the bottleneck. Along the southern wall of the pass, catapults fired steadily, sending boulders and large burning projectiles into the fray. The dwarves' large mounted dragonbows had been turned downward, and now rained long metal bolts into the ranks.

A dwarven horn blared in the distance, and dwarven warriors answered the cry as they began to pour forth from the northern wall. Aurora bellowed orders to the Chiefs of the Seven and the barbarians began a charge. Her barbarians hit the front line with great momentum, but the dwarves were a strong lot. Where the two armies clashed, the advances of both halted. The dwarves used their squat frames to an advantage against the hulking barbarians, coming in low and hacking at the legs of their enemies. The dwarves had devised many formations to fight their often bigger opponents. A shield wall met the barbarian charge, with each dwarf holding his shield over the dwarf before him. The heavy war hammers and axes of the barbarians crashed down upon the metal shields, but the dwarves pressed on. Utilizing their size and strength, they came up under the front line. Soon many of the barbarians found themselves lifted up on the sea of shields, like insects riding upon the backs of marching ants. They soon disappeared from sight, smothered by the dwarven ranks, and hacked to death by dozens of hatchets.

"Up and over!" Aurora ordered the Chiefs, and the command was relayed to the armies. She knew they could not stand toe-to-toe with the avalanche of dwarven shields. But, they could clamber over the shield wall and begin to break up the ranks from within. The command was a death sentence for any barbarians who complied, but they cared not.

A boulder flew from the northern wall, missing Aurora by only inches. Beside her, Orthan Skyflame of Hawk Tribe was not so fortunate. The boulder crushed him and his mount and rolled away, leaving them both broken and bloody. Aurora stood upon her mount and scanned the dwarven ranks. She found no catapult, and guessed another dwarf with powers akin to Roakore must have hurled the stone. Another boulder came crashing through the barbarian ranks, felling many, and Aurora cursed the dwarf.

"Find the stone-mover and kill him!" she ordered Zander, as more boulders came flying from the wall.

"Yes, Chieftain Snowfell," said Zander.

Raene blocked the spear of a Draggard with her heavy shield and cracked its right knee with her long mace. The Draggard went down on top of its shattered leg, which had bent backward under the weight. Raene brought her heavy shield down hard, crushing its throat and snapping its neck.

She looked out upon the sea of shields the dwarves had created. The barbarians were being held at bay. All around the sea of shields, Draggard wreaked havoc. Raene turned her attention on those beasts who were leaping from the northern wall to land among the dwarven ranks. She formed a connection with her metal shield and, with a heave, sent it whirling through the air at the attackers. The shield hit one of the Draggard who had scaled the wall and turned to leap; it fell crumpled to the ground below. Raene mentally pulled the shield back and spun it faster as it made a wide circle. She guided the spinning shield to slam into and snap the lower back of another climbing Draggard. Again she struck, crushing the head of another.

Sudden movement in her peripheral vision alerted her to danger. She mentally called the shield to herself once more and turned on a charging Draggard. The shield whizzed past her helm on its descent and she guided it to skip off the ground and take the Draggard in the stomach. Together, Draggard and shield flew high into the sky and the screaming beast fell to its death. Raene called back the shield and continued her work to clear the wall.

"Raene! What in the name o' Ky'Dren ye doin' here!" asked her twin brother, Ky'Ro.

"What it be lookin' like I be doin'?" said Raene.

Ky'Ro ducked a spear slash and killed the wielder with a growl. "Pa be shytin' gold bars when he catches wind o' this!" he said. His voice contained more mirth than scorn.

"Just watch me back!" said Raene as she strained to maneuver the shield.

She slammed yet another Draggard against the stone, and at the same time, a dark elf spell from beyond the sea of shields slammed into the northern wall above her and her brother. The wall exploded, sending chunks of stone both large and small raining down upon the dwarves. Raene instinctively ducked and focused all of her energy above her. Jagged rocks and boulders fell from the hole in the wall and covered all nearby. Raene found herself straining under tons of fallen debris. With her power over stone, she created a kind of shield above and around her, but she could not hold it for long. Redoubling her efforts, she heaved the stone with everything she had. Sunlight blinded her within the hole that remained of the stone tomb, she climbed out coughing and looked around at the carnage. The small avalanche had not taken as many dwarves as she guessed.

"Gods damn them dark elves!" her brother cursed from behind her.

"Ky'Ro," she said with relief as she clambered down from the pile of stone.

Her brother did not hear her, too busy cursing the dark elves, the Draggard, the undead humans, and the barbarians. Covered in dust and dirt, his dented armor no longer shone in the sunlight. He kicked a rock and lifted a large slab. Beneath the stone, a dwarf lay dead. Most of the dwarves had leapt clear of the falling stone, but many had not made it. The sight of the fallen dwarf only infuriated her brother more. He reached out with his calloused hands and, with a cry of rage, sent the fallen stone hurtling hundreds of yards into the enemy ranks. It had taken Raene a lot of energy to both shield herself and push the fallen stones away from her, but she dug deep and joined her brother in the stone throwing.

All around them the battle raged. The brigade of dwarves under Ky'Ro's command circled the two and held the Draggard and undead at bay. The human undead were relentless, and where an ordinary man would not be able to withstand the crushing blows of the dwarves, the undead kept on coming. The only way to put them down was to sever the head; crushing it worked for only a few moments. They came on whether legless or armless; even with no legs, they clawed forward stubbornly and groped at the boots of the dwarves.

Raene growled with effort, heaving a stone half her size with her mind. She faltered and fell to her knees exhausted. Her brother, however, seemed tireless as he spewed curses and sent stones flying into the enemy ranks beyond the sea of shields.

Ky'Ro's last stone flew through the air, but began to slow and glow bright red. Stopping completely in mid-air, the stone shot back in their direction.

"Ky'Ro!" Raene yelled and brought her hands up to take control of the flying stone. Her brother did the same and together they forced the projectile to stop. Raene could feel the will of another pushing the stone against their efforts, likely a dark elf.

The stone exploded and sent thousands of small, red-hot pebbles flying in every direction. The concussion threw Raene and her brother back many feet. A black wisp of smoke parted the dust cloud of the destroyed stone, and solidified into a dark elf before Ky'Ro. A dwarf leapt at the dark elf's back with his war hammer cocked back in a powerful blow. The dark elf twirled in a quick circle as the dwarf descended, and he unsheathed his blade and struck three times before turning to face Ky'Ro once more. Behind him the dwarf fell to the ground in three pieces, his armor, skin, and bone having been cut through easily. Blood dripped from Zander's curved blade that he now pointed at the dwarven stone-weaver.

Ky'Ro shot his hands out forward, and dozens of stones heeded his will. He sent the stones flying through the air in a blur. Zander moved a hand in a wide circle, taking control of them from the exhausted dwarf easily. The stones twirled a circle away from Zander and sailed like leaves on the wind, slamming into Ky'Ro and dropping him to the ground. Raene gave a cry and charged Zander with her heavy shield leading the way. She slammed into the dark elf with all her might and stopped dead, as if she had hit a stone wall. Pain shot through her body as the dark elf easily sent her flying, end-over-end, to slam into the northern wall.

Raene slowly opened her heavy eyes and saw her fallen brother lying motionless upon the rubble. The dark elf was circling Ky'Ro. He looked down upon his victim with a pleasant grin on his face, as one might admire their own artwork.

"Ky'Ro," Raene tried to scream, but less than a whisper escaped her battered body.

The dark elf raised his blade and stabbed her brother through. Raene screamed in rage within, but her body could only respond in chaotic spasms, and blood-gurgling grunts. The dark elf retracted his blade and began a low chant. Raene could not hear the words as a translucent, shimmering energy shield enclosed them in silence, a shield upon which many dwarven weapons pounded in rage. Spell-light began to glow in the palms of the dark elf, and soon, large, green balls of pulsing energy swirled in the palms of the dark elf. He clapped his hands together and snaking green energy shot like lightning and hit the chest of her brother. To Raene's horror, Ky'Ro rose from the ground within the embrace of green, writhing tendrils. His eyes began to glow the same hellish light, and he stood on his feet once more. Ky'Ro's dead eyes looked to Zander, and waited, unmoving, as if awaiting orders.

Dirk and Chief protected Krentz from all sides, as she in turn extended her consciousness to connect with the dwarven army. When she sensed a wound, she found the victim and quickly set his body to healing. It was not intricate work, patchwork really, but it would do. If the dwarves won, there would be time for more personal treatment. She excelled as a healer in her youth and learned how to heal large groups. This was her largest by far, for she watched over nearly a hundred dwarves, and they took their share of injuries.

Dirk soon found himself idle. Krentz remained far from the main force as the dwarves held them back.

He whistled to Fyrfrost and left Krentz to her healing. A disturbance in the dust and smoke above told him Fyrfrost heard his call. When she swooped for him, he leapt into the air to be caught by unseen talons.

Fyrfrost lifted Dirk into the air and performed an aerial somersault throwing Dirk high into the air. He twirled like an acrobat as Fyrfrost leveled out below. Tucking his legs in and quickly kicking them out again he twirled, spun, and fell into Fyrfrost's saddle. Dirk howled triumphantly and gripped the saddle's horn.

"Let's find some trouble," he called to Fyrfrost.

They flew high over the Ky'Dren Pass, getting a good look at the battle below; the fight did not go well for the dwarves. The collective armies of the dark elves, Draggard, barbarians, and undead had driven the dwarves back nearly a mile into the pass. For the moment, a bottleneck in the pass held the dark hordes at bay. Farther back awaited another such bottleneck, this one with a large metal door. Dirk doubted the door would hold long against the dark elves.

Below, a collection of shields like the giant, metal shell of a turtle protected the dwarves. Over the dwarven shields, stones flew to land among the attacking Draggard. The stone-wielding dwarf reminded him of Roakore; he stood upon a pile of rubble surrounded by his dead kin. Big hands reached out into the air, and stones and boulders alike flew through the air killing many.

One of the dwarf's hurled boulders sailed past a decorated Barbarian women: Aurora Snowfell. She had indeed made her choice, Dirk realized. On a large horse, she watched the advancement of her barbarians. Beside her, on a steed of black, sat a dark elf lich lord with a staff of bones in her left hand. The stone-wielding dwarf had gotten their attention. The lich lord pointed, and the dark elf at her side leapt from his horse, turned to black smoke, and shot off toward the dwarf.

Looking back the many hundreds of yards into the pass, he determined that Krentz was still safely behind the dwarven line aiding the warriors in their attempt to hold the narrow expanse. He spurred Fyrfrost into a dive and flew toward the northern wall. The dark elf landed and was met by flying stones and boulders that he easily turned back on the dwarf. Another dwarf barreled in shield-first. The dark elf sent him flying into the northern wall. Fyrfrost brought Dirk directly over the elf and he leapt from the saddle.

Dirk landed as Zander dove to the side and came up in a defensive stance. The assassin was on the dark elf in a flash, striking with sword and dagger. Zander growled and summoned a spell to his right hand. Dirk dove to the left, avoiding the fireball, and hurled a dart at Zander's feet. The dart was one of Krentz's newest creations, made to absorb any nearby spell energy. A humming globe opened beside Zander as he backed from it cautiously. Dirk threw another dart, this one exploding near his head. With a cry of rage, Zander shot spells from each hand in rapid succession. They flew toward Dirk, but soon curved and surged into the globe of Dirk's enchanted dart.

A call went out nearby, "Ky'Ro has fallen!"

Dozens of enraged dwarves rushed toward Zander with weapons held high. Dirk attacked the dark elf, not wanting the dwarves to mistake his allegiance. A cry of alarm went up from the dwarves as they learned of Ky'Ro's fate. The fallen dwarf now stood before them, his eyes lit with the hellish green light. Zander deflected a slash from Dirk and twirled away. He shot a spell from his right hand that quickly turned and disappeared into the globe. Dirk pressed the attack, knowing the dark elf was frustrated and confused by the spell-absorbing energy globe. The globe would gain power with every spell, and soon pull the dark elf's energy shield into it as well.

"Kill them all!" Zander ordered the undead Ky'Ro.

The angry dwarves reached Zander and struck wildly, sparks exploded with every blow to Zander's back as the dark elf fended off Dirk's attacks as well. Zander leapt over Dirk when he found himself trapped, but the leap brought him too close to the energy globe. He landed and his energy shield was pulled into the globe. Dirk attacked mercilessly, his sword and dagger coming from all angles too quickly for Zander to block. The dwarves pressed the attack as Dirk scored a hit to Zander's face leaving a long slash from chin to ear. Zander called Ky'Ro to him, and the undead dwarf charged to his master's side. He had taken up a dead dwarf's mighty double-headed axe, and cleared a swath to his master, felling any dwarf in the way.

Zander rushed to Ky'Ro and quickly put the undead dwarf between himself and Dirk. Lich lord and undead slave fought back-to-back. Zander killed any dwarf that dared get too close, and Ky'Ro tried to chop Dirk in half with the big axe. The dwarves could not take it upon themselves to strike their fallen prince, but Dirk had no qualms about it. He dodged the lumbering strikes and stabbed the dwarf through the chest with both sword and dagger. The blows had no effect on him and Dirk quickly rolled to the side to avoid the swing of the axe. Again the axe came and Dirk leapt into the air flipping twice to land ten feet away. A Draggard jumped from the northern wall and Dirk swatted the leading spear to the side and struck twice, leaving the Draggard to land legless. He threw an explosive dart at the dwarf that hit him in the shoulder and exploded. Through the smoke of the blast, Ky'Ro came on still. His right arm and shoulder were gone, yet he came on.

Raene was left to watch helplessly as the man in black fought off the dark elf who killed her brother. Ky'Ro rose from the dead and turned his blade against his kin. The man in black possessed a magic about him, it was in his armor and blades, and in his darts. Frustrated with her inability to move, she was yet entranced by the man's attack. He opened a globe of energy that seemed to pull the dark elf's spells to it, and eventually stripped him of his energy shield. Ky'Ro came to the dark elf's side just as the man in black was about to deal the final blow.

Beside Raene sat a large shard of stone. Her body was broken and useless, and though pain wracked her mind, she fought for the clarity that would help her to focus. Determination set her mind aflame, determination to inflict any damage she could to the murderous dark elf. The shard beside her began to vibrate and teeter as Raene focused her will upon it. Through the pain and tears, she took hold of the shard of stone with her mind and floated it just above the ground. She gathered what strength she had left and waited for the moment.

An explosion shook the earth, and dozens of dwarves and shields flew through the air, mangled and broken. Another blast sounded, sweeping more dwarves aside. The ground rumbled as the barbarians and undead charged the broken line.

Dirk ducked an axe and managed to throw a dart at Zander past the one-armed dwarf. The lich lord twirled away from a dwarven war hammer and swatted the dart away into the dwarven ranks. A surge of human undead hit the dwarves and chaos ensued along the northern wall of the Ky'Dren Pass.

Zander chopped down a mace-wielding dwarf and turned to strike another. Behind him came the cry of Raene, and he turned her way as a shard of jagged stone flew into his chest. The dark elf staggered back and gripped the shard with one hand whilst parrying the blow of a dwarven axe. With a cry of pain Zander pulled the shard from his chest and broke it over the head of a dwarf.

Aurora charged through the sea of shields with twenty undead soldiers leading the way. Something forced her to disregard Veolindra's advice to stay back: Dirk Blackthorn. He stood on a pile of rubble battling an undead dwarf. A strange glowing globe tethered to the dark elf Zander as he frantically fought off the dwarven attack.

Aurora's undead guards cut a swath through the dwarves as more explosions sounded behind her. The dark elves began peppering the sea of shields with fireballs, and the dwarven line faltered. Chaos ruled the Ky'Dren Pass as the dwarves fought frantically to hold the enemy at bay.

Along each wall, similar battles played out, as the Draggard and dark elves attacked the dwarven towers and balconies from which dwarven harpoons, spears, and metal bolts rained down upon the enemy ranks. The dwarves fought bravely, but the overwhelming numbers and the spells of the dark elves proved too much. The Ky'Dren Pass would be lost in short time. Already, thousands of dwarves had poured into the Pass from the southern wall, and a steady stream of warriors poured still. But the dark elves began to concentrate their spells on the dwarven tunnels and doorways into the mountain. Fireballs blasted chunks of stone from on high to rain down the side of the wall, closing off many of the passages. Water too was used by the dark elves. They summoned it from their surroundings and forced it to creep into the cracks and crevices along the wall. The water was then frozen solid, splitting the stone and causing deadly avalanches. Worse yet for the dwarves was the raising of their fallen kin. Dark elf lich lords walked the smoldering battlefield, which glowed green in the dreary sunlight. Their ragged cloaks blew in the hot wind of the ravaged land, and, everywhere they went, the dead rose behind them, Draggard, barbarian, and dwarf alike.

Aurora spurred her mount and undead on faster and was soon plowing through the dwarven ranks like a tidal wave. A lone dwarf recklessly leapt to block her path and planted his heavy axe into the chest of her horse. Her mount lurched forward and threw her through the air, but Aurora was ready, she used the momentum to her advantage. She leapt high and came down with the Dragonlance of Ashai upon the head of a dwarf. Leaving him bleeding on the stone, she hurried on to Zander's aid.

Krentz redoubled her efforts as the dwarves–led by King Ky'Ell–pushed the Draggard back from the bottleneck. Dwarves rushed from the southern wall and joined their king in the charge. Krentz became hard pressed to cover them all and refocused her efforts on the king and the front line. She flew as a wisp around the battlefield, making sure to steer clear of the dark elf necromancers. She had sent Chief to aid Dirk, seeing that he had engaged a dark elf. Ever confident he could hold his own, she still felt better knowing Chief had his back. She had seen the barbarian woman take notice of him as well. She saw too that Chief was almost to them. The spirit-wolf glided as glowing mist over the battlefield, his sights set on the charging barbarian.

Dirk cut through the leg of the undead dwarf and severed his head. Three undead soldiers rushed at him as the dwarf fell to the ground. Dirk withdrew a dart and hit the center soldier in the chest. The three undead exploded in a shower of blood and gore, and through the fine mist and smoke of the explosion, Aurora

Snowfell charged. She thrust forth her long dragon-lance, which Dirk prepared to deflect, but before the weapons met Chief slammed into Aurora from the side, and the two went tumbling over the pile of fallen rock.

Zander turned from the dwarves as the undead soldiers and barbarians crashed into the scattered dwarven ranks. He charged Dirk, heedless of the energy globe that absorbed his energy shield. The spell couldn't reach him now. Dirk sprinted to meet the charge, but came to an abrupt stop as a shadow moved across the sun. Zander noticed it as well, but too late. A giant slab of stone soared through the air and crushed him. Dirk followed the direction the slab came and found King Ky'Ell and his dwarves charging toward him.

"All dwarves to me!" the king bellowed, his voice no doubt lent strength from Krentz.

Dirk leapt over the stone pile Chief and Aurora had disappeared behind, and came face-to-face with the barbarian Chieftain as she climbed to meet him. Dirk ducked low as Aurora's dragonlance sailed over his head. Beyond her, he saw Chief in the clutches of a dark elf necromancer.

CHAPTER
THIRTY-THREE

Deeds of Legend

Whill flew over white peaks, approaching the Ky'Dren Pass from the south. He pulled back the power of Adromida and slowed as he approached. With mind sight, he peered through the stone of the mountain to the living creatures within, and observed thousands of dwarves deep inside. The army was steadily filing north to the Pass. Whill came to land upon a ridge overlooking the pass, and what he witnessed infuriated him.

A grand battle took place below him. The banners of Shierdon and Uthen-Arden flapped violently in the spell winds. Even from the height of the ridge, he sensed something not right about the human soldiers. With his mind sight, he peered into them, but did not find the usual glow of life-force, but, rather, a dull-green, pulsing light. Green tendrils of energy tethered them to their masters, the dark elves. The undead soldiers numbered in the thousands. They, along with the hordes of Draggard and barbarians, had taken the eastern mouth of the pass and drove the dwarves back with spells of fire and ice.

Whill leapt from his perch and descended toward the line of skirmish casting fireballs in every direction. The spells engulfed the circling draquon, sending them flailing and screeching to the stone below. He landed like a lightning bolt atop a group of Draggard just inside the enemy line. His energy shield crushed them into the earth, and the shockwave that followed his landing knocked down any within a hundred yard radius. Adromida glowed at his command, radiating like the sun itself there in the pass. Silence followed his arrival as everyone in view became blinded by the glow. Confident that he had gained everyone's attention, he let the sword's sheen lessen until it was tolerable, yet still brilliant.

He turned to face the Draggard, dark elf, barbarian, and undead armies. No bodies remained on the ground in the dark elf army's wake, for they had all been raised from the dead, and now stood before him. A shrill voice bellowed out in a foreign form of Elvish. The undead and Draggard responded by rushing Whill. Dozens of spears sailed toward him, along with arrows and streaking spells from the dark elves. Adromida's power coursed through him as he brought up his left hand. A web of energy formed before him that trapped the spears and spells. Whill chanted a spell learned from one of the Elven Tomes, a spell that would send back the projectiles to their wielders. A small shockwave rippled through the air before him, and the missiles floating in place turned and shot back toward their owners. The spells erupted in explosions, and the spears and arrows found their marks.

Inside his pulsing energy shield, Whill conjured a fire spell. He held the form of the spell in his mind and forced ever greater amounts of Adromida's vast power into it. Soon, a storm of fire formed above his head. Like storm clouds of flame, spewing lightning and licking fire, the spell grew above him in a vortex, reaching high above the Pass walls. Whill unleashed the spell of whirlwind fire and lightning upon his enemies.

"Veorack un arrek var talthous!" Whill bellowed, his voice shaking the earth below him.

The cyclone of fire and lightning grew nearly as wide as the Pass, and rolled over the attacking army, cutting a swath through the center all the way to the mouth. When the flame and lightning receded in a rumbling of thunder, thousands of charred and smoldering Draggard, human undead, and barbarians littered the ground.

"Charge!" the dwarven cry rang out in many voices.

The dwarven army split off on both sides of Whill like a parting river, and crashed into the armies that remained along the southern and northern walls.

Dirk ducked below the dragonlance and leapt into a backflip as the tip came flying past once more. Aurora wielded the lance with great agility and strength, but Dirk was faster. Undead climbed the pile of rubble and reached for him with milky green eyes. He held his ground, easily felling the slow abominations as Aurora stalked toward him with hate-filled eyes. Dirk threw two darts in her direction that she batted away with the tip of the lance. The darts exploded on contact and bathed her in flame. Aurora kept coming, unhurt by the explosion. A shimmering energy shield surrounded her, the work of a dark elf.

All around them, the dwarves clashed with the invaders. One hulking dwargon stomped past, and Dirk leapt to the side to avoid the giant's feet. On the dwargon's back rode a dozen dwarves, chopping and hacking away at its scaled flesh as they took it down.

Aurora swatted dwarves away with the long lance as they rushed her, and Dirk took the opportunity to scale the pile of rubble. At the top, Chief was frantically trying to attack the dark elf woman assaulting him with a spell of the same green light burning in the eyes of the undead. He threw four consecutive darts at the necromancer, two of which exploded against her energy shield. Each of the other two landed on either side of her and pulsed to life. Two globes flashed and instantly began to leach the green spell from the dark elf. She turned from Chief, infuriated, and blasted the globes with spells of fire and lightning. Her assault had no effect, however, and her energy was absorbed.

Dirk leapt from the rubble as Aurora's lance shattered the stone he had been standing upon. He pulled the timber wolf figurine from his pocket as he went, and summoned Chief. The infuriated dark elf abandoned her spell attacks fueling Dirk's energy globes, and rushed him with two curved blades held out wide. Aurora leapt at him from behind with her lance pulled back to skewer him. Chief floated past the dark elf in a flash of light and returned to the figurine. Dirk landed and blocked the two blades of the dark elf as they came in from on high, and then twisted under the blows and behind his assailant as Aurora came down on him. She pulled her lance up short so as not to hit the dark elf, and Dirk found himself facing them both. Dirk frantically parried the dark elf's two swords and Aurora's long lance as he backpedaled closer to his energy globes. When he was between the pulsing globes, he bellowed the command Krentz had taught him. The absorbed energy from the globes lashed out and hit Dirk in the chest where, long ago, a gem had been embedded to store energy. Dirk stopped in his retreat and suddenly rushed his assailants. He leapt into the air over the lance as it stabbed for his chest. In a blur of movement aided by the energy from the globes, he slapped aside the dark elf's swords and landed a heavy boot to her chest. Aurora spun a tight circle, bringing the lance around to slice Dirk in half; he brought up his sword and dagger in a successful cross block. The force of the blow sent him flying backward into a horde of undead. Aurora charged once more, as he hacked and slashed his way toward her.

Breaking free of the reaching hands and blades of the undead, he charged to face Aurora and the dark elf once more. An explosion behind him leveled the nearby armies, sending dwarves, undead, Draggard, and barbarians alike flying to the ground. Dirk found himself high upon the pile of rubble where the conflict had begun. Searching for the source of the disturbance, he found Whill standing inside a shallow crater. Sudden, blinding light shone from the ancient elven blade in his grip, and everyone was forced to turn their heads from the brilliance. The light finally lessened, and the dark elf Dirk had been fighting bellowed a command to her armies. The nearby enemies charged Whill, but their attack proved short lived. He let loose a spell of fire and lightning, engulfing the dark elf armies in flame.

Dirk's attention was drawn to the dwarven woman he had saved from the dark elf. As the fire and lightning cascaded out through the Pass, he leapt with flames licking his heels and landed on top of her covering them both with his enchanted cloak. When the rumbling died down, he dared a glance beyond the cover of his cloak. All around them was smoldering waste. Aurora and the dark elf had disappeared. There was not much to be seen as the smoke and flames blocked visibility beyond ten feet. Dirk brought his hood over his eyes and gazed upon the carnage Whill had wrought.

The dwarves took the opportunity to charge the scattered enemy ranks, and Dirk summoned Krentz to him through the power of the timber wolf figurine. She came to him in an instant in the form of smoke and soon stood at his side.

"Can you help her?" he asked Krentz, indicating the broken female dwarf.

Krentz bent to Raene and laid a hand on her forehead. "She is a tough one," said Krentz as she smiled down upon the dwarf woman, who gasped for her final breaths like a fish out of water. Her vacant eyes shimmered with tears as they stared at her fallen twin brother.

Blue tendrils of healing energy engulfed Raene, and she sucked in a greedy breath as her body was healed.

"Raene!" cried a dwarf. Turning to the sound, Dirk discovered King Ky'Ell. The old dwarf ran to her as Dirk moved to intercept him.

"Outta me way lad!" Ky'Ell warned.

"Please, Krentz is healing her. Let her do her work," said Dirk.

The dwarves filed past them after the retreating armies. Their war songs filled the pass with deep, booming voices.

"What happened?" Ky'Ell asked, shrugging off from Dirk's grip, but not pressing ahead.

"It was a dark elf," said Dirk.

"Me King!" yelled Dar'Kwar expectantly. The dwarven forces pushed back the invaders with Whill of Agora leading the way. The king was needed.

"See she stays put," he commanded Dirk and turned on his heel with one last lingering gaze upon his injured daughter.

Ky'Ell finally turned, mounted a large, armored mountain goat, and rode toward the mouth of the Pass.

The retreating armies fled from Whill's awful power. The dark elves fought back against him, but Dirk doubted they stood a chance. Gazing out over the smoldering battlefield, Dirk found no sign of the dark elf woman who had attacked Chief, or Aurora. But, he knew they were out there somewhere, and he intended to find them.

Aurora lay upon the smoldering ground in more pain than she had known in her life. Her body would not respond to her mental commands; she could not move. Her skin was charred a dark, blistering red. When Whill released the spell of fire and lightning, she was engulfed in flames and stabbed by the crackling blades of light. The lightning burned a hole in her side, and though it had been cauterized by the heat of the blast, it was deep and long.

She wondered why Eadon had failed her, why his power had forsaken her in her time of need. As she lay dying, she saw the lich, Azzeal, come to her then. He reached down and took her burnt and bloody body in his arms.

"Eadon has not forsaken you, Lady of the North," the undead elf whispered in her ear. "You shall never be free of his gift."

Aurora was carried away from the smoldering battlefield by Azzeal. She watched with heavily blinking eyes as her barbarians were engulfed in flame and the incredible spells that flew from Whill. She shed a single tear as she was whisked away. Regret filled her heart as she took in her last breath. The hot winds of destruction blew from the mountain pass, melting snow and ice. All around Aurora, the rhythm of the dripping world played like drums of war in her mind. The air, though smoke-filled and carrying with it the stench of death, smelled to her like the shores of her homeland. She exhaled, and, for a moment, she looked upon her ancestors, and they greeted her with open arms.

And Aurora Snowfell died.

CHAPTER THIRTY-FOUR
Prisoners

High above the Thendor Plains, inside the looming crystal spire, Avriel fought against her chains. Roakore too thrashed against his restraints, so much so, the blood began to trickle from the circular, open wounds about his wrists. The blood ran down his bare arms and sides; some was absorbed by his thick, red-brown beard, while the rest dribbled down to his feet and dripped on the floor, creating a small pool beneath his dangling toes. In normal circumstances, he would have been able to open or break the chain links, but these were enchanted by elven magic.

Roakore stared at Tarren all the while, sensing something was not right about the lad. No tears came to the boy's eyes, and he seemed not the least upset with their situation. He hung from biting chains as they all did, but he gave no indication he was uncomfortable. Avriel had tried to speak to him, but he only stared blankly at the opposite wall. Roakore thought perhaps the lad had gone into some sort of fit, or fear-induced trance. From Whill, he had learned that humans did not do well with torture, unlike dwarves, who went through such pains as basic training. The dark elves had beaten him, and tried their mind invading tactics; they even took the whip to his back, and Roakore had laughed in their faces all the while. He figured they were not often mocked whilst torturing people, which made the sessions all the more enjoyable. The only begging he had done was for them to continue when they brought him back to the cell. Avriel had not fared so well. To think they had put their dirty hands on her infuriated him. Bloody cowards they were, torturing a woman.

"How you holdin' up?' he asked Avriel, who, like he, was hanging from chains in the small, crystal-walled cell.

"I am okay," she said, mustering a smile.

"It be all right, he be comin', they all be comin'," Roakore assured her.

"I know…" Avriel's voice broke into gentle sobbing, and tears fell to mingle with the blood at her toes.

"What did the dirty, rotten devil do to you?" Roakore growled.

"He took her memories," the Tarren-Watcher answered, when she could not.

Roakore and Avriel both looked to Tarren.

"Tarren, where you been lad, are you all right?" asked Roakore.

"Tarren is in a safe place," said the Watcher.

"What did they do to him?" Roakore asked Avriel, but she only stared at the boy, as if reading something of his face.

"Who…who are you? Where is Tarren?" she asked.

"Tarren is in a safe place, you know who *I* am," he responded.

"Watcher," she breathed, dropping her voice as her eyes darted to the cell door. "How can this be? The practice of soul joining is forbidden."

"Forbidden it may be, though necessary it was," he said with a sly grin.

"But you are benign in all things, you are Morenka."

"Yes, child, however, when one of evil heart wishes to do pain to an innocent, 'tis only right to spare the innocent, and to bear their burden for them."

"What in the hells you be talkin' about? Where be Tarren?" Roakore demanded.

The Watcher regarded Roakore kindly, with a serenity unknown to a human Tarren's age. "He resides within my body for the time being."

"You switched out your brains?" asked Roakore, shocked and wide-eyed.

"In a sense, yes, but quite unlike what you imagine, I assure you," said the Watcher.

"So he be walkin' round in what, an old, crusty elf's body?"

The Watcher laughed with a voice of boyish glee. "Old indeed, but not so crusty I hope."

"You tricked Eadon," said Avriel, suddenly aware of the implications.

Roakore was not lost to the meaning, and his face lit up. "You sly, old tree hugger, you tricked the devil right good! Bahaha! I always told me boys Eadon weren't all powerful. Every damned thing be havin' a weakness, I told 'em. Everything."

"What if Eadon learns of the deception?" Avriel asked.

The Watcher shrugged. "He is too busy with his own plans, and too blinded by the future he *sees*. All is clear to me now that I am so near to him. I understand his design, that which he has staked eons on. He is single-minded in his vision, and has blinded himself to all others. Many possibilities still remain; it will inevitably come down to Whill's choice, which is something Eadon has forgotten."

Avriel began to cry, and Roakore wondered why. The Watcher hinted the dark elf could indeed be beaten.

"What is it?" Roakore asked.

Avriel was wracked with sobs, and took a long time to compose herself. When she finally did, her voice was laden with loss.

"I don't know who he is," she said in a near whisper.

"Who?" Roakore asked.

"Whill," she said. "I don't remember him. I know I should. But, every time I try to remember, I see only Eadon's face. I feel his mind inside mine, like an army of insects eating away the memories."

Roakore peered at the floor, offering her a little privacy in her sorrow. She would not want pity, but a friend. He looked again to her tear-filled eyes and offered a grin.

"Then let me tell you 'bout the man they call Whill o' Agora, the bravest human I ever be knowin'," he began.

Roakore told Avriel all about Whill: how he had first met him and Abram, their shared battles, and many escapades. Avriel laughed when he told the story of the bar brawl they had all gotten into in Kell-Torey. She could not help but laugh at the tale. He told her of the prophecy, and of the recent battles. How Whill had claimed the thrown of Uthen-Arden, and was to face Eadon at Felspire. It took him hours to recite it all, but hours they had, and the Watcher too seemed enthralled by the tales. Some of the stories he chuckled at or nodded in nostalgia, as if he had been there. Roakore figured with a name like the Watcher, he probably had.

"He sounds like a charming young man," she said when Roakore was through.

Roakore laughed, "I'll say, seein' as you two got somethin' goin' on, always have."

"Preposterous," she laughed. "I am over six hundred years old, and he is what…twenty? *And* human."

"I ain't for arguin'," Roakore chuckled, "but you two be carryin' flames for each other and ain't no doubt."

Avriel was taken aback by the idea. She searched the Watcher for clarification. He only smiled with a shrug.

"What is this you say about Eadon?" she asked the Watcher. "You see his plans clearly now?"

"Indeed," he replied.

Avriel and Roakore both waited expectantly.

"So?" Roakore finally blurted.

"Everything makes sense now," said the Watcher. "Whill's torture, the invasion of Agora, our capture, the hunting and killing of his Eldalonian kin. Eadon wishes to be him."

"Come again?" said Roakore.

"Eadon cannot take the power of the Sword of Power Given; it must be given to him. If Whill strikes Eadon with the blade, which is his very own, he will, in essence, be giving the power to Eadon. If, on the other hand, Whill defeats Eadon, which he can only do by taking Eadon's power, I believe he will simply do what I have done with Tarren: Eadon shall become Whill, and, therefore, a god-king."

CHAPTER THIRTY-FIVE
The Lich Lord

The Ky'Dren dwarves rallied together and steadily pushed the invading armies back toward the eastern mouth of the Pass. Reinforcements poured from the northern and southern mountain walls as the dwarves viciously defended their home. Whill could not target large groups of enemy soldiers due to the proximity of the dwarves, who had filled the gap created by Whill's fire spell. Instead, he set his sights on the dark elves blasting the dwarven ranks with spells and cutting through them with their glowing weapons.

Whill charged a dark elf who was slicing through dwarven shields and armor with his flaming sword. The dark elf must have sensed his approach, for he turned, and a spell erupted from his right hand, vaporizing any dwarf standing in the way. The spell hit Whill's energy shield and was absorbed harmlessly. The look of terror on the dark elf's face electrified Whill. He swatted aside the dark elf's defensive block, and the sword went flying.

Whill shot his hand forward through the elf's energy shield. He grabbed the dark elf's head and ripped the life force out of his body. The dark elf's armor fell to the ground in a clatter, and his body fell in ashes. Whill shook with the exhilaration of such unrestrained power.

To his right along the southern wall of the Pass, an explosion sounded. Chunks of broken stone and one massive slab broke away from the sheer wall and fell down toward the dwarves charging out of the many passages below. Whill shot out his left hand and took control of the falling slab. Keeping the slab aloft with a force of will, he leapt into the air and flew the few hundred yards toward the dark elf responsible for the blast. A circle of dead dwarves lay at the dark elf's feet, and still more charged the dangerous spell caster with reckless abandon. The dark elf began to turn in a quick circle creating a whirlwind around him that drove back the dwarves in all directions. Whill forced the floating slab to fly toward the dark elf. With a great resonating boom, the slab landed on top of him and drove itself halfway into the hard earth.

Whill leapt one hundred feet into the air along the southern wall and came down on another dark elf; this one stood amid hundreds of undead soldiers whose eyes glowed with a green mist to match her staff.

Veolindra noticed Whill coming, and froze in place as she beheld the sword Adromida. She had only ever seen such power within Eadon's blade. As Whill landed, she turned to mist and seeped into the ground. She came out many feet behind him, and sent her undead after him. Whill tore through the undead soldiers sending limbs and heads flying from the edge of his blade. He circled as he fought, looking for her. She studied his energy shield and nearly laughed at his novice incantation. The shield was quite basic, simply a force of will surrounding him and fueled by the immense power of the ancient blade. The spell showed Whill's lack of knowledge of Orna Catorna, but, while not intricate, it was fueled by Adromida and was therefore impenetrable to magical and physical attacks. But Veolindra existed not in the physical plane: she was a lich lord. Death had been given to her centuries ago by Eadon, and she was reborn a powerful master of the undead. Eadon chose her out of dozens, and for good reason. Aside from him, she was the most proficient in the necromantic arts. She proved loyal, though not because of her constitution, but rather because she had sworn a soul oath to the dark one. The oath remained the only thing holding her back from possessing Whill's mind and body, and wielding the power of legend.

Their eyes met, and his mental grip tightened around her body. At once, she turned to mist and freed herself. With a mental command, she sent more of her undead, humans, barbarians, Draggard, and lumbering dwargon alike to descend on him. Veolindra found a high perch and watched from afar with glee, as Adromida destroyed them all. Whill clumsily wasted energy with his overzealous attacks, but his methods proved effective all the same.

Dirk ran to the northern wall where he had seen the big slab of stone being manipulated by magic. The stone looked too big for one dwarf to handle. The undead converged, bringing with them the green glow of the cursed. Where the undead were hording, he would likely find the female necromancer who had attacked Chief. Behind him and Krentz, Raene followed. The other dwarves had tried to stop her, but she was quite insistent upon making her own decision. The king had asked Dirk to see she kept put, however, Dirk did not answer to the King of Ky'Dren. He answered to no one. Raene could do whatever she pleased as far as he was concerned, and she seemed to like him all the more for it.

"Thank you," Raene said to him, catching up.

"T'was nothing I did, Krentz healed you,"

"Not the healin'," she said, her shorter legs pumping to keep up with him as they ran the back of the dwarven line.

"For puttin' me brother to rest is what I be meanin'. Thank you."

"You're welcome," Dirk told her over his shoulder.

They came to the southern wall, and Dirk stopped beside one of the many tunnels opening up to the Pass. Toward the mouth of the Pass, hundreds of dwarves stood between him and the green light. He needed a quicker route, lest he run atop the dwarves' shoulders.

"Do you know your way through?" he reluctantly asked Raene, hating tunnels.

"Aye," she said eagerly. "You be after them who killed me brother?"

"Aye," said Dirk. "Lead the way," he said, extending his open arm toward the dwarven tunnel.

When they came out of the shortcut through the stone, Dirk found she had brought them at least five hundred yards through the mountains, and into the thick of the undead horde. Veolindra remained out of sight, but in his searching, he found Whill.

"You should let this go," Krentz warned.

"She is out there somewhere," said Dirk from the shadows of the dwarven tunnel. Krentz turned him around with her hand to his shoulder.

"And what will you do if you find her? Even with my power, I cannot defeat her. You are mighty, Dirk Blackthorn, but not *that* mighty."

"Don't be ridiculous." He grinned. "Of course I am."

"You two be talking all night, or we be killin the demon witch?" Raene asked behind them. The residual energy of Krentz's healing coursed through her still, and she bounced from toe to toe in anticipation.

"I have a plan," Dirk told them both. "Krentz, you still possess the gift of power from your father, correct?"

"Yes?" she answered hesitantly, her eyes darting to Raene.

"Right, and the lich lord, she commands the entire army. She has no doubt received similar gifts from her master."

"Go on," Krentz told him, a spark of realization in her eyes.

"And your father does not allow his power to be used against itself, therefore preventing infighting," he reminded her.

"Exactly!" she said, becoming excited. "We will cancel each other out."

"And the fight will come down to good old steel," said Dirk. Unsheathing his blade, he turned to Raene. "Stay closer to Krentz than the demon witch, and you will be protected. Do otherwise at your own risk."

"Got it, now get outta me way before this pent-up energy makes me piss meself," she said, shoving past him. She exploded from the tunnel, shield leading the way, mace cocked back and ready to bash heads.

Raene slammed into an undead soldier, sending him flying back into the others. Her mace split the head of another, and when two more lunged for her, Dirk and Krentz dealt with them. The two danced and weaved around each other, dashing in to strike, and dashing out to be covered by the other. Dirk's darts shot out randomly as they plowed through the ranks. Behind them, Raene's spinning shield severed heads as the power of Krentz's residual healing energy coursed through her. Raene's mace crushed skulls and shattered bones. Her mind controlled the flying shield as easily as her hand controlled the mace.

Dirk scoured the undead hordes, looking for the necromancer. A spell shot out from the crowd and exploded upon the southern wall behind him. Floating in the glowing green fog was the dark elf.

Veolindra turned to green smoke and shot down toward the battleground. Whill slashed the air with Adromida, but missed as Veolindra flew around the ancient blade, through his energy shield, and into his body.

Whill bent at the waist and fell to his knees. He clutched his chest, gasping for breath as the lich lord tore at him from the inside. He sent writhing tendrils into his own body, desperately trying to pry loose the evil spirit within him. But, she would not relent; she clawed and tore at his soul. She dug deeper into his mind and spirit. Something snapped in Whill's mind; she had awakened the Other from his deep prison. The Other wrestled with the spirit of the lich lord, reveling in the pain she inflicted, and returning it to her threefold. It was now Veolindra who begged for escape; she summoned her hordes to her in a desperate attempt to distract Whill and his maniacal inner demon. Adromida surged as he pulled more power into himself and the Other. Veolindra fled from the Other through the dark caverns of his mind like a swimmer reaching for the surface lest they drown. She overtook what parts of him she could, and successfully lowered his energy shield in hopes to loosen his grasp on her.

Dirk and Krentz fought their way to Whill and Veolindra. The two stood motionless within an energy shield that sparked and rippled as it repelled the attacks of the undead around them. The dark elf necromancer had somehow gotten inside of Whill's energy shield, and stood with her hand to his forehead, her body bent with exertion, and his hunched in pain. Dirk knew if he was ever to make up for what he had done, now was the time.

"To Whill!" he told his companions, and threw four darts to land next to Whill and Veolindra.

Undead bodies flew in all directions as the darts exploded, but the gap quickly filled with more of them. They frantically clawed at Whill's energy shield. A barbarian undead hit the shield with his massive war hammer, and the ground shook. Whill's shield dissipated and the heavy war hammer swung toward his head. Raene gave a cry and, with a raised hand, sent the barbarian's war hammer flying high into the air. Her hand changed directions, and the weapon came hurtling down to plant the confused undead warrior's head in the ground. A large blast issued from Krentz's extended hands, and a whirlwind sent the undead warriors falling back from her. She raised the whirlwind and increased its power. All around them, undead were lifted high into the air by the tornado she had created.

Dirk struck the necromancer with sword and dagger, but the weapons had no effect. Raene too struck with shield and mace, but the blows moved through the necromancer harmlessly.

"She is not of the physical plain," Krentz said, cringing against the effort of her storm. "Like the figurine, her soul is tethered…hurry."

Dirk searched frantically for the trinket that might connect the necromancer to this plain. The trinket might have been anywhere in her flowing robes and tattered folds. His eyes were drawn to the staff she held in her hand. Many gems and bones dangled from the glowing staff, including a jawless skull. He reached for the skull when Whill suddenly gasped and stumbled back from the dark elf, writhing in agony. She too seemed to come back to herself, for she grabbed Dirk's wrist and, with a quick jerk, broke his arm. She hit him in the chest with the other. A bright flash exploded from his chest as his armor absorbed the blow. Raene flew at the lich lord with her mace and shield cocked back. Veolindra twirled and slammed her with the end of her staff. A green explosion blew Raene back to be engulfed by the whirlwind.

Dirk came on again with his good arm, slashing at the staff. Veolindra raised a clawed hand, and Dirk was wracked with pain and raised off his feet to float before her.

"The skull!" Dirk screamed at Whill through the pain. But, if the man heard him, he gave no indication. He writhed on the ground as if two beasts raged within him.

Veolindra whirled on Krentz, who remained stuck, controlling her immense whirlwind that kept the undead at bay. An ear-piercing shriek escaped her as she cast a green spell, engulfing Krentz. Instantly, the whirlwind died down and, like Dirk, Krentz was raised by a green spell that tore through her being and clawed at her soul in an attempt to devour it. Dirk felt himself slipping, his soul being torn from his body. He fought the spell with everything he had, though it seemed hopeless.

Through hazy eyes, he watched Whill get to his feet and attack Veolindra with a long glowing chain that looked to have torn through his wrist. Half of Whill's body became a scarred, bloody, and wild-eyed reflection of himself. The chain wound around the lich lord and held her fast. Dirk and Krentz fell to the ground as the undead rushed at them from all sides. With his left hand, Whill pulled the skull from the staff to him, and it exploded on contact. The lich lord disappeared with a violent shriek that echoed through the pass for miles.

Dirk reached for Krentz, who seemed no more than a shadow by then. She had come dangerously close to being absorbed by the lich lord.

"Back to the spirit world, my love," he whispered, and her spirit returned to the trinket in his pocket.

Whill stared down at him. All around them, the undead had stopped in their tracks, a dim, green light glowing in their eyes. With their handler dead, they did nothing, having no mind of their own. Whill scowled at Dirk. "You,' he said accusingly.

CHAPTER THIRTY-SIX

Reunion

Whill grabbed Dirk by the throat and lifted him off his feet. Dirk's good hand clutched Whill's firm grip, and the assassin's words choked out along with his breath. Whill shook with rage and threw him to the ground once more. He held the tip of Adromida to Dirk's chin, as the assassin coughed and tried to find his voice.

"Go ahead," he finally said. "I had no choice in the matter, he would have killed her."

Whill told himself not to listen to him; he was a trickster, a weaver of lies. The assassin was just trying to save his own hide.

"Who is *he?*" he asked, keeping the blade where it was.

"Eadon," said Dirk, rubbing his throat. "He held my woman hostage."

"When did you come into Eadon's employment?"

"Before the fight in the arena, I was captured snooping around the castle where she was being kept hostage. Had I not made the deal to spy on you, he would have killed her. What was I to do? You were a stranger to me at the time."

Whill didn't want to believe him, but he recognized enough truth in his eyes to lower his sword.

"Why are you here?"

Dirk stood hesitantly, dusted himself off, and showed his empty hands. "Krentz and I came here with one General Reeves of the Eldalonian army. We met up in southern Eldalon and helped a band of refugees to the Ky'Dren Pass. He is here somewhere to back up my story, unless he has been killed. Would be a shame really, good man that one."

"Why did you help me against the necromancer?" Whill asked.

"She tried to kill a friend of mine. I took it personally."

Whill eyed Dirk for a long while. After a time, he turned his attentions to the smoldering battlefield. The sun was beginning its descent, and nighttime would be upon them in only a few hours. His mind drifted from Dirk easily; he didn't care about the man's motives. Soon, he would have to face Eadon. Such trivial things as the assassin seemed to not matter. He turned back on Dirk; the assassin had not moved a muscle while his back had been turned. Whill could not trust the man, and should have killed him where he stood. However, he could not kill a man in cold blood, not this one, at least. Dirk had betrayed him, but he had also possibly saved him from the necromancer.

Whill remained shaken by that experience. The dark elf had gone through his shield too easily. He had no idea how to fight against such dark magic. He realized once again how helpless he still was against some of the powers of the elves. Though he possessed one of the most concentrated sources of power in Agora, he did not possess the invaluable experience that came with time, nor did he possess the wisdom. He had crammed the knowledge of the Elven Tomes into his mind, but he had never performed most of the spells, and had not the privilege of learning from his failures as he went. He was a freak of nature and magic as well; the bastard child of a prophecy gone awry.

"I do not trust you…cannot," said Whill. "Neither can I kill you."

"I ain't for thinkin' you be killin' this one. Hell o' a fighter," said Raene, walking toward them from the battleground.

The undead led by Veolindra had fallen, or continued to stand in place, absently staring into the distance. Groups of dwarves traversing the pass eagerly sent the soldier's souls on their way. Raene walked toward them, taking the time to crack two of the undead soldier's skulls. The second one she spent a good deal of time on, and when she finally stood before Whill and Dirk, she was covered in blood and gore.

"Where the elven lady go to?" she asked as she absently wiped her bloody hand on her armor.

Whill remembered seeing a dark-haired elven woman conjuring the whirlwind and then later fighting with the necromancer, but, by the time he recovered from the dark elf's strange attack, she had disappeared.

"She is recovering," Dirk told her quickly.

"Aye," said Raene. "As we all be. Was a right bloody battle, eh? The men be sayin' different, but if you hadn't arrived, the Pass might have fallen," she told Whill.

Raene slammed her fist to her chest and offered her hand in the human greeting, Whill shook it. "Name's Raene, daughter o' King Ky'Ell o' the Mountains Ky'Dren."

"Whill…Warcrown," he said with a nod as they shook. "Well met."

"Well met, indeed. I be knowin' who you be. Not a year ago, you met with me pa in Dy'Kore, eh? He told us all bout ye, says ye be a good friend o' Roakore o' the Mountains Ro'Sar."

"That I am."

"Where he be at?" she asked, looking around. "From what we be hearin' as o' late, you two be thicker than the fur on a snow goat."

"He has been captured by Eadon, he and friends of mine," said Whill.

"Captured!" Raene repeated, shocked. "Then best we be goin to get him!"

"You ain't goin' nowhere, young lady!" Ky'Ell yelled as he approached on his war goat.

The king dismounted deftly and landed sure footed on the scorched ground before her. His gaze moved from her and fell upon Dirk. "I thought I be tellin' you to mind she be keepin' put."

Raene stepped forward with a grave expression on her usually rosy-cheeked face.

"Pa, me King," she bowed and tears found her eyes. "Me brother, Ky'Ro, fell, he be dead."

Ky'Ell closed his eyes and began to shake.

"I found the body. How did it happen?" he asked in a shaking voice of barely controlled rage.

"A dark elf, you killed him when you threw the big slab o' stone on his head."

Ky'Ell's eyes went wide and shot in the direction she meant. His gaze turned back on his daughter and his already angry face turned to a snarl. "He still lives; the stone slab has been moved. Saw it when I went to Ky'Ro's body. No dark elf lay dead under the stone."

"Then we will track him down." Raene said with a patting hand on her father's shoulder.

Ky'Ell flung off her hand. "I done told you to keep put. Be a direct order from your King you disobeyed, be it not?"

"Pa-"

"Be it not?"

"Yes, me King."

"If you woulda done what I told, then we woulda been alerted to the dark elf gettin' away!"

"Yes, me King."

The King raised his calloused hand to slap her.

"Ky'Ell!" Whill yelled.

Ky'Ell turned on Whill with murder in his eyes. "This be a family matter, mind your tongue, and your business."

He turned back on Raene. "Get your arse back to southern Ky'Dren, and report to your mother. 'Bout time you be gettin' a husband and start actin' like a gods damned woman!"

"Pa…" she begged.

Ky'Ell slapped her so hard that she fell to one knee.

"Now!" he screamed.

Without another word, Raene got up and left them for the tunnels to the south.

"I got other things to be tendin' to," he said to Whill. "I wish you to remain to sup at least. We've much to discuss."

Whill nodded, having lost some respect for the dwarf.

"You too, man in black. The help o' your elf friend is much appreciated. You both be named dwarf friend in Ky'Dren," he told Dirk.

"Honored," Dirk said with a nod.

The king mounted his war goat and charged off to the east, and Whill turned on Dirk.

"What are you playing at?"

"Sorry?" said Dirk.

"First you are a prisoner of Eadon, then his spy, and now what? You work for the dwarves? If Roakore ever sees you again, he will likely kill you, just on principle."

Dirk laughed. "Indeed, he would, he proved quite successful the first time around."

"So what is your game?" Whill pressed.

Dirk's eyes searched the ground in retrospect; Whill thought he was either acting, or truly looking inside himself for the answer. Dirk seemed to notice his broken arm again for the first time, hanging limply at his side and turned at an awkward angle.

"You mind?" he asked Whill.

"Yes," he replied.

Dirk's brow raised and his face said, *I don't blame you.* He sighed and produced the timber wolf figurine. "I'm not sure how it works. But, I don't think it is the magic of dark elves. The trinket is a link to the spirit world. From it, I can summon the spirit of a timber wolf of Volnoss. I suspect the relic is barbarian make."

"Humans have no magic," said Whill.

"Perhaps we do. *You* do," Dirk retorted. "The barbarians have witch doctors. Perhaps there is some magic about them after all."

Whill shrugged.

"Anyhow. My woman, Krentz, swore fealty to Eadon. I tried to trap her in the trinket until I could figure out a way to break the vow without killing her."

"And?"

"And she died when pulled into the trinket by the wolf. She is now like he, a spirit who can conjure her physical form."

"Why did she swear fealty to Eadon?" Whill asked.

"She did it on a trade. My vow for hers."

"And you only made your vow to save her in the first place?"

"Correct, but it seems she didn't want saving," said Dirk.

Whill thought about his story. Dirk had taken a bit of a risk admitting his woman had become essentially an undead, or lich, or whatever she might be now. Whill could take the trinket from him at any time; they both knew it.

"Show me," he found himself saying.

Dirk sucked in air between his teeth. His face said *I don't know.*

"The wolf was nearly absorbed by the lich, I dare not summon him as of yet."

"And the woman?"

"Krentz needs to recuperate as well. She can hold her own against any, but it seems these necromancers can inflict real damage to spirits."

Whill believed him; the warning voices in his head had begun to fade. However, he still didn't think Dirk told him the whole truth.

"Why did Eadon kidnap her in the first place?"

Dirk held his gaze. "He caught wind of my reputation, wanted me to work for him."

"Why not just force you?"

"You've met the elf; he likes willing servants over mindless slaves."

True, but Whill remained unsatisfied.

"If he wanted you so badly, why would he trade your fealty for hers?"

Dirk said nothing, as if he had wondered that very thing. "He is a great deceiver. I cannot begin to understand his motives in anything. Perhaps he thought he could keep me snared, dangle her over my head to keep me in line. He sent a dark elf after me after releasing me. I believe he meant to rein me back in."

Whill smelled a rat. He didn't invade Dirk's mind for his answers, but he listened intently for Dirk's projected thoughts.

Silence.

Either the assassin had a great amount of control, he felt guilty about nothing, or he told the truth.

Sensing what Whill was doing, Dirk stretched out his good hand. "Go ahead, read my mind if it will get us anywhere faster."

"Who is she?" Whill asked.

"I don't trust you any more than you trust me," Dirk answered.

"Then you have something to hide, or rather, she does?"

"Don't we all?" Dirk countered, not backing down.

Tension filled the silence as they both stared at one another. Finally, Whill reached out his right hand. Dirk didn't flinch. Whill nodded to his broken arm, and Dirk hesitantly walked toward him. Placing his hand on Dirk's broken arm, he surrounded it with blue healing energy. He delved into the wound with his mind sight, healing torn tendon and muscle, and setting the bone in place with a force of will. He touched upon an energy coursing through the assassin's body and armor. The wound had already begun to heal itself, and Whill followed the energy flow to a gem set in Dirk's chest. Elven magic was at work inside him.

Dirk pulled his arm back and Whill returned to himself with a jerk.

"Thanks," said Dirk, flexing his hand and rubbing his healed arm.

"We are even," said Whill, watching him closely.

"Agreed," Dirk replied.

CHAPTER
THIRTY-SEVEN

Judgment

Aurora stood before her father, head bowed and tears streaming from her like flowing rivers after a long winter thaw. Around them stood the shadows of their ancestors, and, beyond them, the great pillars that made up the glowing entrance to the barbarian paradise, Val'Kharae. She knelt upon her knees in shame, her every deed laid out bare before her ancestors.

"My daughter, what have you done?" her father asked, anger and sorrow etching his booming voice.

Aurora wanted to explain herself, wanted to make them understand that she had had no choice, but it was a lie. She had had a choice, and now she would pay the price. She had led her greatest warriors to a slaughter at the hands of Whill of Agora. The future of Volnoss had been destroyed the moment she killed Azzeal and chose her path. She had tried to lead her people to their lost homeland so they might once again know glory and honor. Instead, she had sealed their doom. Volnoss would be seen as the enemy now.

"Aurora Snowfell!" a voice boomed throughout the murky glow. The shadows of her ancestors turned their heads upward, and her father slowly stepped away from her.

Aurora's armor was ripped from her violently. The furs of the Seven Tribes went up in flames, leaving her quivering naked beneath the looming face of Thodin, the father of the gods.

"You are the coward at your people's back. You have disgraced your tribe. Stand and receive!" Thodin bellowed.

Aurora tried to stand on her shaking legs, but she was suddenly falling. The glowing pillars of Val'Kharae faded in the distance above her, and the shadows of her ancestors went with it. Aurora screamed in the void as she fell, thinking she had been cast down to the Underdeath. The sound of strange chanting surrounded her. She didn't understand the words.

Pain crashed into her, and she screamed for death. Her eyes shot open, and she lurched and flailed. Strong hands held her down, and the chanting rose to unbearable levels. All around her a glowing green fog akin to Azzeal's dead eyes surrounded her. She realized what was happening, and her screams of pain became keening sobs.

Aurora sucked in a frantic breath and opened her eyes to Zander standing above her. His arms shot to the heavens and a crackling bolt of lightning hit her in the chest. The power of the strike jumpstarted her still heart, and air flooded into her burning lungs.

"Rise, Aurora Snowfell, my undead beauty. Rise!" Zander bade her, and she was compelled to comply.

She floated to her feet and stood on strong legs. She saw everything differently through her glowing green eyes. Nighttime had come, and yet everything was as clear as if it were day. The faint moonbeams shooting out between the clouds showed with the same green tint. All about the forest, the glowing outlines of every living creature and every tree gave them away. But, her own flesh didn't glow with life force, but rather a dark swirling fog.

Zander smiled upon her and sat to rest on a large stone set beside a green fire.

"You can thank Azzeal for bringing you to me, and just in time. You were nearly lost to my efforts," said Zander.

Azzeal's eyes never wavered from hers. She realized he had been staring at her the entire time. There was yet a hint of the elf she had known in the milky gaze, a shadow of who he was.

"Why do I remember everything? Why am I not like…him?" she asked Zander, holding Azzeal's gaze.

She thought she saw the slightest of smiles at the corner of his mouth.

"I was able to preserve your mind...actually, Azzeal was. Seems a bit of magic remains in the sun elf," Zander said, amused.

Aurora didn't share his amusement; she was horrified. She had become one of the undead, a pawn to be used at Zander's disposal. The connection between them pulled at her heart, at her soul. Sorrow permeated through her, washing against her tortured mind like an eternal ocean upon the sands of the world. She believed some part of Azzeal had kept her mind intact on purpose, as a final retribution for her sins. In the back of her mind, his croaking voice echoed across the oceans of despair. Before she had awakened, she thought herself cast down to the depths of the Underdeath, and how she wished that was her fate instead.

"You have served our master well. We would have been successful had it not been for Whill. Your people's sacrifice will not be forgotten," said Zander.

"My people..." Aurora's voice trembled.

"They are all dead I am afraid. The wielder of the ancient blade utterly destroyed our armies."

"Where are we?"

"About ten miles east of the Ky'Dren Pass. We travel to Felspire. Eadon shall pass judgment on our failings as he sees fit."

"But, it wasn't our fault," Aurora protested, cringing at the idea of standing in judgment before the dark elf. But, then again, what could possibly be worse than undeath, she wondered.

"Eadon has no patience for such excuses as fault. Failure, to Eadon, is failure," said Zander.

"Where is Veolindra?" Aurora asked.

"She has been destroyed," said Zander without feeling. "Come, you've no need for rest now."

"Where are we going?" she asked, though she knew the answer.

"Felspire."

CHAPTER THIRTY-EIGHT

Ancient One

elzendar stared at the Watcher's body, and, from within, Tarren stared back. They had been holed up inside Del'Oradon castle seemingly forever, and Tarren had not even begun to get comfortable in the elf's body.

"You really in there?" asked Helzendar with a hint of skepticism.

"For the hundredth time, yes, I am *really* in here," Tarren answered. Hearing the Watcher's voice was still strange. Thankfully, his own voice narrated his thoughts.

"Must be weird. You got any o' the old crazy elf's magic in ye?"

Tarren thought about that. It definitely felt weird, but if there was magic in him, he couldn't tell. "I think he took the magic with him," he finally answered.

Lunara had insisted they remain inside the castle, in one of the lower chambers used as a lock-out room for the royals in times of invasion. Outside of the windowless room's single door, a half dozen elves stood guard. Tarren figured the guard was pointless, given Eadon's incredible power, but she insisted all the same. A few of the elder masters had been in to inspect him. They all hummed and nodded to themselves, but didn't find it prudent to share what they had learned with Tarren, to his growing annoyance. Though it was not his body, they poked and prodded with their hands and their minds, and the inspections felt quite uncomfortable all the same. He was glad when the last of them left.

Despite all of the annoyance and strangeness, he was glad he was not inside his own body, and he was thankful for the Watcher's sacrifice. He could not imagine what the elf was going through in his stead, and he cringed to think what had been done to his own body. The entire affair had the air of a bad dream he could not wake from. He wished he would wake up in a soft bed in Cerushia, or Ro'Sar, or, better yet, back in his bed next to the window in his family's inn.

"How you thinkin this all be turnin' out?" Helzendar asked as he anxiously paced the floor of the large room.

"Who is to say how a dream will end?" Tarren replied, wondering where he had come up with such words. Helzendar seemed to notice the difference too, for he stopped his pacing to regard Tarren.

"Think the elf's crazy brain be getting' to ye," he said, and went back to his pacing.

"There are worse things," said Tarren.

Zerafin and the army of elves met with others from Elladrindellia near the town of Harrow, at the end of the eastern branch of the Ky'Dren River. They came in bird and animal form as it suited them. Others rode upon the majestic horses of southern Elladrindellia. Bred for speed and endurance, and fueled by the magic of the elves, the elven horses could travel long lengths before tiring.

With the help of Zionar Master Ornarell, and the network of speaking stones the elves possessed, word had been spread throughout the land to converge on Felspire. Many bands of elves heard the call and had begun the journey from all corners of Elladrindellia. Elves remained spread out across Agora, spies of the Queen Araveal who had been stationed strategically throughout the land. Many of the elves had remained behind in Elladrindellia to fight the hordes of Draggard who came through the portal outside of Cerushia.

Zerafin had been in contact with the queen. He was pleased to learn she and many others had survived the attack. The city however had not been so fortunate. The dark elves laid Cerushia to waste, though they had lost many in doing so. It was the largest attack, and the greatest loss for the Elves of the Sun, in Agora to date. But, the elves had recovered from the surprise of the attack quickly, and had successfully routed the enemy to the shores of Elladrindellia.

Like those in the other kingdoms of Agora, the attack on Cerushia had only been a distraction, a way to keep the kingdoms busy defending their own lands while Eadon and his hordes gathered at Felspire upon the Thendor Plains. Reports were coming in from the druid scouts that the dark armies moved steadily in the direction of the spire.

Zerafin thought of Avriel as he gazed out over his growing elven army, the largest gathering of elven warriors they had mustered since the Drindellian Wars, and it well may have been the last. He remained unsure how the war would all play out. Once, he was confident the prophecy was true, and that Whill of Agora would end the centuries-old war. But now, given what Kellallea had said in the cavern, he was not so sure. He wished to speak to her to discover the truth. He had tried to contact the ancient elf, knowing she was in Agora, but to no avail.

He rode away from the main gathering by the banks of the Ky'Dren River where the horses drank their fill, and dismounted a mile away upriver from them. He left his horse to graze and unsheathed his blade as he sat in a meditative stance among the high grass of the bank. He focused his will on Kellallea and called to her with his mind. Tapping into the power of his blade, he called to her through the water and earth and wind. For nearly an hour, he tried to make contact with the ancient one, but, to his dismay, she either did not hear him, or refused to answer.

Reluctantly, he sheathed his sword and stood beside the banks of the river. He had used much of the power of his blade in calling, but he had to try again. He was possibly leading his elves to slaughter, and needed all of the wise council he could get.

"Kellallea!" he screamed to the heavens. "I am King Zerafin of Elladrindellia, son of King Verelas of Drindellia! Hear me!"

Just when he had given up and began to mount his steed to leave, the wind picked up and blew the thin snow cover up in small twisters of churning white. His horse whined and shuffled nervously, but he paid it no mind.

"Ancient one?" he asked the wind.

The snow began to swirl more violently, and Zerafin soon found himself in the midst of a snowy whirlwind. Ahead, through the whiteout, a form appeared. The wind quickly died down altogether, and the powdery snow fell lazily around him.

"Hello, my child," a voice spoke to him through the snowfall.

He moved closer and inspected her with his mind sight, and gasped when he saw the power she possessed.

Quickly, he turned away and closed his mind's eye. She came to stand before him in a long flowing dress of vine and leaves. Like the falling snow surrounding them, she glowed with the sunlight. Zerafin took a knee before her and bowed his head.

"Kellallea, Lady of the Tree," he said in reverie.

"Zerafin, my child, rise."

He stood before the ancient elf of legend, she who had ended the Great War and stripped the elves of all knowledge of Orna Catorna those eons ago. He stood before her, humbled. Words fled from him and his mind knew only her beauty.

"Kellallea," he said in a broken voice.

"I understand, my child. You fret for our people, for your sister. You have given much of yourself in this fight. Rest now, and be at peace. For things are as they should be," she said, lifting her hand to rest upon his crown. Waves of soothing energy washed through him and his heart and mind found peace.

"Will you come with us to Felspire? Will you help your people as you once did, long ago? Or have you forsaken us; have we fallen from your grace?" he dared ask.

"I meant to teach the elves a lesson those eons ago, a lesson that has been forgotten. How then shall I help you now?" she asked.

Zerafin fell to his knees once more. "Please, Kellallea, we beg of you. Many among us have headed your words, who live by your lessons. Always there will be those who do not. How are we to fight such evil?"

"Fret not, child, I have not forsaken you." She reached out her hands, which Zerafin took as he stood before her once again. "Go with my blessing, Zerafin, son of Verelas. And know that I am with you."

There was a brilliant flash of light, and a surge of power was transferred from Kellallea to Zerafin. His inner gems and his blade were filled with the power of the ancient one, and she was gone.

CHAPTER THIRTY-NINE
The Western Door

Whill sat with King Ky'Ell and a few of his generals around a large fire near the eastern mouth of the Pass. Dar'Kwar was among them. Whill had healed those dwarves he could, and had saved many from the clutches of death. The Ky'Dren dwarves had taken many casualties during the invasion, but the Draggard had been routed, the day had been won. The dwarves were in a celebratory mood after the victory. Ky'Ell did not share the jovial spirit around him. He had lost a son and many other good soldiers during the battle. Many of his cities had been destroyed, and all under his watch.

"What can you tell me of the invasion of Eldalon?" Whill asked Ky'Ell, putting down his bowl of stew.

Ky'Ell regarded Whill as if he had been torn from deep pondering. "Not much, lad. I been fighting my way here from Northern Ky'Dren these last few days.

You be findin' more answers at the western mouth o' the Pass."

"If I might interrupt, me King, I come from the west recently," Dar'Kwar offered.

Ky'Ell nodded and the dwarf went on.

"I been there, on account o' that Dirk Blackthorn and his flight from Uthen-Arden. Eldalon be in shambles, far as the refugees be tellin'."

"Blackthorn?" Whill asked.

"Aye, the man came to the Pass like a bat outta hells, said he knew o' a plot to kill the royal family o' Eldalon, and said he been tryin' to stop it. I left him at the western mouth, ain't for knowin' where he went from there, but if he was trying to stop the slaughter, he ain't been successful. Be true bout yer kin, sir. Last came to me ears, the King o' Eldalon and his family been killed. I ain't for knowin' how many survived."

Whill only nodded at this. He had heard as much, but clung to the possibility that the stories were false. How had Dirk known of such a plot? Better yet, why would he care to stop the assassinations? He searched for the assassin, but saw no sign of him in the nearby dwarven camps. He began to regret his decision to let him go. Another question burned in his mind: Why would Eadon bother exterminating his line? Was he simply trying to goad Whill into fighting him once and for all? Surely, that was the reason he kidnapped Roakore, Avriel, and who he thought was Tarren.

"Might I ask what your next move be? You plan on facin' Eadon?" Ky'Ell asked, and took a long pull from his metal flask. He offered the liquor to Whill, who declined.

"I came here in hopes of learning the fate of my kin. I suppose I will travel to the western mouth and see what might be learned. I will face Eadon in due time. I had hoped to rally the kingdoms of Agora against him, but it seems his ultimatum will leave little time for such a feat. The elves of Elladrindellia move toward Felspire as we speak."

Ky'Ell nodded grimly and lit up his pipe. "What o' the Uthen-Arden armies? You be king o' them now, ain't ye?"

"Yes, though I am not known to them. I have no power to move them to action, not with so little time. If the undead we faced earlier are any indication, I doubt many of Uthen-Arden's soldiers are still…themselves."

"Aye, Laddie, be dark magic we face. Not for you, our dead woulda been raised against us to take the Pass. We be in your debt, Whill. Any way we can help rid Agora o' this scourge once and for all, just say the word."

Whill pondered the offer. He didn't want anyone else to die because of him, but he could use all the help he could get at Felspire.

"I had intended to unite the races against the dark elves. I think Eadon understands this, and I believe it is one of the reasons for the recent invasions. I would be honored, Ky'Ell, if you and your dwarves stood with me during the final battle."

"The honor be ours," said Ky'Ell. "The dark elves and their abominations need be dealt with, once and for all!"

"Hear, hear!" Dar'Kwar cheered, and many dwarves joined in, ever ready to toss back a drink.

Ky'Ell took another shot from his flask, and, this time, Whill joined him. "This Felspire you speak of. Seems it be seen from the mountain lookout posts. It be bout fifty and a hun'red miles from here. You says you got four days? Then, by the gods, we'll muster what we can and be there with ye. Between us 'n the elves, we'll give em a right wakeup call."

"Hear, hear!" the cheer went up again, and the spirits flowed.

A man strode forth from the edge of the fire glow, and stopped before Whill.

"Is it true? The one named in legend is here before my eyes?"

"Well met," said Whill extending a hand.

"General Mick Reeves of Eldalon," said Reeves with a wide smile.

Dirk listened to the conversation through the enchanted studs in his ears, and he was glad he had not been near when Dar'Kwar mentioned him. Whill would have more than a few new questions for him, questions he could not answer. He was glad to learn that Reeves had survived the battle. The general had a few cuts and bruises, and his armor was dented and dirty, but he was alive. Dirk considered waiting for Reeves to be away from Whill, but that would likely be a long time indeed. They were talking in depth about the fate of Eldalon.

Dirk decided it was time to be on his way. He turned from the cliff of the southern mountain range and climbed the rocks up to the ledge Fyrfrost had landed upon.

"It is time we were on our way, Fyr—"

A noise came from somewhere above him on one of the jagged outcroppings of stone. He put up a cautious hand for Fyrfrost to stay hidden. The dragon-hawk had taken on the likeness of the surrounding stone, and even Dirk could hardly find him perched against the mountainside.

"Who goes there?" he asked the night.

"I be goin' here," Raene called back.

Dirk sheathed his dagger as the dwarf's silhouette peeked out over the stone. She made her way down to him deftly, scaling the stone with surprising agility.

"Ye be on your way then, aye?" she asked as she came to stand before him.

"What if I am?"

"I'm thinkin' it be time I be on me way as well. You headed to this…Felspire?" she asked.

"What if I am?"

"I would go with ye, be a good three days march to the strange spire. The lookouts be sayin' they can see it from the peaks. Long walk that be, me thinks you could use the company anyway."

Dirk stared at the feisty dwarf warrior, confused. "You want to go with me?"

"'Tis where they be holdin' Roakore, ain't it?"

"I thought your father ordered you to report to your mother?"

"So? I ain't for a life o' cookin' and cleanin' and birthin' an such. And pity on me father for not seein' me for what I be."

Dirk laughed. He liked Raene, and wouldn't mind having her along. Though, she would never ride on the back of a dragon-hawk.

"I am afraid you would not agree with my means of travel."

"If'n you be meanin' the magic dragon-bird, you be wrong. He be your mount, then he be good enough for me," said Raene.

"You don't even know me," Dirk protested.

"I be knowin' ye saved me hide today, and ye put me brother to rest. If nothin', I be owin' ye the benefit o' the doubt," she told him as she eyed the spot where Fyrfrost hid.

Dirk realized she had been spying on him for a while without his knowledge, and he was more than a little impressed.

"You would ride a dragon-hawk?" he asked skeptically.

"I be meanin' on bustin' me cousin Roakore outta Felspire. Even if it means ridin' your dragon-bird," said Raene.

"You don't share your people's beliefs about the dragons?"

"I be believin' everything ain't as it appears. Me people believe women can't be warriors, just as they believe all dragons be evil. Who's to say they always be right?"

Dirk considered her for a long while. "And if I say no?" he finally asked.

"Then I be screamin' dragon," she threatened, and Dirk had to laugh.

"I thought you might say that."

Raene peered over the ledge to the Pass below, a hint of apprehension on her face. He couldn't be sure what this kind of defiance meant for the daughter of a dwarf king, but he guessed it wouldn't be good. For a fleeting moment, her face showed sorrow, regret, and longing. Raene's expression quickly hardened as she gave a single nod. She had said her goodbyes.

She followed Dirk to Fyrfrost's side and mounted the dragon-hawk. To her credit, Dirk sensed no fear of the mount.

"Best hang on tight," he told her, and Fyrfrost took four powerful strides and leapt off the side of the mountain.

Whill bid the king and his soldiers farewell and was about to leave for the western mouth of the Pass, when something in the sky caught his eye. A shadow had passed in front of the illuminated clouds. With his mind sight, he made out the glowing life force of a dragon and two riders. Upon closer inspection, he realized one to be Dirk, and though he couldn't believe it, he thought a dwarf flew with him. He pondered the idea of confronting the assassin once again; he had a few more questions for him. He decided to let it go for the time being, sensing that this was not the last he would see of the man.

Good riddance, Dirk Blackthorn, he thought and took to the sky.

Fueled by the power of Adromida, Whill flew to the western mouth of the Pass before the sun had come up. He passed over legions of dwarven soldiers marching from the mountain. At what must have been the middle of the Pass, the soldiers broke into two directions, east and west. He guessed there had been, or would be, trouble near the Eldalon border.

He reached the western mouth of the Pass and found a smoldering city of tents and an army of humans and dwarves standing shoulder to shoulder. Beyond the mouth waited an army of Draggard, draquon, and dwargon. With his mind sight, he determined at least a dozen dark elves among them, judging by the bright glow of their stored power. For whatever reason, the dark elf army was not advancing.

Whill landed before the front line to a chorus of surprised exclamations and shouted warnings.

"I am Whillhelm Warcrown, King of Uthen-Arden! I come in peace!" he said, holding up his empty hands to the crowd.

"I ain't for knowin' no Whillhelm Whatsit!" yelled a dwarf, pushing through the crowd to face him.

"Whill of Agora," Whill clarified.

"Whill o'…" the dwarf began, and his face lit up with recognition.

"I heard o' the name, what you want?" he spat.

Whill walked forward despite the spears and hatchets aimed at him. Another dwarf pushed past the first and slammed his fist to his chest with a bow.

"Whillhelm Warcrown, be an honor. Word o' your exploits an friendship to our cousin Roakore be legend. Orzor Brightstone, at your service."

The first dwarf scowled at Orzor. "I be the rankin' dwarf round these parts, shut your gabber and mind your place!" He squared on Whill once again. "Name's Griznor, I be General o' the Western Door."

"Well met, Griznor," said Whill with a slam to his chest that seemed to put the dwarf at ease a bit.

The dwarves and humans alike had begun to stir; his name was whispered by a hundred voices. An Eldalonian knight broke through the ranks and stood before Whill with a shocked expression on his face.

"Now, here is a sight for sore eyes," he said, extending his hand

Whill didn't recognize the man, but he shook the hand nonetheless. Seeing his searching eyes, the knight introduced himself.

"Theolus Klemus, I met you in Kell-Torey."

"Ah, yes, Rhunis's friend. You led us to the castle. You were a city guard at the time, if I remember correctly," said Whill, regarding the knight's armor.

Theolus lit up at Whill's recognition. "Seems I have been promoted again, sign of the times, I suppose," he replied humbly. "We have lost so many, soon enough farm boys will be knights if they can only hold a blade steady."

"The losses have been great, indeed," said Whill, thinking of Abram and Rhunis.

"Take the reunion behind me front line, will ye?" Griznor growled.

Theolus led Whill back through the standing armies. "General Steely will want to speak with you," he said as they walked. "What of Rhunis, is he with you?"

"He is not, he and Abram fell in Del'Oradon," said Whill.

Theolus stopped short, as if he had been punched in the gut. His jovial demeanor was lost at once, and a shadow spread across his face that seemed to cause him to age before Whill's eyes.

"Grave news, indeed," he said as he began to walk with Whill once more.

"Yes, they were both good men, and good friends," Whill replied.

They walked in silence for a while, Whill remembering his old friends with a smile, and Theolus with a frown of sadness. The dwarves and Eldalonian men alike craned their heads as they went. Word of Whill's arrival had already spread throughout both armies. Many stopped him to shake his hand, both men and dwarves.

"What of Fendale?" Whill asked hopefully, but Theolus's face told him all he needed to know.

"I am afraid Fendale has fallen, the Light of the North shines no more."

Whill's heart sank. He had only been in Fendale for a short time. However, the city held a special place in his heart. In Fendale, he had won his weight in gold sparring against Rhunis, and it was the last time his life had been relatively normal...back before prophecies, pirates, dark elves, and ancient elven blades. He thought of Freston and his three sons, hoping by some grace of the gods they had survived. He guessed the old ship builder and his sons would have escaped by sea, if nothing else.

"'Tis a time of dark tiding, indeed," said Whill.

They came to a large tent well inside the mouth of the Pass, and Theolus recited Whill's title to the standing guard. After a moment, the dumbfounded guard slipped through the tent flap and informed his general.

"Enter," he told Whill, unable to meet his gaze.

Whill entered the tent, followed by Theolus. A big man stood from behind a large wooden desk and extended his hand in greeting.

"General Steely."

"Whillhelm Warcrown, King of Uthen-Arden," said Whill, shaking his hand.

The general stopped dead. "King, you say?"

"Yes. I am the son of the late King Aramonis. I have slain my murderous uncle and reclaimed the throne from the imposter Eadon."

Steely gestured to one of the seats opposite his desk, and absently sat after Whill.

"I have not heard a whisper of this," he said, regarding Whill with puzzlement.

"You wouldn't have, I claimed the throne nigh on three days ago."

"I met your father once," said Steely, searching his face for resemblance. "Good man."

"So they say," said Whill. "What can you tell me of my Eldalonian kin?"

The general stared, stone-faced.

"My mother's family…the Eldalonian Royals?"

"Pardon my rudeness," said Steely with a raised hand. He looked to Theolus. "You know this man to be the son of Aramonis?"

"Sir, yes, sir," Theolus answered with a sincere nod.

"How do you know such a thing?"

"Sir, I was introduced to Whill by Rhunis the Dragonslayer, in Kell-Torey. They traveled with King Roakore of the Ro'Sar mountains, and two elves, a prince and princess, I believe, and one by the name of Abram, sir."

The general nodded and seemed to be mulling over the information. In the blink of an eye, he seemed to make his decision and all suspicion left his face.

"Well met, Whillhelm Warcrown."

Whill nodded. "What can you tell me of Eldalon? Of my kin?"

"Eldalon stands upon the brink of collapse. Kell-Torey has fallen, and we lost Fendale recently to a massive naval invasion. Gods damned dark elf ships blasted the city to rubble. Our forces are scattered throughout the kingdom. What word reaches us, comes with the refugees. As for your kin…I am sorry to say the king has fallen, gods bless him."

"The others?" Whill asked.

"Many of the king's family have been assassinated," said Steely, and Whill immediately thought of Dirk.

"A man came round a few weeks back, claiming that he knew of a plot to kill the royal family. T'was likely he who thwarted the attack on Lord Carlsborough. The lord and his family arrived here in one piece a few days back."

"What was the man's name?" Whill asked.

The general seemed to become uncomfortable all of a sudden; he shifted in his chair and reached for a bottle of rum. He gestured with the glass to Whill who nodded. Steely poured two glasses and took a sip of his.

"I don't know his name," he said, finally.

"What did he look like?"

Steely shifted again. "I hear he wore leather armor of all black, and some kind of fancy cloak made of gods knows what."

"You *hear?*" Whill asked puzzled. "Did you not say he came to you?"

The general squinted and pursed his lips. "I am told he did."

Whill eyed the bottle of liquor with a raised brow, suspecting the early-morning-drinking general might not be the best source of information.

Steely followed Whill's eyes to the bottle. "Nothing like that," he assured him. "The devil must have laid some sort of spell on me. I don't remember a thing about him."

"Sounds like Dirk Blackthorn. Did he have a flying mount?"

"They say he left Carlsborough Castle on one. Got it from a pair of dark elf twins. Who, they say, he killed."

"They?" Whill asked.

"The soldiers who witnessed the fight. Seems the dark elves were after Lord Carlsborough and his family. The mystery man, your Dirk Blackthorn, saved them all. They may well be the only ones left," said the general, and tossed back another shot.

Whill tried to hide his surprise. Why would Dirk care about the fate of the Eldalonian royal line? Whill had come here for answers, but seemed to find only more questions.

"I would like to meet Lord Carlsborough."

General Steely nodded to Theolus Klemus, and the man swiftly left the tent to fetch the lord.

"What can you tell me of the wider world?" asked Steely.

"Much, but first, how long has the dark elf army been out there?"

The General glanced to the side with a scowl. "Three days. They attack randomly, and have killed every soldier and citizen seeking refuge. They taunt us by dropping the bodies throughout the camp at night."

Whill told General Steely about the dark elf necromancers and the undead soldiers. He spoke of the recent battle in the eastern Pass, among other things.

Lord Carlsborough came shortly and was pleased to meet him.

"Seems you might be the heir to the Eldalonian thrown," Whill informed him after they had become acquainted.

"Let us hope that isn't true," said Carlsborough sincerely. "My family has suffered a grievous loss. Our line goes back nearly a thousand years, and farther back still if you take into account tales of lost records and such.

I still can't believe it myself. Eldalon has never seen a king as great as King Mathus, gods bless his soul."

"I'll drink to that," said Whill, and the three tossed back a drink.

"Now, what can you tell me of the man that saved your family?"

Lord Carlsborough told him all about his encounter with Dirk, but the tale shed no light as to why he had helped them. Carlsborough only reiterated the assassins had been sent to kill his mother's family; the question was why. Why would Eadon want him to be the sole heir to the Eldalonian throne? Why had he allowed Whill to reclaim the throne of Uthen-Arden? Had the assassination attempts been completely successful, Whill would have been rightful king of two countries.

He left the tent with more questions than answers and set his sights upon the Draggard army blocking the way into the Ky'Dren Pass. He boldly made his way through the dwarven and human armies, walked to the halfway point between the two forces, and drew Adromida. The blade surged brightly with power, and the ring of the blade coming out of its sheath echoed loud and long. Draggard began to charge across the snow covered ground at the command of their handlers. He saw many dark elves take to the sky, transforming into large birds and even dragons.

Whill stopped before the charging horde and summoned the power of Adromida. He held the form of the fire spell in his mind, seeing it clearly, visualizing the release, and letting the power gather. The Draggard closed in to less than ten feet, and Whill shot his open right palm toward them, casting the devastating spell with a cry of rage.

Silence followed in the wake of his echoing voice, and time seemed to stop. The Draggard who had been charging toward him froze in place and floated slowly off the ground. Abruptly, they fell as sound returned to the world and a concussion like crashing thunder rolled over the Draggard army. The ground exploded beneath them and rolled on like a wave folding over itself and the Draggard, and continuing on to engulf the lot of them. The shockwave was followed by spells of fire and lightning that blasted from Whill's right hand in rapid succession, peppering the trapped Draggard and leaving nothing but smoldering bones in their wake. Behind him, the dwarves and humans charged, and Whill took to the sky after the dark elves.

CHAPTER FORTY

Green Wood

Fyrfrost carried Dirk and Raene away from the Ky'Dren Pass steadily eastward toward Felspire. With his hood drawn tight against the blustering wind and the protection of his enchanted cloak, Dirk was not chilled by the biting wind. Raene had no such protection as she sat, pressed against his back. The night had gotten steadily colder since they left the mountain range of her birth, and Dirk new they needed to put down soon. When asked, Raene insisted she was fine, but her chattering teeth told him the truth.

Sparse forests and outcroppings of trees dotted the northern parts of the Thendor Plains, but Dirk was able to find a suitable location from their high vantage point. He steered them toward a thin coppice running the length of a ridge, and put down at its edge. Raene leapt from the saddle and landed square. She crouched, looking and listening to the surroundings.

"We are alone," Dirk assured her. "I scouted the area before we landed."

"Bah," Raene replied in a near whisper as she scanned the area. "I been right behind ye when ye did, and I ain't sure there wasn't nothin' down here."

"Trust me, I have means to see what you cannot. We are alone. Gather what wood you can find," said Dirk.

"This wood be green," she said, breaking a small tree in half and having to peel it apart at the middle. "Doubt any deadwood worth tryin' to burn be 'round here."

"We aren't starting a fire with striking stone and tinder; we have a dragon. Trust me, the greenwood will burn."

Raene shrugged and went to chopping the small trees with her hatchet. Like her male counterparts, she carried four of the weapons strapped to her thighs.

Dirk walked to the ledge of the ridge. Many such rims and rolling hills dotted the plains. In the moonlight, the smaller hills looked like nothing more than snow dunes blown by the wind, stretching off for miles in the quiet night. The ridges reached higher, and stretched west to east: roots of the distant mountain range. They were still in the shadow of the mountain, having traveled only a few hours and with no haste.

From his pocket, he withdrew the wolf figurine and summoned Chief; he dared not bring Krentz forth yet. Chief swirled out of the trinket and solidified before him. From behind, Raene gasped. Dirk turned to find Raene standing wide-eyed twenty feet away. She had dropped many of the felled trees when she stopped in her tracks, and now stood with her arms out, holding a few of the remaining branches.

"What kind o' devilry be this?" she asked, shocked.

"This is Chief," Dirk laughed, and the spirit wolf wagged his bushy tail and cocked his head at the dwarf. He playfully pounced on the ground before him and suddenly sprang at her.

Raene backpedalled and tripped, falling on her backside and sending the small branches flying. She had left her shield and axe where they had landed, and now frantically scrambled away from the big wolf. "Call off your dog, or I'll kill him!" she screamed, brandishing a hatchet.

"Be nice, Chief," Dirk laughed. "He won't harm you."

"Stop right there!" Raene commanded the playful wolf as she got to her feet and cocked back her hatchet. Chief heeded her command, stopped, and sat a few feet before her, wagging his tail lazily in the snow. She slowly extended her hand to pet his head. Soon, she had put her hatchet away and was scratching behind his ears, though she still cocked her head back from getting too close to his mouth.

"Chief," said Dirk, and the spirit wolf came bounding over to him, panting happily. "Is Krentz all right?"

To Dirk's disappointment, Chief gave a small whine and licked his paw.

"Still recovering, huh?"

Chief gave a small bark.

Dirk realized he had saved her from the necromancer at the last moment. Krentz had become translucent, and had begun to glow with the green light of the lich lord's spell. He decided to give her another day to recuperate.

"Chief, watch the perimeter until morning."

At once, the spirit-wolf turned to mist and disappeared among the surrounding coppice.

Raene had gathered a big bundle of trees and thin branches. Dirk built up the firewood and stepped away as Fyrfrost shot a jet of dragonsbreath, igniting the green wood quickly. The dragon fire melted the thin snow cover around the fire pit, leaving blackened earth and scorched patches of grass. His job done, the dragon-hawk leapt up into the sky, leaving a small blizzard of displaced snow whirling around the camp.

"Chief and Fyrfrost will guard us while we sleep. Morning will come quickly; I suggest you get some shut-eye."

Raene didn't argue, though her stomach growled for food. She had gotten little sleep in the last week since the invasion of the northern mountain range. She laid her bedroll opposite Dirk's on the scorched earth and soon fell into a deep sleep.

Dirk fed the fire enough to last until he woke, and lay back looking up at what stars could be seen peeking between the quickly passing clouds. He worried for

Krentz. She had recovered quickly from the effects of the necromancer on the road to Ky'Dren, but the latest foe had been much more powerful than the other dark elf. He hoped she had suffered no permanent damage.

He had been impressed by Whill's display of power during the battle for the Pass. He seemed to have learned much since the last time he had seen him. Still, with the powerful elven blade in his possession, Whill had been vulnerable to the necromancer and her otherworldly powers. This disturbed Dirk greatly, for surely there would be other such dark elves in and around Felspire. Likely, Eadon possessed such necromantic powers, and even though Whill wielded Adromida, it would be useless against the dark elf if he attacked Whill as the necromancer had. Thinking back on what he had witnessed, he realized the dark elf woman had been trying to possess Whill.

A thought came to him, and he sat up with a jolt at the grave revelation. The answers to the riddle came rushing to him. He finally understood why Eadon had cared to make Whill the sole heir to both Uthen-Arden and Eldalon, why Eadon had created a blade that he himself could not wield, and his true intentions in trying to corrupt Whill with those months of torture... Eadon wanted to become Whill.

Dirk believed Eadon's plan likely would succeed, given what he recently had seen of Whill's behavior. He thought back on the fight scene again and again, paying attention to what he had seen of Whill's use of the elven arts. He remembered now clearly how Whill had pulled the life force from his victims as Dirk had seen Krentz do many times. Whill did not follow the sun elves' strict codes and magical laws. He took from his victims as readily as any dark elf might. He thought back on what he knew of the two blades of power. One was the greatest power given, and, as such, could not be taken, but only given. The other was the greatest power taken, and, as such, could not be given, only taken. The nature of the power of the blades was balance, and seemingly a failsafe against the attainment of both. Whill would never voluntarily hand over the power of Adromida, and Eadon understood as much, for it would mean a defeat worse than death. Neither did he have the power to defeat Eadon. How then, Dirk wondered, would Whill destroy the dark elf?

CHAPTER FORTY-ONE

Teera

The days passed in a blur of rushing landscapes and circling stars. Whill had solicited the help of the Ky'Dren dwarves; they would be marching to Felspire and converge upon the final battle with the elves from the south. Whill had intended on uniting the three races against the dark elves, but Eadon had successfully neutralized the human Kingdoms. Uthen-Arden had not officially accepted Whill as their King, and the scattered Uthen-Arden forces who had not become the dark elves' undead were beyond his influence. Shierdon was under the rule of the imposter Travvikonis, and Whill had seen many of their soldiers among the undead. Isladon would be no help to him either. The kingdom had barely survived the initial invasion by Uthen-Arden under Whill's uncle. A new king sat upon the Isladonian throne, an inexperienced king half the age of his father, who had inherited a kingdom in shambles. He would have enough of a challenge seeing the kingdom through the coming winter, let alone offer any soldiers to the battle of Felspire. He had no time to move such an army anyhow. For the same reason, the Elgar dwarves would be of no help. Likely, a rift had opened within Elgar as well, and they would be busy fending off the attack. Lest they had preemptively set out more than a week before, they would not make it in time.

Whill wasn't sure how the fight with Eadon would end; he was not confident he would succeed. All he could do was try. He owed the people of Agora that much, at least.

He had resisted the urge to go immediately to the aid of Roakore and Avriel, knowing it was a trap. Imagining what was being done to them was agony, especially Avriel. Neither she nor Roakore would want Whill to fall for the trap on their account. Too much was at stake to be controlled by impulsive emotions. He had agreed to face Eadon with Zerafin, and he would abide by his promise.

He flew all day and night, east from the Ky'Dren Pass toward his childhood home, Sidnell. He had not seen Teera and the girls in years, and he wished to say his goodbyes and warn them of the coming doom.

By nightfall, the eastern coast of Shierdon came into view, along with its many lighthouses dotting the rocky cliffs, warning sailors of the jagged rocks along the unapproachable parts of the shoreline. He drew back the power of Adromida and slowed considerably, lest he crash into the earth like a meteor from the heavens. He came down on the sands of the quiet beach, sands speckled with the recently fallen snow.

Whill had seen many burnt out towns and destroyed villages across both Uthen-Arden and parts of Shierdon. The warring had not reached these parts. There was little need for the dark elves to attack here; Shierdon had been compromised nearly twelve months ago.

He walked from the beach and up the road leading from the harbor. The village was quiet at this time of night—nearly an hour before the sun would rise. The only lights coming from the shops he passed came from the baker's and few others. Teera would still be asleep at this time, but he doubted she would mind the intrusion. He soon came to the cottage he had spent the first half of his life. Those days seemed to be a life-time ago, as if memories from a dream not his. To his surprise, the lights were on inside. He knocked on the door three times, loud enough to be heard, but quiet enough as to not disturb the neighbors.

"Get the door, Ella," Teera called from inside. Her voice was music to his ears.

Someone approached the door from inside the house. "If it is more sick, we will need to begin mov-ing them to the healing ho-" Ella opened the door and froze as she saw Whill.

"Hey, sis," Whill smiled.

Tears pooled in the corners of Ella's eyes and, for a moment, she was speechless. Finally, she flung the door wide and threw herself into his arms.

"Whill!" she shrieked and hugged him tight.

She backed once more to look at him with wonder in her eyes, and again she hugged him. "By the gods, Whill, it is good to see you," she laughed wetting his cheeks with her tears.

Over her shoulder, Teera turned the corner. Their eyes met, and she stopped and wavered. One hand went to the table to steady herself, and the other clutched her chest.

"Whill?" she smiled and came rushing to him with the sudden agility of a woman half her size and age. She wrapped her arms around him in a crushing hug, leaving Ella trapped between them.

The two women ushered him into the cottage. A kettle was set upon the hearth for tea, and as always, Teera fussed over him, offering drink and food or anything he might need.

"Tea will be fine, for now," said Whill, looking to the sickrooms off to the right. "What's going around?"

"Some fear it is the beginnings of a plague, but I am not sure yet. Started about a week ago, after the voice spoke from the heavens," said Teera, looking to Whill with concern.

"The voice spoke your name, Whill," Ella said in a hushed voice, as if relaying secret information.

"It is a long story," he began.

Whill told Teera and Ella everything that had happened since Fendale, when his life had so utterly begun to change. He told them he was the son of the fallen king of Uthen-Arden, and saw no surprise in Teera's face. As he had guessed, she had known all along. What did surprise her was the story of the prophecy, and, when he mentioned the blade Adromida, her eyes darted to the sword at his hip in amazement. The tale eventually led to the battle in the Del'Oradon arena, and Whill reluctantly told them about Abram. Teera had not asked where Abram was when he arrived. And, when he told her of his death, she seemed less shocked than sorrowful, as if she had guessed as much, but been too afraid to ask. Newfound tears fell for his lost mentor, but rather than relive the pain of the loss, Whill turned to stories of fond memory.

They talked well into morning, until Teera's sense of duty forced her to the sickrooms to tend to the ill. Whill went with her and found four cots in each room. They were all full of children who looked to be on their deathbeds.

"These are the worst of them. There are dozens more throughout the village. The sickness starts as a small cough, and soon turns into dehydrating expulsions of every sort. It is hard to treat them, as nothing can be kept down," Teera informed him as she wiped the forehead of a six-year-old with a damp cloth.

"I can help them," said Whill.

Teera's glance fell to the blade at his hip, and her eyes lit with wonderment. She stepped aside and looked on with anticipation. Whill laid his hand upon the forehead of the dying child and slowly stretched his consciousness out and into her body. With his mind sight, he found the intrusion, and the damage the sickness caused. The disease spread throughout her entire body, and though she tried to fight it off, her body was losing the fight quickly. Through the contact of his hand, he sent a blue, writhing tendril of healing energy into the child, and eradicated every trace of the disease in her system. Whill opened his eyes and found the girl's big, bright ones staring up at him.

"Are you magic?" she asked, and sat up with all the energy of a normal child.

Teera could not help but cry tears of joy as all of her frustration over not being able to help the dying children dissipated in an instant. Whill healed the rest of them, but asked Teera to keep them as long as he was in town, lest his healing cause the kind of riot he had seen in Sherna after healing the stillborn infant.

Bella soon fetched her sisters, who, like her, had grown into strong, handsome women. The eldest, Mael, had four children, and Elzabeth, the middle daughter, had two. Ella, though a year older than Whill at twenty-one, had not, as of yet, taken a husband, a fact Teera did not hide her disapproval of. Like her mother, Ella was a born healer, and did not have the time to devote to such romantic endeavors, choosing rather to focus on the arts of the craft.

Whill spent the day with his family remembering old times, often until they were all laughing until they cried. The loneliness he had been carrying with him dissipated, and he forgot he was Whill of Agora and Whillhelm Warcrown. To them, he was plain old Whill, magic sword or not.

They enjoyed a dinner of chicken and biscuits, and emptied a few bottles of wine Teera had been saving for a special occasion. Soon, night was upon them once more, and Whill was reminded that he had to leave. He wished he could stay, he wished it had all been just a bad dream, and Abram would come through the door any minute. The women sensed the moment coming as well, and again the tears began to fall.

"I don't know how this is all going to turn out. I may never see you again. You must be prepared to leave these lands," he told Teera.

"Where will we go?" she asked. "If this Eadon is as powerful as you say, and all of Agora comes under his rule, where shall we hide?"

"Find passage to the elven lands. Tell them who you are. They will protect you as well as possible," he offered.

"I am too old for all of that. Besides, I am needed here."

Whill began to argue, but Teera took his head in her hands as she had when he was little, when she wanted his full attention. "I believe in you Whill. I always have. Since the day my brother brought the son of King Aramonis home to me, I have believed you would one day grow to become a great man, and that man stands before me now. Abram would be so very proud of you, Whill, as am I."

Whill broke down, and Teera held him as she so often had in his youth. Though he did not share her assessment of him, her opinion meant a lot to him. He got a hold of himself, and as she once had, Teera wiped his tears.

"You are the bravest man I have ever known, Whill. I am sorry your life had to be one of such peril. I think you were chosen for a reason. If there is anyone out there who can do it, you can," she said with a loving smile.

"I love you, Aunt Teera,"

"I love you too, son."

Whill left them standing at the door, waving their goodbyes, and never looked back.

CHAPTER FORTY-TWO
The Only Way

Aurora, Zander, and Azzeal entered Felspire and made their way to Eadon's audience chamber. The dark lord sat upon a throne of crystal which hummed and pulsed like the surrounding spire.

"It is with ill tidings that you come to me now," said Eadon.

Zander bowed at his feet, Aurora followed his lead. "Veolindra has failed you my lord. We would have taken the Pass, but Whill of Agora showed up and destroyed our forces."

Eadon didn't seem bothered by the news. He looked to Aurora and she turned her gaze to the floor.

"You have both failed me," he said, standing.

Eadon towered over them, and Aurora prayed that he would strike them down. He did not.

"The end draws near. You shall have a chance to redeem yourselves," Eadon promised.

Whill left Sidnell, at peace for the first time in a long time; he had said his goodbyes, and he was ready. He flew toward the Thendor Plains from the northeast and mentally recited the elven tomes of Orna Catorna he had put to memory. He had not attempted any of the shifting spells, afraid he might not be able to turn back from whatever animal he changed into.

He came back to the Morenka tomes again and again, and, every time he did, the teachings of the peaceful monks resonated with him more. They spoke of acceptance of life, peace and harmony. The monks believed that by resisting the reality of one's life, pain was created, and only through acceptance would the cycle be broken. They did not believe in war, for, if everyone thought as they did, war would not exist. Whill thought their s a dangerous mindset. The very notion caused its share of wars, but the Morenka at least did not invade their neighbors and force their beliefs upon them. They were enemies to none, and friends to all. A true Morenka would share his water with an enemy, and forgive them while they drank. But Whill remained unable to embrace the way of the Morenka. To him, it would mean to stand down against Eadon, and that was something he just could not do. *That is why you shall fail,* a voice spoke in his mind, one that sounded quite similar to the Watcher.

The land sped by below him, and the sun rose behind. The darkness of the distant horizon turned from dark to lighter shades of blue. To his left, hues of pink and orange turned to blazing red and yellow, as the sunlight seemed to race him across the sky.

He flew all day, and, by nightfall, he passed over the border between Shierdon and Uthen-Arden. He flew at a slower pace than he had whilst traveling from Del'Oradon to the Ky'Dren Pass, slow enough that he did not have to expend so much of the sword's power on the energy shield.

Whill did not remember the last time he had slept. With Adromida at his side, he did not need sleep; he was constantly refreshed, and stronger than ever. Flying took some getting used to, but as Abram used to say, "When you get it, you got it." Though, Abram had been speaking on the topic of knife throwing at the time.

The hours and the miles raced by, and Whill thought of Avriel. *If, by some grace of the gods, we get through this together, I am going to marry that woman,* he promised himself. He wondered how the elves would react to such a thing, and inevitably his thoughts turned to children. Could humans and elves even have children? He was not sure. He could just imagine the hard time a half-human/half-elf would have getting along in the world. And, what problems would arise from having a half-elf as the heir to a human throne? He doubted the people would stand for such a union; they would cry of elven occupation and human sovereignty. Whill cared little about what the people would think, and the more he thought about it, the less he cared for the idea of being king. Royals were bred for their station from birth, and, though he might be an able warrior, an able warrior does not a great king make. He understood nothing of taxes, or trade, or the multitude of other things that a king had to deal with. *Or does the king just appoint people to do all those things for him?* He wondered. *Probably not, if they want to remain in the know, and in power.*

Whill was torn from his ponderings as he came upon the Thendor Plains. In the distance, like a lance jutting from the earth to pierce the heavens, stood Felspire, glowing with vibrant energy from within the earth and pulsing and throbbing in the darkness before the dawn. He drew steadily closer and began to hear the low hum of Eadon's crystal creation. The dark elf was indeed intent on gaining the attention of the gods. Felspire was impossibly tall, splitting the sky with its peak and continuing on beyond the swirling clouds churning around it.

Was Kellallea right? Was Whill doomed to fail against one of such incredible power and unrestrained magic? What if Whill died in the fight? Would Eadon simply take the sword and find some other fool human to give the power of the weapon to him? If it was that easy for the dark elf, why hadn't he already? He chose Whill for a reason, but he could not think of what the reason might be.

He thought of everything he had learned about Eadon, and Adimorda, the elf he had once been. Avriel and Zerafin said Adimorda was the most powerful seer of his age, looking farther into the future and with more accuracy than anyone else. Once it was learned that the two were one and the same, Whill had dismissed the stories of Adimorda as fictitious lies, an elaborate hoax created to ensure the creation of the Sword of Power Given. Perhaps Eadon had seen himself attain both blades as the prophecy stated. If indeed he was the most powerful seer who ever lived, how was Whill to change the future that he had witnessed? Could one truly change the future? Eadon needed to convince Whill to hand over the power of Adromida and fulfill his destiny, but how? Whill was determined not to; he would gladly die first. Perhaps he could simply empty the blade of all of its power and strike Felspire with such a blast that it came tumbling down upon the gathered armies at its base. Kellallea offered him a way out, a way to be free of his burden, once and for all. But Whill could not hand over such power, would not. He did not trust Kellallea or her motives. She had allowed for the rise of Eadon and the destruction of Drindellia for the sake of becoming a god herself.

Whill pondered another notion; what if he attained the Sword of Power Taken? Unlike Adromida, the other sword *could* be taken. He possessed no desire to become godlike, but it would be better than Eadon attaining such a high station. And, what of the gods? If indeed they existed, would they allow a rise to power by one of such evil heart as Eadon? Whill laughed at the very notion. He had no reason to believe the gods were real, and, if they were, they seemed not to care about the plight of the good peoples of Agora. Where had the elven gods been when Eadon destroyed their homeland? Where had the dwarven gods been when Roakore's mountain was invaded and his people slaughtered? Where were the human gods now? Whill gave no stock to the thought of divine intervention. The gods either did not care, or did not exist. It was up to him to stop the future Eadon witnessed those eons ago. He would have to take from Eadon all of his power. It was the only way.

CHAPTER FORTY-THREE

Felspire

As Whill approached Felspire, he realized the grandeur of the army Eadon had summoned to him. Like a dark stain upon the snow-covered earth, the army spread around the base of Felspire in a wide circle. Thousands of draquon swarmed the towering spire, circling with the churning of the storm clouds about its crown. To the south, the elven armies approached, undoubtedly led by Zerafin. Their numbers were greater than Whill had expected, thousands more than had come with them through the portal to Del'Oradon. He was also surprised to see an army of Elgar dwarves to the west. For them to have made it to Felspire, they would have had to begin their march at least a week ago. He was heartened to think they had set out immediately after Eadon's proclamation. To the east, he saw the gathered armies of the Ky'Dren dwarves: Ky'Ell had kept his word.

His allies numbered in the tens of thousands, but Eadon's armies were many times more. Whill knew the fate of them all, indeed, the fate of all of Agora, lay in his hands.

He was terrified.

Never before had he cursed his fate more than he did at that moment. Never before had so many stood by his side.

Never before had he felt so alone.

Dirk, Krentz, and Raene spied Felspire and the Draggard armies from the high ridge of jutting stone, under the cover of Krentz's concealment spell. The ridge was high enough for Dirk to view the many armies advancing upon Felspire, and the huge Draggard force at the base. He had thought perhaps a chance for victory remained, albeit a slim chance. Now, he was not so sure. Eadon's forces outnumbered the allied races three to one, and, when he gazed upon the looming spire before him, he knew nothing but despair. Eadon's power was beyond all comprehension; surely greater than the power Whill's lone sword held.

They had been scouting the battlefield for two days, and had watched with growing foreboding as the dark armies gathered from all directions. Dirk and Krentz had argued in private about the futility of fighting on the side of Whill and his allies. He believed Whill would fail. Eadon had set this all in motion eons ago; he could not be stopped. She argued they had to try.

"To what end?" Dirk had asked the night before. "What is to be gained by risking our lives for those who would not even welcome us to their side?"

"Must it always be about gain with you?" asked Krentz. "Look what he has done to me!" she said with open arms.

Dirk took her raised hands and held them in his. "He is beyond our power, beyond anyone's. Eadon will succeed in his plot. We have helped where we could. We should be far from here,"

"And where would we go?" she pressed. "If he attains the two blades, there will be nowhere to hide in Agora."

"Then we should leave. Your people have discovered other lands across the seas, you said so yourself."

"We have not the means or the direction to do so. Would you so quickly abandon your own people?"

"I have no people," Dirk reminded her.

"Then, go if you like. But I intend on doing what I can. I will see my father pay for his sins."

"Krentz…" he said, reaching for her as she turned from him. His hand went through her arm and she stalked off.

"I can command you back here with the trinket!" he yelled after her.

Krentz stopped and whirled around on him, shocked. "You wouldn't dare!"

"Wouldn't I?" he teased.

She crossed her arms and offered him a cocked brow and a distasteful look. He approached her, offering hands of truce.

"I believe Eadon means to become Whill, and I think he will succeed. Whill has the power of Adromida, but he is far from a master of anything but impulse," he explained.

"Then, we must warn him," Krentz insisted.

Dirk knew he would not win this one, and they were both likely doomed. She insisted they get in the middle of a dogfight, one in which the dogs wielded ancient blades of incredible power. Dirk's instincts screamed at him to flee this battlefield. There was only death and destruction to come. But, he could not leave his Krentz.

The Sun Elves of Elladrindellia filed toward Felspire and fanned out east and west. The river of energy below raged violently. Its hum caused the stones upon bare patches of windblown earth to dance and vibrate. Eadon had tapped into the power of the ley lines, and the air hung thick with its power. The sun elves would not take from the flowing power, but they would accept what was offered. They opened their hands to the magic-rich air and absorbed the pulsing energy around them. The Krundar utilized the power within the earth, and caused mammoth creatures of stone to rise up.

Druids flung sparkling seeds from their pouches that sprang roots in mid-air, and, fueled by water weavers, took root and grew into writhing plant creatures with long, reaching vines. Others conjured creatures of living flame, and swirling pools of water. Druids turned to bears, panthers, wolves, eagles, hawks, and even small dragons. The Zionars among them began to target the minds of their victims, and, then, upon finding the minds of the dark elf Zionars protecting the feeble-minded Draggard, they began to size each other up, planning attacks and counter-attacks, building their defenses, and preparing mental retreats. The Aklenar Seers walked among the elves, touching foreheads and reading futures: they gave warning where they saw ill fate. The Seers were often generals as well, as they were best able to predict the outcome of military maneuvers. They were mentally linked to their subordinates, and could warn or instruct more efficiently. The network of thought strings was also protected by many Zionar. The master healers cast their many enchantments upon the others, and created connections to those that they were responsible for healing.

Zerafin looked to the sky beyond Felspire, to the northeast. He had seen a quick reflection many miles off. He looked with his mind sight and saw the unmistakable energy signature of the blade, Adromida. It streaked across the sky like a comet, surging toward Felspire. The dark elves would see it as well.

"Prepare yourselves!" he commanded his army.

The stone creatures slammed the ground before them causing it to rumble and shake; they pounded their chests and punched their palms. The plant creatures twisted their vines in tight and crouched like cats ready to leap after their pray. The conjured fireballs and globes of swirling water grew in size, and energy shields erupted with a crackling report around their conjurers.

Ky'Ell looked across the barren plains of jutting rock and crystal, beyond the spire. There, to the west, he saw the dwarven armies of the Elgar spread out north and south. The red banners flapped angrily amid the ocean of pointed halberds. The Elgar Dwarves had come to his call. He had sent runners immediately after learning of the rift. He guessed that they too had been invaded, but, regardless, it had been agreed upon by the dwarf kings, in light of the taking of the Ro'Sar Mountains twenty years before.

He looked to the sky as something caught his eye. A streak of fire was flying toward Felspire at great speeds. He saw the elves begin to prepare for battle to the south, and informed his dwarves to do the same. Whill had arrived.

CHAPTER FORTY-FOUR

The Reckoning

Whill came in low to the ground from the northeast, over snow covered ridges and long stretches of prairie. He did nothing to hide his approach, but came in so fast that flames began to rage against his energy shield. He poured the power of Adromida into those flames and was soon hurtling toward Felspire.

He had no words for Eadon; the time for words was over. Now was the time of reckoning. Whill would hit them with everything he had.

The power coursing through Felspire surged, causing the brilliant shaft to glare brightly in a multitude of colors. Whill let loose his pent up energy upon the gathered Draggard hordes at the base of the spire. From his outstretched left hand, fire rained down on the Draggard, and in his wake was left nothing but ash as his flames turned to a concentrated beam that decimated all it fell upon.

He let up on his spell when he approached the elves, and, flying over them, turned to make another pass. His attack had spurred the allied armies to charge; even from his high vantage point, he could hear the war cries of the two dwarven armies as they eagerly charged into the Draggard forces. The elven creatures of stone and vine, fire and water, charged before their handlers and crashed into the Draggard and dark elves.

As Whill came in for another pass, he scoured the impossibly large spire before him. Felspire boasted hundreds of ridges and crystal balconies, but Whill did not see Eadon upon any of them. He knew the dark elf was there somewhere, watching, waiting.

Spells erupted from both the sun elves and the dark elves. They streaked across the sky in a multitude of brilliant colors, some colliding, others being absorbed by shields, and some hit their mark. Explosions shook the ground as the armies collided, and Whill knew many good elves and dwarves would die that day.

Whill passed the Draggard and dark elf armies once again and rained death and destruction down upon them. Felspire surged with power, and a brilliant beam of light shot from the base and slammed into Whill's energy shield. Adromida countered the power with its own, but the blast sent Whill hurtling to the ground, unconscious.

He woke, bewildered, and found himself surrounded by thousands of Draggard and dark elves. Eadon approached from Felspire with a victorious grin upon his face. Whill rose and stepped out of the crater his crash landing had created. He unsheathed Adromida and held the sword before him.

Eadon stopped fifteen feet before him, and tossed three glimmering diamonds to the scorched earth. Whill flinched back, thinking it an attack, but the three diamonds hit the ground and flashed with quick light. There, between him and Eadon, floated Roakore, Avriel, and Tarren. They were surrounded by a pulsing force field that held them aloft, bound by invisible chains. Eadon walked to stand beside Tarren, who slowly spun in place within the spell cage.

"Have you come to surrender the power of Adromida?" Eadon asked with an air of superiority.

Whill answered by shooting a thin beam of power at Eadon. It was the most concentrated spell he had ever conjured, and he poured more of Adromida into it than ever before. Eadon raised but a hand, and absorbed the piercing blast effortlessly.

"Very well," he grinned, and laid a hand upon Tarren's head.

"Let go, and you shall know peace," Tarren told Whill with a smile, and his body disintegrated before Whill's eyes.

"No!" Whill cried and was blasted by another surge of power from Felspire.

He flew back through the air as Eadon turned to lay his deadly hand upon Avriel's head. Whill landed

among the Draggard and came up swinging like a madman, his blade glowing with the brilliance of the sun as
it cut through his enemies.

Dirk, Krentz, and Raene flew over the battleground
with their heads low, spells shot past in every direction,
some exploding next to them, others missing by inches.
Fyrfrost did well to avoid most of them, but Krentz's
energy shield still saved the dragon-hawk from many.

Whill had been blasted from the air by Felspire, and
now stood facing Eadon.

"Faster, Fyrfrost, before it is too late!" Krentz urged
as she fought to hold the energy shield in place against
the stray spells.

Dirk saw Eadon kill one of his three prisoners, and
Felspire hit Whill once more. At the same time, a dark
elf spell exploded in Fyrfrost's face and Krentz gave
a cry. The blast had come from the spire and torn
through her shield. Blood flew from Fyrfrost as he
flailed through the sky. They fell, end over end, and
Dirk leapt from the saddle as Krentz turned to mist and
helped slow his descent. Raene and Fyrfrost crashed
into the Draggard as Dirk landed among them, twenty
feet from Whill.

Krentz was a blur of sword and smoke as she cut a
path through the Draggard. Dirk followed in her wake,
blasting those who got too near with explosive darts.

Whill had risen once again, and was cutting through the Draggard in a rage. His eyes glowed bright white to match the elven blade.

"Whill!" Dirk yelled over the tumult. If he was heard, he did not know, for Whill surged forward and slammed into Eadon.

Their energy shields sparked and hissed against one another as Whill slammed into Eadon and drove him back through the air to collide with the sheer wall of Felspire. They crashed through the wall and into a dark chamber and across, blasting through the back wall five hundred yards away. Eadon laughed all the while. Abruptly, Eadon stopped in his flight and hit Whill with a spell that sent him flying back into the spire. In a blur of shining light, Eadon had unsheathed his blade and was lunging forward. Quickly, Whill brought up Adromida to block, but Eadon hit him with such force that the blade was knocked out of his hands and spun away. Eadon grabbed him by the throat and lifted him high.

"I will have the power of Adromida! How many of your allies must die before you accept your destiny?"

Whill mentally called to Adromida and the blade flew to his right hand at once. He punched out with his left with an energy blast, hitting Eadon in the chest, but the spell was absorbed. Eadon laughed and released him.

He took three strides and turned back on Whill with a smirk. "You cannot kill me with my own blade, boy."

Whill looked to Adromida horrified. Eadon laughed all the more.

"Your purpose had been fulfilled, Whill of Agora. I have made you a legend among men. I have given you not one, but two kingdoms. And this is how I am repaid!" Eadon screamed, and shot a spell that Whill could only brace for. The blast slammed him through Felspire once more, shattering crystal. He landed and rose to his feet quickly as Eadon stalked him.

The power coursing through Felspire hummed and crackled. Through the center of the wide shaft, a beam of white energy shot up toward the heavens. Eadon outstretched his hand and pulled Whill through the air to land at the center of Felspire. Whill looked to Adromida and the power of the ley lines coursing through the spire. A glance at Eadon showed him the dark elf's sudden fear, and Whill plunged Adromida into the power beam.

Raene charged her way through the Draggard crowd, ducking low and running around and between their scaled legs. Finally, she came to Dirk and Krentz who were fending off the Draggard. Raene saw who they were defending and stopped dead in her tracks. Floating above glowing gems in chains of light, was an elf maiden and Raene's cousin, King Roakore. The dwarf had whiplashes all about his naked body. He had only a loincloth for clothes, and blood poured from many wounds. Still, he fought his bondage, screaming obscenities at the nearby Draggard.

At her back a Draggard lunged, and she whirled around and brought her shield up blocking a spear. She shattered her attacker's knee with her spiked mace, and turned to run to her kin.

Roakore wondered if he were dreaming. Possibly he had been drugged by the dark elves. He saw the scoundrel Dirk Blackthorn coming toward him with some sort of ghost elf, and, there, running after them with shield and mace, was a dwarf warrior…a female dwarf warrior! Roakore fought his bonds, thinking the assassin was coming to settle their score once and for all. Before Dirk could reach him, Tarren materialized before his eyes.

"Well, I be the son o' stone! He's alive!"

The Watcher raised a hand, and the spell that bound Avriel and Roakore winked out and they fell to the hard earth. Roakore immediately barreled toward Dirk. The assassin leapt over him, and he and his ghost elf charged on toward Felspire.

"Come back, ye coward!" Roakore yelled after him.

"Roakore! You be all right?" the dwarf woman grabbed his shoulder. He looked at her closer.

"Raene? Ky'Ell's little one?"

"Bah!" she spat. "I be lookin' little to you?"

"What you doing here?" he asked, eyeing her armor and mace.

"Savin' your bloody arse, it seems," she laughed.

The Watcher came to them, holding Avriel's hand as Draggard and dwargon alike pounded on the energy shield he had created.

"Who be the little kid?" Raene asked.

"He be an old elf," said Roakore, to her puzzlement.

"Princess Avriel has not only forgotten who Whill is, but also all knowledge of Orna Catorna. It is not safe for her here," said the Watcher.

Roakore looked to her, and in her eyes he saw none of the elf's ferocity; instead he saw confusion, and fear. Behind them, Felspire rumbled, and the ground quaked beneath it. The power coursing through the spire surged, and large chunks of crystal began to fall upon the gathered armies.

"You will want to be far from here shortly, come with me," the Watcher told them.

"My place be next to Whill, he be needin me now more than ever!" said Roakore, turning to look where Whill had blasted Eadon through the crystal.

"You can offer no help now, good dwarf," said the Watcher, looking to the south. Roakore followed his eyes and saw Zorriaz, the white dragon Avriel had once been, and upon her back rode King Zerafin.

The ground shook once more, and larger chunks of Felspire began to rain down upon the battlefield. Spells streaked through the air from all directions still, and explosions flashed everywhere. The sun had been blotted out by the thick fog of smoke that hung over them, and blackened snow and ash fell slowly to the ground.

Roakore gave a growl of frustration as Zerafin landed, and Avriel and the Watcher climbed on. The Watcher's energy shield melded with Zerafin's, and Tarren's eyes waited patiently for Roakore.

Raene looked from Zorriaz, to the spire, and back to Roakore. "What's it gonna be, cuz?"

"If you do not come with us, you will both die," said the Watcher. "You can offer Whill no help now."

Roakore reluctantly turned from Felspire. For once, he thought about his people over his sense of glory.

"Bah, come on," he said to Raene.

They mounted Zorriaz and flew away from the crumbling monolith.

Dirk summoned Chief on the run as he and Krentz went through the hole Whill had made. He spotted Whill and Eadon at the center of the hollow spire. Whill's blade was thrust into the energy beam coursing from the earth. His eyes glowed with the flowing power, and Eadon backed away.

Dirk sprinted as fast as his enchanted boots would carry him and rushed to Whill's side. Krentz reached Whill first, but was blasted by Eadon. She was thrown back twenty feet with crackling, writhing green lightning surrounding her. Dirk yelled to Whill, who seemed to be draining power from Felspire.

"Eadon wishes to possess y-" Eadon hit Dirk with a bolt of power that lifted him from his feet and sent him crashing to the smooth crystal floor, far away. A hole had been blasted through his side, nearly tearing him in half.

He lay on his back, fighting for breath, with half of his torso missing. He could not move his legs, and when he tried to feel his wound with his right hand, he found that his arm was missing. Dying, his head lolled to the side, and he beheld his beautiful Krentz. She was reaching for him as she flickered in and out of solid form, crawling across the crystal floor. The writhing green tendrils crackled around her, but she inched her way across the floor to him.

"Dirk!" she struggled to say. "Keep your eyes open, baby. Dirk!"

He was tired, and he wanted only sleep. He knew he was dying, but there was nothing to be done. His eyes would not stay open, they were so heavy, so heavy…

"Dirk!" Krentz screamed, closer now. "Take my hand, please, take my hand."

Dirk forced his eyes open and looked down at his left arm splayed out beside him. Krentz reached for him desperately. "Take my hand my, love," she begged.

With the last of his strength, Dirk moved his hand slowly to hers, and she grabbed a hold of it tight.

"Now, send me away," she told him. "Send me away."

Dirk's vision swam, and his eyes closed as his breath came in shorter, more desperate gasps. "Return...to... the spirit world...Krentz," he said with his last words. He felt himself falling then, but falling with Krentz in his arms. His body fell away as they drifted down, down, down...

Whill saw Eadon hit Dirk with a beam of piercing light. The assassin had yelled a warning, but Whill did not understand the words. The power coursing through him crashed in his ears like a raging waterfall. Eadon backed away, and the look on his face quickened Whill's heart: it was fear. Whill turned from the energy beam coursing through Felspire and reached out to the dark elf with a clawed hand. No spell erupted from it; instead, Whill pulled at Eadon's power, the way that he had taken the life force of many dark elves.

Whill felt resistance as Eadon squared on him and held his sword before him defensively. Whill poured all of his hate and all of his rage into the spell, and Eadon began to scream. *The Sword of Power Taken cannot be given, only taken.* The words played across his mind, and he summoned the power of Eadon's blade, Nodae.

"This cannot be!" Eadon cried in rage, and Whill was electrified by his victim's helplessness as he drained the energy from the Sword of Power Taken.

You are being fooled, Whill. Give me the power before it is too late, I beg of you! said Kellallea in Whill's mind. She was suddenly standing next to him. She laid a hand in the power beam coursing through Felspire, and the beam of light shooting up through the shaft dimmed considerably. Whill ignored her plea, and with one last surge of power, he tore Eadon's blade from his hands, and Felspire exploded.

CHAPTER FORTY-FIVE

The Taking

The ground rumbled and shook, knocking all within the shadow of Felspire to their knees. The Draggard and dwargon lurched and shrieked, looking to the spire with fear. There was a surge of power, and, then, sudden quiet, and for a surreal moment, the armies were still. Felspire suddenly exploded with a deafening report that shattered the silence. Shards of crystal and chunks of stone were blasted out in every direction for miles.

Zerafin covered his sister and the others with an energy shield as the spire exploded. Little of the debris landed among the armies, so great was the energy that had been released.

"Kick his arse, Laddie!" Roakore screamed throughout it all, and Raene cheered right along with him.

With his mind sight, Zerafin looked to what had once been the base of the spire and saw Whill floating high

above the ground. In each of his hands, he held a brilliant sword of power, and Eadon was nowhere to be seen.

Felspire exploded with an earth-shattering force, and
Whill felt the power of the two blades come together
around him. Eadon disappeared as the power of the ley
lines winked out and the walls of the spire exploded,
leaving him standing within the eye of a storm of swirling debris. Above, the heavens split wide and a beam of
purest white shone down on the battlefield. Kellallea
remained standing were she had been. Whill looked
up expectantly, wondering if the prophecy of the two
swords were true. He felt the power of the blades coursing through him, and realized that he now possessed
the power of the gods.

Pain exploded in his head, and he dropped to his
knees. *You have served your purpose, Whill of Agora,* Eadon's
voice came to him then. Whill cried in torment, and
the voice echoed ever louder in his mind. He instinctively summoned the power of the blades, but he could
not focus an attack on the dark elf, who had invaded his
body. Eadon tore at his very soul, as their spirits grap-
pled within the caverns of his mind.

Whill's body floated above the ground, and beams of
white light shot from his eyes and mouth as he screamed
to the heavens. Random spells erupted from the two
blades as he and Eadon struggled for possession of his

body. Whill felt himself growing weaker, and Eadon stronger. He was losing the battle for dominance. In his mind, he knelt before Eadon as the dark elf took over his body.

Quickly, before it is too late, Kellallea urged him. Eadon grinned and the suffering threatened to shatter Whill's mind.

He is mine, ancient one. The gods come.

"Let go, and you shall know peace." Tarren's words echoed in his mind in the Watcher's voice.

Whill felt himself fading. He was losing his grip on the power of the blades. The great, pressing weight of Eadon's presence crushed the life out of him. Their souls began to merge, and it was more agony than Whill had ever known. A brilliant light illuminated the dark storm of Whill's mind as his soul was devoured. A sudden surge of energy coursed through Whill, and he felt the presence of his inner demon, the Other.

The Other attacked Eadon's soul with all of the pent up rage Whill had carried all his life. Images of his torture replayed in his mind, but rather than Whill strapped to the torture wheel, it was Eadon. The dark elf's spirit lessened his grip on Whill's, as the Other attacked with everything he had.

Whill's eyes shot open, and he beheld the destruction he was wreaking upon the land. Lightning and fire whirled all around him, as a tornado of jagged chunks of crystal and large pieces of earth torn from the ground below spun in a wide circle. The ground had opened up beneath him and was falling into itself, swallowing up everything around it. Brilliant stars shone above, and Whill knew that the gods bore witness to the battle.

Kellallea stood amid the tumult, seemingly unaffected. She reached out an offered hand, and regarded Whill with a pensive brow.

Eadon wishes to possess you! Dirk's words came to him then.

The Other was being destroyed, it would not be long before Eadon once again focused his attention upon him fully.

Whill, let go, said Abram in his mind.

Whill understood then Eadon's design, the link between their souls laid out his thoughts as if they were his own. Eadon had seen this battle unfold eons before when he went by the name Adimorda. He knew Whill would not voluntarily hand over such endless power, and that would be his doom.

Whill felt the Other being devoured by Eadon's soul, and he knew he had only moments. Mustering everything he had, he pointed the two elven blades at Kellallea.

"Kellallea, I give to you all the power that I possess!" he bellowed in a voice that shook the earth.

Eadon screamed in his mind and tore at his soul like a ravenous beast. From Adromida, Sword of Power Given, a bright blue beam of power struck the ancient elf as she raised her hands to the heavens and floated into the air. A red beam erupted from Nodae, Sword of Power Taken, and Whill felt Eadon tear his soul apart. Whill fell to the earth, dying, Eadon's scream echoing in his shattered mind.

Zerafin and Roakore flew over the battlefield upon Zorriaz The White. The Draggard had begun to flee when Felspire exploded. Those who had been near the blast had been disintegrated. The dwarves and elves pressed the charge in the wake of the blast, but they dared not get too close. Whill floated above the earth radiating with power, spells shot out in every direction as he arched back facing the heavens. Suddenly, the swirling storm around him subsided and the debris rained down upon the battlefield.

"Kellallea, I give to you all the power that I possess!" Whill cried in a voice that echoed for miles.

Zerafin and Roakore watched wide-eyed as the power of the two blades flew from Whill to Kellallea, and Whill fell to the ground, dead. Zorriaz steered them toward Whill. Through raining debris and streaking spells they flew, and, together, Zerafin and Roakore leapt from the saddle. They landed mere feet from Whill and were forced to avert their eyes from the brilliance of Kellallea, who shone before them like the sun come to earth. When Zerafin could stand to look once more, he noticed that every dark elf and Draggard upon the battlefield was dead.

"My Elves of Drindellia," she said in a booming voice as she floated above them. "Long ago, I took from the elves all knowledge of Orna Catorna. It nearly destroyed us then, and it has nearly destroyed us now. I allowed the elves the knowledge of magic once again, in the hopes that the lesson had been learned, but alas, it was not. You are not ready to wield such power. You may never be ready."

"Kellallea, no," Zerafin whispered, knowing what was coming.

Again, there was a brilliant explosion of light, and Zerafin felt the magic and stored power torn from his mind and body.

Thousands of glowing orbs of energy flew from every elf in Agora, and were absorbed by Kellallea as she floated above them. She opened her arms wide to accept the power she stole. All knowledge of the craft, and all of the stored energy the elves possessed was taken from them.

Zerafin dropped to his knees as his tears fell upon the scorched earth. He searched his mind for the vast knowledge he had once possessed, but he remembered nothing. He felt as if he had lost a piece of himself.

"You shall live as mortals once again, and you shall find peace. I am sorry, my children, it is the only way. Remember what happened here for all time. One man, a human, gave up the power of a god, so the world might know peace. Those of you with such righteous hearts might once again find the magic that was lost, and have the blessing of your goddess, Kellallea."

The heavens above opened wide, and beyond the tear in the clouds, brilliant stars shone brightly. The stars below the clouds converged, and Kellallea rose up to meet them.

Rise, Whill of Agora. The words came to Whill through the infinite darkness, and he gasped for breath. He found himself lying upon the ground. Above him, brilliant stars rose up through a tear in the heavens. He rose to his feet and gazed upon the elven blades in his hands. Roakore and Zerafin ran toward him, and, standing before him a stone's throw away, was Eadon. The dark elf stared at his empty hands in disbelief. Just as Whill and the elves remembered nothing of Orna Catorna, neither did Eadon. He was now as mortal as any human.

Zerafin and Roakore came to stand beside him, and Eadon regarded them with fear. He looked around at the approaching elf and dwarven armies, and he saw no allies. He raised his hands up as the tear mended itself, and Kellallea ascended to her godly throne.

"This is not how it happens!" he cried to the heavens.

Eadon fell to his knees, and Whill stalked toward him. Suddenly realizing his doom, Eadon jumped to his feet and began to run the other way toward the advancing Elgar dwarves.

"Not so fast, ye dark elf piece o' shyte!" Roakore yelled, and threw a stone that sailed through the air and struck Eadon in the back of the head. Eadon went down hard, but found his feet quickly as he frantically searched for a weapon. He took up an abandoned Draggard spear and with fury in his eyes charged Whill.

Whill's heart pounded in his chest as he rushed to meet Eadon's charge. He had fought as a mortal all his life, and, unlike Eadon, he was not afraid to die.

Eadon stabbed forward with his spear, and Whill knocked it wide with Nodae. Eadon twirled away from Adromida as Whill slashed. The spear darted for his head, and Whill knocked it aside once more. Eadon had no magic left, but, in his long lifetime, he had mastered more than just Orna Catorna. Whill struck with the two swords, keeping Eadon backing defensively. The fire in the dark elf's eyes had been replaced by fear. As he parried, Eadon looked for a way out, but none was to be found. Whill struck with all his might and Eadon blocked with the tip of the spear, just as Whill had hoped. With the other sword, he chopped the wooden shaft in half. Eadon took up the spear's shaft like a staff and began a twirling dance that pushed Whill back, blocking the flurry of strikes.

Eadon turned and dove into a roll, coming up with a discarded sword. The dwarf and elf armies watched on as Whill and Eadon battled near the edge of the deep hole left by the destruction of Felspire.

Whill charged Eadon once again with a flurry of slashing blades. The dark elf ducked the first and parried the second and quickly spun away.

"There is nowhere to run, Eadon, you are defeated," said Whill, stalking him.

Eadon began to chuckle. "You have not defeated me, boy! You can never defeat me! I am the most powerful dark elf that ever lived!"

He charged Whill and lunged forward with a powerful thrust. Whill parried the blade wide with one sword and stabbed Eadon in the gut. He stumbled back as his shocked gaze regarded his bleeding stomach. Whill retracted his blade and slapped the sword from Eadon's weakened grip. He clutched his stomach and looked at the blood in his hands, confused as he fell to his knees.

Whill tossed the blade Nodae to the side and brought Adromida to bear on Eadon's neck.

"This is not how it happens," Eadon pleaded, blood dribbling from his lips. "I ascended to the heavens, I became a god."

Whill cocked back Adromida, and, with a swift strike, lopped off Eadon's head.

Whill stared into Eadon's shocked, dying eyes as his head rolled and settled upon the scorched earth.

"You forgot about choice," said Whill. The dark elf could only stare up at him, and a look of utter shock became his death mask.

CHAPTER FORTY-SIX
A New World

Whill stood panting, looking down upon the corpse of Eadon. It was finally over. Time seemed to slow as he gazed upon the armies of the elves and dwarves surrounding him. Roakore took him up in a one-armed bear hug and pumped his fist into the air victoriously. He was let down and met by pats on the back and shakings of his hand. All the while, his eyes remained locked on his defeated opponent.

"You have done it, Whill," Zerafin told him with a wide smile. He shook his hand and patted his shoulder with the other.

Whill peered to the now clear sky. "She has ascended to the heavens, she has become a goddess," he said of Kellallea. He remembered that she had once again taken all knowledge of Orna Catorna from the elves. His eyes met Zerafin's, and the elf knew his mind.

"Perhaps it is for the best," Zerafin offered, but Whill saw the pain of loss in his eyes. They had won the day, but at great cost. The ancient enemy of the elves had been defeated, but they were now mortal.

"Where is Avriel?" Whill asked, but then saw her over Zerafin's shoulder, standing among the elves.

He let go of Zerafin's hand and ran to her. Avriel met his gaze without recognition as he approached, and Whill stopped short before her.

"Avriel?" he said through his fading smile, "What is it?"

"Eadon robbed her of her memories. She does not remember you," Zerafin said behind him.

A tear found Whill's eye to match those welling in Avriel's. She offered Whill her hands, and he took them in his. "Eadon may have taken my memory of you, but I know that I once loved you."

Camp was made among the ruins of Felspire. Crystal shards littered the Thendor Plains for miles. Some were no bigger than a small dagger, while others were hundreds of feet long. They jutted out of the landscape in all directions, casting a multitude of lights upon the land. As was tradition, the dwarves had brought barrels of ale with them, and that night the spirits flowed like rivers. Both dwarven and elven scouts reported no dark elves or Draggard for miles. Those who had gotten away were far from the ruins of Felspire.

As jolly as the dwarves were about the victory, it was a bittersweet win for the elves. Their faces held a mix of emotions. Joy at finally being rid of the dark elf threat, and sorrow for the loss of a magic they had used all their lives. Not one of them remembered the ancient knowledge, including the Watcher, who seemed to be trapped within Tarren's body forever, as the boy was likewise trapped in his.

The dwarves and elves alike had many injured and dying, and Whill spent the night tending to those in need, and though the elves no longer possessed magical healing abilities, they had retained a vast knowledge of the working of the body. Ointments and bandages replaced spells and mind sight, and the wounded were tended to in the old ways.

Raene avoided the dwarves as well as possible. She kept her head down as she searched for wounded throughout the ruins of Felspire. It would have been nice to take part in the celebration with her kin, but she would not be accepted by them for what she was. Her father would be furious to find her here, and she didn't care to have that conversation. As she lifted a shard of crystal from the pile, something echoed strangely as it fell and slid down the smooth surface. She looked closer, carefully removing debris as she searched, and then she saw it. Unbelieving of her eyes, she reached for the object carefully and extracted it from between two crystals. She raised Dirk's timber wolf figurine to the light and quickly clutched it to her breast, looking around for any who might have seen. She stashed the trinket in her pocket with a smile and wondered.

Aurora, Zander, and Azzeal stared out over the destruction of Felspire. Aurora couldn't believe her eyes; Eadon had fallen. Zander seemed less concerned than he should have been, he even grinned.

"Your master has been defeated, your magic taken. Why do you smile so?" Aurora asked the lich lord.

"Do you not feel it within you?" he asked, regarding her. "Orna Catorna has been lost to us, but the power of the spirits remains."

Aurora glanced at the silent Azzeal. His eyes still glowed with the same green light as hers. "In a world without magic, we shall be powerful indeed," said Zander turning from the ledge. "Come, there is much to be done."

Aurora could not help but follow him. She reluctantly turned from the celebration of the allies and followed her master into an unknown future.

The following morning, the dwarves and elves went their separate ways. Ky'Ell and his Ky'Dren dwarves headed west, and the Elgar to the east. Whill traveled with the elves, along with Roakore, Raene, and the Watcher.

"Will you be able to return Tarren to his body?" Whill asked as he walked beside the Watcher

"Kellallea has taken all knowledge of such things. I am afraid she is the only one who might," he said, peering up at the sky.

Beside them, Zerafin looked to the clear, blue sky as well. "And she, like the gods, remains silent to our prayers."

Whill felt bad for Tarren. How long would he have inside the body of one so old? Without Orna Catorna, the Watcher's body was as mortal as any. Whill reminded himself that had the Watcher not switched places with him, Tarren would have died at Felspire. Still, he had paid a dear price.

Looking to Avriel, Whill felt a pang of loss in her pleasant, but distant, gaze. Her every memory of their time together was gone; he had lost her. He could only hope that someday, somehow, the memory of the love they had shared would come back to her. Until then, he would search for a way, and he would wait for her.

Two days into the march south, Raene snuck away from the armies and found a place to be alone. There was barely a tree to be found along the plains, and the grass was weighed down with snow. But Raene found a suitable location along the deep banks of a small stream. With her back to the high wall of the bank, she took the timber wolf figurine from her pocket. Hesitating for a moment and looking over her shoulder in all directions, she listened but heard nothing. She held the figurine before her, simply staring at it. She had overheard Whill, talking about how Dirk and Krentz had tried to warn him of Eadon's plans, and how Dirk had died.

"Dirk Blackthorn, you in there?" she whispered to the trinket and waited. She glanced around again feeling silly. What had Dirk said to bring forth the wolf?

"Dirk Blackthorn, come to me!" she hissed in a whisper.

She was about to pocket the trinket when it began to glow. She squealed and dropped it in the mud as shimmering fog slithered out of the trinket and Dirk Blackthorn solidified before her eyes. She quickly scooped up the trinket and backed away from him. He looked as real as he had in life, his armor and weapons intact. Dirk stared down at his own body in wonderment, and his eyes quickly went to Raene and the trinket in her hand.

"You are a clever little dwarf," he said with a smile.

He offered her an outstretched hand and indicated the figurine. "May I have that?"

Raene pulled back the figurine and held it behind her. Dirk cocked an eyebrow.

"The holder of the trinket controls the spirits within, correct?" she asked.

Dirk scowled and withdrew his hand without an answer. Raene fondled the trinket in thought.

"Such a trinket would come in handy for a dwarf warrior. They say that there is no magic left in the world, yet this remains," said Raene.

"I put your brother to rest, remember? You owe Krentz your life," he reminded her.

Raene nodded, and reluctantly handed Dirk the trinket.

"Thank you," he said to her. He held the trinket aloft and summoned Krentz and Chief.

Nothing happened.

Dirk cocked his head and stared at the trinket. "Chief, come to me!"

Still nothing.

"Krentz I summon thee!" he yelled shaking the trinket in his fist. "Something is wrong."

Raene offered her hand. "May I?"

Dirk ground his teeth and gave her back the trinket.

Raene coughed and cleared her throat. "Chief, Krentz, I summon thee."

The timber wolf figurine began to glow, and their spirits swirled out of it and solidified beside her.

Krentz looked from Dirk to Raene and to the trinket, in turn. "What?"

"I was unable to summon you myself," said Dirk.

"It seems that only the living may control the spirits within," said Krentz, staring at Raene.

"You mean I be controlling you three?" Raene asked, eyeing the trinket with newfound wonder.

"Controlling? No, but it seems that we are at your mercy. You are now the guardian of the wolf relic," said Dirk.

"Thank you, Raene, we are forever in your debt," said Krentz. "But, tell us, what happened, how did you find the trinket?"

Raene took the better part of an hour filling them in on what had transpired after they went into the trinket. Krentz listened with a pained expression when she told them of Kellallea's taking of power, and Dirk grinned to hear that Whill had killed Eadon after he tried to run away like a coward.

"The son of a bitch did it," he said in wonderment when the tale was through.

"You seem surprised," said Raene.

"Indeed, I am."

Chief had scampered off to frolic in the snow, and the three of them climbed the bank and took in the sight of the marching armies.

"Now what?" Raene asked them both.

"Well, seems you are stuck with us," Dirk replied.

Raene gazed out over the plains of jutting crystal. "There be many dark elves and Draggard out there still. And there ain't no magic left, none but what be in that trinket."

"I suspect that non-magical powers, such as necromancy and that which fuels the trinket, were unaffected by the Taking," Krentz clarified.

"Right," Raene nodded. "I says we hunt down and kill as many o' the surviving dark elves and Draggard we can find," she added.

Her mind was racing with possibilities. She was now the 'Guardian' of the wolf figurine, and, as such, had the power to summon not only a ghost wolf, but also a powerful elf and deadly assassin. She would be the most powerful dwarf warrior who ever lived.

Whill and the elves traveled for two weeks, mostly by foot, as there were not enough horses to carry them all, and they were no longer fueled by their magic. When they came to the fork in the road leading to Ky'Dren, he and Roakore reluctantly said their goodbyes.

"Well, ye did it, Laddie. I never had a doubt about it," said Roakore.

"Well, then," Whill chuckled, "that makes one of us."

Roakore laughed and hugged him, patting him on the back so hard that Whill's breath was nearly knocked out of him. They parted, and Roakore slammed his fist to his chest and bowed low. Whill returned the gesture.

"Come and visit me mountain when your duties permit," he said with shimmering eyes and a wide smile. "Whillhelm Warcrown."

"I will," he promised.

Roakore said his goodbyes to Zerafin and Avriel as well, and the three watched the dwarf king begin down the road leading to his mountain.

CHAPTER FORTY-SEVEN

The End of a Long Road

Whill stood before the city gates of Del'Oradon, unable to believe he was now the king of Uthen-Arden. He realized he had never really believed that he would ever serve as king. Now that the war was over, he began to dread his newfound duties. Once again, he wished Abram was with him.

The elves had marched farther south than they needed to, and would soon make their way east to Elladrindellia.

"We shall visit in the springtime," said Zerafin, and beside him, Avriel smiled reassuringly at Whill. His heart broke when he realized that she would be going with her people. He forced the lump in his throat down and hugged them both.

"It has been an honor to have known you both. Thank you for all that you have done. Without your help, this would not have been possible," said Whill. He waved to them as they rode to catch up to their people, and Zerafin yelled back to him.

"It is the dawn of the age of peace in Agora. Long live King Whillhelm!"

"Long live King Zerafin!" Whill yelled after him.

When they had faded beyond the horizon, Whill walked through the gates of his city and was met by Alrick and the cheers of his people. He was home.

The winter months passed by, and the peoples of Agora got by the best they could. The four human kingdoms had seen great loss during the war, as had the dwarves of the three mountains and the elves of Elladrindellia. Magic had been lost to the elves, and those first months of adjustment were hard on them. They soon realized just how much they had relied upon magic to do everyday things.

The dwarven descendants of Ky'Dren retained their ability to move stone, though they did not share this information with the elves. To Roakore, it was a welcome testament to the power of the gods.

There were few reports of Draggard or dark elves within the borders of Agora, and the barbarians had not pressed their initial invasion from the north. The winter went by slowly. Heavy snows fell that year, and the freeze lasted longer than usual. Just when the people had given up hope for spring, the weather turned, and the worst of the winter passed.

Springtime came to Agora, and the new age of peace was celebrated by all. The dead were properly buried, and the rebuilding process began. Nearly everyone in Agora, be they human, dwarf, or elf, had known loss due to Eadon and his dark armies. Many cities no longer existed, their people all but wiped out. New cities cropped up around the old, and people went on living. There were many births during the spring and summer. It was a time of healing and new beginnings.

Whill's official coronation took place on his twenty-first birthday, one year to the day that Abram had given him the wolf-hide jacket while they sailed to Sherna upon Old Charlotte. So much had happened during the year that it felt as though it were a lifetime away. He thought of Abram often, and was comforted by the knowledge that his old mentor smiled down upon him.

Kellallea came to him the first night he was officially king, while he was reading by candlelight in his chambers.

"And so, the reign of Whillhelm Warcrown has begun," she said as she suddenly appeared before him.

Whill jumped with a start. "What do you want?"

Kellallea walked around the desk with a frown. "You have a strange way of showing gratitude."

Whill scoffed at that. "Had you helped when I asked, many lives might have been saved!"

"Likewise, had you handed me the power sooner," she replied, and Whill turned from her, disgusted.

"Why are you here?" he asked as he gazed out the window at the still-gathered crowd standing before the castle. They were chanting "Long live Whillhelm Warcrown!"

He wished they would stop.

"You have spoken to me in your thoughts, and your prayers have been answered."

Whill reeled around to face her. "I do not pray to you. You are not a god of mine!"

"Pity," she said as she lazily caressed the back of the chair he had been sitting in. "With power such as mine, Tarren could be returned to his body, and Avriel..." she teased, and Whill hung on her words, "her memories could be returned to her."

"If?" he asked, sensing she would not offer such things for free.

"You are a wise one, Whillhelm Warcrown. Ours shall be a glorious friendship."

Whill was reluctant to enter into any bargain with the devious goddess. But he knew that she held the ancient knowledge of Orna Catorna, the loss of which had haunted him as surely as it did the elves. He thought often of the power he had once wielded, and Kellallea knew his heart. He yearned to once again wield power as he once had. He dreamt of teaching humans to use magic as the elves had, so that they would never fall victim to one such as Eadon ever again.

"A glorious friendship, indeed," said Kellallea with a wry grin.

The End

Sample Chapter

The Windwalker Archive
Book 1
Talon

PROLOGUE
Plagueborn

*As recorded by Azzeal, Ralliad of Elladrindellia,
Keeper of the Windwalker Archives*

**Born by a Dogstar Moon, shunned, they see only with
their eyes. Righteous vengeance shall be his.
—Gretzen Spiritbone, 4975**

Volnoss
Winter (*Vetr*)
4980

The wind blew across the frozen world, sending phantoms of snow dancing and twirling in the half-moon light. In the night the cry of the timber wolf echoed throughout the wood. Stars twinkled brightly in the clear winter sky. All but the hungriest of predators huddled in nest and burrow.

The cold of Volnoss killed men without shelter and fire; the freeze crept through stitched seams and clung to the bones. The winter was one of the coldest and harshest told by the elders, and none disputed their claim. The fall crops had long been eaten, and the ice grew thick upon the waters. Fishing spots had to be moved, often by more than twenty thrown stones. Every day the catch was less, partially due to illegal fishing near barbarian territory. Each season disputes erupted between the barbarians of Volnoss and the Kingdom of Shierdon, and every year the elders called for patience.

A sickness had taken hold of many of the children and elderly of the tribe. The terrible sickness had come with the harsh cold and, as such, had been named the Frozen Plague (*Frjosa Mien*). The disease came in the night with a high fever and nightmares that left victims thrashing in madness. By morning the victims slept as if dead, their skin cold to the touch. About their hands and feet started a discoloring of the skin like frostbite, which slowly crept across the body until death.

The sickness had taken hold of a tribeswoman by the name of Kvenna Windwalker, wife of circle member Kreal Windwalker. Kreal had been tending his sick and pregnant wife for nearly two weeks. The frozen plague had crept along her limbs to her shoulders and waist. Nothing the shaman or witchdoctors tried did anything to slow the sickness.

Kreal had been beckoned by duty to a gathering to address the issue. The women of the tribes had become furious in their demands for action, but the men remained impotent to do anything about the sickness. The people demanded answers from the chiefs, but they had none.

Being no good to his wife fretting by her side, Kreal finally took his old mother's advice to go to the *Samnadr.* When he entered the long tent, he found his tribesmen in chaos. A few fights had broken out; men and women alike screamed and cursed each other, while others cried at the spectacle or clawed at their hair to announce their grief. Babies cried and children mimicked their parents. Teen boys full of wolf piss and fire pleaded to be sent to Agora on a quest for medicine; others promised they would bring back ships full of food, supplies, and medicine if only given a chance.

The elders, however, knew the truth. No help was to be found from any of the nations of Agora, and should they seek to steal its resources, they would be met with devastating force. What trade agreements they did have with pirates and smugglers were tedious enough, and war with Agora—namely its most northerly nation, Shierdon—would break those trade ties. If Shierdon set embargoes on Volnoss, the kingdom would need only wait until the dead of winter, at which point the starved barbarians would be forced to return to the negotiating table. Once again they would sign an unfair treaty they must adhere to whilst Shierdon never did. Always the Agoran kingdoms broke treaty, and ever more the barbarians raged for war. No love for the barbarians was to be found within Agora; the wounds of the past were still too fresh.

Kreal looked upon his once-strong people now gripped with fear and panic, and he pitied them and was ashamed.

To gain the gathering's attention, he grabbed the closest man and punched him in the face, sending him backward into the crowd. Charging across the tent screaming, he tackled two men who had begun fighting. He pummeled one unconscious, and as the other scrambled to get to his feet, Kreal pulled the man back down and beat him until his eyes rolled. With powerful arms and legs, he heaved them both into the crowd.

Kreal gained the crowd's attention.

Most barbarians stood heads over any Agoran; even so, while the tallest of the mainlanders stood only to a barbarian's shoulder, the tallest of the barbarians stood only to Kreal's eyes. The man looked up to no one. His broad shoulders and thick arms were a testament to the might of Timber Wolf Tribe. Such was his size and strength that he could wrestle a snow bear to the ground and break its neck, as he had once done during a hunting trip in which two tribesmen had died. He wore the snow bear hide as a reminder to his kin and to other bears. Four long, deep scars ran the length of the left side of his face from brow to chin, as a reminder to him.

The room became quiet and all eyes fell upon Kreal. There were nearly three hundred in attendance in the

Sudroen Hall on this night. At the center of the large tent, logs burned, sending smoke twisting steadily up and out of holes in the peaks. Bones of ritual hung from the high ceiling, along with other herbs and enchantments of the shaman. Each of the tribes was represented within the Sudroen. The skulls of the snow cat, timber wolf, bear, fox, and dragon hung, respectively, above each tribe's designated space, along with the beaks and feathers of both eagles and hawks.

Kreal walked behind his chair at the circle of the seven tribes. Each tribe had seven seats at the circle, and in the center sat the seven chiefs. Each tribe's people dictated to their seven members sitting in the outer circle, who in turn dictated to the chiefs. Men and women sat within the outer circle, though only men could be chiefs. Kreal eyed his chief, Winterthorn; as usual, the grizzled man wore no expression.

Kreal addressed the crowd with a deep, snarling voice that demanded to be heard.

"I too feel the pain of hunger; I too tend to dying kin; I too see no end to this winter of death. I feel as you feel, and I would feel it no more! Long have we sat waiting for this circle to decide upon a course that might lead us from our miseries, but *neinn*! More talk! We vote down measures that might bring us food and medicine. And why?"

The pain of his sorrow showed on his face and in his voice; he was a man come undone. He glared at the seven chiefs and pointed a shaking finger. "I am done waiting; I leave tomorrow to search for a medicine that will save our people, and I will not be stopped." He eyed the gathering slowly; many eyes found the floor, unable to match the intensity of his gaze. "Any who share my mind would do well to join me—any from all tribes."

Amid the howls and cheers of the people, Chief Winterthorn stood so quickly that the many necklaces of bone danced loudly against his barrel chest. Without gesture or word, he quieted the gathering. All eyes fixed themselves on him as he stared back at Kreal; there was no love upon his face.

"This matter is settled, Kreal Windwalker of Timber Wolf Tribe. The circle has spoken."

"And the people have spoken! If the circle's will were truly that of the people, we would not sit idle while we starve to death and die slowly from the *Frjosa Mien!*" Kreal yelled, and many of the barbarians nodded and cheered in agreement.

Winterthorn walked slowly and purposefully until he stood before Kreal. He was not as tall; his shoulders, however, were as wide as a pony's body was long. The large tent fell silent for many breaths as the two stared each other down. Kreal wanted nothing more than to challenge his chief for his title and once again bring honor to the tribes. But he could not. Barbarian custom dictated that only a man with a strong heir could challenge a chief. Kreal's wife was pregnant with their first child. Kreal had not yet a son, while Winterthorn had two grown sons. Winterthorn knew this, as did everyone else within the tribes. Kreal could not challenge his chief—at least not openly.

"You would defy the counsel of the circle *and* the will of the chiefs?"

"I would defy any who stand in my path, for I will find a cure, or I will not return to this land," he promised.

Kreal left the gathering, followed by the cheers of the tribesmen. Those within the circle eyed each other. Few of them spoke; the people already had.

The next morning Kreal kissed his dying wife's forehead for what he knew may be the last time, gathered his things, and left for the docks. He said nothing to his old mother but accepted a kiss upon his cheek when she pulled him down to her.

At the docks he was met by the cheers of nearly two hundred men and women. They boarded four icebreaker boats and headed south to the shores of Shierdon. Word had come from pirates to a man of Bear Tribe that a similar plague had devastated much of western Shierdon, and a cure had been found. Rumor held that the cure had been discovered by the distant Sun Elves of Elladrindellia; whether the rumors spoke the truth or not, Kreal hoped to find out.

He and his men were gone for three tenday and returned by the next crescent moon. They had been successful in their quest and brought back the plant that was used to make the cure, forever after it grew along the coast of Volnoss and was incorporated into many new remedies.

Kreal and his men had saved the tribes, yet he had not been quick enough to save Kvenna Windwalker. Just as he was returning to administer the elixir to his wife, she died. So close to seeing her alive was Kreal that he witnessed her extended hand fall to her death-bed even as he raced into the tent.

A wailing cry escaped the big man as he ran to his wife and took up her frail, discolored body in his arms. He sobbed into her chest and screamed with fury, cursing the gods and the women who bore them children.

A baby's cry pierced the air, instantly silencing Kreal. He jerked his head and looked to his mother-in-law, Gretzen; in her arms she held a bundle wrapped in furs. From the top edge of the furs, a small, clenching fist shook with the baby's wailing.

"It's a boy," said Gretzen, her dark, leathery hands holding the bundle tight. "Kvenna name him before death. He is Talon; your son."

Kreal went to the infant's side quickly. The gods had taken his wife from him, but they had blessed him with a son, an heir who might stand beside him against

Winterthorn and his sons. As Kreal looked upon his newborn son, the hope and awe on his face disappeared, and he was left horrified and quaking. Talon was born at only seven months and was small—too small. Kreal could have held him inside one palm.

Kreal backed away from the baby, shaking his head.

"That's no son of mine; he's a Throwback, a *Draugr*, a *Skomm*! He's small, weak. This Draugr will never bear my name; he must die. He must be cast to the stones as was the way in the past!"

Searching around frantically, he finally found a skinning knife and turned back on Gretzen and her bundle.

"I seen his stars," she said, turning the baby behind her defensively. "He was forced into world on night of Dogstar Moon!" Gretzen screamed, furious at his words.

Kreal began stalking toward them, staring at his dead wife. "Throw him into the ocean. We do not keep the weak."

"I've right to keep him if you refuse him. Until he stands for his *Miotvidr*," Gretzen proclaimed. "His life be legend one day; I foreseen it. It in the bones and in the stars; he will do glorious things. Songs will be sung of man he becomes; mark my words, Kreal. Talon will make legend the name Windwalker!"

"Give him to me," Kreal growled.

"Kvenna kiss him before she die; she smile on him, she loved him," said Gretzen, circling around the tent away from him.

"Shut your mouth!" Kreal flipped over the small table in his way, stalking her.

"Would you kill child your wife loved?" she pleaded, reaching down quickly to scoop up the iron fire poker.

The fury died in Kreal and he hunched, defeated. To Gretzen he seemed small.

"Do what you will, old lady; I will not have him. He will not live to see the summer," he said in a low, faraway voice and left the tent.

Gretzen wiped her grandson Talon with a soft cloth and sang the very song she had sung to his mother; she cried as she sang, yet she smiled as she cried.

End of Sample
Now Available on Amazon

Made in the USA
Lexington, KY
03 September 2014